LOVE & MARRIAGE AT HARPERS

ROSIE CLARKE

Boldwood

First published in Great Britain in 2020 by Boldwood Books Ltd.

I

A CIP catalogue record for this book is available from the British Library.

Paperback ISBN: 978-1-80048-134-3

Ebook ISBN: 978-1-83889-185-5

Kindle ISBN: 978-1-83889-184-8

Audio CD ISBN: 978-1-83889-247-0

Digital audio download ISBN: 978-1-83889-182-4

Large Print ISBN: 978-1-83889-708-6

Boldwood Books Ltd.

23 Bowerdean Street, London, SW6 3TN

www.boldwoodbooks.com

1

'Have you heard the stunning news?' Rachel Craven asked Sally Ross when she entered the kitchen of the apartment they shared with Maggie Gibbs and Beth Grey on the morning of 21 February 1913. All of them were employed at Harper's, the new department store in Oxford Street, and the arrangement to share a flat had worked out well for the four friends who had met when applying for posts at the prestigious store.

Sally took off her coat and flung it over the back of a chair.

'I don't believe I would have the courage to do what Emmeline Pankhurst did...' Rachel went on as she turned down the gas under the saucepan she was tending.

On 19 February, Emmeline Pankhurst – and some unnamed accomplices – had blown up a villa being built for Lloyd George near Walton Heath Golf Club and the papers were filled with the atrocity and up in arms at the way the suffragettes had become so militant. The story had knocked the news of Captain Scott's failure to reach the North Pole off the front page.

'I'm not sure I'd want to.' Sally flicked her pale blonde hair back from her eyes. The wind had blown it all over the place, because it was longer than usual. 'It was brave, of course, because she could easily have blown herself up instead of Lloyd George's new villa – but what does it achieve? She will go to prison and I don't believe she has advanced the Women's Movement one inch. In fact, she will have a lot of influential men thinking we're a bunch of lunatics... and if she'd been a few minutes later, innocent workmen would have died.'

Rachel agreed with Sally, though her loyalty to the leader of their movement made her reluctant to give voice to her opinion, even though Emmeline had become too militant of late. They had both joined the Movement for Women's Rights the previous year and often attended meetings. Lately, however, some of the speakers had been too fiery and were often booed by men who came just to disrupt the proceedings. Sally had gone on to the stage at one point at a recent gathering and told the listeners that she thought they should have non-violent protests and march to Downing Street and the palace with their banners, but she drew the line at using bombs. She had been shouted down by some of the more vociferous members.

'I think the Women's Social and Political Union is going too far, Rachel, and I shall not attend their meetings again – only those of the less militant branch, the Women's Rights Movement, which is what we all thought we were part of when we joined...'

'Yes, you're right, of course you are. The Women's Social and Political Union is far too militant for us and I shall not attend their meetings in future either.' Rachel smiled at Sally approvingly as she deftly changed the subject, not wanting to get bogged down in politics. 'I like the colour of your new blouse – what do they call that colour exactly?'

'York tan – at least that's what the salesman called it. I bought some stock for Harper's fashion department and liked them so much when they arrived that I purchased one for myself...'

'Very smart!' Rachel turned back to the gas cooker where she had some potatoes boiling for the supper they would share with Beth and Maggie, when they arrived. 'I bought some boiled ham for our tea to have with mashed potatoes and sliced carrots.'

'I'm glad it's your turn to cook supper and not mine.' Sally sighed heavily.

'Are you all right, Sally?' Rachel asked, because the younger girl looked tired. 'It was a bit much, Ben Harper and his sister Jenni making you the buyer for Harper's without enough training, but now they're both in America and that makes a lot of work and responsibility for you.'

Ben Harper, the owner of Harpers store in Oxford Street London, had been gone for more than five months and Rachel thought that was disgraceful. It seemed to her that he'd simply abandoned ship, leaving it to his managers and Sally to cope with the buying and running of the shop, which Rachel believed unfair.

'Jenni Harper writes me long letters giving me advice and if I need anything urgently, I send her a telegram and she always helps.' Sally shook her head dismissively. 'When Jenni was last over just before Christmas, she told me that her brother is anxious to return but can't at the moment.'

'What sort of business could keep him from the store he professes to care about?' Rachel muttered.

Sally shook her head. 'Jenni said it was very important... But she approved everything we're doing and says she doesn't think Mr Harper could do better if he was here. Besides, we've taken on a new buyer for the men's department and it seems to be doing better again...' At first the men's department had struggled, because the stock was not ideal for the British market but that had been adjusted after Sally's advice had been sought and given.

'It was Miss Harper's idea to have the sale after Christmas, I suppose,' Rachel said, frowning. 'It made an awful lot of work for the staff and we really didn't have a lot of damaged or unsaleable goods to get rid of.'

'No, we've been lucky that our stock has a good turnover.' Sally looked thoughtful. 'I bought in a few seconds from some of our suppliers. Most of them only had a very small fault...'

Rachel hesitated, then, 'I hope you won't be offended, Sally, but I didn't think that was such a good idea personally. Some of my ladies were a bit sniffy when I told them they were buying seconds.'

Sally nodded her agreement. 'Jenni said it's what they do in their stores in New York, but I think you're right, Rachel; it doesn't work with our customers. I don't think I'll do that again...' She broke off as the door opened, letting in a cold blast from the hall-way. Maggie had a red nose and Beth looked frozen as they hurried inside.

'Oh, it's warmer in here,' Maggie, the youngest of them, exclaimed. 'Sorry we're late, Rachel. We went to buy some tinned fruit for afters and missed our bus so we had to wait twenty minutes for the next one.'

'The wind goes straight through you out there,' Beth said. She and Sally were both in their early twenties and Rachel was in her mid-thirties, a widow and supervisor for the hat, accessories, bags and jewellery departments. Beth was a senior salesgirl but Sally had risen swiftly to the position of buyer because Ben and Jenni Harper had taken a liking to her. 'Are you two going to that suffragette meeting this evening? I intended to come, but I'm not sure I can face that bitter cold again...'

'The meeting has been cancelled until further notice,' Rachel told her. 'Because of the arrest and coming trial of Emmeline Pankhurst, the sisters think that there will be agitators in the crowd. So we're waiting until some of the fuss dies down... and both Sally and I have decided not to attend the WSPU meetings in future.

What Emmeline did was just too much... too violent. Innocent men might have been hurt.'

'Yes, I saw something in the paper...' Maggie put in. 'A man left his evening paper lying on the seat when he got off the bus so I brought it home. I haven't read the whole article but it says she looked pale but calm as she was arrested. She pleaded guilty to the bombing and to other disturbances.'

'They will put her in prison,' Sally said. 'I just don't see the point of what she did – and I think it puts men who might agree with our cause, against us.'

'I agree,' Rachel said, 'but you know that Emmeline thinks we have to do something drastic to make them listen to us, otherwise they will just go on ignoring us. I spoke to her a few weeks ago at one of our meetings because I wanted to know her opinion – and she is always open to all members, as you know. She said that even those who are not against us treat us like children or pets to be humoured. I asked her if she thought it worth the risk personally and she said she was willing to give her life if she had to... I admire and like her so much, but I fear she will lose support for both branches of the Movement if she goes on this way...'

Rachel looked at Beth, sending her a silent plea, because Sally was evidently angry and she wanted an end to politics. 'Will you make the tea while I mash the potatoes? The carrots have butter on them already...'

'Lovely, I'm hungry,' Beth said and went to pour boiling water into the teapot. 'I definitely want to join the Movement instead of just attending the meetings once they start again, Rachel, but not the WSPU...'

'Yes, me too,' Maggie agreed. 'I think it is time women had equal rights with men. Why shouldn't we? They've had it all their own way for too long...' She looked angry, pink spots in her cheeks.

'However, I agree with you and I do not want to see innocent people hurt...'

Rachel understood that some of the anger in the younger girl's voice was because of her break-up with her boyfriend Ralf the previous autumn. After a big quarrel over Maggie's visit to her dying and estranged mother, Ralf seemed to have disappeared from the picture. Yet it was ironic that the trouble between them had been caused by Ralf's mother, who had wanted to dominate the girl she thought would be a docile bride for her son. Maggie had a mind of her own and she had not put up with Ralf's mother's interference for long. Instead, she'd left her lodgings at his home and come to join her friends at the flat. Although Ralf had tried to apologise, Maggie had refused to accept his remorse and told him she did not wish to see him, since then he'd stopped coming to the store where she worked and waiting for her outside when she left at night. However, she was still smarting from his refusal to take her side and her anger sometimes came out in other ways.

Rachel reflected on the changes in the young girl since she'd started to work at Harper's. The death of her father and the suspicion that her mother might have had something to do with it had helped to turn her from the shy child she'd been to the determined young woman she now was, a woman quite capable of standing up for herself.

Maggie's arrival at the apartment and then Beth's after her aunt's marriage, had made them a little crowded, for there were only two bedrooms, a kitchen, bathroom and sitting room. Each bedroom had two single beds, but there wasn't a lot of room for personal possessions. Their efforts to find a larger flat had been unsuccessful for the reason that landlords preferred married couples or families and tended not to trust women living together.

Fortunately, they had the use of a shed in the yard at the back in which Rachel had stored some things that she'd kept from the home she'd enjoyed before her husband had died so painfully and bitterly. His illness had gradually become worse over several months, causing her much grief and distress until his death and after. It was just some boxes of mementoes she was reluctant to throw out and a few bits of furniture.

'I saw an advertisement for a larger flat today,' Sally said as they all sat down to eat. 'I think we might just have afforded it between us, but when I rang from the office they said it had gone...'

'Do you think it really had?' Rachel asked. It had taken time to find a landlord who would let to them in the first place and Sally was pretty sure they'd got their present flat because Mr Harper had stood guarantor for them and it was situated just round the corner from Harper's in Berwick Street, making it easy to walk into work on fine days.

'I'm not sure,' Sally replied and made a wry face. 'I think next time I'll lie and say I want it for my husband and myself...'

'Your non-existent husband would have to sign,' Rachel said with a sigh. 'That's why we have to get recognition that women are more than just their husband's belongings...'

'I'll go on a march for women's rights,' Maggie said. 'I won't throw bombs or anything, but I'll hold a banner and shout slogans.'

'I think that would be enough to get you arrested at the moment,' Sally cautioned. 'The police will be hard on us all if we give them the chance – that's why I think Emmeline was misguided...' The others nodded, because it wasn't easy being a woman in these troubled times but they were all determined to do what they could to make the situation better for women as a whole.

2

Sally lay in bed reading the latest letter from Jenni Harper. She'd retired early, leaving the others talking and laughing in the sitting room, because she had been feeling down all day. For weeks she'd expected the owner of Harper's to return; she'd been certain he would be back in London to see the wonderful Christmas windows that she and Mr Marco had planned together. There was a themed snow scene, showing mountains in the background and snowmen, with children playing in the foreground, and in another window, Christmas trees, parcels and a huge cardboard Christmas cake with a table laden with imitation food. Unfortunately, they didn't sell either cosmetics or toys at Harper's yet and Sally felt they had missed the Christmas trade that might have brought in. However, the crowds had been three deep for days because of Mr Marco's magical displays, but Mr Harper hadn't been there to see it and he hadn't written to her for weeks, leaving his sister Jenni to keep the avenues of communication open. Something that made Sally wonder at his neglect, because she'd understood the store was all-important to him.

It was strange, just as Rachel had suggested. What kind of busi-

ness could keep Mr Ben Harper from London and the store he'd
seemed so keen on. Had he tired of it already? Was he the kind of
man who liked to start things and then sell them and move on? She
knew it was what was being whispered in the various departments.
After all, he was an American, and even a few months of steady
trading were probably enough for him to sell at a good price... but
surely he wouldn't? She couldn't bring herself to believe that he
would let everyone down that way. There must be a valid reason
why he hadn't returned to London as he'd planned, surely?

Sally enjoyed her job as buyer for the fashion, jewellery and bag
department at Harper's, and she'd discussed bringing in cosmetics
and a small toy department with Jenni, but at times it made her feel
lonely. Being in an office wasn't the same as being on the shop floor
working with Maggie and Beth and the days she didn't meet buyers
sometimes seemed long when she was concentrating on her sales
sheets. She'd felt like one of the girls when she worked in Rachel's
department, but now she often only spoke to the others at night
when they came home.

It wasn't really her job that was getting her down though,
because she loved every minute. In her heart, she knew it was
because Mr Harper hadn't been in touch. Before he'd left for America, Sally had been drawn to her employer, fascinated by his
dynamic personality, even though she knew it was foolish. He'd
seemed to show an interest in her at times, but at others he'd
seemed indifferent and she knew it might be better for her if he
never returned. If the shop was sold, her experience at Harper's
should help her to get a good job somewhere. However, she didn't
think many places would give her the opportunity to buy for the
store, as Jenni and Ben Harper had.

Sometimes, Sally wished she was back on the shop floor with
her friends, but that was daft. She earned more than she ever had in
her life and Jenni said she would get a raise soon. The profits for the

store had been good – though Sally wasn't sure about the January sale results. Some of the seconds had just stayed on the shelf and she didn't know what to do with them. For her that was a bad decision and she saw the small margin of profit on the sales as being a failure. Yet even that was not responsible for her black mood.

Sally pounded her pillow in sudden anger. She wasn't going to be upset over her employer. No man was worth it! She forced herself to think positively. She had a couple of days off next month and it was time she did something for herself – maybe she would go and visit some friends... it was a while since she'd seen her friend, Sylvia, and she'd seen nothing of Mick, the manager of the pub near the hostel where she'd lived before moving into the flat with Rachel. He'd waited outside the store one evening before Christmas to give her a card and a box of special chocolates and wished her Happy Christmas. Although she'd sent him a card, Sally hadn't bought a gift. And, as she'd been going out that evening with Beth, when Mick asked if she had time for a meal or a drink, she'd had to refuse him. Afterwards, she realised she hadn't explained why and wished she'd told him it was just a girls' night out at the music hall, because she thought he might have taken her refusal the wrong way. He probably thought she was courting strong, which was far from the truth. Mick was a friend, a bit like the brother she'd never had; she enjoyed his company and she wouldn't like to hurt his feelings, so perhaps she should get in touch.

Sighing, Sally turned over restlessly, wishing she could just go to sleep and wake up to find all her personal problems had melted away – but, of course, that never happened in real life.

Hearing Beth's voice bidding the others goodnight, Sally closed her eyes and clutched the silver cross that the nuns had told her was her mother's. It lived beneath her dress all the time and was hardly ever taken off. She hoped Beth wouldn't want to talk, because she wasn't in the mood that night...

* * *

Beth crept into the room, because Sally seemed to be sleeping. She'd sat up late to make a new skirt for herself on Rachel's sewing machine. Rachel allowed her to use it whenever she wished and Beth made things for all of them. She'd just finished sewing a beautiful lace bed jacket for Rachel's mother-in-law.

'It's Mother-in-law's birthday,' Rachel had told her, 'and she likes good things. To buy something like this from the shop would cost several guineas, Beth. It's absolutely lovely and much better than I could do...'

'Aunt Helen taught me,' Beth had said, smiling. 'As you know, she was a seamstress for years and made a good living out of it. She didn't like me using her machine and said I wasn't good enough to be professional. I suppose I've always compared myself to her and found I was lacking – but I'm pleased with the way your bed jacket turned out.'

'I think you're better than you imagine with lots of things,' Rachel had encouraged her. 'Everyone enjoys your cooking and I've noticed that customers like you serving them in the department...'

Beth had smiled. 'Jack loves my cakes and pastry. Fred says I'm a better cook than his wife was and I cook Sunday lunch for them all at least once a month – more if Jack is home.'

Her boyfriend, Jack Burrows, was a steward and worked on the ships going back and forth between America and England. He'd sailed on the Titanic's ill-fated maiden voyage and miraculously survived, saving two women and a child before he was dragged unconscious into a half-empty lifeboat just as the order was given to pull back before the current from the sinking ship dragged the boats under. When he'd recovered in hospital in New York, he'd changed to working for the Hamburg-American Line and was currently away on one of his frequent trips. He and Beth had got together when he'd come back from America and saw each other whenever he was home.

Jack was Fred Burrow's son. Fred worked as head porter at Harper's and was responsible for getting the new stock out to the departments, which was a big job for one man and he'd been given a junior to help him. Beth had met Jack because of her friendship with Fred and still spent her tea break with the older man in the basement most days. Fred was proud of both Jack and Tim, who was now a member of the Royal Flying Corps, but she knew Jack's experience with the Titanic had made his father especially proud.

'One day I'll retire from the ships,' Jack had told Beth when he was talking of the future. 'I'll have enough saved soon and then I can either look for a small hotel or pub we can run together – or, failing that, a job as manager just until I get my own place...'

Beth had just smiled and let him talk. Being with Jack made her feel happy and helped her forget the disappointment she'd had when her former boyfriend had walked out after she'd told him she couldn't leave her ailing mother to marry him. To be fair, it had been as much her mother's fault as Mark Stewart's, but he hadn't stayed around to see what happened after Beth's mother had used emotional blackmail to force her to refuse him. To her surprise, he'd gone overseas and then he'd come back married. For a while, Beth had felt her heart was broken, but she'd got over Mark and now she was enjoying life with Jack.

Getting married wasn't Beth's priority, because she loved the freedom and independence her work gave her after the years spent nursing her mother before she died and Beth went to live with her Aunt Helen. She wasn't ready to leave work to become a wife and mother yet, though she knew that marriage couldn't come soon enough for Jack.

A smile touched Beth's mouth as she got into her bed and snuggled down into the warmth of the covers. Modern girls could afford to be a little more independent than their mothers, who had in many cases had no future other than marriage open to them.

'Goodnight, Beth...'

'Goodnight, Sally. I'm sorry if I woke you.'

'You didn't. I've been thinking...'

'You all right? Anything I can do?'

'No, just work – how about you?

'Jack is coming home this weekend so I'm feeling good about that...'

'Lucky you,' Sally said. 'I think I'll visit some friends...'

'Goodnight then...'

Beth closed her eyes. Jack was only ever away for six weeks at most, because, given decent weather, they could be there and back in no more than four weeks, though sometimes there were delays to the return journey due to bad weather or for repairs needed to the ship. Even if he was home on time, though, it always seemed ages to Beth and she hadn't seen him since the New Year, perhaps because of atrocious storms in the Atlantic.

He'd told her she would love America, but Beth was too busy, too tied up with her own life, to think about travel. Besides, she couldn't afford the price of a ticket, and even if she'd joined the line as a maid, there was no guarantee she would be assigned to Jack's ship. No, she would rather be at Harper's and it was lovely when he got home. They would have so much to talk about...

3

Maggie tidied her hair, tucking a wisp behind her ear and smoothing her dress. Rachel Craven was a friend and they shared an apartment, but at work she was her supervisor and expected her staff to be smart, and Maggie tried to do everything well. At sixteen years of age, her life had turned upside down the night she got home from work and discovered her father slumped on the floor of his bedroom, an empty bottle of laudanum near him and her mother vanished. When her mother had been found dying in the infirmary months later, Maggie had found the courage to visit and forgive her for leaving her father to die and for taking her father's compensation money to squander on her lover – but she could not forgive Ralf's betrayal. Ma had been misled and her foolishness had cost her her life and Maggie's father's life too, but Ralf had no excuse for his betrayal. He'd sworn he loved her, but when his mother had tried to forbid Maggie to visit her dying mother, Ralf had stood aside instead of supporting the girl he was supposed to love. Maggie had felt betrayed and hurt. So she'd broken off her relationship with him and now enjoyed living with her friends. Maggie was conscious that as the youngest she earned the least and could only contribute a small amount to their combined expenses. Maggie was earning a little more than she had when she'd started at Harper's, but still not as much as Beth, who had been given a rise at Christmas, and nowhere near as much as Rachel or Sally. Sally was the highest paid and earned more than a lot of men did. She contributed the largest amount to the rent and the housekeeping pot and seemed happy to do so. Maggie sensed that Beth felt she did not contribute enough sometimes and Maggie could afford even less. Therefore, she must be of use to the others, and on her best behaviour at work.

Rachel gave her a nod of approval as she took her place behind the counter selling scarves and leather gloves. Maggie was relieved that the January sales were over and her stock now only consisted of the quality silk scarves and beautifully made leather gloves that their customers expected. She had hated the recent sales because Rachel had insisted that, when something was damaged, the fault was shown to the customer so that they could make an informed choice. Three women in particular had complained and Maggie had been embarrassed to explain that the sale goods were not regular stock.

'Well, I think that is disgusting,' one irate lady had declared when Maggie had told her the cheaper scarves were seconds.

Another customer had marched straight off without a word and a third had told her that she considered it was cheating to offer second-rate goods at sale prices rather than giving a percentage off the regular stock. Maggie had agreed with her but had to bite her tongue. She doubted they would see any of those customers in the department again.

Seeing a lady approaching, Maggie tensed because she thought she'd served this customer recently.

'Good morning, madam,' she said politely. 'How can I help you?'

'You can show me some good quality silk scarves please, miss,' the woman said. 'I don't want any of that rubbish you were offering during the sales.'

'No, of course not,' Maggie said. 'They have been removed from stock now that the sales are over. Have you any colour preferences?'

'Yes, I want greens or turquoise,' the customer replied. 'It is a present for my daughter and I want something nice...'

'Yes, of course.' Maggie opened the drawer and began to select the colour choices. She suddenly saw a sea-green scarf that she knew to be one of those bought in for the sales and drew a quick breath. How had she missed that when she was clearing her counter? She drew it out and attempted to discreetly place it in her top drawer.

'That is pretty,' the sharp-eyed customer said. 'May I see it, please?'

'This one should not be in this drawer,' Maggie said. 'It has a fault...'

'Show me, please...'

Maggie reluctantly opened the scarf and pointed to the tiny catch in the bottom corner. 'This is a fault during manufacture, madam. I apologise because it ought not to have been in the drawer as it was freshly stocked yesterday. I must have placed this sales item there in error.'

'What is the price?'

'Five shillings,' Maggie said apologetically.

'I shall take that for myself, thank you – and now you can show me the quality scarves for my daughter's gift...'

Maggie was so shocked that she obeyed without the normal sales patter and was even more surprised when the customer purchased two silk scarves, one in dark blue and the other in turquoise at fifteen shillings each, and the damaged scarf for five shillings.

Maggie wrapped them all separately in tissue, done up with thin ribbons, and then placed them in a smart Harper's black and gold bag.

'Thank you, young lady.' Her customer smiled at her. 'I couldn't be seen to buy from the sales, because my friends would titter behind my back – but I love a bargain as much as the next person. It was a bit of luck for me that the cheap scarf had got stuck in your drawer...'

Maggie nodded, speechless. It was only much later that she told Rachel what had happened over a cup of coffee in the restaurant.

'That is interesting,' Rachel said as Maggie explained. 'I wonder... Sally is annoyed with herself for buying too much of the sales stuff. We could have a few reduced items on the counter without being loud about it and see what happens. I'll suggest it to Sally this evening and see what she thinks...'

'Providing they are very cheap and don't have much wrong, it might work, but not if they have a bad fault.' Maggie smiled. 'I could have sunk through the floor this morning when she demanded to see that scarf...'

'I understand her reasoning,' Rachel said thoughtfully. 'If she was seen shopping at the sales, her friends might whisper that all her clothes came from them, but if she buys when the sales are over but picks up a bargain, then no one knows.'

'Pride,' Maggie said. 'My mother always worried too much about what the neighbours thought until...'

'Yes, I know.' Rachel placed a sympathetic hand on her arm. 'Back to work, Miss Gibbs, and thank you for sharing this information...'

Her superior's formal use of her name pulled Maggie back from the edge of tears and she smiled. At work she was Mrs Craven's subordinate, but at home they were friends. The arrangement worked well, because Maggie made sure that it did. The thing she dreaded most was losing her friends, for then she would be alone.

'Thank you, Mrs Craven,' she said as they returned to their department. 'I think your idea is a good one...'

When they reached the department, Miss Hart, the floor super-visor, was glowering at Beth. She was a woman of medium height, but thin, with slightly mousy hair pulled back in a tight knot and a pale complexion, her mouth tight with disapproval. 'You left a customer standing at the bag counter for ten minutes and then she left without being served,' she said as they entered behind her.

'The customer I was serving made a large purchase of six new hats,' Beth told her. 'I apologised to the lady who was waiting and explained it was the lunch break period for my colleagues and she said she understood and would return once she'd had a cup of coffee...'

Miss Hart rounded on Rachel. 'Could you not have taken your break singly? Was it wise to leave the department understaffed?'

'We were quiet earlier and we are still a junior short,' Rachel replied in a calm voice. 'I have spoken to you, Mr Stockbridge and Miss Ross about this matter. Our busy period is due in about half an hour when the shop girls have their lunch break and I believe Miss Grey acted in a perfectly proper way...'

Miss Hart frowned in a cold manner, nodded and walked off. It was true that they were one junior short, but Rachel could perhaps have staggered the breaks more. She'd reasoned that trade always picked up again at two o'clock and gambled that Beth could cope on her own for a short time. However, there was no time to dwell on the mistake for Mr Marco, their flamboyant and talented window dresser, had walked into the department.

'Ah, Mrs Craven,' he said and his dark eyes smiled warmly. 'Always, you are so elegant – and I have come to beg for your advice...'

'Mr Marco,' she said. 'How nice to see you, I hope you have recovered from the chill you had last week?'

'I am quite well now, dear madam... and now I should like you to tell me which of your bags you think needs to be featured in my new displays. I am doing my last winter scene before we start on the spring clothes next week when it officially starts. Miss Ross wants to move on some of the winter stock that has lingered, shall we say? I have a cherry red coat with a grey fur collar as the central feature – so which of the bags should my model be using?'

'Oh... well, I think this grey snakeskin is lovely and it would tone well with the coat, but it hasn't sold despite others similar being snapped up...'

'Then I shall feature it,' Mr Marco promised. 'You will have customers asking for it within days...'

'I do hope so...' she said and handed him the expensive bag, before making a note of it in her stock book as being for window display.

'I'm sorry for what happened earlier, Mrs Craven,' Beth said as he departed. 'I mean for what Mrs Hart said to you just now, but I couldn't get to... Ah, here is your customer – she has returned, as she promised.' She smiled as a customer walked into the department.

The smart looking woman nodded to Beth. 'You were so busy earlier. I had a lovely cup of coffee and a slice of cream cake, which was delicious but will do nothing for my waistline.' Since she was willowy slim and very attractive, they all laughed.

'Perhaps I can help you now, madam?' Rachel inquired and took her place behind the counter as Beth turned to a new customer and Maggie returned to her counter.

Maggie spent a little time tidying up and noticed that Rachel sold two expensive leather bags and a silver bangle studded with garnets and pearls. It was a bangle she liked and had wished she might buy for herself, but she had little hope of being able to afford it.

'My customer was telling me how much she enjoys shopping here,' Rachel said, coming up to Maggie a little later. 'She was asking me whether she thought her daughter could get a job here for a few months. Shirley has to do some work experience for her college project. Apparently, she wants to run her grandfather's stores when she is older but she doesn't want to do her work experience course there. I told her that we needed a junior and to apply to Mr Stockbridge.'

'Let's hope she gets the job...' Maggie said. 'I'm glad it wasn't me who got into trouble with the floor walker...'

Miss Hart was sharper than ever of late and Maggie lived in terror of upsetting her and being sacked for some small misdemeanour. When her father had lived, it hadn't worried her quite as much, because she knew that he would never have complained, even if she couldn't contribute to the household expenses, but she had no family now and couldn't expect her friends to pay all the bills.

Maggie wondered what made Miss Hart have such a sour outlook on life. She knew most of the staff at Harper's now, because she liked to browse the various departments when she had time, and most of them were friendly, even the supervisors – so why did Miss Hart always look as if she had been sucking lemons?

Maggie put her worries from her mind and smiled as several customers entered the department at the same time. Three of them went to Beth's counter and started asking about hats and trying them on, one went to Rachel's counter and the fifth came to Maggie. She was an elderly lady, a little plump and didn't look as if she could afford very much for a scarf.

'I want to see your very best silk scarves,' she announced with a twinkle in her eyes. 'My daughter-in-law has just had a little boy and I know she covets one of your scarves...'

Maggie thought quickly, recalling a very pregnant young woman who had looked at her stock recently. 'Does she have dark blonde hair worn in a roll around her head?' she asked and the woman nodded. 'It was these two she was looking at just last week, madam...' Maggie displayed two very pretty navy, red and white headscarves priced at seventeen shillings and sixpence each.

'Did my Daisy indicate which she preferred?' the woman asked.

'She couldn't quite decide and said she would think about it...'

'Then perhaps I'll take both of them,' Maggie's customer said and smiled. 'She's a clever girl – just given me a beautiful grandson. That deserves a present, doesn't it?'

'Yes, it does, madam,' Maggie said, responding with a smile of her own as she wrapped the two pretty scarves in tissue. 'She will be thrilled with such a lovely gift...'

Maggie took the exact money, gave her customer the bag and watched as she left the department. How kind that lady was – so different from the way Ralf's mother had been towards her...

4

Beth's resentment at being unfairly blamed for keeping a customer waiting smouldered until she met Sally when taking her tea break. Sally invited her for coffee in her office and it was served with iced biscuits and fruit cake and was much nicer than queuing in the restaurant. Sally was so generous, sharing her privileges with her friends.

'You're lucky to have this office and a secretary,' Beth said and savoured the taste of the roast beans as she sipped the fragrant drink.

'I'm supposed to share it, of course, but at the moment it's all mine,' Sally said. 'I enjoy my work and the perks are great – but it is hard work, Beth. I sometimes wish I was back in the department. I had less responsibility. If I make a mistake now it could affect the business...'

'Yes, I do understand,' Beth said, because Sally must feel the pressure of so much responsibility. 'I like my work – but not when Miss Hart is mooching around finding fault.' She explained about the customer waiting at the bag counter and Sally nodded.

'Yes, that is the problem when you're dealing with expensive goods. You have to serve each customer. You can't just leave them. At least with hats and clothes, they can wander around and look for a while and try some on – and the assistants will see them to the changing rooms. With bags and silver jewellery, customers either wait or return later...'

'She did return and bought two bags and a bangle – the one Maggie wants and we'd agreed the three of us would buy for her birthday...'

'It's a good thing I bought another just like it and kept it in reserve then,' Sally smiled. 'Maggie will forget it and then it will be a real surprise on her birthday...'

'Oh, that's great,' Beth said. 'I'll give you my share of its cost when Maggie isn't around at home. Not that she goes out much, unless it's with one of us...'

'I haven't heard her mention that boyfriend of hers for ages,' Sally said thoughtfully. 'There's no chance she's still seeing Ralf, I suppose? I know he came to the store to see her, but I didn't think she would go out with him after the way he behaved...'

'At the moment, she says she doesn't want to meet him,' Beth said. 'He has tried to speak to her a couple of times since Christmas, but she's still angry at the way his mother acted. He should have stood up to her and protected Maggie at a time like that...'

Sally shook her head. 'He certainly didn't behave well...'

'I don't like him and I hope she doesn't take up with him again,' Beth confessed. 'I got a postcard from Ireland this morning. Jack's boat stopped there because of storm damage for repairs. He is on his way home and he'll be on leave all next week.'

'Lucky you,' Sally smiled. She liked Beth's boyfriend.

'Thanks for the coffee,' Beth said. 'I'd better get back. Miss Hart got out of bed the wrong side and is on the warpath today.'

'When isn't she?' Sally laughed. 'I know she has a job to do, but so does Mr Stockbridge and he always manages to be pleasant to everyone.'

Beth agreed and left, acknowledging the secretary, Miss Summers, as she walked through the outer office. She didn't really envy Sally this job, even though it was well paid and there were extras like having your morning coffee brought in on a tray.

As Beth walked to the lift, Mr Stockbridge was just leaving his office and speaking to Mr Marco and Mr Brown, the new buyer, a man of a similar age, small, dark and a little anxious looking. He was now in charge of the buying for the men's department, which was the least successful in the store, though doing better than it had at the start.

'Good morning, Mr Stockbridge, Mr Marco – Mr Brown,' Beth said as she walked past.

'Good afternoon, Miss Grey,' Mr Marco replied, a look of mischief in his eyes as he reminded her that it was now well past noon.

'Yes, sir,' she laughed as he gave her a discreet wink.

Mr Brown looked on as if he had toothache and she wondered how two people could be so different – but Mr Marco had a job he loved and was very successful and perhaps Mr Brown wasn't as happy in his work. It was better if you enjoyed what you did, she thought.

Selling hats was enjoyable and Beth could do it well and easily. She wouldn't have minded Rachel's position as head of the department but did not resent her. It was just that her own work was not always enough and she would have liked to be a supervisor and earn a little more money so she could help Jack save for his own business. He was so enthusiastic about the hotel he wanted and she loved it when he was home. When he was away at sea, she would've been lonely if she hadn't been living with her friends.

Beth returned to her counter just as they started to get busy and spent the next three hours serving customers. She tidied up her display, bringing in fresh stock. Sally had bought quite a bit of pale straw for the spring and they were already selling well, despite the prolonged cold weather. Women had had enough of the long winter and a new hat was one way of cheering yourself up.

Beth didn't need to cheer herself up with a new hat now that Jack was coming home on leave again. They would go out several evenings, even if it was just to the pub for a drink or to his home. Beth smiled at the thought. She would pop in and speak to Fred Burrows before she went home, let him know that she'd heard from his son and he would be with them by the weekend if not before.

* * *

Fred grinned broadly at her when she popped into the basement, which was his domain. He was one of the last in the store at night and would make sure everything was secure before he locked up for the evening. Like Mr Stockbridge, he had a key to the staff entrance and he checked every door and window with the manager every night before they both left. He now had a young lad named Willie Jones to help him, which took some of the workload from his shoulders. Willie was just fifteen and it was his first job. Freckle-faced and eager to please, Beth liked him and was glad Fred had help.

'That's grand news, Beth,' he said when she told him the news of Jack's return. 'You'll come to supper one day when Jack is home and Tim might turn up if we're lucky. He'll want to see his brother...'

She smiled. 'I'll bet Tim will be made up now the Royal Flying Corps has its first military airfield in Scotland.'

'I'm not so pleased with him being based up there half the time...' Fred sighed. 'I know he's a man, but I'd like him nearer me...'

'Let's hope he gets leave soon then. We'll get some fish and chips as a treat,' she said, 'and some of those pickled onions your friend, Martha, sells on the market...'

'Aye, Martha makes the best pickles,' Fred agreed. 'Best I've tasted leastways.'

'Best I've had too,' Beth said, smiling at him. 'I'll get off now, Fred. I'm going to a lecture on women's rights this evening – it's not one of the big rallies, just a meeting of friends to talk about the way things are going. We have to be a bit careful at the moment because of what Emmeline Pankhurst did...'

'Ay, poor lass,' Fred said. 'They will send that lady to prison this time and the way they treat you ladies is terrible sometimes; that force-feeding is wicked. You just be careful you don't get yourself into trouble and end up behind bars.'

'It's just Mrs Craven and me this evening, but we're not going to Mrs Pankhurst's branch of the Movement anyway; ours isn't militant, but they think we're all the same...' Beth acknowledged. 'I'll see you tomorrow, Fred...'

'Goodnight, Beth,' the porter replied. 'I shall look forward to seeing you for supper next week! And be in nice and early tomorrow, because I've got a load of stuff to bring up to your department first thing...'

She waved to him and hid her smile as Willie winked at her broadly. Her life seemed so much fuller these days than it had when she'd lived at home with her invalid mother...

5

'It is with regret that I tell you that Christabel Pankhurst will be leaving England to live in Paris for a while,' the speaker said. She was standing on stage at the small hall hired for their meeting and it was crammed full of ladies, who hung on her every word. 'Her presence will be greatly missed, but because of that beastly Cat and Mouse Act she cannot remain here...'

The Act had been devised by Mr Asquith's Liberal government to overcome the suffragettes' defiance in going on hunger strike. Because of the outcry against force-feeding women who refused to eat when arrested for standing up for women's rights, Parliament had come up with the idea of letting the women go when the alternative would be starvation or force-feeding and then, a few months later, when they had recovered their strength, re-arresting them. Unless they were extremely strong-willed, it was believed that it would break their resolve and was hated by the Movement as a whole, whether the militant or the passive section.

An attractive, clever and dedicated woman, Christabel Pankhurst was the daughter of Emmeline and an extremely devoted father, who stood with them in their cause. She had been

educated to high standards and was responsible for forming the
Women's Social Political Union, or the WSPU as it was generally
known, thereby almost splitting the movement in two, by dividing
the militants from those who favoured more passive protest.
However, she was seen as an inspiration, even by those ladies who
did not wish to use force, and it was agreed that her absence would
be keenly felt, but as she'd been imprisoned several times, she
needed to stay away from Britain for a while to regain her health
and strength.

'Our sister will of course stay in touch and she will guide us
from Paris,' the speaker went on. 'Dear Emmeline is once again
facing the brutality of the law and I ask you to pray for her with me,
sisters...'

Everyone stood and repeated the prayer that Emmeline
Pankhurst would come through the ordeal of trial and imprisonment safe and well, and then the meeting was over. It had been
suggested that a march through London take place quite soon and
the word would be sent out to all branches of the Movement.
Banners and sashes would be needed to show support, but it would
be a peaceful protest this time.

'We should not give the authorities cause to treat us so badly,'
the speaker said. 'In other countries we are listened to with more
respect, but here our leaders seem blind as well as deaf to our
requests for equality.'

'I think things are better in America,' Rachel said as she and
Beth walked home after the meeting. 'Why do you think the men
who sit in parliament are so blind? Why can they not see that it
would cost them almost nothing to give us the right to vote?'

'Perhaps they think that once we have that we shall want more,'
Beth suggested. 'Women have always obeyed their husbands and
worked for masters who treated them no better than servants. If we
can vote, then we can ask for equal rights at work and play...'

'I do not see where it harms a man if a woman has the same rights...'

'And the same rate of pay...' Beth said. 'Those who employ women in the factories would never be prepared to pay as much as they pay the men...'

'Why not, if they do as much work as the men?'

'A man would say that was not possible, and I suppose in some forms of manual labour it would not be,' Beth said with a smile. 'I do not think either of us would do well at digging up the roads nor building houses, do you?'

'No, I don't,' Rachel laughed. 'But we are just as good at serving customers in the store...'

'Perhaps better,' Beth replied. 'However, I do not think the men that work at Harper's would be happy if we were paid the same as them...'

'No, they would not.' Rachel agreed and they reached their bus stop. There had been no trouble outside the meeting that night, for it had not been advertised openly. Together they felt quite safe, though neither would have liked to be out at night alone.

As they boarded the bus taking them home, both were thoughtful. They had agreed to take part in the peaceful protest, but, as all the ladies at the meeting had known, such marches were not always allowed to remain peaceful occasions. Hecklers would try to provoke a reaction and if there was violence the police would use it as an excuse to break up the meeting and arrest the women taking part... and it made no difference whether you belonged to the pacifist side of the movement or the militants now.

* * *

'I'm so glad you're home safely,' Beth said when Jack was waiting for her to leave work the next evening. She ran into his arms and embraced him, feeling the thrill of being so close to him. Each time she saw him, she fell more and more in love with him.

'I couldn't wait to see you,' he'd said. 'I've got my car – shall we go for a little drive before I take you home?'

'Yes, please...'

Jack opened the door and she climbed in. He smiled at her and drew away from the kerb.

'I miss you so much when you're away, Jack...'

Jack didn't answer, merely smiling at her until he pulled into the courtyard of a public house that did good food.

'And I miss you,' he said and drew her into his arms, kissing her sweetly but with passion. 'I read your letters in turn and make them last the voyage out, but then I read them all again on the way home.'

'I love you and I'm glad you're home...'

'Let's go and have a few drinks and a nice meal,' Jack said, getting out and opening her door. 'I only have a week's leave and I don't want to waste a minute...'

'I had a letter from Aunt Helen this morning,' Beth said as they went into the pub. 'She wants me to go for tea on Saturday when I leave work. I'll finish about four this week and I can catch the bus to her home, but if you wanted, you could fetch me at around six and just say "hello" to her.'

'Yes, why not?' Jack replied. 'I've got some things to do on Saturday and I might have some news when I come...'

'What do you mean?' Beth asked. 'What kind of news?'

'It will be a surprise if it comes off...' he said mysteriously.

Beth laughed because Jack liked surprising her.

He treated her to a lovely meal of ham, egg and chips, and then later drove her back to the apartment she shared with her friends.

'I'll see you tomorrow,' he said. 'I'll be waiting when you leave work and we're going to my home for supper...'

'All right...' Beth leaned in to kiss him again and he caught her, holding her tight against him. She felt the warmth of his breath on her face and a shiver of wanting went through them both. 'Jack... I do love you...'

'I love you, want you so much,' he said, and nuzzled her neck. 'I hate it that you have to leave me, Beth. I want us to be together. I want to have you next to me in bed and love you...'

She hugged him and then kissed his nose in a teasing way. 'We have to wait for a while, Jack. We can't afford our own business yet and unless we save, we never shall. Once we have children, the chance will be lost...'

'Yes, I know.' He sighed reluctantly and moved back, looking at her longingly for a moment before getting out of the car and holding the door for her. 'Sometimes when I'm close to you I forget to be sensible...'

'I could easily forget too,' she whispered. 'But I know how important it is to you, Jack.'

'Not as important as you,' he replied and sighed. 'You are right and I'm too impatient. I'll see you tomorrow, Beth...'

Beth left him and let herself into the apartment. She could hear laughter coming from the sitting room and when she entered saw Sally showing the others some magazines. They had cups of cocoa on the table and looked comfortable and happy. Beth went to sit on the spare chair and picked up one of the magazines, which had pictures of various new outfits and hats ready for summer. Living with Sally, you always knew ahead of time what was going to be in the shops next season.

'Did you have a lovely evening?' Rachel asked and Beth nodded. 'Far more interesting than our meeting the other night then...'

'Yes, much,' she said. 'I shall be going to Jack's home for supper tomorrow and on Saturday I'm having tea with Aunt Helen. Jack will fetch me afterwards and we'll spend the evening together –

because that will be his last on shore for a while.' She sighed because his shore visits were all too short.

'I would say you were a gadabout, except that Jack's visits are always short,' Sally said and smiled. 'Truthfully, I'm envious. I was just telling Maggie about a play I saw last year and trying to persuade her and Rachel that we should go to a theatre on Saturday...'

'Why don't you all go?' Beth asked. 'It would be a lovely treat. Is there a good play or a nice musical show?'

'There's something about Irving Berlin in the paper,' Rachel said. 'I think his hit song – "Everybody's doing it!" – is still very popular, and there's a concert of his songs and others on at the Lyceum, I think...'

Beth left them discussing the possibility of a visit to hear the concert on Saturday evening as she went into her bedroom.

She looked at herself in the bedroom mirror and thought that her mouth looked thoroughly kissed. Had the others noticed? No one had said anything. She felt heat tinge her cheeks as she recalled how close she'd felt to giving into the urgency of Jack's kisses.

'Something wrong?' Sally's voice made her start. 'You looked a little sad?'

'No, not sad, just thoughtful,' Beth said, and turned to smile at her. 'Have you ever wanted to do more than kiss a man, Sally?'

'Once or twice I've wondered what it would be like,' Sally nodded, 'but not enough to make me forget myself. Is Jack becoming a little impatient?'

'Just a little. He wouldn't... you know... but he wants to be married...'

'And you don't?'

'Yes, I do love him,' Beth said. 'Even so, I'm just not sure I'm ready for children and being just a housewife. I enjoy my life here with all of you...'

'We do have fun,' Sally agreed. 'I hated living alone and I was often unhappy before, but living with you and the others is so much better. If you wanted to come to the concert, we could go another night...'

'Oh no, you should all go on Saturday. You will enjoy it.'

'You're lucky to have Jack,' Sally said, surprising Beth. 'Don't hesitate too long and lose him, Beth. Living with friends is fun, but a husband, love and a family is worth so much more. I want that more than anything...'

'With the right man... you wouldn't just marry for the sake of it?'

'No, of course not, and I too love my life as it is, for the moment. I'm just saying that you could have something more, Beth. Don't lose it unless you really don't want it...'

'I've wondered...' Beth looked at her and suddenly the thought struck her. 'Is it Mr Harper, Sally? Is it because of him that you've been a bit down for a while?'

Sally hesitated and then, 'It's stupid, I know – and I've nothing to hope for, but I was rather attracted when he was here...'

'The way he swept in and transferred you to the top floor, just like that, took my breath away,' Beth said. 'I thought he was going to try and seduce you...'

'No, he didn't – though I thought he was interested once or twice, but he never said anything. Sometimes, I think he'll just stay in America and leave the store to his managers...'

'But you must hear from him,' Beth said. 'He wrote a letter to Mr Stockbridge thanking us all for making the store a success. Mr Stockbridge read it out at the Christmas staff meeting – and we were told to have a sale after Christmas...'

'It was Jenni Harper who advised me to have a sale,' Sally told her sadly. 'Mr Harper wrote to Mr Stockbridge about the store and Jenni writes regularly to me. I can't understand why he doesn't come back...' Her voice caught with emotion.

Beth felt bewildered. 'I don't understand it, Sally. He seemed so keen on making a success of Harper's...'

'Well, it is a success,' Sally said. 'I think we could make a few changes here and there, but overall it is doing well... but...' She shook her head. 'I'm a fool. I don't know why I liked him so much; it's just a silly crush, I suppose...'

'I'm so sorry you've been hurt. I know it does hurt when someone lets you down...'

'He didn't, not really. It was all in my mind.' Sally shrugged and raised her head. 'I've decided I shan't waste any more time thinking of him! I'm going to visit some friends on Sunday. You'll be feeling a bit down after Jack leaves – why don't you come with me? It will be a day out. We could have lunch and then a nice walk before we come home...'

'Yes, all right,' Beth said and impulsively threw her arms about Sally and hugged her. 'Let's make it a day out, just the two of us, and forget our worries for a while...'

6

'What is wrong, Aunt Helen?' Beth took her aunt's hand and held it, feeling the faint tremor. She'd sensed something immediately she entered her aunt's neat parlour and now she was certain Aunt Helen was troubled. Glancing round, Beth recognised some of her aunt's furniture, but there were other things that must belong to her new husband, Gerald. 'I can see you're upset – do you want to tell me about it?' Aunt Helen's marriage had happened so quickly and Beth had never been quite certain she liked Gerald. There was something about him that made her uneasy, though she couldn't put a finger on it.

'There's nothing wrong,' Aunt Helen said gruffly. 'Don't bother about me, tell me what you've been doing – are you still courting that young man?'

'Yes, I'm meeting Jack later,' Beth replied. 'He is coming to pick me up – and then he's back to sea tomorrow...'

'As long as you're happy...' Beth's aunt sounded so down that she knew something was badly wrong, because she'd always been such a strong and confident woman. 'I know you're upset – is there anything I can do?'

Her aunt shook her head.

'Surely, there must be something...'

'I made a foolish mistake, Beth,' she said, the words coming out of her in a rush. Tears were in her eyes and her hand trembled. 'I should never have married him...'

'What has Gerald done?' Beth asked, seeing the pain and hurt Aunt Helen was valiantly trying to hide. 'I thought he loved you – and you seemed to care for him.'

'I imagined his courtship meant love, but I was wrong...' Aunt Helen looked at Beth for a long moment. 'Gerald was looking for a rich widow and he thought I had more money than I did... I suppose he believed the house was mine. When he discovered I had no more than two hundred and fifty pounds in the bank and lived on the interest from a trust that dies with me, he changed towards me. He has been... most unpleasant...' Her voice sounded close to breaking and Beth reached for her hand and held it tightly. They had not always been the greatest of friends while Beth lived with her, but she could not bear to see her aunt in such distress.

'Will you leave him?' she asked, for it seemed the best thing.

'Oh no, I couldn't,' Aunt Helen looked shocked. 'What would people say if I walked out so soon after my wedding? Besides, it would make him look a fool or worse and he would never allow that...'

'Has he threatened you with violence?'

'No...' Aunt Helen denied it, but Beth sensed the uncertainty in her voice. 'Not in so many words; he contents himself with scorn...'

'I am so sorry,' Beth said. It was only a matter of months since the wedding and her aunt was a proud, independent lady. For her to have told Beth of her husband's mistreatment, it must be harsh. 'Is there anything I can do? Could I speak to him or...?'

'No! That would be the worst thing you could do,' Aunt Helen said and her voice caught. 'I just wanted you to know in case...' she hesitated and then shook her head. 'No, I am foolish... he would not...'

'He wouldn't harm you...' Beth touched her arm gently. Aunt Helen winced and as she moved her arm, the sleeve fell back and Beth caught sight of a dark bruise. 'Did Gerald do that to you?'

Beth thought her aunt would deny it, but then she nodded and a tear trickled down her cheek. 'I have taken out another insurance policy on my life. I had one before I married, but he said it wasn't enough... he asked me to take a new policy out and it is for a large sum of money. When I questioned him, he told me it was compensation for his disappointment and that I should be glad to protect his future and mine. He took out a policy on his own life too, naming me as the beneficiary, so I could hardly refuse.' She blinked hard and then said, 'Oh, Beth, he accused me of deceiving him, of making it appear I had more savings than I did...' Aunt Helen swallowed a sob. 'I think he would be glad if I died...'

'Oh, Aunt Helen,' Beth said and put an arm about her shoulders. Was it her imagination or had her aunt lost weight? 'He wouldn't do anything terrible, would he?'

'No, for if I was murdered he would get nothing from the insurance...' Aunt Helen paused, then, 'He will not get it, though, I've made certain of that... Gerald has taken much of what I had, sold my best things and my savings have gone – and only a few hidden things remain...' She blinked hard, her eyes misted with tears. Yet in that moment she was more like the woman of old – determined and a little angry.

Beth listened in angry silence. Gerald had clearly bullied Aunt Helen into giving up her money and her precious things, but for the moment Beth was more concerned with her aunt's suffering than what she'd lost.

Beth would have liked to pack her aunt's things and take her away before anything terrible could happen, but even as she tried to think of a way to persuade Aunt Helen to leave the brute she had married, they heard the back door and then Gerald entered the parlour. For a moment, his eyes narrowed in displeasure and then he smiled with his mouth but not his eyes.

'Beth, how nice of you to visit Helen,' he said. 'Had I known you were coming, I would have stayed at home and put off my business...'

Beth's mind worked quickly. 'I called on the off-chance that I would find you both at home,' she lied and saw gratitude in her aunt's eyes. 'I was just about to leave, but I am glad to have seen you, Mr Greene.'

'Oh, surely you will call me Gerald now,' he said and the look in his eyes made Beth want to grit her teeth. She remembered the way she'd felt excluded at their wedding and the coldness in his eyes as he'd looked at her. Why hadn't she warned her aunt then – but it had already been too late and at the time she'd dismissed it as being her imagination...

'Of course, Gerald, if you wish,' she said. 'I must go now...'

'No, stay a little longer and I shall hear all your news,' he said and smiled at his wife in a way that held no warmth or love. 'Please, Helen, make a fresh pot of tea, and I shall have a piece of this lovely cake. How fortunate that you had made one of Beth's favourites today – I seem to remember, did you not once tell me that you particularly like ginger cake, Beth?'

'Yes, quite possibly,' Beth replied. It was another half an hour to six o'clock and she thought that two could play Gerald's game. 'I was telling Aunt Helen that I had joined the Women's Movement, though not the militant branch...' It was a calculated guess that Gerald would not approve and it gave him the opportunity to lecture her on the folly of allowing women to have a say in the running of the country. He informed her that women did not have the right kind of minds to run successful businesses and harangued her about the superiority of the male species in all things.

Beth allowed him to rant and did not attempt to disagree, though she thought him biased and stupid in his blinkered attitude. However, it seemed to please him that Beth allowed him to lecture her and he appeared to forget his earlier suspicions.

When Jack came to the door and rang the bell, Beth was able to take leave of her aunt and, though she could say little, a squeeze of the hand told her that Aunt Helen had understood the reason for her meek acceptance of the lecture and thanked her for it.

She kissed her cheek and whispered, 'Leave him, dear aunt, I beg you...'

Aunt Helen said nothing, just smiling and waving as she left.

Beth did not ask Jack into the house and he looked at her oddly as she gave him a little push down the path.

'What is it?' he said once they were sitting in the car. 'I know that look, Beth – something has made you angry.'

'That insufferable man!' she said between clenched teeth as they drove away.

'Your aunt's new husband?'

'Yes, unfortunately. She made a terrible mistake, Jack. He thought she had money – much more than she did – and he has taken out a large insurance on her life.'

'Lots of husband and wives take out big insurances...'

'You didn't see the way he looked at me when he came in, Jack. Aunt Helen hadn't told him I was visiting and the expression in his eyes was murderous. I let him think I called on the off-chance, but he knew the truth. Aunt Helen had prepared cakes and sandwiches I like...'

Jack was silent for a moment. 'All marriages have their ups and downs, Beth...'

'Yes, I know.' Beth nodded. 'But she had a bruise on her wrist she tried to hide from me and she is very unhappy. I wished I might help her, but she wouldn't leave him; she seems broken, resigned to her fate.'

'It would be difficult for her to find a new home...' Jack frowned. 'I'm sorry, Beth. I know there are men like that – men who prey on rich women who live alone and are not married...'

Beth nodded, thoughtfully. 'If I could find her somewhere to go – somewhere out of London where she could start again...'

'For that she would have to agree,' Jack reminded her. 'Your Aunt Helen is a stubborn lady, Beth. I cannot see her leaving everything she took to the marriage behind – and that is what it would mean, because he would stop her taking the furniture. He may even have control of what money she has...'

Beth looked at him anxiously. 'I'm worried about her, Jack. Supposing he means to murder her for the insurance?'

'That is a bit dramatic,' Jack said, and frowned. 'He would need to be very careful, because if there was any suspicion, he wouldn't get a penny of the money and he could hang for murder.'

'Yes, I know...' Beth sighed. 'Gerald thinks that women are inferior beings and believes we don't have the sense to run a successful business – a man like that probably believes he could commit murder and get away with it...'

'Yes, there is a possibility that he might,' Jack said and a glint of anger flicked in his eyes. 'Next time you visit your aunt, Beth, I shall come with you. I'm not saying I could prevent him doing whatever it is he intends, but at least I could help persuade her to leave him if she's really unhappy. Dad would take her in until she sorted things out for herself...'

'Oh Jack, you're a lovely person,' Beth said and kissed his cheek. 'Thank you for listening and understanding. It upset me for a while, but, in truth, I think Gerald is probably just a bully. He will go on making Aunt Helen's life a misery, but I don't really see him as a murderer. He would have to be clever to have any chance of getting away with it...'

'Then he probably won't do it,' Jack said. 'He has underestimated both you and your aunt, and in my book that makes him a fool – a bully and a fool...'

'Yes, perhaps you're right. I'm just being silly, because I don't see him as a cold, calculating murderer,' Beth said and immediately felt better. 'I'm glad I talked to you, Jack – and now we should enjoy our evening, because it will be our last together for a while.'

'I shouldn't be away much more than four weeks next trip, but if you're worried, remember you can always talk to my father...' Jack said.

'Yes, I know,' Beth said and kissed him. 'I'll keep an eye on her and that's all I can do for now...'

7

Rachel and Maggie had gone to church together that Sunday morning. They were taking some flowers to the graves of Maggie's parents and Rachel's husband. They were buried in different churchyards but only a bus ride apart. Beth and Sally had decided to visit some friends of Sally's and they caught the bus to Pimlico at just after ten o' clock.

Sally had bought a box of Fry's chocolates to take for her friends. 'I haven't visited in a long time,' she told Beth. 'I'm glad you came with me – it's nicer than going alone...'

'I should only be moping at home and worrying,' Beth said. 'I'm glad to be out with you...'

'Are you worried about Jack?'

Beth shook her head and then told her some of what her aunt had confided about her marriage.

'They'd probably had an argument,' Sally suggested. 'Most marriages go through bad patches, so I've been told...'

'Yes, I'm sure that's true,' Beth agreed. 'I don't remember my parents ever having a serious disagreement, but Dad was so patient and loving with Mum. He was the one that did everything for us... that's why it was such a shock when he became so ill and died...'

Sally nodded. 'I wish I'd got some memories to share, Beth, but mine were none of them good – just discipline from the nuns and lectures from the priests. That's if they didn't try to grope you. I know some of the girls were in tears after they had to visit the priest's office. One of them tried to touch me once and I bit him. I broke the skin and he ran away to get it bathed with antiseptic. He called me a vixen but never tried to touch me again...'

'How wicked of him!'

Sally laughed as Beth looked at her in horror. 'It happens all the time at these orphanages, Beth. I think it is why the kids can't wait to get out of them, even though it's hard to manage alone.'

Beth nodded. Sally didn't often speak of the past and when she did it made Beth see just why she valued her friends so much. She'd had a hard life and it must have been lonely much of the time.

Changing the subject, they spoke of Emmeline Pankhurst, who had been sentenced to prison for three years for inciting arson. In the past, Emmeline would have gone on a starvation diet, knowing the prison authorities would let her out rather than see her die. Because of the Cat and Mouse Act, she would know that even if she used her trump card, they would re-arrest her as soon as she was well enough. It was another way of bending the suffragettes to the will of Parliament.

'It's a wicked way to treat the suffragettes...' Sally said furiously.

'Yes, it is, but I can't agree with what Emmeline did,' Beth said and decided to change the subject. 'Tell me, Sally, how do you know Sylvia? Was she from the orphanage too?'

'No, we met at the hostel. She came up from the country to find work,' Sally explained. 'We became friends for a while – I didn't know her well, but she found a job at the pub of a woman named

Marlene through Mick. He ran the pub opposite the hostel and was a good friend when we needed him – and then Marlene said I could work for her if I chose...'

'You wouldn't think of leaving Harper's?'

'Not at the moment,' Sally said. 'It depends how things are in the future – but I might be in need of a job when Mr Harper comes back... if I find it too difficult to work with him.'

Beth nodded. Sally didn't often show she was restless, but despite her successful job, she wasn't as happy as she should be and Beth wondered if this visit was to see whether she would enjoy working there in the event she needed a new job. Beth knew Sally had feelings for Ben Harper, even though she pretended they were nothing more than a silly crush.

The ancient pub was a short distance from the river in Pimlico and had a restaurant overlooking the riverbanks. It looked beautiful despite the dull morning, its grey walls half covered by creeping roses that would look wonderful in summer, and surprised Beth, who hadn't expected anything as impressive.

'This is lovely...' Beth breathed. 'When you said a pub, I never thought it was like this...'

'I didn't either. I suppose I ought to have visited before, but there never seemed time,' Sally said. 'I feel a bit guilty now...'

The public bar was closed, because it was Sunday, and the only drinking allowed was in the restaurant with the purchase of food. The notice in the glass door enabled the customers to see what was available before they entered.

'Can I help you?' a girl asked as they went in. 'Have you booked a table?'

'No, we haven't,' Sally said. 'I didn't realise it was necessary...'

'We're always busy on Sundays,' the girl explained. 'We might be able to squeeze you in – I'll ask Marlene...'

'It seems they're busy even on Sundays...' Sally looked surprised.

'I think it's because they serve alcohol,' Beth said. 'Not every café has a license...'

A well-dressed woman with bleached hair came out of the office. She was looking at her bookings and, Beth thought, about to refuse them a table when she saw Sally and her face lit up with a smile of welcome.

'Sally! As I live and breathe it is you, darlin'. Sylvia ain't 'ere today– but I'll find a table for you and your friend and you can sit and tell me everything. Come into my office while Jean gets your table ready...'

They followed her into a comfortable office. It was crammed full of antique tables, chairs and a magnificent partner's desk. On the wall were paintings of river scenes and birds flying and there were two great vases of flowers that smelled gorgeous.

'Sit down, both of you,' Marlene said and beamed at them both. 'Please tell me the name of your friend, Sally.'

'I'm Beth Grey,' Beth said. 'I work at Harper's in the hat department...'

'That's nice, dear,' Marlene replied. 'Mick told me you've got an important job, Sally. Gone right up in the world he says...' Her eyes went to Sally's left hand, as if seeking something. 'He thought you might be wed...'

'No, I'm not engaged or married,' Sally laughed. 'Mick doesn't change then?'

'Mick never changes,' Marlene said and rolled her eyes. 'He'll make some lucky girl a fabulous husband, but unfortunately I'm old enough to be his mum.' She laughed as if that were a great joke.

'Of course you're not,' Sally responded with a smile. 'I refuse to believe you're a day over thirty-five, Marlene, and Mick must be thirty or more...'

'He's twenty-nine and a bit,' Marlene said, eyes dancing with mischief. 'I may not be too old, but I might as well be – that lad has eyes only for one lass...'

Beth saw the colour rise in Sally's cheek. Marlene was teasing, but she was near the mark, because Mick had obviously shown interest in Sally. Beth wondered if Sally had any interest in him. She'd thought Sally was breaking her heart over Mr Harper but hadn't known anything about this other man.

'Well, you can ask him yourself if you like, Sally love. Mick has a table booked for four friends today and he'll be coming with them. You'll say "hello" of course. He'll be surprised to see you here...'

'I wanted a day out,' Sally replied, oddly defensive. 'How is Sylvia getting on here?'

'She's a very popular young woman,' Marlene said but frowned. 'One of the customers insisted on taking her to the country for the day. He's promised to take her to a marvellous restaurant and Sylvia is interested in sampling some of the food. We're always looking for new ideas here...'

The receptionist knocked, entering to tell them their table was ready and Marlene took them through herself. As soon as they were settled, she wound her way in and out of the tables, speaking to all the customers and asking them if the food was all right. Everyone seemed pleased and Beth looked in awe at the menu when it arrived. They settled on roast duck, sautéed potatoes and red cabbage with red wine sauce. For pudding she was torn between a sherry trifle in an individual dish with a cherry on top or a brandy-snap basket with home-made ice cream and peaches.

It was as their coffee was brought that a man Beth thought attractive came up to their table.

'Excuse me,' he addressed her. 'I don't mean to be rude, but I want to say "hello" to Sally...' He had a slight lilt to his voice but not enough to make him stand out as being Irish, she thought.

'Mick, nice to see you,' Sally said and smiled up at him. 'This is my friend, Beth Grey.'

'Pleased to meet you, Miss Grey,' Mick grinned. 'Did the two of you enjoy your meal then?'

'It was lovely,' Beth replied. 'I can't ever remember having anything as delicious.'

'Well, you must come again,' Mick said. 'Marlene will always find a table for friends – and if you will permit me, I should like you to accept this lunch as a gift from me to both of you...'

'No, you can't do that,' Sally said. 'It's kind of you – but I'm paying. It's my treat for Beth...'

'Well, I shan't keep you any longer,' Mick said, seeming to accept her words. 'Enjoy the rest of your day, ladies...' He nodded and walked away. Beth watched and saw he went into Marlene's office.

'He seems nice,' Beth ventured when Sally was silent. 'It was generous of him to offer to pay for the lunch – but I'm sharing the bill with you, Sally. I didn't intend you to pay it all.'

'No, I asked you to come,' Sally said and frowned. 'Mick is too much... if you give him an inch he will take a mile...'

'He didn't seem that sort to me...' Beth replied.

'He was always too familiar,' Sally continued. 'I like him. He can be a good friend – but he wants too much...'

'You mean he thinks a lot of you and you don't want to get involved,' Beth said, seeing more than Sally realised. 'You like him too, but he isn't the kind of man you'd want to get involved with...'

'No, he isn't,' Sally admitted. 'I do like him, you're right, but – that's it...' She frowned. 'I didn't expect him to be here...'

'I think he knows Marlene very well,' Beth said, having observed them. 'Do you think he is a partner in the business?'

'What makes you ask that?'

'Oh – just the way she spoke to him and he followed her into the office. I don't know anything, Sally. I just wondered...'

'You might be right,' Sally looked thoughtful now. 'I thought he just managed the pub near where I lived, but perhaps...' She shrugged. 'It makes no difference.'

'I suppose not...'

Beth broke off as two men entered the dining room together, glancing at Sally to see if she'd seen Mr Marco with the younger man. Sally didn't seem to have noticed and the two were shown to a discreet table in an alcove and out of sight of most of the diners. It was hardly their business. Beth decided not to mention it because Sally seemed lost in her thoughts.

Beth finished her coffee. She was convinced that Sally was more interested in the Irishman than she would allow. Sally kept her secrets, but she liked Mick, whatever she said...

* * *

It was pleasant walking by the river that afternoon, because a weak sun broke through the clouds. Although they were in March, it wasn't really spring yet, but neither was it as cold as it had been for a while and they watched swans and ducks gliding by on the dark waters of the Thames.

When they were ready, they caught a bus home and had tea with Rachel and Maggie by the fire. Rachel had bought some crumpets the previous day and they took turns toasting them and spreading lots of butter and thick honey on top.

'These are the times I shall always remember,' Sally said as she brought a tray of fresh tea through for them. 'It has been a perfect day... but a bit bittersweet for you and Maggie, Rachel.'

'I'm over the loss of my husband now,' Rachel said and glanced at Maggie. 'It will take a little longer for Maggie – but I think it helped today, visiting their resting places.'

'Yes, it did,' Maggie agreed and smiled. 'I think I'm so lucky to have good friends.' She looked at Rachel, who nodded. 'We saw some other friends after church and we've agreed to go on a march with the Women's Movement next Sunday morning. Rachel already has a sash to wear and I've been promised one – shall you both come?'

'Yes, I'll come,' Sally said. 'I think it's time we demonstrated in a peaceful manner again. I don't think there's much sense in bombs and violence, but I'm happy to march or to chain myself to the railings of Hyde Park...'

'I think we'll stick to marching with banners,' Rachel said and laughed softly. 'None of us want to end up in prison. I agree with Sally that a peaceful protest is the best way forward.'

8

Fred brought up several boxes of new spring hats to the department on Monday morning. He winked at Beth and carried them into the stockroom for her. 'My Tim was sayin' how nice it was havin' you over to supper, Beth. We thought you might like to come to lunch on Sunday?'

'Yes, I would – but it depends how long the march goes on for, Fred. I'll pop over when I can – but don't wait if you're hungry. I can always stay for tea...'

'Right you are,' he said and hesitated, then, 'Take care, Beth. I reckon the coppers and those who stand against women's rights will have it in for you ladies this time. They won't care that you don't belong to the militant branch of your union; if you're wearing the colours, they will brand you all as being the same. Make sure you don't get into hot water, love.'

'Yes, I shall. I'm only going to march behind the banners. I shan't throw anything or break any windows...'

'Sensible girl,' Fred said, smiling. 'If they were all as sensible, mebbe the Parliament lot would listen to what you have to say...'

'We all think the same, but the members of the WSPU are more militant,' Beth acknowledged and nodded as he departed to fetch up more goods for the other departments. His assistant, Willie, was seeing to the disposal of empty boxes by loading up a van that had come to collect them, because of the constant flow of packaging, the basement would otherwise soon overflow with cardboard.

After Fred had been up, Miss Hart visited the department and walked round, inspecting everything. She ran a finger over both Beth's counter and Maggie's, but since there wasn't a speck of dust, had nothing to say.

Mr Marco was the next to visit. Beth was serving customers and she only had time to notice that he had a long conversation with Rachel, but he glanced her way and winked as he left. Rachel came up to her later and told her that Mr Marco was going to feature spring hats in one of his windows that week – a complete window with nothing much else but hats, so he'd hinted.

'He said that he would like some of your new stock and some of the old. He's going to do something with flowers – but he wouldn't tell me any more, because he likes the windows to be a surprise.'

Beth nodded, mentally thinking about the hats in stock. She had some pretty straw creations and some felts that were bright and pretty. Mr Marco's wink had been because of the window he was planning and she knew that whatever he used would bring in the customers, so she needed to choose hats that she had more than one example of, unless she wanted to ask for them to be removed from the display every time a customer wanted to try one on.

She started to unpack her boxes of new stock in her lunch break. She had a bottle of lemonade and a bun with her and would consume them a little later when she was allowed a few minutes' comfort break.

Rachel entered the stockroom as she finished unpacking the first box. Some really fancy straw hats with lots of veiling and silk roses were lying amongst the tissue they'd been packed in.

'Oh, these are beautiful,' she said.

'Yes, and all of them are individual,' Beth said enthusiastically. 'I can tell the customers that we have only one of each in stock...'

'Miss Ross has such good taste,' Rachel agreed. 'I think she charms these firms into giving her something special.' She looked about her. 'You shouldn't have done this in your lunch break, Miss Grey...'

'I don't mind. I'll have a drink and a bun later...'

'I'll give you an extra ten minutes to make up for it,' Rachel said and smiled. 'I'll do a bit for you now while you have a cup of tea...'

'All right, thanks,' Beth said, and took her lunch to the basement, where Willie was holding the fort. He'd made a mug of tea and handed her one with a grin, telling her that Fred was upstairs in the men's department.

She was no longer than fifteen minutes and when she returned Rachel had unpacked the second box of new hats and was busy writing up the stock list.

'Miss Grey, you're needed – and you, Mrs Craven...' Maggie alerted them to customers and all of them were busy for the next hour or so.

The afternoon was well advanced by the time they had unpacked all three dozen hats and Beth had written all the new stock into her records. The styles were fresh and colourful and Beth liked some of them far more than the previous spring stock.

She rearranged two of her main displays and was still busy when it was time to close the department.

Rachel came up to her and watched for a moment, nodding her head.

'Time to finish now, Beth,' she said, and the use of her first name meant they were done with work for the evening. 'We've all had a busy day, but you've worked extra hard.'

'I love seeing the new styles,' Beth said truthfully. 'Sally has bought some wonderful hats. I think she was thinking of weddings, because they're much too fine for everyday wear. Look at that gorgeous creation of pink tulle, straw and silk roses...'

'Yes, I noticed that she was buying more of the really fanciful stock this time,' Rachel said and looked doubtful. 'I know summer is coming, but I hope she hasn't gone a bit too far...'

'Several women admired them,' Beth said, 'but no one has bought new stock yet.'

'Say nothing to Sally,' Rachel warned as they left the department. 'She has worries enough with all the buying for the various departments and tomorrow you may sell loads of them.'

'Yes, I hope so,' Beth agreed. 'I know Mr Harper pays Sally good money, but I wouldn't want her job for all the tea in China...'

* * *

Beth sold ten hats the following day, but only one was from the new stock. Several young women tried them on, but then bought something more sensible than the 'flights of fancy', one matron called the lovely straw creations.

'If I had an invitation to Buckingham Palace, I'd buy that one,' another customer told Beth, 'but I feel I've nowhere to wear it...'

Beth smiled and said it looked lovely for a wedding and the customer agreed but left with a red felt cloche trimmed with a single rose.

However, on the Thursday, a mother and daughter came in and made a beeline for the display of straw creations. They both asked to try them on and exclaimed excitedly over each one. In the end, the mother bought two for herself and her daughter bought six.

'We have two weddings this next month,' the mother said, 'and Jilly is getting married at the end of the month. These hats are just right for her honeymoon – she and her husband are going on a trip to Paris and then to Rome and Greece...'

'How exciting,' Beth said, slightly envious. 'It must be wonderful to travel.'

'Jilly is marrying a baron,' the mother said proudly and her daughter blushed. 'He's not English, of course – Prussian, but such a lovely man...'

'Mummy – Arnulfo wouldn't like you to tell everyone...'

'Of course he wouldn't mind,' her mother said. 'He is proud of his heritage – and of you...'

They chattered away as Beth packed their hats into the smart boxes and sent their money up to the office in the pulley system. After she'd given change and was tidying her display, Rachel came up to her.

'It seems I was wrong about those hats after all...'

'A mother and daughter bought them for a wedding. I think they do not usually shop here. They must have been attracted by the window display...' Mr Marco had taken five of the new hats for his window display, which was hats set on stands in amongst flowering plants and bushes, seeming to say they were like blooms themselves – and he'd hung jewelled bees and pretty blue birds, that he'd created in his room on the fourth floor, from the ceiling. Everyone agreed it was another magical window.

'Yes, it does look lovely,' Rachel said. 'I was surprised to see those ladies buy so many...'

'I'm just glad they did. I was afraid they might stay on the shelf for ages.'

However, the sun decided to shine for the next few days and with thoughts of weddings and garden parties, the sales of pretty hats soared and soon Beth was telling Sally that they needed more stock.

'I wasn't sure those new hats would sell,' Sally confessed. 'I'll buy some more of them, but I'll buy more of our normal stock again. It doesn't do to put all your eggs in one basket.'

'No...' Beth looked at her thoughtfully. 'Have you had any word from Mr Harper yet?'

Sally shook her head, but she was smiling. 'No, but the good news is that Jenni is on her way over. She sent a telegram to tell me that she would be here at the end of next week. It will be good to see her – and I shall feel better once she's had a look through the accounts and approved some of the new stock...'

'Yes, of course you will. I'm pleased she is coming for a visit – it wasn't fair the way they both deserted you, leaving you to sink or swim on your own. It would have served them right if you'd walked out and let the store go to pot!'

'Beth!' Sally laughed at her vehemence. 'It really wasn't that bad, love. Jenni has kept in close touch all the time and done nothing but encourage me. She felt responsible for her friend's death because she let her have her ticket on the Titanic and the little boy needed someone to help him get over the shock of losing his mother and being snatched from the sea. Luckily, she thinks he doesn't remember the sinking at all when he is awake, though he cries for his mother... but he has bad dreams, which she thinks is due to the sinking.'

Sally paused. 'I've spoken to Mr Stockbridge and he and Mr Marco think we should have a minute's silence in the store next Tuesday for the anniversary of the sinking of the Titanic, just as a mark of respect.'

'Yes, I'm sure Miss Harper would appreciate that – although she won't be here, will she?'

'No, but Mr Marco intends to put something in the window and it will remain for a week or two, so she'd see it then...'

Beth nodded. She could excuse Jenni Harper for returning to America, but not her brother. Mr Harper had decided Sally was the

right person to buy for his store, made much of her and then
deserted her, and if Beth had had her way, he would have been
punished for causing her friend distress. However, she knew things
didn't work that way. The Ben Harpers of this world usually got
whatever they wanted. She smiled and gave Sally a hug, deciding to
say nothing about it; after all, it was Sally's life and she was the only
one who could make changes.

9

Sally woke from a pleasant but muddled dream. She'd been walking down the aisle of a country church wearing one of the fancy wedding hats she'd purchased for the store. As she went outside into the sunshine, she turned to smile at her husband and saw that it was Mick – and then she woke up with a start.

What on earth had put that idea into her head? Sally laughed as she dismissed the dream as nonsense. It was seeing Mick at Marlene's pub and what Beth had said about him being a partner in the business. Was it possible that she'd underestimated the Irishman? Surely she wasn't that mercenary she could suddenly see a man as her husband just because he half-owned a restaurant? No, it was just a stupid dream. She didn't dislike Mick now, but her heart still pounded when she thought of Ben Harper.

Where was the wretched man?!

Sally shook off the lingering thoughts as she washed and dressed for work. It hardly mattered if Mick had half a dozen businesses. She was attracted to Ben Harper and she couldn't get him out of her head, even though she knew he'd never given her any reason to hope he might care for her. She might daydream about him, but her common sense told her not to be foolish. She had a good job, friends she liked and trusted and life was better than it ever had been. It would be foolish to give all that up for the sake of a man who had shown no romantic interest in her.

At her office, she glanced through the post which had been put on her desk for her attention, then read a few paragraphs of the daily paper, looking at an advert for the new Morris Oxford car and thinking how helpful it would be if she had one and could drive herself rather than waiting for cabs or buses, which were paid for from her expense account as the buyer for Harpers. She would have to purchase the car herself and that was more than she could afford just yet.

The day ahead was busy. Sally had three appointments with travelling salesmen, all of whom worked for garment manufacturers. She had found that it was best to invite the salesmen to the store and take them to the department. If they showed their new styles to the supervisor and she liked them, it helped Sally to decide whether or not they were likely to sell. She did not always follow the advice of the women who worked in the department, but often they were broadly right.

That day, she chose six evening gowns, two dozen day dresses for spring and summer and an assortment of skirts, several short jackets that fitted into the waist and a whole range of fine silk blouses; all of them would be in size 36 through to 42. Above that size needed a different style and cut and would be purchased from yet another firm that specialised in larger sizes.

The salesmen who came regularly knew that she drove a keen bargain and the sensible ones gave her the best price without haggling. Sally had learned, during the strike of clothing workers, that there were many layers in the business and now went to the firms that produced the garments rather than wholesalers whenever possible. Most were happy to deal with Harper's, though a few still insisted that she go through their chosen wholesaler. These were the named brands and more expensive, and though it was necessary to stock them, especially in the larger sizes, she'd discovered that a good range of medium priced goods turned over faster and pleased their younger customers.

That day was a good day, though much of it was spent dealing with figures and sales reports and Sally was feeling tired when she left Harper's later that evening. She was startled when she saw a man get out of a car just ahead and come to her, but then saw it was Mick and relaxed. He gave her his easy smile.

'I thought you might let me take you out for a quiet supper?'

Sally hesitated, a little surprised he should ask, and then nodded. 'Why not?' she said, smiling. 'To be honest, I'm tired and I'd like to relax over a glass of wine...'

'Right you are, me darlin',' Mick said and grinned from ear to ear. 'I know just the place. I was wantin' to try it out and I think it's just what you need, Sally.'

Sally let him hold the door of the smart De Dion car for her and slid into the passenger seat. Of French manufacture, the seats were covered with smooth leather and it smelled nice, as though it had been polished with lavender beeswax.

'What made you think of taking me to supper tonight?' Sally asked as he drove off into the traffic.

'Sylvia wants to see you. She asked me to pass on the message and here I am,' Mick replied without glancing her way. 'She was sorry to have missed you when you visited and she has a day off next Sunday week. She wondered if you would meet her and have lunch somewhere – enjoy a day out with her...'

'Yes, that sounds lovely,' Sally said, smiling as she looked at him. 'You didn't have to take me to supper to ask me that, Mick.'

'Sure and couldn't I have asked just for the pleasure of your company, Sally Ross?'

'Yes, if that's true,' Sally said. 'I've had a hard day at work and I shall enjoy being looked after by a friend.'

'And what else should I be thinkin'?' Mick teased. 'If it's after romance you are, my love, then we'll choose another day when neither of us has been working fit to kill ourselves...'

His words piqued her interest and she looked at him properly. 'I don't really know what you do, Mick.'

'Sure you do, Sally. I'm the bar manager across the way from the hostel...'

'Yes, but that's not all, is it? Do you have an interest in Marlene's pub, Mick?'

'Now what in the world put that into your head?' he said, but laughed softly, sending her an appreciative glance. 'I could never fool you for long, could I?'

'So why are we going to supper this evening?' Sally was amused as she saw his mouth twitch. 'You want my opinion about somewhere you're thinking of making an offer for...'

Mick gave a shout of laughter. 'You'll be the end of me, Sally Ross. I may even have bought it already and want you to see if you'd like to work there...'

'I have a good job where I am, Mick...'

'Aye, that you have,' he agreed. 'But you're not happy at present and if I could put the smile back in those lovely eyes, I'd give the world and count it well done...'

'Mick! You're a charmer and a flirt,' Sally said, but she was laughing. The worries of her day seemed to slough off and she felt relaxed. 'Yet there is a lot more to you than I first thought...' He was a businessman and an entrepreneur and Sally was seeing a whole new side of him.

'I'm after thinkin' that you put me down as a worthless rogue, and mebbe you were not far wrong.'

'No, I was wrong,' Sally told him. 'You're a good friend, Mick. I shall never forget what you and Bridget did for us that night. If you hadn't fetched Bridget, Sylvia would have had to go to the hospital because the bleeding wouldn't stop – and we should both have been in trouble over an illegal abortion.'

'I only wished you'd told me what you needed in the first place,' Mick said. 'Sylvia is better now, but she may never have a child because of what that butcher did to her and that's a sad thing for a woman...' He looked grave and Sally felt remorse strike her. Why had she gone to Soho and found a woman who could tell her where an abortion could be done?

'I didn't know what to do for the best. Sylvia was crying and desperate. I advised her to have the baby and let the Sally Army give it to a deserving couple for adoption, but she wanted to get rid of it – so I asked someone and was told of that woman...'

'And Sylvia might have died,' Mick said. 'It's a crime against God to kill a babe that way, but if it must be done, then Bridget will do it safely. She's as skilled as most doctors and she only does it if it's safe – but she tries to talk the mothers into having their babies if she can.'

'If society didn't blame the woman every time an unmarried girl became pregnant, more of them would have their babies out of wedlock and keep them.' Sally sighed. 'I've known girls try to kill themselves rather than let anyone know they were in trouble...'

'Was that at the orphanage?' Mick asked, looking at her intently.

'Yes, I had a friend called Janet. She was fifteen and she fell in love with a young traveller off the fair. When he moved on, she discovered she was pregnant and there was no way she could marry. Janet was terrified of telling the nuns and she tried to cut her wrists in the bath...' Sally took a sobbing breath. 'They found her and she was sent to hospital and then away to a place in Ireland. I never discovered what happened to her, but she was a Catholic and she had committed unforgivable sins. I was told that she would be punished and that her child would be given to a good woman to bring up...'

'You had a hard upbringing.' Mick said, and looked at her sadly. 'My mother was a good Catholic woman and I know how unforgiving the church can be, especially to women they believe have sinned. Eve has a lot to answer for, so she does,' he said in a lighter tone. 'Getting Adam thrown out of Paradise.'

He pulled the car into a parking space. The restaurant was in Putney and the exterior looked old; covered with ivy, it had an air of permanence and solidarity that spoke of quality. A short distance away, Sally could hear the sound of the water and somewhere in the darkness the horn of a riverboat sounded.

Inside, there was the smell of cooking and coffee brewing and, overhead, were lanterns that gave off a gentle sparkle. The tables were covered in red and white checked cloths and set with small lamps and posies of spring flowers that added to the welcoming atmosphere and gorgeous smell.

'This is lovely, Mick,' Sally said. 'Really pleasant and comfortable...'

'Let's hope the food is as good,' he said and a wicked smile lit his eyes. 'I booked a table for us, but they have no idea who I am...'

Sally laughed. She was genuinely enjoying herself and glad she'd agreed to come. Once, she would have turned him down without giving him a chance, but she owed him at least this for what he'd done for Sylvia and her that night, when Sylvia looked like bleeding to death.

They were shown to their table by a smart waiter, who held the chair for Sally. A menu was presented and they were left to peruse it for a few minutes. It was varied, with dishes ranging from steak, chips and mushrooms to veal done in a special sauce and lobster bisque with home-made rolls and butter.

'I should like the home-cooked ham, salad and jacket potato,'

Sally said to Mick. 'I like it that they have simple food as well as some fancy dishes.'

He studied the menu a little longer and then nodded. 'It could be a little more adventurous with some dishes, but it depends on how they cook the food...'

'What made you buy without trying it first?' Sally asked.

'I know that the atmosphere is right and I can make it a success,' Mick replied, sounding confident. 'I did it with Marlene's place and I can do it with this – it just takes the right people to run it...'

Sally nodded and smiled as the waiter returned for their order. Mick ordered a bottle of white wine that Sally liked and her choice, choosing a breaded veal cutlet with sautéed potatoes and peas for himself. She would have thought he was a steak and chips man and realised that she didn't know him at all. She'd thought him just the manager of an East End pub, but he was a businessman.

The starter, when it arrived, was all that she had expected and beautifully cooked and presented. Sally enjoyed it very much – listening to Mick telling her stories about his devout Catholic mother, who went to church every day of her life, and his less than devout father, who had had to be driven to confession once a month, made her smile.

'My father spent his nights drinking and my mother spent her days praying for him to be forgiven his sins,' he quipped. 'Between the two of them, we kids didn't get much of a look-in, but it taught us to be independent...'

'At least you had a good mother,' Sally said. 'I never knew mine.'

'I preferred my father, for he was a cheerful soul, though I vowed never to follow his path and I left Ireland as soon as I could...' Mick laughed softly. 'My sister became a scold, but I sent her money to look after Mam, which she did until my mother died.'

'You had a family; I envy you that,' Sally said. 'With all their faults, they were yours.'

'It's right you are,' Mick agreed. 'One day I hope to have sons and daughters of my own, but they'll have a loving home and a mother who spends her time caring for them, not on her knees on a stone floor.'

'Then you must choose wisely,' Sally said and smiled at him.

'Aye, I will...' He gave her a long, considered look. 'And now let's see if this food is as good as it looks...' He watched the waiter set their main meals in front of them, nodding as Sally tasted and smiled.

'It is good...' She glanced up as two men walked in and were shown to another table, recognising them instantly. It was Mr Marco and the same young man he'd been with when she had lunch at Marlene's pub. As they sat down and looked at each other over the wine list, Sally knew instinctively that they loved one another.

'Something wrong?' Mick asked and Sally shook her head. She would not draw his attention to the two men any more than she had Beth's, even though she'd been aware of them being shown to a discreet table at the time.

'Nothing – it's all perfect.' Sally smiled at him and avoided looking across the room so as not to embarrass Mr Marco.

After they had eaten, Mick paid the bill and tipped the waiter generously but said nothing to the staff about having bought the place. He'd told Sally there was a time and a place for everything and he would make changes in his own time.

'So what did you think?' he asked as he drove her home.

'I liked it very much,' Sally said. 'I think it could have been a little busier and I don't know why it wasn't...'

'At the moment they fall between two stools,' Mick explained. 'The food is well cooked but not adventurous enough to tempt the regular diners – this is more for folk who just want a quick supper because they're hungry, but the prices are a bit high to ensure that all the tables are filled every night. So we either retain the high prices and make more effort with the menu and increase the range of the wine list, or we make it cheap and cheerful...'

'So which are you thinking of doing?' Sally asked.

'Which would you do?'

She thought for a few moments. 'I think it is too nice a place to go cheap and cheerful. I would put white tablecloths on the tables and bigger flower arrangements about the room, improve the menu and the wine list and keep the prices about the same or slightly higher for the top-of-the-range dishes...'

'Agreed,' he said and looked at her as he stopped the car outside her apartment block. 'So – when do you take over?'

Sally laughed and shook her head. 'My advice I give for free,' she said, 'but I'm not ready to leave my job at Harper's.'

'Then I thank you for your advice and a pleasant evening,' Mick said, smiling as he got out and opened the car door for her. 'If you change your mind, you know where I am...'

'Yes – and thank you,' Sally said. She hesitated, then leaned towards him and kissed his cheek. 'Thank you for caring, Mick. You're a good friend and I shan't forget.'

She left him, knowing that he watched until she was safe inside the flat.

Going out with Mick had helped her over the tiredness that had made her feel down when she left work. He was good company and there was far more to him than she would ever have guessed.

10

'Miss Gibbs, would you take these stock sheets up to Miss Ross on the top floor please?' Mrs Craven requested that Friday morning. 'She wanted them as early as possible because she has a meeting with a representative later...'

'Certainly, Mrs Craven,' Maggie said and smiled at the woman who was her friend, head of department, and sometimes a substitute mother, all rolled up in one. 'I'll be as quick as I can...'

'No need to rush,' Mrs Craven said. 'You may take a tea break before you return if you wish...'

Maggie thanked her and went through the department to the lift area. It came almost immediately and she was soon being whizzed up to the top floor by the friendly operator, Emmie Jones, who was a woman in her thirties. She smiled at Maggie but didn't speak, so Maggie didn't either. When she got to Sally Ross's office, the secretary told her to go straight through. Sally was on the telephone and she motioned to her to put the lists on the desk and smiled, mouthing 'thank you' and continuing with her phone call.

Feeling a bit disappointed, as she'd hoped she might get invited for coffee, Maggie left immediately and set off down the hall, past

Mr Marco's room, which was tightly shut, and then Mr Stock-bridge's office. His door was slightly open and as she was about to go past, Maggie heard a deep sobbing sound. She paused, trans-fixed by the pain in that sound, because she understood that kind of grief. Mr Stockbridge was in distress.

Maggie only hesitated for an instant before entering the office. Mr Stockbridge was sitting at his desk, his head in his hands, his shoulders heaving, and she was drawn to him inexorably, forgetting the fact that he was the manager and she a lowly salesgirl. Without even thinking, she placed a gentle hand on his shoulder.

'Is there anything I can do, sir?' she asked softly. 'Are you very ill – do you need a doctor, Mr Stockbridge?'

He stiffened and then looked up; his eyes, red-rimmed, held a look of desperation, and for a moment she wondered if he would shout at her and send her away.

'It's my daughter, Becky,' he told her in a long shuddering breath. 'We rushed her to the hospital last night with appendicitis… the doctors don't know if she will come through the operation.'

'Oh, I am so sorry, sir,' Maggie said, and she was, because she knew that if the appendix had burst, it could be extremely dangerous and people died with it. 'Would you like a cup of tea? I could fetch it for you?'

'You are very kind,' he said and for a moment he smiled sadly. 'You are so like my Becky, Miss Gibbs. It was the reason I gave you the job immediately last year. Becky is my only daughter and all I have since my wife died…'

Maggie felt devastated for him. He must be absolutely desperate over his daughter's condition. 'Wouldn't you be better at the hospi-tal?' she asked tentatively.

'I was there all night,' he told her. 'Matron asked me to leave. She said I should go home or to work… I couldn't bear the house without Becky…'

'No, it is awful to be alone in a house once the people you love have gone...' Maggie had experienced the utter loneliness after her father died and her mother disappeared.

'You would understand, of course,' Mr Stockbridge said and looked sad. 'You lost both your parents last year, I believe...'

'Yes, sir, I did,' Maggie agreed. 'Are you sure I can't get you anything – do you need anyone at all?'

'No, I shall be all right,' he assured her and she saw his shoulders straighten. 'Thank you, Miss Gibbs. You have helped more than you realise – please return to your department...'

'Yes, sir,' Maggie walked to the door, hesitated and looked back. 'I shall pray for Becky, Mr Stockbridge – and I believe God will answer our prayers...'

She walked out quickly before he could answer. Her heart was thumping now and she felt shocked at herself for being so daring. Mr Stockbridge was the manager and she'd had no right to speak to him the way she had, and yet he'd needed help and she'd given him what she could.

Mrs Craven was busy serving when she returned to the department and Beth had two customers. Maggie went to her counter and stood behind it ready. A few minutes later she had a customer for gloves and then two more for scarves, but even though she was busy, she did not forget Mr Stockbridge and her promise to pray for his daughter. She just hoped that the doctors would save the girl that meant everything to her father... just as she had to her own father before he died.

It was just before closing time that evening when Mr Stockbridge entered the department. He came straight to her counter and she knew immediately that he'd had news.

'Your daughter, sir?' Maggie asked and he smiled. 'She has come through the operation?'

'Yes, Miss Gibbs,' he replied. 'I am delighted to tell you that the doctors are pleased and believe that we've been lucky and she will make a full recovery...'

'That is wonderful news,' Maggie said, conscious that Beth and Rachel were looking at her. 'I'm so pleased for you both.'

'I knew you would be.' His smile said so much. 'And now I want a present for her – what do you ladies suggest?'

'A piece of jewellery or a pretty scarf,' Maggie proposed. 'We had some sweet enamelled pendants in just this week... Mrs Craven, would you mind showing Mr Stockbridge the pink heart...'

'Yes, of course...' Rachel got out the pendant and he looked at it, smiling and nodding. 'Yes, exactly what my Becky would like. I knew you ladies could help me...' He looked at Rachel. 'My daughter has just had an operation for appendicitis and Miss Gibbs realised I was very worried earlier...'

Rachel served him with the bracelet and he paid her, carrying the little bag carefully as he left the department.

Maggie felt the curious eyes of her friends on her as they prepared to close for the night. 'I bumped into him after I gave Sally those stock lists,' she said, deciding to keep the fact that she'd discovered their manager in tears to herself. 'I could see he was worried and he told me about his daughter... apparently I remind him of Miss Stockbridge...'

'Yes, well, it seems everything has turned out well,' Rachel said, frowning a little. 'He seemed pleased with the pendant you suggested...'

Maggie nodded. 'Well, it was very pretty and if she is a bit like me, it will suit her. Besides, he just needed a bit of help...'

'Yes...' Rachel said drily. 'I seem to remember he is a widower, Miss Gibbs, just be a little careful...'

'It was just a Christian kindness, Mrs Craven,' Maggie blushed and shook her head. 'Don't think wrong of him please... he has always been pleasant to me, but he is to us all. Anyway, he's old enough to be my father...'

'Yes, he is,' Rachel said, 'and don't you forget it...'

'I shan't,' Maggie assured her. 'I'm not interested in anything like that...' she said as they left the building. 'I'm far more interested in our march this weekend...'

* * *

The sun had decided to shine on the women who marched that Sunday morning. It was a fine sight as the banners waved and the colours of the Movement glowed in the sunshine. A large crowd of women had assembled at Hyde Park and were addressed by three speakers, all wearing green, white and mauve sashes and large hats with little bunches of flowers in the bands. These ladies were members of the peaceful branch of the Movement and the cheering was spontaneous and loud, before they set off to march round the streets, singing and chanting defiant slogans, with the intention of halting in front of the Houses of Parliament to deliver their petition to Mr Asquith.

It was after the women had been marching for some minutes that the crowd became ugly and started jeering and throwing things. A stone hit Maggie on the face and she cried out in pain. Beth looked at her anxiously and took out a clean handkerchief.

'Here,' she offered. 'Let's try to get to somewhere quiet and wash that cut...'

Before Maggie could answer her, there was a sudden surge as some men with cudgels attacked the women and the crowd broke before them, screaming as they ran to avoid the heavy blows. Maggie tried to stay with her friends, who were running just ahead of her but she was caught up as frightened women and onlookers were pushed into an undignified panic and women fled in fear of arrest. Suddenly, someone took her arm and she found herself being propelled through the mass of crying, screaming people, out of the chaos and into a quiet lane.

Maggie had known who had come to her aid immediately he took hold of her arm and so she allowed him to force a way through, holding in the desire to cry or scream as he forged a path to safety for her.

She looked at her former fiancé as they stopped and breathed deeply. 'Thank you, Ralf,' she said when she could speak. 'That was most unpleasant...'

'You're bleeding,' he said and tipped her head to one side, dabbing at the cut with his own clean white handkerchief. 'It isn't deep. Let's find somewhere to sit down and I'll ask for some water to bathe it for you.'

'My friends will be worried. I should look for them...' Maggie looked at him uncertainly. She was grateful for his help but not sure how she felt about meeting him again.

'You'll never find them,' Ralf said. 'Please allow me to help you. I'm not your enemy, Maggie. I came to support your movement...'

Maggie decided not to protest. The mood on the streets was still ugly and she wanted nothing more than to sit down with a soothing cup of tea and get over the shock of the unprovoked attack.

'We were not doing anything illegal,' she said as Ralf took her arm once more and steered her towards a small tearoom just at the end of the street. 'Why did those men attack us like that?'

'Because you're fair game wearing those sashes,' he replied. 'Let me take it off for you, Maggie. It might provoke some idiot to try and harm you again. The mood is against the suffragettes at the moment. Unfair perhaps, because you're not all militant, but, after what Emmeline Pankhurst did, probably not unexpected...'

Maggie was silent. She allowed him to undo the little silver pin that held her sash. He rolled it up and put it in his pocket and then steered her into the small café. It had just six tables, five of which were occupied. The yellow tablecloths were bright and there was a glass cake stand with luscious cream cakes on display. Ralf pulled a chair out for her. Maggie sat down and he ordered tea and a plate of cakes. She shook her head, but he ignored the silent protest.

'You've had a shock and something sweet will be good for you.'

The waitress brought a little bowl of warm water and a small cloth. 'Thank you,' Ralf said, smiling at her. 'My young lady had a little accident and she is feeling shaken.'

Maggie thanked the girl and bathed her face. Ralf watched and nodded and she dried it on his handkerchief.

'Yes, it has stopped now. I dare say it feels sore, but it wasn't a bad cut. You won't have a scar...'

Maggie nodded.

When the waitress returned with their order, she removed the bowl and cloth. Ralf poured their tea and selected a strawberry tart with a dollop of cream on top for Maggie.

'Eat that,' he instructed. 'You will feel better for something inside you.'

Maggie took a bite, realised that she liked it and ate the whole thing. Funnily enough, it did make her feel better and she smiled at him.

'Thank you, Ralf. It was kind of you to rescue me – and to bring me here. I was feeling a bit shaken.'

'That is only to be expected,' he said. 'I couldn't stand by and see you get hurt, Maggie. I was afraid you might get crushed in that surge. It was lucky that I happened to catch sight of you just as the trouble started...'

'They were paid bullies,' Maggie said. 'They will try to blame it on us, but we were having a peaceful march...'

'Yes, I expect it will result in bad press for your movement,' Ralf said and looked at her sadly. 'I've been hoping to see you, Maggie. I wanted to apologise for what my mother said to you. It was wrong of her and unkind. I wanted you to know that I did not think ill of you for going to your mother when she lay dying. It doesn't matter what she had done – or hadn't done – she was your mother and it spoke well that you cared for her, even though she deserted you and your father.'

'I was angry with her when my father died,' Maggie said, a little break in her voice. 'But she was dying. I had to go and I had to forgive her. I wasn't showing disrespect to your mother, though she thought I did.'

'My mother has high standards,' Ralf told her. 'Sometimes, she expects too much and I think she was wrong to speak to you as she did – but she is still my mother. I could not quarrel with her and shame her in front of you, but I spoke to her in private later and she apologised to me. She knows she was wrong, Maggie. I am truly sorry for what happened.'

Maggie was silent for a moment. She had broken her heart over this man for weeks, but now she felt nothing. 'You let me walk away alone,' she said quietly. 'My mother was dead and I was grieving. You did nothing to help me. I'm sorry, Ralf, but if you truly cared for me, you would have stood by me, as my friends did. They might not have agreed with my forgiving my mother after what she did, but they cared for me and helped me grieve. Where were you when I needed you?'

'Yes, it was ill done of me. Please don't hate me, because I still care for you,' Ralf said. 'I was going to come and tell you. I've left my job and I'm joining the Royal Flying Corps – I want a different life and I think we might have war quite soon...'

'War?' Maggie stared at him as if he'd gone mad. 'What on earth do you mean? Why should we have a war?'

'I dare say you do not read the papers very much?'

Maggie frowned. Was she imagining it or was he being condescending? Did he imagine she was a child to be humoured? 'Sometimes, I do – when there are articles about the Movement or the King and Queen...'

'You have read nothing about trouble in the Balkans or in Serbia?'

Maggie shook her head. Rachel often talked of world affairs, but she'd heard nothing of this or any hint of war. 'If there is conflict somewhere in Europe, it cannot affect us – can it?' she asked, perplexed.

'As yet nothing is certain,' Ralf told her. 'I decided to make a change in my life because I no longer wish to reside at home. My sister is soon to marry, as you know, and I want something different...' He frowned. 'I wanted to tell you that my mother will not rule my life – or yours if we were together. I know that I hurt you, Maggie, but I was torn two ways. I have regretted what I did a thousand times and I am asking – begging – you to give me another chance...'

'Oh, Ralf, please don't...' she said, feeling distressed by his words and knowing that he'd tried to approach her sooner, but she'd refused to see him. 'I'm not sure how I feel. I don't know what I want. I thought it was to be your wife, but I could never live in your mother's house.'

'You wouldn't have to...' He looked at her eagerly. 'If you would let me take you to tea sometimes, we could perhaps make it up...' He took a box she recognised from his pocket. 'Will you take back your ring?'

Maggie shook her head. 'No, Ralf. I need to think about this – and I *am* grateful for what you did this morning – but I can't just go back to what we had...'

Ralf looked disappointed and replaced the box in his pocket. 'Will you at least think about meeting me sometimes?'

'I will consider it,' Maggie agreed reluctantly, but his attitude had shown her that she'd been right to break off their engagement. Ralf claimed to love her but he thought of her as a little girl, not a sensible woman. 'Don't ask for more yet, Ralf. I was very hurt and I'm not certain I can trust you now...'

He looked disappointed and she had to resist the urge to touch his hand and tell him she didn't mean it, but she held back because she truly wasn't sure how she felt now. A part of her responded to his smile and his words of love, but she was no longer the innocent she'd been when they first met.

'There is a concert in the park next week,' Maggie told him. 'We shall all be there and we'll have a picnic. If you come, you may be able to take some of us for ice creams – and that's all I am offering for now, Ralf.'

'It is as much as I deserve,' he admitted and signalled for his bill.

When he had paid it, they left the café together. The streets were quiet now, but Ralf insisted on seeing her home on the bus. They parted outside the flat where she lived with her friends and she offered him her hand to shake.

'You were gallant to rescue me,' she said. 'I may see you on Sunday next week then...'

'Yes, thank you,' he said. 'I'm glad I was there when you needed help, Maggie. I couldn't bear it if anything happened to you...'

She shook her head and left him, hurrying upstairs, anxious now about the friends she'd lost when the march broke up. Sally and Rachel were waiting when Maggie got in. Beth had gone to Jack's home.

'Thank goodness you're all right,' Rachel said, hugging her in relief. 'We were so worried and we tried to find you afterwards. Beth said she thought she saw you with Ralf?'

'Yes – he rescued me from the crowd when we were parted and took me for a cup of tea. It steadied me and made me feel better...'

Maggie looked at Sally. 'I'm sorry if you were worried, but Ralf said
we would never find you...'

'He was right. We all ran for safety and came straight here.
Good thing he saw you,' Sally said. 'I know he let you down when
your mum was dying, love, but at least he took care of you today...'

'Yes, he was kind,' Maggie said but didn't tell her friends that
Ralf had asked her to go out with him again. 'It was such a shame
the march was ruined – and we missed the concert too...'

'It was so unnecessary,' Rachel said crossly. 'We never intended
to cause trouble and those louts ruined it... and if it weren't for Ralf,
you might have been badly hurt, Maggie...'

'Yes...' Maggie was thoughtful. 'Ralf has joined the Royal Flying
Corps... he says there may be trouble in Europe and he thinks we
might become involved. Is he right, Rachel?'

'Oh, I doubt it,' Rachel said lightly. 'There have been rumblings
in the Balkans for ages, but it always seems to go away after a while.
I mean, the King of Greece was assassinated only last week. Things
like that can cause conflicts to flare up at any time – but I prefer to
think it won't happen.'

'Surely it is nothing to us if there were a war in Europe,' Sally
said, frowning as she picked up a trade fashion catalogue and
immediately changed the subject. 'I've been trying to decide
between these two new lines, Maggie – which do you like?'

'This one,' Maggie said, pointing to an evening gown with
diamanté straps over the shoulders. It clung to the model's figure,
making her look slim and glamorous.

'We have treaties with Russia...' Rachel said, answering Sally's
original question. 'I suppose that is what Ralf was meaning. We
might possibly be drawn into a little war if there was a conflict, but
it isn't likely...' She then retrieved the catalogue from Sally and
endorsed the gown Maggie had chosen. 'Yes, this is the best one –
but both are nice. I think the more stylish gown is for a woman in

her thirties, while the other is better for a mature woman of fifty or so...'

'Yes – so perhaps I should try both,' Sally said, the conversation now steered completely away from conflict and war. 'Our evening collection needs a bit of a shakeup. Jenni erred on the conservative side and I think some women are ready for something a little more daring...'

'I agree,' Maggie said. 'It wasn't a very good day what with the riot and being hit by that missile – I'm so glad I've got friends I can rely on. Being here with you three and sharing things like this is all I want right now.'

11

'You've done wonders, Sally darling,' Jenni Harper said as she swept into the office in a cloud of perfume later that week. 'I love that marvellous display of summer hats in the windows and the ground floor looks very busy as I passed through. I can't believe you've done so well – and after both Ben and I deserted you...' She reached out to embrace Sally. 'It was really too disgraceful of us!'

'Jenni,' Sally returned her hug. 'It's so good to see you. I've missed you and I did need your advice, but I tried to remember all you'd told me and when I urgently needed to know something I telegraphed you, as you asked...'

'Ben is delighted with the way things are going,' Jenni went on. She took off her expensive wool coat with an astrakhan collar and tossed it over a chair, together with her bag, gloves and smart silk hat and then fluffed out her hair. 'That's better; I didn't realise it would be this warm. We're having a cold snap back home.'

'It has only just turned a little warmer here,' Sally told her.

'I noticed the window in memory of the Titanic,' Jenni said. 'I would've been here last week, but I attended a memorial service at home...' She blinked away her tears, changing the subject to stop herself crying. 'My brother was sorry not to get back here before Christmas but hopes to come soon now...'

'So that means you and Mr Harper intend to carry on the business.' Sally managed to keep her voice steady, despite her inner turmoil. 'I know the staff have been wondering because of his prolonged absence.'

'Yes, of course. That was never in doubt, Sally. I know things have been hectic, but we still care about Harper's as much as ever, I promise you. Ben has asked our aunt if she will loan us some money should we need it to continue trading, though the cash flow seems reasonable at the moment – but she has promised to help if we hit a problem... and my brother can't wait to get back. I'm the advance cavalry...' She laughed in delight. 'I assure you he will come the moment he can...'

Sally let out a sigh of relief. 'I'm sure the whole staff will be relieved to hear that their jobs are secure.'

'In business nothing is ever completely secure,' Jenni said. 'We're only as good as our last sales sheet – and for the moment that is very good.' She frowned. 'Sadly, things are not good back home. Prohibition has hit a lot of businesses and as a result we have rising crime. The government should realise folk will drink even if it is banned...'

'Yes, I'm sure if people want to drink they will...' Sally said because the British papers had a great deal to say on the problems prohibition had caused in America.

'It costs the economy huge sums,' Jenni said, 'and you can never be certain what will happen. The criminals have too much power. However, this is a more civilised country and I wish I could spend more time here...' She sighed. 'So, by the looks of things trade is bearing up well? You've all done a splendid job, keeping us going when we couldn't help much...'

'We dipped a bit during the January sales,' Sally told her. 'The spring and summer season looks like being excellent, at least it has begun that way, but, of course, we've hardly started. Last Christmas was good – but you had those figures...'

'Yes, we did,' Jenni agreed. 'I wished that I might have come over to celebrate with you, Sally, but Tom's father begged me to spend the holiday with them.'

'How are the General and his son?' Sally asked, because the family had been caught up in the tragedy of the Titanic and the boy had lost his mother, the General his wife.

'Little Tom is beginning to sleep better,' Jenni said and the animation had left her pretty face. 'For months he woke having nightmares about the ship going down, though when he's awake he remembers nothing; his dreams are muddled and he doesn't know what is actually happening, just that it's dark and cold and he's lost his mother, but fortunately he has just started to get through the night without dreaming. Henry is wrapped up in his work and I have no idea how he feels...'

Sally nodded. She knew that Jenni felt more than friendship for her lost friend's husband, but she wouldn't ask personal questions. It was for Jenni to tell her if she wished.

Jenni had picked up the latest spreadsheet, which Sally had prepared, showing the takings during the sales fortnight. 'Yes, I see why you were concerned. We learn by our mistakes, Sally. What works at home may not work here. Perhaps we should have done more discounting on end of lines or regular stock...'

'I do not think I would buy in seconds again,' Sally said. 'Rachel Craven came up with an idea for selling some of the unsold stock and it has helped to get rid of things I regret buying, but some of it will never sell...'

Jenni ran her finger down the columns, doing the sums in her head. 'It cost us a couple of hundred at most,' she said and nodded. 'I don't think it matters, Sally. I could get rid of whatever is left to a clearance house for a nominal sum and then just write it off against the profits. It would balance out the taxation.'

'I thought you might think I'd bought badly...'

'No, not at all,' Jenni said. 'You acted on my advice and no one will blame you for a small loss on sale goods, Sally.'

They discussed the profits for a while longer and the window displays, which were not actually Sally's responsibility, though she discussed what should go into them with Mr Marco once a week.

'I should like to see some themed windows again,' Jenni told her. 'I wasn't here to see the Christmas displays, but a friend of mine on a visit to London took photographs and showed them to me when she got home and I certainly liked what I saw...'

'Good,' Sally felt relieved. 'I've ordered some of next winter's stock, but I'm still in the throes of choosing ladies coats – so if you would like to sit in on the meetings I have for today you're welcome... and Mr Marco has a lot of ideas you might like to discuss with him while you're here.'

'Yes, I'd love to, though you're doing very well.'

'But might do better with your advice...'

'Only if you feel you need me,' Jenni said and smiled at her. 'I came straight here from the train – but now I'm going to Ben's apartment to change and get settled. He has asked me to open it up for him and I'll be staying there until he gets back...'

'Of course...'

'I'll be back later and I'll arrange some meetings this next week – but I'm sure Ben will pleased when he sees what you've done.'

'Is he coming soon?' Sally asked, deliberately keeping her voice light.

'As soon as he finishes the business that has kept him in New York,' Jenni said and hesitated. 'Ben has talked to me more recently – and there is a lot of stuff I didn't know about, Sally. I told you once to be careful of my brother, but I didn't understand...' She sighed.

'He made me promise not to tell you, so I can't – but don't think too badly of him for leaving you in the lurch. I know he thinks highly of you professionally and personally.'

'I've simply done the job you gave me...' Sally kept her eyes on the balance sheets, not wanting to give her feelings away. 'I'm just an employee...'

'No, you're not.' Jenni laughed. 'He believed in you, Sally, and...' She shook her head. 'Ben will tell you himself when he comes – and now I'm dying to have a bath and put my feet up. Shall I call for you at seven this evening and we'll have dinner – unless you have another engagement?'

'I should enjoy that, Jenni,' Sally said. 'I'll pop home and change and then meet you back here...'

'I shall very much look forward to seeing you this evening.' Jenni impulsively kissed her cheek. 'We must seem ungrateful wretches, throwing you in the deep end and leaving you to swim on your own, Sally, but we saw something special in you, believed in you, and you managed splendidly.' Jenni was a whirlwind, accustomed to sweeping up all before her.

Sally gathered up the various spreadsheets and accounts and locked them in the safe. She had an appointment almost immediately with a jewellery manufacturer in Hatton Garden and needed to get going or she might be late.

The department that Rachel Craven was head of was thriving and getting larger. They were now selling a selection of carefully chosen gold and silver jewellery, some of which had semi-precious stones. Thus far Sally had not ventured into rings and that was one of the decisions she had to make today, whether or not to begin a range of dress rings to complement the other jewellery. It would depend on the range she was shown and whether or not the price offered would keep them within her parameters so that her prices were still competitive with other jewellers in the area.

In the end, Sally decided to try a small range of gold rings set with precious and semi-precious stones. They were what was often described as gypsy rings, which meant they were a band, set with either three or five stones, such as garnet and pearls or sapphires and diamonds, but surrounded by the gold of the actual shank rather than a prominent claw set. Rings of this design set well with wedding bands and were often bought as eternity rings, but men could wear them and sometimes did, with just one diamond set in the thick band of gold, and many ladies wore them on the middle finger or on the right hand.

Sally bought a ring pad that held eighteen rings, with another six rings in reserve. She spent nearly two hundred pounds on the stock altogether and hoped the rings would sell, though the jewellery maker had told her that he would be willing to exchange for bangles or brooches if she decided that they did not sell in sufficient numbers. Display space was limited and everything had to earn its place because they needed a constant turnover.

Most of the afternoon was spent in carefully pricing the rings and Sally herself took the stand down to Rachel and saw it locked in the display cabinet.

'I shall put this in the safe at night together with the spares,' Rachel told her and smiled. 'These are gorgeous, Sally. Funnily enough, I've had two requests for rings this week – both by men looking for gifts. They both bought bangles from me and leather bags from Maggie... but I think they might have bought one of these if they'd had the chance.'

'They are the most popular sizes according to the designer,' Sally said. 'Of course, they can be sized to fit and we have a ring sizer who can undertake the work for a modest fee. Actually, I can just order the same ring in the right size...'

'I think that's an excellent idea,' Rachel said. 'We'll see how it goes. I've been amazed by how this part of the department has expanded. I mean, why come here to buy jewellery rather than one of the other jewellery specialists?'

'I think it is because we're reasonably priced and more accessible,' Sally suggested. 'I've done a bit of research at some of the nearest jewellers on Bond Street and at four of them I had to ring a bell to be let in. Once inside, I had to ask to see whatever I wanted and they showed me one thing at a time and I felt as if I were under scrutiny the whole while Here, we are still careful not to get out more than two pieces of jewellery at a time, but the displays are easy to see and people walk in and out of the department as they choose. Rich men may wish to be asked to sit down and be shown expensive jewellery, but the man in the street wants to make a quick purchase in his lunch break...'

'Yes, I agree – and you seem to have the knack of choosing what people like,' Rachel said. 'I always feel intimidated when I enter an expensive jeweller's and I don't get to see half of what I'd like to see – because the stock is so expensive I dare not ask to touch it.'

Sally nodded agreement. 'I'm always pushing for something different and I asked Jenni to bring a few pieces of American silver. I'm hoping for something exciting...'

Leaving the department, Sally went home to change out of her formal skirt and blouse into a pretty dress. It was a pale grey silk with three-quarter sleeves, a white collar and a wide belt that accentuated her narrow waist. Her ankles were on show and, though not quite a hobble skirt, it was rather narrow. She wore it with a short boxy red jacket and a smart red cloche hat with a rose at the front.

There was still more work to be done when she returned to her office and Sally was deep into a report from the men's clothes department when Jenni opened the door and walked in. She was wearing a smart black silk dress and coat trimmed with white fur at the sleeves and hem, and she had a little white cloche trimmed with a black rose at the front. Seeing Sally's hat ready for her to put on, Jenni laughed delightedly.

'I knew we had the same tastes,' she cried. 'That dress is just perfect for you, Sally. Are you ready – surely you've done enough for today?'

'Yes, I was merely looking at the sales in the men's department. The new range of jackets Mr Brown bought seems to be selling well – particularly the tweeds...'

'Yes, I haven't met our new buyer yet,' Jenni said. 'Mr Stock-bridge said he was well recommended but, between you and me, didn't have your flair...' she winked at Sally.

'That's a bit unfair actually,' Sally said. 'The sales have certainly had a steady increase since he arrived – not huge but definite...'

'Enough work for now,' Jenni announced and swept the remaining paperwork into the safe. 'We're going out to enjoy ourselves. The work can wait until tomorrow...'

Inevitably, their conversation turned to the store as they ate. Sally told Jenni of the changes made to the jewellery department and Jenni smiled.

'Strangely enough, I've brought some rings for you to approve,' Jenni said. 'The stones are amethysts, onyx, blue topaz and moon-stones, and they are all set in silver. It will be interesting to see how the prices compare...' She took a ring from her pocket and showed Sally; it was a large square stone set on a thick silver band and looked almost too heavy for a woman to wear on her hand. 'What do you think?'

'A little clumsy...' Sally said. 'I think our customers might prefer something smaller...'

'Like this...?' Jenni drew out a pretty pale moonstone oval ring, set in silver, that had been chased with unusual markings and Sally exclaimed, taking it to try on her own hand.

'Yes, this is lovely, Jenni.'

'It's just as well I bought more like this than the large stone,' Jenni smiled. 'They sell well at home, but I've learned that it is two different markets. The suits you couldn't sell here sold out in days at home. I gave them a small mark-up and could have sold twice as many.' Jenni put the rings back in her handbag. 'I've left the rest in the safe at Ben's apartment,' she said. 'I'll bring them in tomorrow – and that really is enough shop, Sally. I want you to tell me what you've been doing on a personal level. I hope you've had time for some fun?'

'Yes, I have,' Sally said and smiled at her. 'I've been out to lunch with friends and I had supper at a nice pub that another friend has invested in – and I've joined the Women's Movement... not the WSPU, but the peaceful branch... although the police don't seem to know the difference.'

'Ah,' Jenni said. 'That is interesting. I'm a member of the Women's Movement back home and I really think we're making progress, what about over here?'

'They've brought in that awful Cat and Mouse law and it has put some of the members off attending the meetings as well as refusing to go on the marches, for fear of arrest and imprisonment...' She frowned. 'I sometimes wonder if King George V knows what his ministers do in his name...' The way the Act allowed the prison governor to let the women almost starve themselves and then let them go free only to re-arrest them a few weeks later was cruel.

'It's quite wicked,' Jenni said. 'I think our members are a little more civilised at home, less inclined to acts of violence, but our members are getting organised and we intend to march and to lobby our government more...'

Sally smiled and they talked eagerly, comparing notes and discovering how much alike they thought on all manner of subjects. It was a pity, Sally thought, that Jenni's life was in America, because she would have liked to see more of her. They worked well together and they were also friends, something that didn't always happen.

* * *

Jenni's stay in England was to be all too brief. She had a week of visiting new suppliers with Sally, lunching or dining out with her and discussing the stock. They also found time to visit the theatre together one evening and the ballet another. It was a new world for Sally and one she was beginning to enjoy.

Sally was allowed to choose those things she liked best from the jewellery and bags Jenni had brought over. She trusted Sally's judgement and if Sally thought it wouldn't sell, the article went back in Jenni's trunks to return to New York with her. If it was approved, Jenni would order larger quantities to be shipped over when she returned home.

'I love seeing what you bring and everything is refreshingly different,' Sally told her when they'd made their final choices and three quarters of the new lines had been accepted into the London store. 'But there is no doubt that as people we do have different tastes in fashion and matters of style.'

'And that's good,' Jenni said. 'I'm taking three new lines you've sourced home with me, and if you find anything more of the same quality, you can send me some samples.'

The exchange of ideas and sources was proving helpful to both buyers and now that they knew each other better, they could laugh and talk without fear of embarrassment or offence.

However, one thing happened that distressed both of them, and that was when the Home Secretary, Reginald McKenna, had public meetings by suffragettes banned.

'How dare they do something so outrageous?' Jenni demanded when she saw it in the newspaper.

'Possibly in retaliation for the cricket pavilion in Royal Tunbridge Wells being blown up earlier this month...'

Jenni frowned. 'I'm not sure violence is the right way...'

'Even when the Movement is peaceful, they won't let us march. There was an unruly crowd that broke up one of our meetings just before you arrived and I think that was probably the excuse they used to get the law through.'

'Well, we shan't tolerate it in New York,' Jenni said, with a look of determination. 'We have to stand together, Sally. Women must be free to speak their minds and to own their lives.'

Sally agreed, but it seemed the opinion in England was against them for the moment and she attributed that to the more militant actions of some members. However, she knew that they would continue to meet, but in secret.

The week seemed to fly by and Sally wished they'd had more time to go out together, but it was a working trip and Jenni had commitments back home.

'Perhaps I can come over for longer at Christmas this year,' she told Sally the night before her ship was due to leave. 'I should like to have a holiday with you, really have time together. We might even go skiing together...' She smiled. 'I'm booked on the Cunard liner, the Aquitania, this trip...'

'I've no idea how to ski,' Sally said, laughing.

'I can teach you,' Jenni hugged her. 'This has been fun and I learn something every time I come, Sally. I'll write and I'll send the stock you've chosen – and we'll keep in touch...' Jenni looked wistful, as if she would have liked to stay longer.

'I hope you do come over for a few weeks at Christmas or next summer. I'd like to take you on an English seaside holiday,' Sally teased. 'We'll walk on the sand with no shoes and eat fish and chips on the beach and candy floss...'

'I shall miss you,' Jenni said. 'Don't give up on us, will you,

Sally? I promise it will be worthwhile in the end...'

Sally promised to look after the store and they finally parted late at night the evening before Jenni was due to board her ship. Jenni insisted on calling a taxi to take Sally home, because of the late hour. When she crept in at past eleven, Beth was sitting up in bed writing letters.

'I thought you would be asleep,' Sally said, but Beth shook her head.

'I couldn't sleep until I heard you come in,' she said. 'Did you have a good evening?' Sally nodded and Beth smiled. 'Shall you see Jenni again before she leaves?'

'No, she will leave for Southampton first thing,' Sally said. 'Her ship sails the following day, but she wants to be there in plenty of time and it takes several hours on the train and then boarding is hectic, so she told me...'

'You've had a busy time while she was here, Sally.'

'Yes, I have, but it was fun – and Jenni approved all I've done, Beth. It made me feel so much more confident, lifted a weight from my shoulders. I've been working in the dark for months, but Jenni's approval means that I can trust my judgement and go on as I have been.'

Beth nodded her understanding, her gaze steady as she watched Sally's expressive face. 'And Mr Harper – when is he coming over?'

'Jenni didn't know, but she thought soon...'

Beth nodded and yawned. 'You'll be glad when he comes; he can take some of the work on his shoulders,' she said and settled down, snapping out her bedside light.

Sally undressed, climbed wearily into her own bed and switched off her bedside light. Jenni was fun, but she was very energetic and it was tiring just keeping up with her...

Sally's last thought before she fell asleep was that she would be glad when Ben came back.

12

That weekend, Sally got ready for her day out with her friend, Sylvia. She wore a simple skirt and blouse with her red jacket and the cloche hat Jenni had admired. They had agreed to meet at the Lyons Corner House on Shaftesbury Avenue and Sally was the first there, standing outside in a chilly wind, waiting for ten minutes, before Sylvia arrived. When would the spring get here? It was the end of April and still cool sometimes.

'I'm sorry,' she exclaimed, 'have you been here long? My bus was late...'

'I was just thinking of going inside,' Sally said. 'I could do with a cup of tea and a bun...'

'Yes, it is time we ate something,' Sylvia said and smiled. 'Thanks for coming, Sally – I wanted to tell you some news and to ask a favour...'

'Let's get inside first,' Sally said. 'That sun is bright, but it's cold in the breeze.'

'Yes, I know. It's nearly May and officially spring,' Sylvia agreed, 'but it doesn't feel much like it at the moment.'

Inside, they were shown to a table by one of the bright-faced girls who kept the popular restaurant running efficiently. Lyons had opened their first restaurant four years previously and others had blossomed since then, because they were cheerful, pleasant places and served their customers with courtesy and efficiency. Within moments of an order being given, a pot of tea for two, some toasted teacakes and a plate of little cakes was on their table.

'That looks lovely,' Sylvia remarked. 'Good thing I had a raise this week...'

'This is my treat,' Sally replied firmly. 'Tell me, have you been to the Chelsea flower show?'

'No, I'd like to though.'

'Yes, me too. Now, tell me your news...'

'I've received a proposal of marriage,' Sylvia said and gave a little giggle, 'and I wanted to ask if you could lend me nine pounds...'

Sally stared at her in silence for a moment. She'd lent Sylvia money before and had never seen a penny of it back. 'Firstly, congratulations on the proposal,' she said. 'Are you going to accept?'

'Yes, I am,' Sylvia nodded. 'Frank is a travelling salesman and he says he's mad about me. He wants to get a flat in London and I'll live there and he'll come and go rather than living in hotels...'

'Do you care for him?'

'He's all right – yes, I like him,' Sylvia replied. 'He's generous and he doesn't expect too much – and I'd have security. He's got a big insurance on his life and I'll get the money if he dies...'

'But you're not in love with him?' Sally wasn't sure how she felt about Sylvia's revelations. Her shallow nature had shocked Sally. She realised that she'd never really known her and that living with Beth, Rachel and Maggie had given her high standards. Sylvia seemed to realise that Sally was disapproving and blushed slightly.

'I'd look after him if he was ill and I'm not after his money, but I'm fed up with being on my own. Marlene is all right, but she can be a bitch if things aren't just right – and with Frank I'd have a real home...'

Sally nodded, not sure how to take what Sylvia was saying. Perhaps she was too ready to condemn for she had a good job and true friends. 'And why do you want me to lend you nine pounds?'

Sylvia looked uncomfortable. 'I know I never paid you what I owed you before – but you said it didn't matter...'

'And it doesn't, but I'm not sure I can afford to lend you nine pounds – that's a lot of money, Sylvia. I work hard for what I get and I don't intend to throw it away.'

'I'll pay yer back once I'm wed,' Sylvia said, looking sulky. 'I've got to buy Frank a wedding present and the ring I want for him is six pounds – and I need a new outfit...'

'I'm sorry,' Sally said. 'If that's what this is all about – asking me for money – then I wish you had made that clear. No, I'm not going to give you nine pounds, Sylvia.' She hesitated, then put her hand in her pocket and brought out three pound notes. 'I have enough to pay for our meal and this – and it's all I'll give you. I don't want it back. You can call it a wedding gift and do what you want with it, but that is all I can give you.'

Sylvia looked peeved but took the three pounds. 'I thought I could rely on you – after all, we know things about each other...'

'Is that a threat?' Sally looked at her hard. 'My employers know all there is to know about me, so do your worst – and I think I've had enough of this...' She waved her hand at the waitress and summoned the bill. 'Don't ask to see me again, because I'm not interested...'

'You needn't fly up into the boughs just because of a measly nine pounds...' Sylvia muttered. 'Sit down and finish your tea...'

'No, thank you,' Sally said. She paid the bill and walked out, leaving Sylvia sitting there. Inside, she was angry and hurt. She'd thought they were friends, but it seemed that Sylvia had just seen her as someone to use, a meal ticket when she was short of money. She'd given Sylvia help in the past and she'd thought to get more from her under the guise of friendship.

Shaking her head in disgust, Sally caught the next bus to draw up. She felt sick with disappointment and got off a couple of stops from home, intending to walk her mood off before she joined her real friends. As she approached the apartment she shared with Beth and the others, she saw a car drawn up outside. Mick got out and came towards her, looking grim.

'I take it you've just got back from meeting Sylvia?'

'Yes. I didn't stop long...'

'Marlene just told me why she sacked her,' Mick said and looked annoyed. 'I'm sorry, Sally. I wouldn't have brought her message if I'd known what she's been up to – Marlene says she's been stealing money and drinks. She confronted her when she told her she was going to get married and asked for some money to buy her clothes.'

'She asked me for money too,' Sally said. 'I wasn't inclined to do it again...'

'Nor was Marlene.' Mick shook his head in disgust. 'We've both tried to help her, Sally. She won't keep a job five minutes wherever she goes. Marlene is generous and gave her the benefit of the doubt, but she was ten pounds down in her takings this week and she said enough is enough.'

'I shan't meet Sylvia again.'

'Good, I should think not. She's forfeited any right to your friendship...' He hesitated, then, 'Would you like to go out to lunch with me?'

'Yes, why not?' Sally said. She was feeling thoroughly fed up and the prospect of a nice meal in his company was appealing. 'I don't have a penny on me. I should go in and get some...'

'You won't need it, I'll be buying lunch...' Mick frowned and then raised his eyebrows. 'You gave Sylvia money?'

'I gave her three pounds as a wedding gift, which was considerably less than she wanted.'

'She didn't deserve that much, if you ask me,' he said. 'I'm sorry that wretched girl asked you for money. It seems we all trusted her too much...'

'I thought she was a friend, but she tried to blackmail me,' Sally replied, 'so I walked out on her. I shan't get caught like that again...'

'Forget her, Sally. Let's go out and enjoy ourselves. I'll take you somewhere different – and you can tell me what you think...'

'Not more property?' she asked with a teasing look.

Mick smiled mysteriously. 'Well, you never know,' he said and opened the car door for her. 'It depends how good the food is...'

* * *

The food was exceptionally good. They both had Dover sole, pan fried with a delicious prawn sauce, soft creamy mounds of potato, petit pois and asparagus tips. Savouring every mouthful, Sally sipped the cool sparkling white wine and then ate her brandy snap with black cherries in kirsch and cream with equal pleasure.

'Now, that really was a delicious meal,' she told Mick as they drank coffee afterwards. 'Where do you find these wonderful places?'

'I ask my customers where they like to eat and then I try the menu for myself,' Mick said and she knew he meant the customers of the pub he managed. 'I was told about this place the other evening. The food is excellent, but the manager was dishonest and left his employer in the lurch when he ran off with his wife and most of his money...'

'Oh, how terrible! The poor man must be devastated...' Sally was all sympathy.

'I imagine so,' Mick agreed. 'I dare say he was relieved to get an offer of a silent partner and some cash to keep him afloat...'

Sally quizzed him with her eyes. 'Are you showing me how little I know about you?'

'I'm trying to make you smile,' Mick said. 'I'm not a secret millionaire, Sally Ross. I simply got lucky – my uncle in Ireland died in May 1912 and left me his property, most of which consisted of two fields and a racehorse. I must have had the Divil's own luck, because the horse won the Irish Derby in June last year and brought me a few bob in winnings – and then I sold him for a small fortune.' His eyes lit with devilment. 'The horse hasn't won since...'

'Did you drug it or something?' Sally demanded, laughing.

'No, I just talked it into winning and making me fortune...'

'Oh, Mick, you idiot!' Sally shed her cares as his teasing made her giggle. 'Seriously, did it only win the one race?'

'Just the one...' Mick grinned broadly. 'Honest to God, I've no idea why – but mebbe Uncle Sean had been training it up for that one race. He'd had it entered for months, so I let it run...' He shrugged. 'Everyone said it was a miracle and for me it certainly was. I used the money wisely and I now own a half share in three restaurants... well, Marlene's place is a pub, but 'tis the same thing...'

'So can I expect to experience more surprise meals like this one?' Sally asked and Mick shook his head.

'I've invested my windfall, and for now I'll just carry on managing the pub and see what happens...'

'You've chosen wisely,' Sally said. 'Everyone likes to go out for a celebration meal sometimes, so you should make a small fortune out of your businesses...'

'I'll just sit back and watch them grow, that's the idea.' Mick laughed softly. 'I might carry on investing when I can; it's become a habit, though I don't always put my money into a place, even if the food is good.' He looked thoughtful. 'I was investigating a pub in Soho the night I saw you being attacked. I decided against that one... but I was glad I was there...'

Sally nodded, remembering the night she'd gone up to Soho Square to locate a woman of the streets in the hope of discovering someone to perform an abortion for Sylvia. She'd wondered why Mick was in what was rather a shady area and perhaps that had coloured her opinion of him without her realising.

'I should never have been there,' she confessed now. 'If I'd known... I shouldn't have got involved with Sylvia's problem at all...'

'You tried to do her a good turn, but she took advantage of you,' Mick said. 'I should stay clear of her in future if I was you.'

'Yes, I shall.' Sally sighed. 'Life is so strange, isn't it?'

Mick raised his eyebrows, but she shook her head. 'I'll take you home now, Sally. It looks as if it might come on to rain soon.'

'April showers bring May flowers...' Sally chanted and smiled. 'You're a good friend, Mick. I was feeling angry and upset when I left Sylvia but now you've cheered me up.'

'Good, that's what I hoped to do,' he said. 'I'll get you back before the storm breaks...'

The sky was getting darker by the minute as they drove. Suddenly, lightning struck across the sky and there was a roll of thunder. Rain was driving down, making the roads slippery and puddles were forming everywhere.

Outside Sally's flat, Mick drew the car to a halt and turned to look at her. 'Thank you for having lunch with me,' he said and then leaned forward. His lips caressed hers softly for a brief moment and then he sat back. 'Get in quickly before you drown...'

'Mick...' Sally hesitated and he shook his head.

'Go on, Sally Ross – there's nothing to say...'

Sally nodded, opened the door and got out. She ran quickly to the small block of apartments, used her key and disappeared inside without looking round. She did not notice that Mick watched until she was safely inside – nor did she notice that across the road, another man watched from the shelter of a shop doorway. She did not see his frown or the look of hurt on his face as he walked away...

13

Sally was in her office early on Monday morning. She wanted to catch up on the stocktaking that she'd left while Jenni was over. It wasn't necessary to check the lists as often as she did, but Sally liked to be on top of things. If something wasn't selling it was important to know and if a line sold out quickly it was sometimes worth restocking the same item.

Sally's head was bent over her work when the door of the office opened and she assumed it was the secretary.

'Yes, please, I'm more than ready for coffee...' Sally said and looked up with a smile. A chill went down her spine and the smile froze as she saw who was standing in the doorway. She got to her feet, staring at him. 'Mr Harper... welcome back...' Her words were scarcely above a whisper. 'You didn't let us know you were coming...'

'Thank you, Miss Ross. I got a passage sooner than I expected and thought I would surprise you – I hope it is a good surprise?'

'Oh yes, of course,' she replied and her cheeks were warm. She was finding it hard to breathe and her chest felt tight. He was smiling, but the smile didn't reach his eyes and Sally had a feeling that he was angry. 'Is something wrong?'

'Why should there be anything wrong?' he asked, his voice icy. 'I know that I owe the success of Harper's to you – at least that is what Jenni tells me and I always believe my sister...'

Why was he so cold? He hadn't asked her how she was or said it was nice to see her and she could feel his disapproval, see it in his eyes, so what had she done to displease him?

'I could hardly have run this place alone,' Sally said, feeling hot and uncomfortable under that piercing gaze. 'I believe I've helped things on their way by choosing the right stock for my departments, but you have a lot of good people here, Mr Harper.'

'Yes, I know,' he said and his smile was now a few degrees above freezing. 'I intend to do something to reward everyone for their loyalty – especially when I wasn't sure of the future...'

'Jenni said you'd solved the problem?'

'Yes. My aunt has agreed a loan of a hundred thousand dollars should I need it, but I hope we shan't have to use it.'

'At the moment we're showing a tiny overall profit, I think?' Sally ventured as her pulse returned to something like normal. Whatever was getting at him it didn't seem to be the store?

'Yes, we are,' Ben agreed and now he was almost cordial. 'That is why I want to show my appreciation – and I'd like your advice, Miss Ross. Would the staff appreciate a small raise in their wages or a party?'

'I'm not really sure,' Sally replied, wrinkling her brow. 'Most of them would be happy with a raise, but some might like a party... something that shows you realise how hard they've worked.'

'So a small rise in wages and a few drinks and canapés here after work rather than a lavish do at a hotel?'

'Yes, that sounds about right,' Sally agreed and smiled. His down-to-business attitude had slowed the rapid beating of her heart and she was almost calm. 'It's nice to see you back, sir, and I'm glad it all went well for you in America...'

'What did Jenni tell you?' He frowned and looked wary.

'Jenni said you were busy – and that your aunt was talking about a loan in the future if you required it. What else would she tell me?'

'Nothing...' He turned away from her and she saw the tension in his broad shoulders. Something was bothering him, but he was controlling it. 'Tell me, Miss Ross, have you been well? What have you been doing with your life?'

Sally hesitated, unsure of what to say; she decided to stick to work. 'Nothing much except keeping busy here. We had a dip in sales during January,' she said. 'I think it was because we bought in seconds. In future I think we should sell end of lines at reduced prices and perhaps a percentage off regular stock...'

'And is that all?' As he faced her again, his eyes seemed to bore into her, making Sally wonder what she'd done wrong.

'Have I done something?' she asked. 'If I have, I do not know how I've offended—'

'You've done nothing you're not entitled to do,' he said, a glimmer in his eyes. 'I should like a copy of all the accounts and current stock lists by the end of the day. If you will arrange to have them on my desk by this evening please.'

'Yes, of course, sir.'

His eyes seemed to snap at her. 'My name is Ben – Mr Harper if you have to, but please do not call me sir. It sounds as if I'm old enough to be your grandfather...'

'I'm sorry...' Sally began, but she was talking to thin air. Mr Harper had gone, shutting the door with a sharp click. She had the feeling that he'd been keeping his temper on a tight rein but had no idea why.

She'd been so happy to see him, but his attitude upset her. If she'd addressed him formally, it was his fault. He was the one that had closed up on her. He'd gone back to America without a word and she'd heard nothing from him. Now he was snapping at her because she called him sir – how was she supposed to act when he was around? Ben Harper wanted to be her friend one minute and the next he was glaring at her as if she were the enemy...

* * *

Ben walked the length of three blocks before he cooled down enough to think clearly. He was a damned idiot, allowing his feelings on seeing Sally, her beauty and her poise, to erupt into unwarranted temper. He wasn't sure why he'd lost his control, except that the previous night he'd seen Sally in the arms of another man and it had made him want to break the so-and-so's neck and shake her until she came to her senses. He fingered the object in his pocket and his expression darkened. Ben Harper had been to hell and back and he'd been looking forward to surprising Sally when he returned to the country he now thought of as home – but he'd waited outside her apartment for her to come in after he'd learned that she'd been meeting a friend and then he'd seen her kissing that damned fellow and his anger had become white hot.

Maybe it was his fault he'd lost her. He should've let her know he thought she was lovely and that he was falling for her – but he couldn't have done things differently. Ben hadn't been free to say the things he'd longed to say and Sally had made it clear that she was the kind of girl who wanted marriage or nothing. Was that what her escort had offered her? She'd smiled when he kissed her in the car and looked happy when she ran across the road in the rain and his heart had stopped until she was safe on the other side, because it reminded him of another girl and another time, and a tragic outcome.

Ben had been too anxious and too frustrated to go after Sally the previous night. He'd intended to be cool, calm and dispassionate when they met this morning, but it seemed that was impossible for him where she was concerned.

It was too late for him to speak now, but he had to come to terms with seeing her every day, because she was damned good at her job and he didn't want to lose her. Sally had made her choice and he was a fool to let it get to him. He should be grateful for all that she'd done. He was at fault, not Sally. Ben should have stayed in touch more, sent her a cable or written, instead of just leaving her in the dark. He was the fool and Sally was not to blame – and yet seeing her with another man rankled...

If she allowed that rogue to kiss her, what more had she allowed him? Ben had expected her to be wearing an engagement ring that morning and it angered him that she wasn't. He remembered when he'd offered to help her pay her rent and she'd acted as if he'd made a move on her virtue – was that just a show of modesty for him, because from Ben Harper she wanted marriage? Did she see him as a good prospect – the right kind of husband material? Perhaps her other friend was just a friend and he was misjudging her – but if so why had she allowed the kiss and why look so happy about it?

Perhaps he was just jealous? Ben knew he was capable of jealousy and wasn't proud of himself and yet he couldn't stop the maggot eating away at his insides. In his head, Sally Ross was his. He'd thought she must sense that, feel that invisible string he'd felt pulling them together from the start – but if she'd given herself to someone else... The sickness rose in his gut and he wanted to tear the man who had despoiled her limb from limb. She should have waited... she must have known he would come back when he could.

No, hell! How could she have known when he'd never hinted or said a thing to tell her that he admired her more than any woman he'd ever known? He'd kept it all inside, even though it had been difficult at times, but he'd done it because he had no right – and if he'd kissed her he would probably have ended up in bed with her and that would have ruined her life, so he'd kept a discreet distance. More fool him! He should have made her his own while he had the chance...

Ben wasn't sure whether he was more upset with Sally for not waiting or with himself for not telling her the truth. Yet he hadn't been free and the bitter despair had made him hold back and keep his secrets when he should have been open. Sally had no idea how he felt about her. He should have told her about Maribel... but it was too painful and he was too guilty to talk about what he'd done – the tragedy that had ruined his life and Maribel's too.

His young wife had been pretty, full of life and excited to be marrying a man who could take her away from the poverty of her life, only his father had disowned him for choosing the daughter of a hillbilly, as his father had so rudely called her, and Ben hadn't been able to give her all the things she'd wanted.

Ben felt wet on his cheeks and angrily brushed it away. All the tears had been shed a long time ago when he'd left Maribel in the hospital, knowing that she would never run or laugh or make love again, but just lie there like a cabbage and stare accusingly at him whenever he visited. She was in there somewhere, inside that useless lump of disfigured flesh; he knew she was still there, and she blamed him for the waste of her young life and Ben knew he was to blame and that was why he had to stand by her and pay for her to be washed and fed and kept alive, even though it was a living death. And he had to live with the knowledge that it was because of him that Maribel, and all that she had been, was lying there waiting for death.

Ben had hated himself for such a long time. There had been other women in his bed since Maribel, but only because he needed the release of sex. He'd chosen the women he slept with carefully and took nothing from them they were not willing to give or sell. He neither offered love nor asked for it and he knew he had the reputation of a bastard. Uncle Gerald had disliked that in him and it was the reason he hadn't given him full control of Harper's.

'I like you, Ben,' he'd told him once, 'but you're a heartless bastard and I'm not sure I can trust you to look after my baby...'

The stores were like children to his uncle and Ben had laughed, promising that he would treat the store like a lover.

'That's just the trouble,' his uncle had said. 'I'm not sure you know how to love.'

But Ben did know how to love. He'd loved the sweet, shy, spoiled girl that was Maribel, but because they were both headstrong they'd quarrelled and she'd had a temper. She'd run from him in anger over a stupid trifle and, in the blinding rain, straight into the path of the truck that had knocked her down...

Ben had never told anyone the truth about the young girl he'd married. Not even his beloved sister, Jenni. It hurt too much and he was too wracked with guilt, too remorseful to allow himself to seek understanding or sympathy. He took what he needed from life and visited the shell of his wife and told no one nor asked for anyone's help. The hospital took every dollar he had to spare for years and everyone thought he must be a fool or a gambler when he had no money to buy new cars or houses and it was only when he started to work for his uncle that he managed to save a little and think of a future.

He hadn't felt anything but the release of sex with a woman for years – and then an English Cockney girl smiled as they looked at a shop window together and for the first time the ice cracked. It thawed a little more each time he saw her and the wanting became an ache inside him, but Sally Ross wanted marriage and Ben Harper was married to a girl he'd run off with when he was nineteen...

He'd been a fool not to tell Sally! Perhaps if he'd revealed his story, Sally would have understood and then it wouldn't be too late, because Ben was free at last, but now it meant nothing. The only woman he wanted had been in another man's arms... but he could only blame himself and somehow he had to live with it.

14

Rachel served her customer with a silver bangle and a gold gypsy ring set with garnets and pearls. It was the third time he'd been in to purchase goods in the last fortnight and he'd bought something on each occasion.

'Someone is going to be lucky,' she said as she did the packages up for him with ribbon and Harper's distinctive black and gold boxes. 'Are they all for the same lady?'

He smiled and shook his head. 'Last week I bought a gift for my sister-in-law, Wendy, a special bag for my aunt in Hampstead, and the week before that I bought a silver brooch for my sister, Mary – these are for my nieces, Simona and Jacqui...'

'Well, you do have a lot of ladies to buy gifts for...' Rachel said and presented him with the small carrier bag.

'The only problem is I've run out of female relatives to buy gifts for,' he said and looked rueful. 'I'm not sure what excuse I can use to come here again...'

Rachel felt a little shiver at her nape and looked at him. She was startled by what she saw there, because it was unmistakeable. She'd seen admiration in a man's eyes before but not for years – or not that she'd noticed.

'I'm not sure what you mean, sir...' she said, a little flustered.

'I know your name is Rachel Craven,' he replied, 'and one of the girls called you Mrs... but you're not wearing a wedding ring...'

Rachel felt breathless but managed to answer calmly. 'I'm a widow. My husband died nearly three years ago now...'

'I'm so sorry; I know how hard that can be. My wife died five years ago. I have a good family and they try to look after me. My sister-in-law is always introducing me to young ladies – but I would prefer to choose my friends for myself.' He hesitated, then said formally, 'Mrs Rachel Craven – would you allow me to take you to lunch somewhere nice this Sunday, please? I promise that I'm harmless, solvent, clean, and I don't have a prison record...'

Rachel couldn't help the laugh that escaped her. She'd chatted to him each time he came in to buy a gift and realised that she found him pleasant, and short of them both having a mutual friend, they had no other way of being introduced.

'Would you mind telling me your name?'

'Of course, you don't know...' He laughed and shook his head. 'I'm William Bailey; I'm a qualified solicitor – and I'm looking for a friend and perhaps a wife...'

'Well, that was rather more information than I asked for...' Rachel was brimming with laughter now but tried to hold it in. 'Where shall we meet?'

'You mean you will...' His whole face lit up and she felt pleased that she'd trusted her instinct. 'I know of a very nice restaurant near the park... it's called the Cherry Pie...'

'Yes, I know it,' Rachel said. 'I went there with some friends for lunch the other day. Shall we meet there at a quarter to one?' She was glad he'd chosen somewhere she was familiar with, because it was nice but not so posh that she would feel uncomfortable.

'Yes, thank you so much.' He tipped his hat to her. 'I feel very lucky and honoured. Good day to you, Rachel Craven. I shall look forward to Sunday...'

Rachel watched as he walked from the department and then she felt the hot flush of embarrassment rush over her. What on earth had she done – saying yes to an invitation from a man she knew nothing about? It was stupid and brazen of her and of course she wouldn't go... she couldn't, could she? He could be anyone – a murderer or something... and that thought was even more stupid. She'd never seen anyone less like a murderer and this was just a reaction to being flirted with by a man.

She'd made up her mind to put the past behind her. The shadow of her husband's illness had haunted her for a long time, but now she was ready to put that away and find happiness. She was a little uncomfortable that she'd allowed a stranger to invite her out, but she seldom met gentlemen these days and Mr Bailey was a gentleman. He'd visited the department three times in order to ask her out and she was glad she'd said yes, even though it went against all that she'd been taught as a young woman when it would have been frowned on even to speak to a man who had not been properly introduced.

A smile touched her lips. Sunday lunch was hardly decadent and she could always say thank you afterwards and walk away and yet she knew, even as her mind wrestled with anxious thoughts, that she was looking forward to the engagement. It was a long, long time since a gentleman had taken her to lunch...

Her thoughts of the persistent gentleman fled as she saw her employer enter the department with Mr Stockbridge and Mr Marco following behind. Mr Harper came up to her, smiling and offering to shake hands.

'Good morning, Mrs Craven,' he said. 'Your department looks

bright and rather exciting. It seems to have grown since I was last here?'

'Yes, Mr Harper,' Rachel smiled. 'Miss Ross was so pleased with the jewellery sales that she had more cabinets put in and we have twice as much stock as we did when we started last year.'

'That is marvellous,' he replied with a nod. 'And the rest of your department?'

'The hats are always good sellers,' Rachel informed him. 'Gloves are a little more seasonal, though the scarves are always wanted for gifts...'

'I am more than pleased with your sales, Mrs Craven. I want to thank you and your staff for your efforts and to assure you all that your loyalty in looking after my business will be rewarded with a ten per cent pay rise – and a bonus of ten shillings this week...'

'I'm sure everyone will be very happy with that,' Rachel said. She hesitated, then, 'Are you back in London for some time now, sir?'

'It is my intention to make my home here, because Harper's is very important to me and I mean to make it a lasting success,' he answered, a little nerve flicking at his temple. 'I shall be looking for a permanent home now that I've sold what I had in New York...'

'Ah, the beautiful Mrs Craven,' Mr Marco said, coming up to her after chatting with Beth for a moment. 'You will allow me to use some of your best items for my window display, I hope. I want to recreate Aladdin's Cave with jewels and bright scarves, also silver from the ground floor... it came to me in a dream last night. You will permit?' His eyes twinkled at her. 'You will keep this secret on pain of death?'

'Of course, Mr Marco, but you must promise to return everything in pristine condition – no tears in the silk scarves...'

'You scold me so, beautiful madam,' he said teasingly. 'I assure you it was not I that damaged the green silk last time – but a foolish girl I was given to assist me...'

'Miss Brown, I think,' Rachel nodded. 'Still, I shall expect you to sign for everything...'

'For you, I would sign in blood...' he said and his smile was pure mischief.

Rachel shook her head as the three men left the department. Mr Marco was forever flirting with her, but she knew it was merely his sense of humour and an innate charm. She had seen him in the restaurant she liked best with a man some years his junior and from the way they looked at each other, Rachel guessed they were more than friends. She was not shocked as some ladies might have been, for such liaisons were not accepted in polite society, but understood that his personal life was his own.

Her thoughts returned to the gentleman with whom she'd arranged to have lunch. Was she completely mad to agree to meet a stranger? Perhaps she should call it off – except that she had no idea where to contact him and it would be impolite to leave him standing outside the restaurant...

* * *

'What will you wear?' Sally asked that evening when she told the others what had happened. They'd looked at her in disbelief for a moment, but then Beth had smiled and Maggie had hugged her and Sally had taken charge of her outfit. 'If the weather is nice, I think you should wear your blue suit,' Sally continued. 'Your navy shoes are smart and I have a darling little hat you can borrow, Rachel. I bought it this week and I haven't worn it and I know it will suit you...'

'Sally, that is extraordinarily generous of you, but I'm sure I have something I can wear...'

'Not as pretty as my hat,' Sally said and danced around her, tweaking her hair and teasing her. 'I'm so happy for you, dearest Rachel. We all love you and I know you were lonely before we started living together.'

'It is only a luncheon...' Rachel protested.

'It is a start – a new start for you,' Sally said. 'If he's nice and I think he must be – you will have a friend and perhaps more...'

'It's romantic,' Maggie said and looked wistful. 'Ralf did the same thing, you know. He kept coming to the counter until he got up the courage to ask me out...'

'Yes, I remember...' Rachel looked at her sympathetically. 'Do you miss him, Maggie?'

'Sometimes – he came to the park one Sunday when I was with friends and joined us for a while, but it wasn't the same. I can see him again if I want...' Maggie shook her head. 'I don't know if I want to forgive him...'

'Well, this is just a luncheon between two people who rather like the look of each other and need a friend,' Rachel said. 'I think perhaps he'd had enough of his family trying to find him a new wife...'

'Or he fell in love with you over the jewellery counter...' Beth said. 'It does happen just like that, Rachel. Jack says he loved me from the moment he saw me. I'm not sure it's true, but it was soon after that's for certain...' She smiled happily. 'I'm really pleased for you.' She nodded. 'I've got a pretty silk blouse you can borrow if you like, my aunt made it for me...'

'That is kind of you,' Rachel said. 'Tell me, how is Helen now?' She thought Beth didn't see her aunt often and reflected that she had neglected her spinster seamstress friends, Mildred and Minnie of late, making a mental note to visit soon.

'Oh... not too bad,' Beth replied. 'I'm going to visit her again soon...' She looked sad and uneasy for a moment and Rachel recalled that she'd said something about her aunt not being as happy as she'd hoped in her marriage. 'Don't let's think about that now, it's you we're concentrating on, Rachel. What you're going to wear for your lunch appointment...'

'You don't think it was vulgar or cheap of me to accept an invitation from a stranger?'

'No, of course not,' Sally said. 'We're all strangers until we meet, aren't we?'

'I suppose so...' Rachel laughed.

* * *

Rachel glanced around the restaurant. It wasn't the first time she'd been there for a meal but its quiet atmosphere of elegance and quality charmed her each time she came with friends. Now, here with William, it seemed even more special and she was suddenly glad that she had let Sally persuade her into dressing up for it.

'What will you have?' William asked, glancing at the extensive menu – or would you like me to choose for you?'

'I'd rather like the melon starter,' Rachel said, 'and fish please – Dover sole if they have it, pan fried with sauté potatoes and peas...'

'Sounds delicious,' William agreed. 'I think I'll have the same – and then I can have some of that delicious gateau I can see on the sweet trolley...' He patted his stomach. 'I try to watch my weight but just for once...'

'I hardly think you need to diet,' Rachel said, glancing at his spare frame. 'You seem to be one of the lucky ones as far as that is concerned.'

'My aunt thinks I don't feed myself properly,' he said with a wicked smile. 'She tells me I need a wife to feed me up – do you think I do, Rachel?'

Rachel smiled. He was teasing her and she was enjoying it. Her life had held little laughter for some years before she joined the staff at Harper's. Being teased by a man was something she thought had gone forever...

'Perhaps,' she said. 'I should warn you, I am not a particularly good cook...'

'And I like plain food,' he said. 'Besides, it's nice to come out and leave the work to others, isn't it?'

'Yes,' she agreed. 'It is – and I am looking forward to my lunch today...'

William laughed and summoned the waiter. Rachel sipped the wine he brought and looked about her. Life had suddenly become so much brighter...

15

Sally lay in bed and reflected on the day just past. It had started badly for her because of Ben Harper's strange attitude – but she'd had a good day otherwise. Several of the sales people had told her how pleased they were with the new stock – and then Rachel's news had cheered them all up. Sally was really pleased that her friend had a chance to go out with a gentleman. Perhaps she was taking a risk as she knew nothing of him, and some people might say she was behaving in a fast way, but Sally knew how easy it was to misjudge people on first acquaintance. Take Mick for example...

Mick had seemed to be an impertinent barman without much to recommend him, but he'd turned out to be a good friend. Whereas she'd taken to Ben Harper from the first moment and now she didn't know what to make of him. Perhaps she was a poor judge of character; she just hoped that Rachel wouldn't have her heart broken if things developed with her new friend.

Turning her back to Rachel's bed, Sally buried her face in the pillow and let the tears slip quietly into its softness. Damn Ben Harper and his moods. She would put him out of her mind and concentrate on her work and if she couldn't work in the same office as him, she would ask Mick to find her a job...

* * *

Ben was at his desk and reading the reports she'd put out for him when Sally got in the next morning. He looked up at her, hesitated and then offered her an apologetic smile.

'I'm sorry if I was a bit off with you yesterday,' he said. 'I'll try not to let it happen again – and you didn't deserve it. I've been reading these sales reports and they're even better than I expected.'

Sally nodded, accepting that it was all the apology she was likely to get. She realised that if she wanted to go on working for him she had to accept that he was the boss and nothing more. It hurt, but she would be a fool to throw away a job she had come to enjoy just because she'd been foolish enough to have feelings for him.

Sally sat at her desk, picking up a list of appointments and looking through them. She had nothing for that morning and decided that she would take a tour of the various departments. It was the best way to tell whether stock was moving or sticking on the shelves. Figures only told half the story, because they didn't tell you that a certain dress had sold out in the first week and another was lingering unloved on the rail.

Standing up, she gathered pencil and book and prepared to leave.

'Where are you off to?' Ben asked. 'I was hoping to discuss various things with you, Sally.'

'Certainly,' she said. 'I was going to walk round the various departments and check the stock visually. I like to do that regularly so that I know what is selling well and needs replacing and what still lingers a couple of months on. Mr Stockbridge likes to hear my opinions...'

'Sounds like a good idea to me,' Ben Harper agreed and stood up. 'Shall we go? Where do you want to begin?'

'The ground floor is where the customers are first attracted into the store,' Sally replied. 'I think the displays there need to change frequently. Some stock is always the same. People come in for the same teapot, cup and saucer or plate regularly. Our blue and white range is popular because if something is broken we always have it in stock for replacement.'

'Yes, that was a good idea,' he nodded his approval. 'I've noticed there is quite a regular turnover on that. The silver tea and coffee pots also sell well as individual items. I remember we discussed that last year.'

'Yes, we did and decided that we would have a range people could add to over time and it has worked well. I've been told customers come back for extra items every so often and they're pleased they can find them in stock and don't have to order.'

'Jenni had some glassware delivered from the States, didn't she?'

'Yes, last Christmas, and it sold well as gifts,' Sally told him. 'I think most of it was sold in December – and Jenni said she would find us something similar in time for the Christmas trade this year.'

He nodded. It was part of shop life that you started to plan your Christmas stock in the spring and early summer in order to have it on your shelves at the right moment. Spring stock was ordered in the autumn, and autumn and winter in the spring or summer. Sally enjoyed seeing the styles that would be coming in the next season ahead of time.

The ground floor was open plan and though there were actually several departments, the customer was not aware of it as they could wander from one counter and display to another. The leather suitcase, briefcase and dressing case display was just inside the door.

Next was a stand of walking sticks with silver tops, umbrellas and parasols. At the back of the store were the glassware, china and silver displays, with three counters and assistants. To one side was a counter with pens, propelling pencils and writing paper, some in leather cases. In the middle of the store was a long counter with a display of table lamps. At the other end were the lifts that took customers up to the next floors, and a very small stand of face creams, soaps and lavender water was tucked in a corner.

'Do we sell much in the stationery department?' Ben asked as they passed the counter.

'Not very much,' Sally replied thoughtfully. 'Mr Benson is in charge of that and the lighting section. I have wondered if we might use that space for something else...'

'Have you anything particular in mind?'

'Well, yes, I do – but Jenni hasn't said any more about cosmetics, so I'm not sure whether we're thinking of opening a perfumery department or not. Jenni said we might have a section selling Elizabeth Arden perfumes and cosmetics – if that firm is actually up and running yet. I believe they were just in the development stage when she mentioned it. There are also the English firms to consider...'

'I'll ask Jenni about Elizabeth Arden, you investigate the English firms,' Ben said and made a note in his book. 'Do you think soaps, perfumes and various things like that would do better than the stationery if given a more prominent position?'

'We could divide the area,' Sally suggested. 'Neither needs a great deal of space at the moment. I suggest we ask Mr Benson to look after the lighting and promote a woman to the counter selling perfumed soaps, Eau de cologne and lavender water I can source here, and anything else Jenni can come up with from America.'

He gave her an odd smile. 'Would you like to sell make-up here?'

'I know some of the older ladies might frown on it,' Sally said, 'but the younger ones are buying cheap lip rouge and powders from places like Woolworths – so why wouldn't they buy a nicer range from us? We could have some pretty powder compacts, lavender water, perfumed soaps at first and then introduce the more expensive face creams as our customers get used to the idea.'

'That sounds like a great idea...' Ben smiled at her. 'We make a good team, you see – putting out heads together was a good idea...' He smiled to himself. 'If I had the room, I'd love a toy department for the kids...'

Sally nodded but wouldn't let herself respond to his smile. Ben was only being the friendly boss. To let him beneath her skin again would be to lay up pain for herself once more. She nodded but was saved from saying more by the arrival of Mr Marco, who took his boss off to look at something he was planning for his latest display. Smiling, Sally went back to her work. She wasn't the only one glad to see Ben Harper back.

* * *

Ben Harper asked Sally if she had time to have supper with him that evening and she said she was busy. He frowned at her answer but didn't push his claim to her time. In actual fact, Sally had nothing to do but wash her hair. She went to bed early with a book and tried to put the memory of his smile out of her head. Damn the man! Why did he have to look at her like that – so reproachfully – when she knew she was just an employee to him?

Beth had been to supper with Fred and his younger son, Tim. She came in at about ten that night and apologised to Sally for keeping her awake.

'I wasn't sleeping anyway,' Sally said. 'Did you have a good evening?'

'Yes and no,' Beth said and grimaced. 'I get on with Fred – but poor Tim is a bit in the dumps. He has broken up with his girl-friend. That isn't the worst news, because Fred never thought her good enough – but now Tim is determined to join the Royal Flying Corps and that has upset his father. He says those flying machines are too flimsy to be safe and he wanted his younger son in a nice safe job... Jack is away for long periods and now Tim will leave home too.'

'Yes, I can see why that would upset Fred,' Sally agreed. 'But young men grow up and don't want to stay at home for ever...'

'They'd had words over it, so there was a bit of an atmosphere,' Beth said and sighed. 'Fred said it was bad enough that Tim wanted to fly, which is dangerous in itself – but he thinks we're in for trouble in Europe before long and he says if there is a war the Flying Corps will be a death-trap for the young pilots...'

'Yes, I think he might be right,' Sally frowned. 'I've heard a few people mention the possibility of war recently, but I can't see why trouble in parts of Europe means we have to fight, can you?'

'No, I can't,' Beth agreed. 'It seems daft to me – but Fred reads his daily paper from cover to cover and he says it is a matter of treaties. We've promised to defend certain countries and if other countries go to war with them, it means we have to fight as well...'

'The politicians who sign things like that should be shot,' Sally said and then laughed. 'Take no notice of me, Beth love. I'm in a bit of a mood...'

Beth sat on the edge of her bed. 'Is it Mr Harper? Have you fallen out with him?'

'No, not really... yes, in a way...' Sally shook her head. 'He was better today, but yesterday he was like a bear with a sore head. I thought I was going to be accused of something dreadful and then he just went off in a temper. This morning he apologised, but he seems to be watching me all the time, Beth. I feel as if I've done something wrong and I don't know what...'

Beth nodded and then thought of something. 'He called here on Sunday – when you'd gone to meet Sylvia. I didn't speak to him myself, but I think Rachel told him you were meeting a friend for lunch. You didn't see him that day?'

'No – nor did he mention it to me...' Sally frowned. 'I wonder...'

Beth raised her brow in enquiry, but Sally shook her head.

'I think I'm going to make a cup of cocoa,' she said. 'Would you like some?'

'Yes, please...' Beth yawned. 'We were busy all day today at the store. I've sold nearly all my green silk scarves, Sally. It seems to be the most popular colour at the moment...'

'I'll see what I can find for you,' Sally promised and went through to the kitchen. Her mind was going round and round in circles, but nothing made sense to her. Why would Ben Harper come to find her on Sunday at home and then act in such an off manner on Monday morning? Unless...?

Sally remembered how the weather had broken suddenly when she'd been having lunch with Mick. Afterwards, when he brought her home, he'd kissed her and she'd thanked him for her lovely meal and then she'd got out of the car and run back to her apartment building. Because it was raining so hard, she hadn't looked back. Was it possible that Ben had been standing in a doorway waiting? Had he got cold and bored of waiting and then seen what he thought was an intimate moment between lovers? Was that the reason for his anger?

Sally tingled all over. If her kiss with Mick had made Ben angry perhaps he did care for her?

She shook her head, because she didn't know if she was just hoping that was the reason and making a fool of herself again. How could she say to Ben Harper that Mick was just a friend unless he asked? She'd been out with Mick a couple of times recently and knew that Mick wanted to be more – much more. Sally was confused. Had she given Mick reason to think their relationship might be more than it was? Should she have pushed him away or slapped him when he kissed her? No, he'd been kind to her and it had been just a friendly kiss. She hadn't felt like slapping him because she did like him – it was just that she felt more for Ben Harper.

She was such an idiot!

It was a horrid tangle and Sally didn't know what to do or say for the best. She couldn't know why Ben Harper had come looking for her or if he'd watched her arrive home with Mick. Besides, he'd left her without a word for months and couldn't complain if she went out with other friends – and despite the kiss, that was all Mick was to her, a good friend.

Deciding that she couldn't solve the puzzle, Sally made two mugs of cocoa and took them back to the room she shared with Beth. Beth was already undressed and in her own bed. Putting the mugs on the little cabinet between the two beds, Sally got into her own and sipped the milky drink.

'Men are a pain, aren't they?' she said and Beth laughed.

'Yes, they can be,' she replied. 'When they're lovely you would do anything for them and when they're not...'

'You could shake them...' Sally laughed. She had made up her mind there was nothing she could do. If Ben had something to say to her, it was up to him.

* * *

Ben Harper didn't come into the office the next morning. Sally asked the secretary to type up the notes she'd made the previous day and put them into a file, which she placed on the desk for Ben when he arrived. She had several appointments with representatives and would be out most of the day.

It was tiring going from one firm to another and she'd had enough by the time she got back to the office at four thirty. Miss Summers came through and asked if she would like a tray of tea.

'Yes, please,' Sally said. 'I ate a Chelsea bun in a taxi and that's all I've had time for today.'

'Mr Harper was looking for you earlier,' Miss Summers remarked. 'He came in twice and asked where you were. I told him you had appointments and he looked annoyed and went off again.'

'Oh dear!' Sally grimaced. She'd not thought to tell him that she had appointments all day and wondered if she would be in his black books again when he got back.

Sally had written up all her notes for the day and was just preparing to leave for the evening when Ben Harper entered the office. He shot a look of annoyance her way.

'So you're back at last then…'

'I've been back an hour or so and I've written my notes up for Miss Summers to type for your files. I've seen two autumn/winter collections today and I spent a long time looking at leather bags for the autumn collection. It all takes time if you do it properly. I haven't been sitting around drinking tea…'

'I didn't doubt you were doing your job,' he said, and looked at her oddly. 'We seem to be off on the wrong foot since I got back, Sally. Can we start again please?'

'Yes, of course,' she replied. 'If I've done something to offend you, please tell me, Mr Harper.'

'It's Ben to you and you know it,' he said. 'I've been like a bear with a sore head and I'm sorry, Sally. I know you've done one hell of a good job here and I'm grateful.'

'I'm glad you're happy with my work,' she replied and then gave a little sigh. 'I don't want to fall out with you, Mr— Ben. I just wish I knew what I'd done wrong.'

'You haven't done anything,' he admitted wryly. 'I'm the fool – so I'm saying sorry. I want us to be friends again.'

'Yes, all right,' she said. 'We're friends and colleagues. I've made notes of what I've bought for autumn and what I saw and didn't buy... you can read my writing or wait until Miss Summers types it for you...'

'Why don't you let me take you for supper and tell me?'

Sally hesitated and then shook her head. 'I think we should keep our friendship to working hours, Ben. I'll have a cup of coffee with you if you wish but not a meal...'

'As you wish...' He moved away from her and the frown was back. 'I shan't take up any more of your time, Sally. You've had a busy day – get off home or wherever you're going...'

'I'm going home to supper and I'll spend the evening talking to Beth and Rachel,' Sally said. 'I have a lot of friends... Goodnight, Mr Harper...'

She went out before he could think of an answer. Sally wanted to go back in there and tell him that she would love to have supper with him, but it couldn't go on this way. He seemed so approachable one moment and the next he was frozen and angry. He should decide what he wanted their relationship to be and stick to it...

It took every ounce of strength she had to walk away but Sally wasn't going to let him break her heart all over again...

16

Maggie went with Beth, Jack and Fred to the park that Sunday afternoon. She and Beth had packed sandwiches and buns and they enjoyed a picnic before listening to the concert. It was after the brass band had packed up and they were deciding where to have their tea when Fred's younger son, Tim, turned up. He was wearing his Royal Flying Corps uniform and looking very pleased with himself.

'You do look smart,' Maggie said and smiled. The sun had come out and it was feeling a little more like spring and he looked so happy that it made her feel better too. She'd wondered whether Ralf would arrive during the concert as he'd said he might one day on the off-chance they would be there, but he hadn't and she wasn't sure whether to be glad or sorry.

'Am I in time to come to tea with you?' Tim asked. 'I thought I might have got here sooner, but we had some new kites delivered to our base and I had to be there, even though I was officially off-duty...'

'I'm sure you can come.' Maggie smiled. The decision was made to visit the small tea shop at the corner of the park and they all walked there together. 'Are you enjoying being a member of the Royal Flying Corps?' she asked.

'Love it,' he replied. 'I've already been up for five hours' training, a few more and I'll get a chance for my first solo flight...'

'That's wonderful,' Maggie said and slipped an arm through his, giving him a companionable smile, because she'd got to know him from the numerous weekends he'd spent with them when his girlfriend, Dottie, had been with him. 'Tell me what it feels like to be up there above the clouds. Is it as exciting as it sounds?'

'The most exciting thing I've ever done...'

'I'm not surprised that a lot of young men are joining up,' she replied. 'Not all of them will get to be pilots, I suppose?'

'We need navigators and gunners and ground crew...' Tim said enthusiastically. 'We do low flying and take aerial photographs and that is really fun...'

'I wish I was a man and then I could join too...'

Tim laughed and shook his head. 'You're much too pretty for me to agree, Miss Gibbs. I would rather you were a young lady I could take to tea sometimes...'

Maggie smiled up at him, because his enthusiasm was catching. She liked this man who seemed to take pleasure in most things. Before this she hadn't taken too much notice of Fred's son, because he'd always had his girlfriend with him, but she knew from Beth that he had broken up with her and that meant Maggie could be friends with him without upsetting another young woman.

'I think you're very kind,' she said, a faint blush in her cheeks.

'Dad told me you broke up with your boyfriend,' Tim said. 'Dottie got fed up with me, so I'm at a bit of a loose end – I know it's too soon to get involved in another relationship, but we can be friends, can't we?' He grinned. 'I had a bet on Covercoat in the Grand National a couple of weeks back and won fifty pounds – so I'll treat everyone today.'

'Lucky you,' Maggie said. 'Fifty pounds is a lot of money – but you don't have to treat us all.'

'I'd like to – and we can be friends, can't we?'

'Yes, of course we can,' Maggie said as they followed the others into the teashop. 'I should like that – and I know you, so there is no impropriety...'

Tim grinned at her. 'We're practically old friends,' he teased and in a way it was true because they'd been meeting in company with Beth and his father and brother for a long time now, but always with others around. Yet Maggie felt easy with him. It wasn't like starting a new relationship, because they'd got used to each other over several weekends the previous summer.

'Tell me,' she said. 'Some people are saying there may be war in Europe – you don't think so, do you?'

'Oh, I shouldn't think so, not to involve us, though that lot out there in the Balkans are always having a go at each other,' Tim said airily, though his eyes didn't meet hers at that moment.

* * *

'I've got an appointment at the Halcyon Hotel in the morning,' Jack said as he and Beth walked a little ahead of the others in the park that afternoon. 'If they offer me the job, I'll have one more trip to America and then I'll be here for good...'

His eyes sought hers. 'It means we could marry quite soon. I can probably find us a little place of our own, but we can always stay at Dad's for a while...'

'Do you think you'll be happy working for someone else in this hotel?' Beth asked, looking at him doubtfully. 'I thought you'd set your mind on a place of your own?'

'Well, I have, and if something had turned up, I would have taken it,' Jack replied. 'But this would be good experience for me,

Beth. If I have a couple of years managing this hotel for the owners I'll be ready to take on my own and I can look round at my leisure and make certain I get the right one for us...'

It did make sense and Beth could only agree, though it brought the prospect of marriage alarmingly close. She loved Jack and she did want to marry him, but he seemed in such a rush and Beth would have preferred a longer courtship. In her mind, she'd thought probably Christmas or the following spring, but Jack was talking of this summer and it seemed all too quick. Marriage and babies was definitely the future, but she was enjoying her life at Harper's – at least most of the time. Her promotion to the hat counter had given her more scope to use her creative flair and seeing all the new creations that Sally bought was exciting. Beth wasn't sure she wanted to give all that up just yet. Had they had a small hotel of their own to run, so that she'd be involved in the business with Jack, it would have felt more exciting. She could have cooked pies and cakes, made it well known for good home-made food.

She smiled at Jack, not wanting him to sense that she had doubts. Losing him was something Beth wasn't prepared to risk, but she would have been happier if he'd stuck to his original plan...

'Well, if you're happy with the idea,' she said and he kissed her enthusiastically. Beth responded to the kiss, feeling a surge of love. Of course she wanted to marry him and perhaps he was right and it was better to get some experience of running a hotel before they took on their own...

* * *

'Tim asked me if I would like to go to the Music Hall with him on Saturday evening,' Maggie told Beth later that evening when they were making cocoa in the small kitchen they all shared. 'You don't think it was wrong of me to say yes?'

'Why should it be?' Beth asked with a smile. 'Tim is Fred's son, perfectly respectable, and we're all friends. I know you believed you were in love with Ralf, but he let you down, Maggie. Unless you want to give him another chance, there is no reason you shouldn't go out with other friends.'

'That's what I thought,' Maggie smiled, happy with Beth's answer. 'Neither Tim nor I want a deeper relationship at the moment, but we get on, and we'd like to go out now and then. I know Ralf would hate it if he knew – but I don't belong to him...'

'You're still not eighteen,' Beth told her with a smile. 'There's no reason you shouldn't make friends with several young men before you decide to marry. You should make the most of the situation, Maggie. Living with Rachel, Sally and me, you have more freedom than I did when I was looking after my mother.'

Maggie nodded. 'It was a lucky day for me when I got the job at Harper's. I should never have known you or Sally or Rachel if I hadn't come to the interview that day...'

'I like living with you all too...'

'But Jack wants to marry you. You're in love – aren't you?'

'Yes, I do love him...' Beth kept her sigh inside. Perhaps most women had doubts before they married. 'I do want to get married and have you and Sally as my bridesmaids...'

'I can't wait to be your bridesmaid,' Maggie said. 'Will you be choosing the dresses soon? I can help pay for it if it isn't too expensive...'

'Sally said she would keep an eye out for me,' Beth said. 'She says I may be able to get them cheaper straight from the wholesaler and she can arrange that – but I could have them made.'

'Your aunt might do it,' Maggie agreed. 'She makes lovely clothes, Beth. Why don't you ask her?'

'I suppose I could,' Beth said doubtfully. 'I'm not sure whether her husband would like that very much. I might pop over on my half day and ask her...' She ought to go soon anyway, because her aunt had been upset the last time and Beth was uneasy about her.

'Have you set a date for the wedding?' Maggie asked, looking excited.

'Not yet. It depends on whether Jack gets the job he's after – and then we'll have to find somewhere to live – but we both know we shall marry soon. I think perhaps in the summer. July or August...'

'That isn't so far off now,' Maggie said. 'Specially if you're going to have the dresses made for us all...'

Beth agreed, because May was well advanced now and two months wasn't long to make three bridesmaids' dresses and one wedding gown. Of course, if Sally arranged for her to get a discount at a bridal gown wholesaler, Beth could choose what she needed and save the bother of finding a seamstress to make them. Once upon a time, she would have asked Aunt Helen without hesitation, but remembering her aunt's unhappiness, she was reluctant to make more bother for her.

However, if she visited to warn Aunt Helen that she was thinking of marrying quite soon, Beth might be able to judge whether or not her aunt was suffering from her husband's unkindness. If only she could do something to help! If she could persuade her to walk out on her bully of a husband – yet Aunt Helen was not the kind of woman to admit publicly that she'd made a mistake and leave him; she would consider it her duty to stand by him, however badly he treated her.

'You're right. I've got the afternoon off on Tuesday this week. I'll pop over and see her and ask whether or not she could make the dresses for us...'

17

Gerald opened the door to Beth's knock that afternoon. He looked annoyed, but then smiled in a false way and she knew that she wasn't welcome, though he opened the door wider and invited her inside. However, they progressed no further than the hall, which smelled of roses and lavender from the pot pourri Aunt Helen always had in the hallway.

'I'm afraid you've had a wasted journey,' Gerald said but didn't smile or look apologetic. 'Had you sent a letter letting us know you were coming, I could have informed you Helen wouldn't be here...'

'Not here?' Beth felt coldness at her nape. 'Where has she gone?'

'She went to visit an old friend three days ago. I expect her back the day after tomorrow...'

'Oh – who has she gone to see?' Beth didn't know why she pushed him, but something told her he was lying.

'A woman called Muriel. She is in some distress because her grandson just died,' Gerald said, but he didn't look at Beth and she knew he had made the story up. Wherever her aunt was, she hadn't gone to see a lady called Muriel.

'In that case, I'll try to get here next week. My half day will be on Thursday next week.'

'Very well, I'll tell her you called,' Gerald said. He held the door for her and she had the feeling he couldn't wait to get rid of her. As Beth was leaving, she thought she heard a sound from above... like a floorboard or a door creaking and she instinctively glanced at the ceiling. 'It's the cat...' Gerald's excuse startled Beth, because she could have sworn that her aunt had never mentioned having a cat.

'I'll be back next week...'

Outside, in the cool breeze, Beth looked at the upstairs window. It was the landing window and she could have sworn that the curtain twitched – as if someone was up there, watching...

Surely that couldn't be her aunt? Aunt Helen would have come down when she heard Beth's voice. She would never have let Gerald deny her – unless he had threatened her with violence? Surely things hadn't got that bad between them?

Beth turned away reluctantly. She was uneasy, unwilling to walk away and leave without getting to the bottom of the little mystery. However, short of calling her aunt's husband a liar, Beth had no reason to demand access and she didn't want to cause a fuss for nothing. Perhaps Gerald had a cat, though he didn't strike her as the sort to have any pets. He was too cold, too selfish to give an animal the attention and love it needed. Besides, her aunt didn't like cats much and it was a surprise they had one...

Walking away, Beth decided to ask Jack to come with her next time. He was going back to sea for two weeks, and if he got the job he was after, that would be his last trip to New York. After that, he would be working nearby and that meant she could see him more often. If she told Jack her suspicions, he would help her to discover the truth.

* * *

The letter from her aunt arrived that Friday morning. Aunt Helen apologised for not being at home when she'd called.

> *It would be better if you could write a week before you come in future. I do like to see you, Beth, but only if I know you're coming. Gerald doesn't like surprise visits and it is better to let me know well in advance.*
>
> *Your grateful aunt, Helen.*

Beth read the short note several times. The handwriting was her aunt's, but it wasn't her phrasing. Aunt Helen would never be so short; her letters had always rambled and been filled with news. Beth still had some from the time of her mother's death, when her aunt had invited her to come and stay. She found them in her things and compared them, frowning over the formation of some letters. It was Aunt Helen's writing and yet it wasn't – and Beth sensed that either her aunt had been forced to write the letter or it had been difficult for her to write.

The idea that Aunt Helen was being bullied was growing in her mind. That evening, she told Jack what she feared and he looked serious, nodding in agreement as he looked at the letter and compared it with others from Aunt Helen.

'I'm sure someone was up there when I visited, Jack – and I don't think she has a cat and this letter looks wrong...'

'It doesn't look quite the same, though it is similar,' he agreed. 'I think you might be right, Beth. I didn't like that chap the only time I met him. I've met his sort on the ships. They seem to imagine that they have the right to ride roughshod over everyone else... charming and polite until someone upsets them and then they react like snarling wolves. One of them was a peer of the realm, but I saw him strike his wife viciously when he didn't realise I was in their suite turning down beds...'

'What can I do to help her?' Beth asked and Jack shook his head.

'I asked Lady Treverne if she would like me to be a witness against her husband and she denied he had hit her – told me I was mistaken and gave me five pounds for my trouble...'

'It's pride, I think,' Beth said. 'Aunt Helen wouldn't have told me anything if I hadn't seen the bruises on her wrist. I just wish I could help her.'

'You can't unless she asks for help,' Jack said. 'We can only surmise something is going on – unless we can find proof...'

'Will you come with me next week, please?'

'On Thursday...' Jack hesitated and then nodded. 'Yes, of course I will, Beth. I'm not sure what we can do even if he is hitting her – but at least we might let him know that we know. He might restrain himself if he thinks we're watching him...'

'Yes...' Beth was thoughtful. 'I'm almost sure she was upstairs that day, Jack. I think she may have had bruises she couldn't hide and so he made her stay out of the way...'

'Men like that are disgusting,' Jack replied. 'I'd like to give him a thrashing – see how he feels on the wrong end of a beating...'

'Please, don't,' Beth said. 'Aunt Helen wouldn't thank you – and Gerald is the sort that would press charges. You would be the one in trouble, Jack.'

'I know...' He looked rueful. 'But one of these days he'll be caught out and then nothing will save him.'

* * *

Beth couldn't wait for her next half day and she and Jack went in his little car to visit Aunt Helen. This time, her aunt answered the door herself, smiling and asking them into the sitting room, where a tea of sandwiches and cakes had been prepared.

'I'm sorry you had a wasted journey last week,' she said. 'Gerald wasn't in the best of moods, I'm afraid. He didn't see why I should visit my friend, but I couldn't ignore her, Beth. She was in such distress...'

'I'm sorry she was in trouble. I hope she is better now, Aunt Helen,' Beth said. 'And how is your cat now?'

'What cat? Really, Beth, you know I dislike them...' Aunt Helen frowned. 'My friend is better now, thank you...'

Her aunt's excuse sounded plausible and her smile seemed real, but Beth noticed that the ruffles at her wrist were tight and she thought she caught sight of a white bandage beneath. She'd assumed the cat was Gerald's but now she was almost sure there had never been a cat, which meant someone had been upstairs and Gerald had lied to her – but why didn't Aunt Helen open up to her and tell her what he'd done? Was she just too upset or embarrassed to talk and did Beth have the right to force her? Surely, Aunt Helen would tell her if she was really scared?

'I wanted to ask if you felt up to making my bridesmaids dresses,' Beth said after a few minutes thought. 'There will be three of them, all adults, and I'll bring their measurements – and they could come for a fitting or you could come to ours.'

'I think it best if I come to you,' Aunt Helen said. 'Gerald goes on little trips every few weeks. For his business, I believe...' She hesitated, then, 'If I came while he's away, it would be better... he doesn't like me to have people he doesn't know here, but he won't stop me coming to you.'

The nervous look in her eyes prompted Beth to ask, 'Is everything all right, Aunt Helen? I know you're not as happy as you expected to be when you married – but if you were frightened or hurt in any way, I would help you...'

'Please do not be foolish, dear,' Aunt Helen said. She glanced nervously at Jack as if wondering whether he would believe her. 'I expect I was a selfish woman set in my ways. I've had to learn that I'm married now and a gentleman expects his wife to do as he asks and look after him. If I said anything stupid last time you came, I was just feeling upset and you should forget it.'

Aunt Helen bent over the teapot, refreshing it with hot water from the silver-plated kettle on the stand that she had beside her chair. Beth shot a look at Jack and he shook his head. She let the words that sprang to her lips go unspoken, because if her aunt did not want to tell her the truth, there was no use in pressing her.

'I am very fond of you, Beth,' Aunt Helen said and pressed her hand as they left. 'One day, you may discover how fond. I regret that I did not show it more when we lived together, but I did not realise how fortunate I was to have such a loving niece. I do hope you and Jack will visit when you can – and that you will have a long and happy life together...'

'Oh, Aunt Helen, take care of yourself,' Beth said a little sob in her voice. 'I do love you and if you need me just let me know...'

Jack looked at her when the door had shut and they were sitting in his little roadster. 'She is nervous, Beth,' he said, 'but she won't tell you what is wrong – particularly not when I'm there. I think he has hit her. I moved my hand towards her as she was reaching for a slice of cake and she flinched.'

'Oh, Jack...' Beth looked back at the house in distress. 'What can I do?'

'Only what you are doing,' he said. 'You will need to see your aunt more often because of the bridesmaids' dresses and that will give her more opportunity to tell you what's on her mind.'

'Do you think it is pride that is holding her back – or fear?'

'Probably a mixture of both,' Jack replied. 'Gerald isn't the only husband who intimidates his wife, far from it. Some of them use violence and some just inflict scorn and belittle their wives. On the ships, we stewards saw it all the time. I should say Gerald has used both scorn and physical abuse to make your aunt fear him.'

'So I'm not imagining it?'

'In my opinion, your aunt has been bullied into submission. Gerald fears that you might go to the police and that is why he has allowed her to see you today. She said he was out, but I think he was in the house, keeping out of the way. He might even have been in the next room, listening.'

'No wonder she lied! He is a nasty piece of work,' Beth said and felt worried. 'I'm frightened for her, Jack, but if she won't let me, I can't rescue her.'

'What could you do for her?' Jack asked. 'If he is the kind of man I imagine him to be, he would fetch her back if she left him...'

'Then she has to stay there and put up with him?' Beth looked at Jack, but he was concentrating on the road as he drove off into the traffic.

'I think she has accepted that,' Jack said and indicated he was turning left with a flourish out of the window. His arm signal was clear and they turned at the next corner into a quieter road. Jack risked a glance at her. 'I think there are a lot of women in your aunt's situation, Beth. Some men are controlling brutes.'

Beth nodded because he was right. 'Some women like to control too,' she said, 'but they use emotional blackmail rather than brute force.'

'And that is just as wrong as the other way,' Jack said. He pulled on the brake, stopping the car and turned to look at her. 'Marriage should be for love and an equal partnership, Beth. I love you and I want to marry you soon, but you have to want it too and sometimes I think I'm rushing you...' His eyes were serious as he looked at her and she found she was crying, the tears trickling silently down her cheeks because he was such a lovely man and she flung herself against him.

'I do love you so much, and I want to be married,' she said emotionally. 'I like my job, but if we had our own hotel I'd enjoy helping you, Jack.'

He smiled and touched her cheek, brushing the tears away. 'You can keep working at Harper's until you're ready to give up,' he said. 'Perhaps by then I'll have something we can either buy or rent ourselves. It's what I want, Beth, to run a little hotel – or a pub – between us, and bring up a family.'

'It's what I want too,' she said and kissed his cheek, because in that moment she felt good with his strong arms around her and it was all she wanted.

Later, when she was in bed, Beth thought about Aunt Helen. It was so sad that she'd waited all those years to marry, looking after her domineering father until he died and then earning her living successfully for years. What had made her choose a man who would seek to dominate her? Was it something in her character that made her pick a man similar in manner and attitude to her father?

Beth tossed restlessly for a while before she could sleep. Jack was right; Aunt Helen wasn't the only wife who suffered the bullying of her husband. Until and unless she spoke out against him, there was nothing anyone could do to help her.

18

Sally was at her desk when Ben Harper walked in that morning towards the end of May. The sun was shining outside and she was feeling pleased with herself, because the new summer stock had come in on time, been checked and was all correct. It was amazing how often items were either missing or damaged and she had to spend time chasing the manufacturers for replacements, but that day everything was just as it should be.

'It is a beautiful spring morning,' her employer said. 'Or is it summer?'

'I think we are officially still spring,' Sally replied. 'However, the weather has got ahead of itself. I shouldn't wonder it will meet itself coming back...'

Ben Harper threw back his head and laughed, seeming genuinely delighted. 'You English do have some quaint sayings...'

Sally looked at him, a sparkle of mischief in her eyes. 'Do you know, Mr Harper, some of us think the Americans have a very peculiar way of speaking at times.'

His eyes met hers and she saw a gleam of something in his that made her heart jump and then beat faster. 'I think that's the first time you've actually teased me, Sally,' he said and smiled. 'I hope it means we're going to be friends – and you'll drop the Mr and call me Ben, won't you please?'

'It doesn't seem respectful at work,' Sally replied. 'I don't want the staff to get the wrong idea...'

'And what if it wasn't the wrong idea?' he asked and his eyes were mocking her. 'I'm afraid this conversation is going to have to wait for another time, Sally, delightful as it is – I have an appointment with my bank...'

'Oh dear, that sounds ominous?'

'Not business, a personal matter. I want to buy a house or a larger apartment and I may need a bridging loan until I can sell the one I have...'

'Well, good luck,' Sally said and glanced at the little watch pinned to her smart black dress. 'I have an appointment with Mr Marco. We're discussing a series of windows for the summer and he asked me if I could source some rowing items he wants for his regatta window...'

'Sounds fascinating,' Ben said. 'I wish I could stay, but needs must when the devil drives...' His eyes narrowed as laughter bubbled up in her. 'Surely you know that one?'

'Oh yes,' Sally agreed. 'One of the nuns at my orphanage was very fond of using it when she made us scrub out the latrines...'

His eyebrows went up and he shook his head.

Sally was amused as she saw him laughing to himself as he went off. At least he seemed in a better mood now...

* * *

'You are so clever, Miss Sally Ross,' Mr Marco said when she gave him the list of contacts for rowing materials she'd made on his behalf. 'I think the store would grind to a halt without you...'

'You're a flatterer, sir,' Sally said, but she was smiling. Everyone liked Mr Marco, because he never seemed to have moods, was always cheerful, helpful and friendly. Only a few of the meaner kind whispered behind his back and Sally wasn't one to take notice of gossips. She turned to the business at hand. 'I think it's a good idea to feature all the main sporting events of the summer in the windows.'

'The English love their cricket, the rowing regattas and the horse racing,' Mr Marco said. 'Also the tennis and the garden parties; it is joyous to dress the windows for summer, but already we must think about the autumn and winter – and this is not so easy I think...'

'I had an idea for an Eastern theme,' Sally said. 'Something similar to a Turkish bazaar or an Ali Baba scene...'

Mr Marco's eyes sparkled with interest and a big smile spread across his face. 'I think Ben Harper was luckier than he knew when he promoted you, Miss Sally Ross. I thank you for your help – to plan so many original windows is not easy, but together we go well – yes?'

'We certainly think along the same lines,' Sally said and laughed. 'Have a nice weekend, Mr Marco...'

'I hope to,' he said, but a shadow passed across his face and for a moment she caught a fleeting sadness. 'We must see what happens, no?'

Sally nodded and left him to his work. Mr Marco was a bit of a mystery, because no one seemed to know where he came from or who he really was, but he was undoubtedly an artist in many ways and in his room were great rolls of silk, paper and all the bits and pieces he needed to set the scene for his fantastic displays. She thought it was almost like the backstage of a theatre, with the para-phernalia of a scene painter. The window dresser created wonderful backdrops for his windows, which made them original and often drew crowds to admire them. Sally had actually seen Mr Harry Selfridge standing outside on a couple of occasions and she knew he prided himself on his windows. It was a wonder he hadn't tried to poach Mr Marco...

* * *

'What will you do tomorrow?' Rachel asked Sally when they left work that Saturday evening. 'I'm going out with friends, Beth is visiting Fred's family and Maggie is meeting a friend for tea – it rather leaves you on your own...'

'Oh, I'll catch up on work, probably wash my hair and then go for a walk in the park...'

Rachel looked concerned. 'You should find something outside work, Sally. I know you love your job – but you ought to be courting...'

'I'm fine,' Sally said, 'don't worry about me, Rachel. I can amuse myself.'

However, after her friends left on Sunday morning, Sally found she was too restless to stay indoors. The sun was shining and she wanted to be out in its warmth, even if she was alone. Shrugging on a light jacket, she left the flat and headed for the park, walking through streets that were frequented by people in holiday mood.

Sally hadn't bothered to pack herself something to eat, so she found a little café and bought a sandwich and a cup of tea and then entered Hyde Park, strolling by the lake and through the gardens, which were bright with spring flowers. The sun had brought everyone out and she was watching a small boy playing with a hoop and smiling when she became aware of an altercation and her eyes were drawn to an ugly scene. Two men were being jeered by a group of men in rough clothing with cloth caps. Even as she watched, one of them threw a clod of earth picked from the flower beds at the two men. In that instant, Sally recognised one of the men as Mr Marco. The other man was younger, had a gentle soft face that was almost girlish and she'd seen them together before.

'Bloody queers...' she heard the louts yell at them and saw the way the young man flinched in fear. Mr Marco looked anxious, his eyes darting about as if he thought they were about to be set upon. 'Filthy buggers...'

Without thinking, Sally marched up to Mr Marco and his friend. She flung her arms about Mr Marco and kissed his cheek. 'I'm so glad you're here, darling,' she said loudly. 'And your cousin – I've wanted to meet you and congratulate you on your engagement to Maria...'

Turning, Sally faced the louts, her arm linked with Mr Marco and his friend, her eyes fierce and glinting with anger, daring the louts to come near her.

For a moment they stood glaring at her and muttering beneath their breath, then their leader turned away and they slunk off without another word.

Mr Marco looked shaken and his friend was shuddering. 'Thank you, Miss Ross,' Mr Marco said. 'Julien was frightened, because his father has threatened to cut him off from the family if he becomes involved in a scandal... and this is not the first time we've been attacked...'

'I'm so sorry,' Sally said. 'I shouldn't have barged in, but I couldn't stand by and let them insult you both...'

'You are a very brave and lovely young woman,' Mr Marco said. 'We are used to the insults, but they looked as if they meant more.'

'Thank you,' Julien said, finding his voice. 'You were kind...'

'I'm glad I was here...' Sally turned to leave, but Mr Marco caught her arm.

'You did us a favour, Miss Ross – may we take you to lunch?'

'Yes, why not?' Sally said and smiled at them. Her presence

would make it easier for them to dine somewhere nice and she was happy to be seen with her friends. 'I'd love to have lunch with you...'

* * *

Mr Marco came to her office on Monday morning. He presented her with a large box of chocolates tied with a ribbon bow.

'These are from Julien,' he told her. 'I said it was not necessary but he really wanted to thank you, because had the police been called it might have meant trouble for him...'

'I'm sorry for what those men said to you...' She smiled at him, because she liked him and had enjoyed her lunch with them. 'It was nasty and uncalled for...'

'It is to be expected,' Mr Marco replied sadly. 'We are different and society says that a love like ours is wrong...'

His honesty struck her to the heart and she felt tears sting.

'Society is wrong and unfair,' Sally said. 'It must be hard for you both...'

'Julien was saying goodbye,' Mr Marco replied, his voice shaking. 'His father is sending him on what you might call the Grand Tour in a few weeks and when he returns, he is to be married...'

Sally saw how distressed he was and her heart went out to him instantly. No wonder he'd seemed so sad about the whole thing. 'I'm sorry...' she said, but Mr Marco shrugged.

'It hurts to love,' he said, 'but we move on. I have work to do, Miss Sally Ross...'

In a moment he was gone. Sally sat staring at the door he'd closed. He was right. It did hurt to love, especially when that love wasn't returned or was snatched away...

19

Sally looked at the evening paper and frowned. The whole of the spring and into early summer there had been reports of trouble stirred up by the suffragettes and now a young woman had died for the cause. Emily Davison had thrown herself at the King's horse, Anmer, intending to bring His Majesty's attention to her cause at the Epsom Derby, but the horse was startled and, when it fell, crushed her and she had later died of her injuries. Several times previously, Miss Davison had been arrested for protesting violently, and force-fed in prison, before being released under the Cat and Mouse Act. Now, she had paid the ultimate price for her defiance.

It was a brave but shocking and perhaps foolish action. And many people would be questioning the reasoning behind it – had she meant to throw her life away or was it merely a thoughtless act that resulted in tragedy?

Sally thought that surely now the men who sat in parliament must understand that the women they seemed to despise as useless creatures, undeserving of a vote, were not going away? They were intelligent, thoughtful women who felt passionately about their cause and these protests would go on and on until the women won what they considered their right to vote. A tiny notice that a Miss Emily Dawson had become a magistrate caught her eye and she smiled. Perhaps some women were beginning to be recognised as sensible, capable beings.

Folding the paper, Sally walked briskly home. Beth's aunt was coming that week to fit the bridesmaids' dresses and she didn't want to be late back. Beth herself had found a pretty white lace dress for her wedding in August and she had the veil which had belonged to her mother, which she intended to wear with a new headdress of wax flowers.

'I think the veil is gorgeous,' Sally had said when Beth showed it to her just before her aunt arrived. 'Your mother kept this for you – what happened to her wedding gown?'

'I think she had it adapted to wear in the evenings,' Beth said. 'I believe a lot of women used to do that, years ago. It was probably the only time they ever had a dress as good as the one they married in.'

Sally nodded. 'I never had any family life, Beth, so I assumed mothers passed things on to their daughters on their wedding day.'

'The veil was preserved,' Beth said, 'but I never saw the dress. My father said she looked beautiful and I think that the dress may have been worn and then eventually cut down to make a christening gown for me. Unfortunately, that was used to bury my younger brother... he was just nine months old, so Dad told me once. My mother never spoke of him, but I do not think she ever got over his death. I've often thought that was the beginning of her being an invalid. We had a maid until my father died and then we couldn't afford it...'

'So you weren't really much better off than me.' Sally nodded. 'I envied girls who had known their mothers, Beth, but you didn't have much fun either.'

'It was better than being brought up by nuns in a church

orphanage,' Beth smiled. They heard the doorbell ring. 'That will be my aunt. I'd better let her in...'

She went to the door, welcomed her aunt and embraced her. She'd lost a little weight but otherwise looked much the same.

'Are you all right, dearest?' Beth asked, looking her over anxiously, though outwardly she seemed fine. 'I'm so glad you came...'

'I'm happy to be here, Beth...' Was there a flicker of something in her eyes? If it was fear it was soon concealed. 'And don't look so worried. Gerald is away and I'm fine...'

Beth smiled at her. Perhaps she'd made more of her aunt's distress that day than was warranted. Jack had said it might just be a tiff between husband and wife.

Aunt Helen had cut out and tacked together dresses for each of the bridesmaids. It was the first stage and she made several adjustments for each, exclaiming over how tiny Maggie's waist was and at Sally's slender hips.

'You have the perfect hourglass figure,' she told Maggie. 'You've bloomed since I last made something for you... and Sally is thinner than I remember, though this is the first dress I've made for her...'

'Are you sure this isn't too much for you,' Rachel said when it was her turn for a fitting. 'Three dresses is quite a lot, Helen. I could do mine if you liked...'

'Oh, no, I really don't have much to do some days,' Aunt Helen told her. 'Gerald has been away on business for the last ten days and I do not expect him back for another week. When I'm alone, I live very simply and so I enjoy my sewing...'

'Yes, well, as long as it isn't too much work for you...' Rachel smiled at her. 'I don't think I've put on weight, have I – though William has taken me out for lunch the past three Sundays and in the evening to dinner twice.'

'Is he your gentleman friend?' Aunt Helen asked, seeming interested.

'Well, we are friends,' Rachel said. 'Mr William Bailey – and he's a solicitor. We've lunched together a few times and on Sunday we went for a walk in Regent's Park after tea... William is very good company.'

'Oh, what a coincidence...' Aunt Helen said. 'Gerald brought a friend home two weeks ago for dinner. His name was William Bailey and he was a solicitor – but he was also a parliamentary candidate hoping to stand in the next election. I overheard him say that he intended to make a series of speeches against the Suffragette Movement...'

'Oh, dear me,' Rachel said and frowned. 'That is odd... although I suppose the name is common enough...'

'Yes, I imagine it must be,' Aunt Helen said and smiled as she fastened a last pin. 'Yes, that should fit you nicely, Rachel. I am looking forward to seeing you all dressed for the wedding. Have you set the date yet, Beth?'

'Jack has,' Beth replied. 'He starts his new job next month and he says he asked his boss for the week of the tenth of August as a week off for us – the ninth is the Saturday so that will be the day of our wedding. We're going to see the Vicar of St Martin's this Sunday after morning service...'

'Then I shall make sure I'm at the wedding,' Aunt Helen smiled. 'I'm not sure Gerald will come – though you will ask him, Beth?'

'Of course I shall.' Beth looked at her anxiously. 'I wouldn't dream of insulting him by leaving him out.'

'Is it to be a big wedding?' Sally asked. She had dressed after her fitting and made tea for all of them, bringing it with a tin of biscuits into their parlour. The tin was from Huntley and Palmer and had a fancy design on the lid.

'We're inviting twenty guests apart from family,' Beth told her.

'Jack has several friends he wants to ask and three cousins and their wives and children. I only have you three and Aunt Helen and Uncle Gerald – I don't mind each of you bringing a friend if you wish. Maggie, you could invite Ralf...'

'Oh no, Tim will be there and I'll spend any spare time with him,' she replied and smiled brightly.

Rachel said, 'I might ask William – but not if he has been giving talks against our movement...'

'Oh dear, I shouldn't have told you.' Aunt Helen looked upset. 'I'm sure it can't be the same man. He wouldn't be your friend and do such a thing behind your back – would he?'

'I don't know...' Rachel frowned. 'I thought he was honest and trustworthy, but if he has deceived me...' She went to her bedroom to take off the bridesmaid gown and Aunt Helen looked at the others.

'I didn't mean to cause trouble. It was just such a coincidence. You see, Gerald thinks the Women's Movement is ridiculous. He says women don't have the brains to decide who should govern and he is very much against them ever being given a vote – and this man, William Bailey – he said much the same thing. He thought it a good theme to gather popularity in order to be elected in the next election.'

'Well, it isn't your fault,' Sally said. 'You can't blame yourself for mentioning it, Helen. If he is a despicable cheat, it is as well that Rachel knows about it now...'

'Oh yes,' Aunt Helen said, even more upset. 'Much better to discover the truth now...' It was obvious to Beth that she was thinking of her own marriage and perhaps wishing she'd thought more before accepting Gerald's proposal.

It was getting quite late when Beth went down and asked the porter to ring for a taxicab for her aunt. Sally was with them and she insisted on paying the fare.

'You came to us and we're all grateful,' she said when Aunt Helen protested. 'I know the dresses will be perfect. Have a safe journey home, Helen.'

'Take care, Aunt. It was lovely to see you,' Beth said. 'When would you like to visit again for another fitting?'

'Probably the week after next,' her aunt suggested. 'I'll write and let you know, Beth...'

'Yes. Take care, dearest...' Beth kissed her cheek. She felt Aunt Helen tremble and looked into her eyes. 'Is something wrong?'

'No, nothing is wrong, my dear. Goodnight, Beth – and you too, Sally. Thank you both for being so good to me...'

Sally looked at Beth as they returned to their flat. 'Your aunt has changed a lot, hasn't she?'

'Yes – I think she isn't very happy in her marriage...'

'That's unfortunate...' Sally said. 'Why doesn't she just leave him?'

'Women of her generation don't,' Beth replied. 'I think you'd have to be brave to face a divorce, Sally.'

'Well, you won't have to because you found a good one.' Sally smiled and squeezed her waist. 'You'll be deliriously happy and have lots of beautiful children...'

'Not too soon I hope,' Beth said. 'I don't want to give up work just yet, Sally. I love Jack, but I don't want to have babies too soon. I had years of staying at home caring for my mother...'

Sally nodded thoughtfully. 'I can see what you mean, and I love my job, but I want a family and I envy you, Beth. I've never known love...'

Her thoughts went to Mick and the way he'd looked at her the last time he'd driven her home; she'd thought then he cared for her, but she hadn't seen him since that rainy night when he'd kissed her and wondered if that kiss had simply been an impulse and then there was Ben. It was clear that he saw her as nothing more than an employee. Why was it that she never found love?

'Are you going to have a holiday this year?' Beth asked her as they went into the kitchen to wash the cups. 'Last year you said you couldn't manage time off because you were too busy. I took mine then, but I didn't go anywhere...'

'It would be nice to go to the seaside if only for a few days,' Sally said. 'Perhaps if we could rearrange the staff a bit, we could go together – perhaps leave early on Friday evening and return on Monday evening...' She shook her head. 'Of course, you're having time off when you marry...'

'It would only mean two days of my annual leave,' Beth said. 'Yes, why don't we do that? Jack is away this weekend and next, but then he'll be home for good to start his new job. There's nothing to stop us going off to the sea for a few days, is there?'

'I'll speak to Mr Stockbridge about cover for your department,' Sally told her. 'We've just taken on a new girl. She has some experience in clothes, so I could request her to take your place – and Mr Harper can see any reps while I'm away...'

Beth looked at her curiously. 'How are things between you two now?'

'We make a good team for Harper's,' Sally replied and sighed. 'He hasn't asked me to supper since I refused – and I think he is seeing someone...' she made a face. 'Last year he was with a different woman every week, but I've seen him with a pretty young woman several times recently...'

'No?' Beth gasped.

Sally was rueful. 'A woman rang the office yesterday when we were talking and she asked for him and I heard him say they were meeting for lunch. I suppose it is my own fault that he doesn't ask me out...'

'Why did you refuse if you want to go out with him?' Beth looked at her oddly.

'I was annoyed.' Sally shrugged. 'Oh, Beth, I don't know what to do – sometimes I think he's going to say something important and then he walks away again. If he cares for me, he should say something, shouldn't he?'

'Yes, it is up to him,' Beth agreed. 'But you might encourage him a little, Sally.'

'I think it is too late...' Sally shook her head. 'Take no notice of me, Beth. I wouldn't know love if it got up and bit me.' But, of course, she did and it had and now she was suffering.

* * *

Their holiday was arranged swiftly. Sally scheduled a replacement for Beth for two days and informed Ben Harper that she was taking a few days off the next morning.

'Oh – going somewhere nice?' he asked.

'Beth and I fancied a trip to the sea,' Sally said. 'It's just a long weekend really. I booked in at a small hotel in Southend...'

'You're entitled to a longer vacation...'

'Yes, but Beth is getting married in August and she wants most of her holiday then...'

'Ah, I see...' His dark eyes narrowed as he looked at her. 'Just a little break for the two of you then...'

'Yes...' She raised her eyes to his. 'You can cancel my appointments if you have other arrangements?'

'No, nothing that matters,' he replied, not looking at her. 'I might take a trip to Paris next month. I thought we might stock some French gowns... what do you think?'

'A few evening gowns might sell,' Sally said. 'You could visit

some perfumeries too and consider stocking perfumes and
colognes.'

'I was thinking you might like to come along,' he said casually.
'They must have their autumn and winter collections ready by
now...'

'Yes...' Sally fought for breath because his suggestion had taken
it right out of her. 'Yes, I should enjoy that. Jenni said once that I
ought to see Paris and I would like to view the new winter collections before I buy too much stock...'

'I'll book two cabins then and the hotel,' Ben said. 'I'll give you
the dates – so you can let anyone you need to know you'll be
working...'

'I'm free to do as I please. I don't have to tell anyone anything.'
Sally's head went up. 'Talking about time off, Maggie, Beth, Rachel
and I will all be away for the Saturday afternoon of Beth's wedding,
but we shan't leave until one, because the wedding is not until three
in the afternoon...'

'Sally, if you wanted the day off you could take it...' Ben said and
the warmth in his eyes made her heart jump. 'Surely you know that
I appreciate all you do here?'

'Yes, thank you.' She smiled at him. 'Miss Hart was most indig-
nant when I told her that we needed cover for the whole department that Saturday, but Mr Stockbridge was kind enough to say
that he would bring in other staff for a few hours. After all, a
wedding is something special, isn't it?'

'Yes, it is, very special,' Ben said and she saw a flicker of pain in
his eyes. 'Have a good weekend with your friend – and now I must
leave, because I have a luncheon appointment with a friend of a
friend...'

Sally watched him go and wondered. Paris in July would be
wonderful. Never in her life would she have expected to be taken to that

marvellous city to view the new autumn/winter collections of beautiful clothes – but she'd never thought she would be able to afford a few days at the sea either. Struggling to pay for a room at the hostel, Sally had never hoped for a job that paid her as much as she earned now. Perhaps she should be grateful for what she had and not yearn for more?

* * *

The weekend came quickly and a surge of excitement overtook the two girls as they took their packed suitcases to work that Friday morning and left them with Fred while they worked.

'I'm glad you're having a little holiday,' Fred smiled at them. 'This weather is lovely, but it won't last. Have a paddle for me while you're there, girls...'

'Yes, we shall, and we'll bring you a stick of rock back,' Sally said, teasing him.

'I'd rather have a box of fudge,' Fred joked. 'I'll break my teeth on that other stuff and it would cost a fortune to have them mended.'

Beth giggled and kissed his cheek. She knew that Fred had a part denture at the bottom of his mouth and it always gave him problems if he ate anything hard or gritty.

'We'll bring you some lovely soft fudge,' she promised. 'It's years since I went to the sea, Fred. The last time was when my father was alive...'

'Well, you have a good time,' he said. 'I wish I was comin' with you...'

Rachel and Maggie said the same when Sally came to collect Beth from the department that afternoon. 'You should take a few days off next week,' Beth said. 'Sally can arrange cover for you both. After all, you're both entitled to a holiday...'

'I should like that,' Maggie said wistfully and looked at Rachel, who smiled.

'Well, why not?' she said. 'I know Miss Hart will not like it very much, but we should be able to go together if we wish...'

It was usually agreed to stagger staff holidays, but Beth knew that there were some of the other departments that could manage with less staff for a few days. Once, when Rachel was away for a while, they'd had a man from the fine china department and he'd sold several bags and a few pieces of jewellery while he was serving on her counter, which seemed to suggest that the female customers did not mind being served by a man.

Sally had arranged a taxicab to take them to the station. She'd popped in the previous day and bought their train tickets in advance, so they went straight to the relevant platform and caught the next train, which was already waiting.

'I'll give you my share of the tickets and the taxi,' Beth said when they were settled on the train. 'Don't you dare refuse, Sally, because I'm not sponging off you all weekend.'

'As if you would,' Sally said and laughed. 'I'll keep count and we'll square up when we're ready. I'm really looking forward to this, Beth. I doubt I would have thought of taking time off if you hadn't said you'd like a few days at the sea...'

'It looks as if it will keep nice...'

'Yes, let's hope so...' Sally smiled at her and passed her a magazine. 'I hope the hotel is all right. I just picked it out of the paper, but it had a good reputation...'

'I'm sure it will be lovely.'

20

Beth was correct and the hotel, which was right on the seafront, was comfortable and clean, though not as modern as Sally had hoped.

'I don't mind it being a bit old-fashioned,' Beth told her as they settled into their room. It had twin beds and was cheaper than having two single rooms, and it also had the advantage of an adjoining bathroom. 'That's a real luxury – saves us going down the hall...'

'Yes, I made sure we had our own bathroom,' Sally replied.' I had enough of queuing for the bath when I lived in the hostel.'

At home in the flat they were more civilised and asked each other when they wanted to use the bath. Fortunately, there was an extra public toilet in the reception area downstairs so if anyone couldn't wait for the toilet, they were able to nip down and use that. Because there were four of them sharing the flat it happened now and then, but they were all considerate and having a separate bathroom and toilet was fortunate.

'We've got a lovely view of the sea and the pier,' Beth said, looking out of the window. 'What shall we do this evening? Have dinner in the hotel – or go out and find somewhere to eat?'

'I think there are several shows on in the theatres,' Sally said. 'Why don't we have a leisurely meal and then go for a walk along the front and see what is on?'

It was decided that was what they would do and they ate a well-cooked but plain dinner of roast chicken, potatoes, two veg and stuffing. Afterwards, they took their jackets and went for a walk on the promenade. The pier was lit up and they could see that a variety show was playing there Beth didn't recognise any of the artists, though one woman was a Marie Lloyd impersonator and the poster said she had her 'to the life'.

'We could book there for tomorrow,' Sally said and linked arms with Beth. 'Smell that aroma – there's nothing like it, is there?'

It was the smell of food cooking mixed with the tang of the sea. A little breeze had stolen the heat of the day and it was lovely just walking past the pier and all the pubs, restaurants and amusements that made Southend the popular resort it was.

'It isn't quite as busy as I thought it might be,' Sally said.

'I expect more people come when the children are out of school,' Beth replied. 'I think that's why you managed to get our room so easily – the end of next month may be busier, because the school holidays start at the end of July...'

Just ahead of them, the door of a public house was suddenly thrust open and a group of rowdy young men erupted into the street. They were all wearing Army uniforms and had obviously been drinking heavily. One of them barged into Beth and trod on her foot and she was jostled by two of the drunken but good-natured soldiers. She gave a yelp of distress and then found herself being pulled back out of the way.

'Are you all right?' a male voice asked and she turned, startled to find herself looking into the anxious face of Mark Stewart – the man she'd once thought she was in love with; the man who had broken her heart. 'Did he hurt you?' Mark said, looking at her in concern.

'It was just the shock...' Beth said. 'Sally, this gentleman is an old friend of mine...'

'We were more than that, Beth.' Mark's soft eyes chided her. He moved towards her as if he meant to touch her, but she stepped back out of reach.

'Thank you for rescuing me, but I think you know what I meant,' Beth said politely. 'We are certainly no more than friends now. Excuse me, please. Sally and I have to be somewhere...'

Mark hesitated, a look of annoyance on his face, but he inclined his head and walked off.

Sally glanced at Beth, noticing her colour and touched her arm. 'You don't like him much – why?'

'That was Mark; I told you, he broke my heart when my mother was an invalid.'

'Ah yes, I remember now,' Sally agreed. 'He went off because your mother wouldn't agree to the marriage...'

'I always thought he would come back after she died,' Beth said, 'but when he did, he was married. Unfortunately, his wife died soon after we met again, I think in childbirth, he seemed to imagine I would go back to him when he wrote and told me. I didn't answer him.'

Sally nodded. 'A bit odd, him being there when that soldier barged into you, wasn't it?'

'Do you think he was following us?' Beth asked, after a moment. 'It is a bit strange...'

'Would he do that – if he saw us?' Sally looked at her and Beth nodded.

'He might. Mark can be a bit intense at times. He didn't much like it when I told him I wasn't interested last year...'

'Maybe it was just a coincidence,' Sally said and hugged her arm. 'He couldn't have known we were coming down here, could he?'

'No,' Beth replied and breathed deeply. 'Of course he couldn't – but it was just a shock seeing him come from behind me like that...'

'Yes, I suppose it must be – but after all, he only tried to help you, Beth. Perhaps you were a little bit short with him.'

Beth looked at her for a long moment and then nodded. 'Yes, perhaps I was. I should have thanked him properly, but he makes me uncomfortable.'

* * *

The next morning, when they went down to the hotel dining room for breakfast, to her surprise, the first thing Beth noticed was Mark, sitting at a table with an older woman. He saw her and his eyes narrowed and then he seemed to catch sight of her engagement ring and smiled in an odd way. What a coincidence that they'd chosen the same hotel, but, of course, it was one of the best available.

She and Sally ordered a luxurious breakfast of egg, bacon, tomatoes, mushrooms and a slice of fried bread, followed by toast and marmalade and coffee or tea. They both chose the coffee because the smell was so nice and it tasted good too.

Mark and his companion went from the dining room before Sally and Beth, but when they eventually left, it was to discover him standing by the table in the hall upon which all the daily papers had been placed for the convenience of the guests.

'Good morning, Beth – and I believe you must be Sally Ross,' Mark said. 'Did you enjoy your breakfast? They provide a decent one here – my aunt certainly enjoyed hers. She has been staying here for years...'

'Oh,' Sally said, 'is your aunt a permanent guest – or do you mean she visits once a year?'

'She resides here all the year,' he replied with a faint smirk. 'Aunt Jane was left a fortune by her late husband and, having been let down by a series of live-in maids, she decided to take a suite here and liked it so much that she has never left.'

'I see,' Sally remarked. 'Well, it was nice to meet you, Mr Stewart. I'm going up to our room, Beth – are you coming?'

'Yes, I am. I want to put on a jacket before we go out...' She hesitated and then nodded to Mark. 'It was kind of you to help me last night. I'm sorry if I was rude – it was the shock...'

'I quite understood,' he replied. 'Have you booked for the shows yet? You should do so, because all the best seats go first...'

'Yes, thank you – we intend to,' Beth said and moved on, following Sally into the lift.

'So that explains why he's at the hotel,' Sally said. 'But do you think he saw us at dinner yesterday and followed us?'

'Perhaps – it is quite plausible,' Beth said. 'I'm not sure why he would but...' She shrugged her shoulders.

'Did you know he had a rich aunt?'

'He certainly never mentioned her to me.' Beth made a wry face. 'What kind of person lives in a hotel?'

'Perhaps a lonely one,' Sally said. 'At least she has company and people to look after her and call the doctor if she is ill.'

'Yes, I suppose so...'

Beth put thoughts of Mark and his aunt out of her mind. She and Sally went out to explore the busy town of Southend in daylight. There was so much more than the piers and the gardens, boarding houses, restaurants and pleasure booths, though they were fascinating enough, but there were also many fashionable shops, a cinema showing a silent movie and several theatres. They booked seats for that night, though could only get them right at the back of the upper circle.

'I should have liked to see another show on Monday, but we'll need to travel back in the afternoon,' Sally said, looking at the bill advertising another variety show in the town.

'We could go to a matinée,' Beth suggested, 'and then catch the late train home on Monday evening.'

'Yes, let's do that,' Sally said and laughed. 'Why don't we go to see that film with Mary Pickford?'

It had come out the previous year and was titled *The Mender of Nets* and was a love story about a young girl who mended nets on the seashore and fell in love, but the man of her dreams was still entangled with a previous girlfriend.

'Yes, all right,' Beth agreed. 'Shall we go shopping now or have lunch?'

They decided to shop for a while and Beth bought some new shoes, which were just right for her wedding. She'd been looking for a leather pair in the pale cream she wanted but hadn't found any until now. The ones she bought were cream suede and had a smart bow.

'I like those,' Sally said. She'd tried on several pairs herself but hadn't purchased any. 'Harper's doesn't have a good shoe department...'

Beth gave her a nudge. 'You're on holiday, Sally. Forget Harper's for a few days.'

'Yes, you're right,' Sally agreed. 'I'm hungry – shall we have something to eat now?'

They found a small café on the promenade and had toasted teacakes and coffee and then went on the pier, walking right to the end, where they bought iced drinks and sat in the sun, watching people go by. The sun was warm and they sat for some time and saw Mark walking with his aunt on his arm. She was laughing at something he said and though he definitely saw Beth and Sally, he did not speak or nod as he passed.

'Something fishy there,' Sally said as they walked back to the hotel in time for cream scones and tea. 'Are you sure she's his aunt – I think she might be a rich lady friend...'

'I really don't mind who she is,' Beth replied. 'I'm not interested in Mark.'

'I should hope not,' Sally said and glanced at her left hand. 'Jack would have something to say if you were...'

* * *

On Sunday, both girls went to church after breakfast. Sally said she saw Mark's aunt, but Beth didn't notice her. Afterwards, they bought a batch of Sunday papers and sat reading them in the hotel lounge over a pot of delicious coffee and some crisp almond biscuits.

The papers seemed full of dire news. In the Balkans, there had been several deaths as Bulgarian and Serbian troops clashed and Russia had warned of its displeasure but no war had been declared. Beth recalled Fred saying that war in Europe might make it difficult for Britain to avoid helping an ally, but even though the troubles rumbled on in various countries, so far nothing had been said of a war that would make Englishmen fight. However, it was a little disturbing that Germany had decided to boost its troops. The Kaiser was still visiting various heads of Europe and spoke of undying friendship towards his cousins in England.

As they went into lunch, Sally saw Mark with his aunt once more. He hadn't been in church, but he was at lunch and they were celebrating something with wine. After lunch, several guests went out for a bracing walk along the front, bracing because the wind was chilly that afternoon.

'Should we brave it?' Sally asked, glancing out of the lounge window. 'I don't think it will rain...'

'Yes, let's go on the pier again,' Beth said. 'I really enjoyed the show last night and it makes me wish we had longer here.'

'Yes, it is so relaxing...' Sally agreed.

As they went out into the hall, they saw that Mark had just come from the lift with his suitcase. He stopped and then came towards them, offering his hand.

'Off home then?' Sally asked.

'Yes, I just came down for a few days and I have appointments in London tomorrow. It was nice meeting you, Miss Ross – and you, Beth...'

Beth nodded, but she didn't answer nor did she smile.

Sally watched as he picked up his case and left.

'I can understand why you thought you loved him,' she said to Beth as they went out, shivering a little in the cool breeze. The sky was overcast and the sea was grey, crested with yellowish foam. 'But I wouldn't trust him an inch – you're much better off with Jack...'

'I know.' Beth smiled. 'I don't think I should have liked being his wife...'

'Too controlling,' Sally said. 'He reminds me of your aunt's husband...'

'Yes...' Beth frowned. 'Shall we buy some postcards from that booth on the end of the pier? I'll send one to Fred, even though I'll be back at work when he gets it – and one to my aunt...'

'Good idea,' Sally said. 'I want to buy some small presents for Rachel and Maggie. They are the only ones I have to take anything back for...'

'What about your other friends?'

'Oh, Mick wouldn't want a box of fudge and I doubt Marlene would either,' Sally said lightly. 'I don't have any other real friends, apart from you and Jenni...'

Beth hugged her arm. 'Let's choose something together. I saw some pretty earrings I thought Maggie might like – they cost more than a box of fudge, but if we bought them together...'

'Good idea,' Sally said. 'I saw a shell brooch I thought Rachel would appreciate. Let's get that for her. After all, we aren't likely to do this again... but we'll get some fudge for Fred and maybe I'll take Mr Harper a stick of rock...'

'Go on, I dare you,' Beth said and they both laughed.

* * *

In the event, they decided not to bother with the matinée on Monday afternoon. Instead, they went for a walk in the morning, had fish and chips on the beach and then afternoon tea in the hotel before catching their train back to London.

'It would have been too much of a rush,' they agreed, 'and we can always see the film in London when it comes round again...'

The seaside break had done them both the world of good. Beth was feeling refreshed and yet pleased to be back at home, and as she told Fred the next day when she visited them, 'I've got all the excitement of my wedding coming up...'

'You can bring whatever you need over to mine when you're ready,' Fred told her, because they hadn't been able to find a home yet that they could afford. 'Even if you just want to store it until you find what you want...'

'Thank you,' Beth said and gave him a peck on the cheek. 'But we've got nearly a month until the wedding and when Jack is settled at home he will have plenty of time to look round...'

'Not once he starts that job of his...' Fred said and looked at his paper. 'I told you there was going to be a war out there, didn't I?'

'I read there was conflict, but it doesn't affect us, does it?'

'Not yet,' Fred agreed. 'It's the Balkans, Greece and Serbia against Bulgaria – let's hope that's where it stops...'

Beth nodded. She was vaguely anxious about the troubles abroad, but it all seemed so far away and she personally had so much to look forward to.

* * *

The papers said it was a mystery. Sylvia Pankhurst, the daughter of Emmeline, hadn't been seen in public for a while and no one knew where she was until she made a dramatic appearance at a public rally and the police tried to arrest her. Women fought them off with umbrellas and hatpins and both sides suffered quite a few injuries in the fracas. Sylvia was spirited away and although the police went to her home and arrested someone, it wasn't her. For a week, it was a game of hide-and-seek and then, on the following Monday, the police found and re-arrested her and she was returned to Holloway prison, where she immediately began a hunger strike once more. It was a cruel policy the way the authorities let the women go before they could starve themselves but then re-arrested them once they'd recovered so they had to go through it all again.

'They're gloating now,' Sally said furiously when she read the report in the paper – 'and just look at this!' Directly under the report of Sylvia Pankhurst's arrest was an advert for a new game called Suffragettes In and Out of Prison. 'They're mocking us with this wretched game! Whoever invented it should be locked away in a dark cell and the key thrown in the river!'

'Oh, yes, I've seen that in a shop,' Rachel said. 'It does make one frustrated – and I am already upset. I've told William that I think he is despicable and I do not want to see him again...'

'Oh, Rachel, no,' Beth said, looking at her in surprise. 'I thought you were going to give him the benefit of the doubt?'

'I was, I did – until I saw this...' Rachel showed them an article in a magazine about William Bailey, the new Conservative candidate who had spoken out about the folly of the Suffragette Movement. 'Read what it says, Beth – it is belittling...'

Beth read the article and gasped. 'It is written as though we are foolish children. Oh Rachel, how hurt and upset you must be – and after you trusted him...'

'I have written to him cancelling our next appointment and I've told him what I think of his deceit...'

'Yes, I should think so,' Beth said. 'I am so sorry...'

'I should never have gone to lunch with him...' Rachel said stoutly, but Beth knew she was putting on a brave face. She'd obviously started to have feelings for him and now she was hurt that he'd betrayed her trust.

'Why don't you and Maggie book your holiday?' she asked and saw Rachel relax, the anger draining out of her.

'As a matter of fact we have. We're going to Skegness. I have some old friends who run a boarding house there and we are going for a week. They've given us very favourable terms and I'm going to pay for Maggie, though she doesn't know it yet...'

'That will be lovely,' Beth said. 'When are you going?'

'The week after next – which means we shall be back in plenty of time for the last fitting for our bridesmaids' dresses...'

21

Miss Hart brought the two new members of staff to the department to show them where they would be working temporarily. One was a junior with no experience of selling at all and the other a girl who had worked in another department store.

'I saw the advert for an experienced salesgirl,' Janice Browning said to Rachel when she showed her their routine. 'The money was better than I was getting, so I decided it was time for a change.'

'We shall be glad to have you at Harper's,' Rachel told her and nodded to Beth. 'Miss Grey, while I'm away, Janice will take over your counter and you will be in charge of my counter. Marion here will work on the scarves and gloves...'

Miss Hart came to take Janice away. She would be working on the ground floor normally, but Marion Kaye was left with them.

'I shall rely on you to give Miss Kaye at least the first idea of what to do before you depart on your holiday, Mrs Craven.' Miss Hart sounded as if she doubted it.

'Yes, of course, Miss Hart – but Beth is very experienced now, you know, and I'm sure she will be able to cope for a week.'

Miss Hart sniffed in disbelief and went off.

Marion stood looking at the counters, clearly lost and frightened until Rachel took her in hand. She kept the girl with her at the jewellery counter, showing her where everything was stored, and how the stock books worked. She explained the way they wrapped the best things in tissue before placing them in the exclusive bags and how to work the cash dispenser to send the money up to the office.

Gradually, the baffled look disappeared and, by the evening, Marion was able to put stock away and tidy up efficiently. Maggie had let her look through the scarves and gloves, and Beth showed her the hats, and she seemed happy to be working with them.

'We always had a junior until Miss Ross was promoted,' Beth told the girl. 'You will be very helpful to us all, Miss Kaye, and I'm glad you've come.'

'I wish you would call me Marion...' she replied a little shyly.

'Well, we shall when we're not at work,' Beth explained, 'but it is the policy of Harper's to address everyone as Miss or Mr, whatever their formal title.'

Marion nodded and smiled. 'Yes, Miss Hart told me – she is rather fierce, isn't she?'

'She is a dragon at times,' Beth agreed. 'She used to be worse than she is, but I've noticed she's less sharp these days...' A frown creased her brow. 'It's odd, but I don't think I've ever seen her smile. Perhaps she is unhappy in her personal life. She never speaks to us and I really know nothing about her, which is a little sad...'

Marion nodded but still looked nervous. She'd been allowed to go to lunch with Maggie and by evening the two were firm friends. So much so that Maggie was able to tell them all about their new member of staff that evening at home.

'Her mother is often unwell and her father works on the ships and is away most of the time,' Maggie said as she helped Beth get their meal. 'Marion has an older brother, who also works on the ships, two younger sisters and two other brothers. Marion gets her youngest sister up and gives them all breakfast. This is Marion's first job.'

'She isn't getting much money for a start,' Beth said. 'I suppose she's trying to help her mother, but she seems an intelligent girl. She picked up the method of stock-keeping very quickly.'

'Marion told me that she'd hoped to stay on at school and become a secretary.' Maggie looked sad. 'She made the decision to leave because her mother could not afford for her to learn typewriting. I think her mother is finding it hard to cope...'

'Now that is sad,' Beth said, shaking her head. Marion Kaye was not the only one who had had to make sacrifices for her family. With the breadwinner gone there was often no alternative than to send girls and boys to work, who might otherwise have continued in education.

'Well, we'll all help her settle in,' Maggie said. 'She is a nice girl and she will fit into our department.'

Beth nodded, because she liked the new junior and thought her a big improvement on replacements they'd had inflicted on them in the past.

* * *

Marion's intelligence and worth was proved when Rachel and Maggie were on holiday. Janice came up from the glass department to help and Marion took over the scarves and gloves. Janice did well enough in the hat department, though Beth thought her artistic skills lacked something and felt the display had never looked so poor. However, she was busy on Rachel's counter and made a mental note to rearrange the hats as soon as she had the department to herself.

However, the next morning, when Beth got in, she found that

Marion had arrived before her and everything had been transformed. There was a stunning display of hats in contrasting colours that she would not have thought of putting together but which looked arresting.

'Did you do this?' she asked and Marion smiled.

'I hope you don't mind, Miss Grey. Art was one of my favourite subjects at school and I was going to take it at college – and I thought the hats looked dull...'

'Yes, they did, and I was going to do them before I started on my own counter,' Beth said. 'You've done very well, Miss Kaye, but it may be best if you don't mention it was you to Miss Browning...'

'Yes, Miss Grey,' Marion's smile was brilliant. 'I would love to arrange some of the jewellery – if that would be a help to you?'

'We'll do it together this morning...' Beth promised, but as it happened, their whole morning was suddenly turned upside down.

It was around eleven when Miss Hart came into the department. Beth had been about to send Marion for her break, but she waited, some inner instinct telling her that something was wrong, though she couldn't have said what. Just that there was a grey look about the supervisor's skin.

'Your department looks very tidy and... rather smart...' Miss Hart looked about her. 'I came...' She blinked several times. 'I came to tell you...' She shook her head, clearly in distress. 'I don't know...'

'Are you unwell?' Beth asked just as the floor supervisor gave a sigh and crumpled in a heap at her feet.

'Miss Hart...' Beth knelt by her side, but Marion was ahead of her. The girl leant over Miss Hart and unfastened the high neck of her dress and then took her wrist.

'Her pulse is weak, but she is alive,' Marion said. She pulled back Miss Hart's eyelid and looked at her. 'She hasn't fainted. I think she has had some sort of a fit, but she's breathing. We should get an ambulance immediately...'

Beth nodded and went into the office, where the telephone stood on the desk. She lifted it and explained to the operator that she needed an outside line.

'Is it a doctor you need?' the girl asked.

'This is an emergency,' Beth told her urgently. 'We think Miss Hart may have had a fit or a stroke... we need help quickly.'

'Very well, leave it to me...'

Three ladies had entered the department. They stared curiously as Marion remained on her knees and stroked the floor walker's head, talking to her softly.

'Perhaps we should come back later?' one of them said.

'Yes, would you mind?' Beth beckoned Janice, 'Could you stand by the door and tell any customers that this department is closed for half an hour please?'

'Yes, of course, Miss Grey.'

Janice did as she was bid and Beth knelt beside Miss Hart once more, glancing at Marion. 'You're sure she's still breathing?'

'Yes, it's very shallow, but she is breathing...'

'How did you know what to do?'

'I didn't, it was just instinctive...'

Beth nodded in appreciation, but her attention was on the floor walker. 'She's unconscious, isn't she? I thought something was wrong – and she hasn't been quite herself for a few days...'

'This has probably been coming on,' Marion said and continued to stroke Miss Hart's head gently, her voice reassuring and calm as she told the prone woman that everything would be all right.

Miss Hart's eyelids flickered once or twice and Beth thought she could hear but was unable to reply.

It must have been nearly a quarter of an hour later when two men entered the department bearing a medical bag and a stretcher. They were a private ambulance firm that Harper's employed in emergencies.

'You can leave her to us now,' they told Marion and she stood up, moving away. Miss Hart moaned and her fingers moved. 'Yes, looks as if she may have had a fit or a stroke...' the man spoke again after bending over her.

'You'll take her into hospital?'

'Yes, we shall,' he said. 'Do you know the name of her next of kin?'

'No. She is Miss Glynis Hart – the manager, Mr Stockbridge, may know more...'

'Very well,' he said and then glanced at Marion. 'Good work, miss...'

Marion didn't say anything, just inclined her head.

'I'm going to inform Mr Stockbridge,' Beth said. 'Tell Janice to allow the customers back in...' She felt quite upset as she made her way swiftly up to the manager's office. Miss Hart was a dragon, but she didn't deserve to be ill like that!

Her visit to the manager was brief. He promised to contact the ambulance driver with Miss Hart's details and Beth returned to the department.

'You should go for your break,' she told Marion. 'You deserve it – and that was most upsetting.'

'Poor woman,' Marion said. 'I wonder if she has anyone to look after her...'

'I don't know whether she lives alone or with someone...'

Marion went off for her break and Beth was busy in the department. She sold three leather bags and a silver bracelet and Janice sold two hats. Beth also served on the scarf counter and sold a pretty red and white silk square. When Marion returned, Beth sent Janice for her break. She was just serving a customer with a silver brooch when Sally entered the department.

'What happened to Miss Hart?' she asked after the customer departed.

'She just collapsed at my feet,' Beth said. 'I think it may have been what is called a stroke...'

'She is young for that, surely?'

'Yes, that is what I thought, but the ambulance men said it can happen at any age if someone is under extreme stress...'

'Poor woman,' Sally said. 'Goodness knows what she will do if it affects her badly and she can't work. She lives completely alone and has no family – at least, none that she mentioned when she gave her personal details to Mr Stockbridge.'

'Then she is going to be in some difficulty,' Beth acknowledged. 'Do you have any idea which hospital she has been taken to?'

'Mr Stockbridge said they thought the London – but I'll telephone later and find out if she's there and how she is...'

'She is going to need help,' Beth said.

Sally nodded. 'Yes, she will – we'll do what we can. She was a dragon sometimes but I feel sorry for her. I know it's no fun living alone...' She wrinkled her brow. 'It's odd that we work with her every day and yet we knew nothing about her life...'

'She didn't encourage anyone to ask...'

'Miss Hart enjoyed telling us what to do,' Sally admitted, 'but we can't just desert her. I shall see what I can do for her.'

'She was worse to you than anyone.' Beth touched Sally's arm. 'But that is why I love you. We'll take it in turn to visit her – and we'll do what we can for her.'

'I'm going to have a collection for some flowers for her,' Sally said. 'Mr Harper has given me five pounds, but I'll put that into an envelope for her. I think she may not be able to work for some time...'

'Oh, poor thing,' Beth said and sighed. 'Jack will be docking later this evening. His ship is a few days late, because of repairs, and he'll have to go straight to his job on Monday. He's the new manager of the Hotel Maddison. We're all so lucky and poor Miss Hart is lying there in hospital...'

'You didn't make Miss Hart ill,' Sally said. 'We'll help her in whatever way we can, but you mustn't let it upset your plans for the wedding...' She smiled. 'Does the thought of being married give you butterflies?'

'Yes, it does a bit.' Beth laughed. 'I love Jack and I want to be his wife... but sometimes I'm scared.'

'Why? Jack isn't the sort of man who bullies or beats his wife...'

'I know.' Beth shivered. 'Perhaps it isn't my wedding that is bothering me – perhaps it is my aunt and now Miss Hart...' Beth sighed. 'Aunt Helen seemed fine when I took her the fudge, but Gerald was there and she didn't say much...'

'Visit her again with Jack,' Sally suggested. 'I'll let you know what I've discovered about Miss Hart later this evening...' Sally then left them to get on.

Beth was too busy to dwell on the events of the morning, but both Marion and Janice looked subdued and she knew the incident had upset them.

'You mustn't worry,' she told them both when they were closing the department that night. 'I am sure Miss Hart will be all right...'

'Will she?' Janice asked. 'My Aunt Sheila lives alone. Her husband died at sea and she has never remarried, though she had chances. She was ill last year and we had her home with gran and me and looked after her. Aunt Sheila told me that if it hadn't been for us, she would have died, because she couldn't have worked or cooked for herself...'

'I think there must be quite a few women who have to live alone,' Beth said. 'I suppose that was what the workhouse used to be for, though everyone hated it and not many go there these days. Well, there aren't as many now...'

'Awful place!' Janice said at once. 'My grandfather was taken in to the workhouse when he got too old to look after himself. My mother was too busy to look after him and her children were all under five, but she regretted not taking him in afterwards. He was only there a week before he died...'

'Oh, poor man,' Beth said. She knew that many old folk lost the will to live if they were forced into what was thought of as the shame of living in the workhouse. 'But Miss Hart is young enough to recover. If she is lucky, she will return to Harper's to work when she's better.'

The girls nodded, but she could see that neither of them were convinced and she wasn't sure she believed it herself. Strokes could impair movement or speech and Miss Hart would have a difficult time getting over it – if she lived.

* * *

Sally was late leaving the office and Beth was home alone when she got in. She'd shopped and had a ham salad with fresh bread and butter waiting for their supper. Her friend's face lit up at the sight.

'It was manic this afternoon,' Sally said and flopped down, accepting the cup of sweet hot tea from Beth with a sigh of relief. 'There was a mix-up over an order and I've been hours sorting it out...'

'So, did you have time to ring the hospital?'

'Yes, I managed that,' Sally replied. 'Miss Hart is still unconscious, but they think she has a good chance of recovery, though she may be affected – either paralysis on her left side or speech...'

'She can't be much more than forty...'

'Somewhere around forty-five,' Sally agreed. 'I wonder what brought it all on. Her job is responsible, but there isn't really much stress attached to it. She is really just a watchdog and her bark is worse than her bite...'

'Oh, Sally!'

'Well, it is true...' Sally gulped her tea. 'Gosh, I needed that, and I'm hungry. There's no point in visiting Miss Hart yet, but I'll go at the weekend – hopefully, she may be conscious by then...'

'Let's hope she is,' Beth agreed. 'Will Harper's do anything for her if she is off sick for a long time?'

'I've spoken to Mr Harper about that,' Sally said. 'He agreed that they will pay her full wages for a month and then half for a further six months...'

'That is very generous,' Beth replied. 'I doubt many employers would do as much.'

'I might have done a little arm twisting...' Sally grinned wickedly. 'He is taking me to Paris next week – and I hinted I might not go if he didn't show a bit of sympathy...'

'You've got him twisted round your little finger...' Beth laughed. 'Well, just be careful you don't get carried away in Paris... moonlight and romance and all that...'

'Oh Beth!' Sally looked up with a wry smile. 'Sometimes I think he really does care, but others...' She shook her head. 'I've tried not to care, Beth, but I do like him so very much. I can't help myself...'

'Is it wise going to Paris with him?'

'Probably not, but I'm going...' Sally arched her eyebrows. 'What can he do – seduce me? If he did, I might say yes...' She winked at Beth. 'Besides, it's Paris; he has all the travel documents sorted for us and I may never get another chance if I don't go now...'

'Sally! You wouldn't sleep with him...'

'Why not? Maybe it will end in tears, but if it's all I can have...' she laughed again. 'We need to live a little dangerously, Beth. I don't want to end up like Miss Hart, living alone in a small flat with no one who cares when she's ill. I can't move on until this thing with Ben Harper is settled – perhaps a passionate affair will clear the air...'

Beth looked at her doubtfully. 'You may get hurt...'

'I've been hurt before,' Sally said. 'Perhaps because I was too careful – next time, I'll throw caution to the winds and see what happens...'

'I don't blame you. I'd love to visit Paris...' Beth nodded. 'Come and eat your tea then. This ham is delicious. I pinched a bit and it was lovely...'

The two girls looked at each other and sat down to eat. They got on so well and enjoyed sharing the flat, but both of them knew that the time to move on was close.

'We'll always be friends, won't we, Beth? When you're married and I'm – well, whatever happens, you'll always be my friend...?'

'Of course I shall,' Beth said and smiled. 'And so will Rachel and Maggie. We bonded when we were some of the first of Harper's girls and that will never change. Life moves on and we'll change, but we shan't forget each other.'

22

Aunt Helen brought the bridesmaids' dresses for a final fitting on the Sunday after Rachel and Maggie returned from Skegness. They had both got a nice delicate colour to their cheeks and the rose silk looked particularly well on Maggie and Sally, though Rachel could have done with a deeper shade. Each of them had a straw hat with a dark crimson rose on the brim, which Sally had bought cheap from the wholesalers, and when the three were dressed, they looked a picture of fresh prettiness.

'Oh, you do all look nice,' Aunt Helen said. 'I've done a good job, though I say it myself.'

'The gowns are lovely,' Beth agreed, thinking that her aunt seemed more her own self, 'and far less expensive than shop bought. I must pay you for your time, Aunt, but the material wasn't ruinous...'

'No, I shan't accept payment – it's my little gift to you,' Aunt Helen said. 'I'm giving you my silver tea and coffee service as a wedding present, Beth. Gerald has his own and prefers that I use that – so I want you to have mine and the gowns are a little extra.'

'You're too good to me.' Beth kissed her on the cheek. Had she been worrying for nothing or was her aunt putting on a brave face? She had certainly chosen a wonderful gift for her. Beth had managed to buy a few bits and pieces for her future home, but a silver tea and coffee set was a desirable gift. She had some linen that had been her mother's, but anything of value had been sold to pay bills when Mama was ill. Because Beth had so few relatives, she did not expect to have many lavish gifts for her wedding. Her friends were putting together to buy her something nice and she knew that Harper's was giving her some money, because Sally had arranged a collection, but the silver service from her aunt was special.

'Your husband still hasn't found anywhere for you to live, I suppose?' Aunt Helen asked.

'Jack says he'd rather wait and buy a place,' Beth said. 'We're going to live with Fred for a while – just until we get straight...' It wasn't quite what she'd wanted, but she knew Jack was right. It was silly to pay rent for a couple of smelly rooms when they could stay in Fred's pleasant cottage – and he was more like a father to her than a work colleague.

'Well, I dare say you will manage,' Aunt Helen said and nodded. 'You're not the only young couple to live with in-laws...'

'Yes,' Beth agreed. 'I'm sure it will be fine...' She looked at her aunt. 'Are you all right?'

'Just a bit tired – and no, it wasn't making your dresses, Beth. Gerald has been away for a month and I don't always sleep well these days. I think I hear noises in the house... and that's foolish. Gerald says it is the house and it creaks...'

'Yes, it does. I heard creaking upstairs the day I called when you weren't there,' Beth said. 'You probably have loose floorboards...'

'Yes, perhaps that is what it is,' Aunt Helen agreed, but her gaze slid away, making Beth wonder. 'I'll get off then – and I shall see you on the day of your wedding, if not before...'

Beth nodded and kissed her again. 'Take care of yourself.'

She went down to the ground floor and called a cab for her aunt, seeing her safely inside before going back up to the flat. After she'd been driven away, Beth's smile faded. Someone had been upstairs at Gerald's that day and she suspected it had been her aunt – had she been hiding because the evidence of her husband's brutality had been impossible to conceal? It was worrying, but until Aunt Helen asked for her help there wasn't much she could do, except let Gerald see that she wasn't going away and would be keeping an eye on him.

Rachel was tidying the sitting room when Beth returned. She smiled at Beth.

'Your aunt is a good seamstress. Those dresses are really well made.'

'Yes, she is...' Beth sighed. 'I thought she looked tired and subdued, Rachel. I wish with all my heart that she'd never married that awful man...'

'It is a shame that he doesn't treat her right,' Rachel agreed. 'I sometimes wonder if any men are to be trusted...'

'Have you seen that man again? William Bailey...'

Rachel shook her head. 'No, and that makes me angry. The least he could do is apologise...'

Beth looked hard at Rachel. 'You really liked him, didn't you?'

'More fool me,' Rachel said, sighing. 'He was such good company and so kind and generous, Beth. I really thought we might have the start of a relationship...'

'Perhaps I'm being unfair, but I don't trust him – and after the way Gerald treats my aunt...'

'Yes, I know.' Rachel touched her hand. 'Don't let your aunt's disappointment spoil your happiness with Jack. I had years of happiness with my husband before he became ill. Things changed then and it hurt me... but I was getting over it until...'

'That wretched William Bailey!' Beth said. 'Just wait until I see him. I shall have something to say to him... and he won't think I'm a mouse or a child...'

'How fierce you are,' Rachel said, smiling. 'I suppose William is entitled to his opinions, but I can't help wondering whether he asked me out simply to find out more about our movement.'

23

The weather was lovely on Monday and Tuesday, though on Wednesday it was overcast and a little cool for August, almost like an autumn day in summer. Rachel was glad of her warm wool jacket when she left Harper's that evening; it was red to match the jaunty felt cloche she wore and suited her mood of determination. She wanted to do some shopping before going back to the flat and had started to walk along Oxford Street, which was still thronged with people, lights twinkling from café windows and the brightly lit window displays of the department stores, when she felt the tap on her shoulder.

'Rachel, please let me talk to you...' Turning, she saw the man who had made her so angry. She took a deep breath, torn between hitting him with her cane shopping basket or sticking her long steel hat pin into his hand but decided against either because he might put it down as childish behaviour. 'I know I owe you an apology. I've been trying to see you – but I think you were away...' William Bailey looked at her, appearing subdued and apologetic.

'I went to the sea for a holiday with a friend,' she said with a regal nod. 'I agree – you do owe me an apology, sir. You may make it and then leave...'

'You're very angry, aren't you?' William looked at her hesitantly.

'I think you might be angry if I had described you as foolish or childlike in your opinions and actions...'

'I didn't say those things,' William said, looking at her earnestly. 'I may have said that certain actions carried out in the name of the Women's Movement were foolish and the actions of wilful children – and don't you think they are, Rachel? Is it really sensible to throw one's self in front of a racehorse in full flight or to put bombs where innocent people could be hurt?'

'Certainly, I do not agree with some of the action taken by the militant members of our group...' she conceded, because she too thought such actions rash. 'Yet I admire Emily's bravery and devotion to the cause...'

'Brave certainly, but also foolish. I knew you could not think it wise or useful...' he said and looked eager. 'I wanted to know more about your movement, Rachel. I'd seen you and your friends leaving the meetings and I wanted to get to know you – but after I'd spoken to you a few times, I realised you were intelligent and lovely and I never meant to hurt you. I spoke at that meeting, but my speech was written for me because I was too busy to do it and I didn't realise how it would look or sound until I saw it in the paper...'

'You deceived me...' she said, still angry with him. 'You got me to talk about the Movement and how I felt and then you gave that wretched speech...'

William had the grace to look ashamed. 'Yes, and I wish I'd cut my tongue out first. I was told it was a popular stance and that I stood more chance of being elected at the next by-election if I took an anti-suffragette stance...'

'Well, good luck to your campaign...' Rachel said coldly. 'Please, let me go now, Mr Bailey. I'm tired and I have things to do...'

'You won't forgive me?' He looked so upset that her heart ached.

'Of course I forgive you,' she said in a softer tone. 'I am a rational, reasonable woman – but that doesn't mean I wish to see you again. Good evening, sir.'

He stood back and let her walk on. Rachel immediately felt a pang of regret. She had enjoyed lunching with him, but he had let her down.

Rachel did her best to put Mr Bailey and his opinions from her mind. Some of the shops were not yet closed and she shopped for food; her basket was filled with bread, fruit, fresh salads and cheese by the time she got home. Inside the door of the flat was a small table where all the post was placed so that they could all find it easily. Picking up a letter addressed to her, she realised it had come from Minnie, one of the two spinster sisters who had lived in Mrs Malone's boarding house when Rachel was residing there. Minnie seldom wrote unless it was an invitation card and Rachel felt instinctively that something was wrong. The sisters had been fine when she'd visited just before her holiday with Maggie.

Taking the letter into the kitchen, Rachel slit the envelope and read the single sheet, gasping in shock as she realised why Minnie had written to her.

'Is something the matter?' Beth asked, seeing her standing with the letter in her hand. 'You've gone white...'

Rachel looked up. 'Minnie's sister has suddenly died. I've told you about them, I know. Neither of the sisters has ever married and they make a precarious living by their sewing.'

'She must be devastated...' Beth said and looked up as Sally came in to the flat. 'Rachel has had some bad news...'

'I'm sorry I'm late,' Sally said. 'I went to visit Miss Hart this afternoon. We're off to Paris in the morning and it's my last chance to visit for a week – but you were saying Rachel has bad news?'

'A friend of mine has died,' Rachel said. 'I think I shall leave my supper and go straight over. I'll take a taxi...'

'I'm so sorry.' Sally touched her hand in sympathy. 'I had some good news today – Miss Hart is very much awake and she knew me. Her speech is a little affected and her left hand is paralysed, but the nurses told me it is a small miracle that she is alive.'

'I'm pleased for her,' Rachel said. 'I'll hear all your news when I get back – but I must go. Poor Minnie will not know what to do...'

'If there is anything I can do – when I get back from Paris...' Sally said, but Rachel hardly heard her as she left. Minnie was such a sweet person and she knew that the death of her sister would leave her vulnerable and alone.

* * *

'I'm so glad you came,' Minnie said, clinging to Rachel's hands. Her eyes looked red and she was visibly distressed. They'd spent two hours discussing the practical stuff. Mildred's body had been taken away for examination, because the death was very sudden. 'They are going to do tests to see why she died...' A sob left her and her hands were trembling. 'What am I going to do without her, Rachel?'

'I'll help you all I can,' Rachel said. 'I can help arrange the funeral once the coroner releases her to you for the burial. I have a little money saved...'

'Oh no,' Minnie murmured, shaking her head. 'Mildred paid into an insurance fund for her funeral – we both do, because there is no one else to do it, you see. Money isn't the problem just yet, though she was the one who dealt with our customers. I can manage – but it is just losing her so suddenly...'

'Yes, of course it is,' Rachel agreed. 'Just let me know when you're ready and I'll come over again. Is Mrs Malone making things difficult for you?'

'She has been kind – everyone is kind,' Minnie said. 'But you are our friend, Rachel. Mildred would have wanted you to know…'

'Just remember that you were your sister's greatest friend. She would want you to carry on as best you can,' Rachel told her.

'Yes, thank you,' Minnie said. 'I'll be all right now – it was such a terrible shock.'

When at last Rachel left her, she felt so sad. Minnie was making the best of things, but she would be lost without Mildred to guide her. Rachel wished that she could do more, but death was final and she couldn't bring Mildred back. If the flat had been larger, she might have taken Minnie home with her that evening, but that wasn't an option. She would have to see what she could manage after the funeral.

* * *

Beth made Rachel a cup of cocoa and a tomato sandwich for her supper on her return. She listened to the sad tale of the sister who was left to cope.

'If I can do anything to help…' she said, and then smiled. 'Supposing, I was to move in with Fred and his sons before the wedding, Rachel? If Maggie shared with Sally, you could take Minnie in with you…'

'Oh, Beth, that is so lovely of you to offer, but I'm not sure what the others would say…'

'I don't mind – if Maggie doesn't,' Sally assured her. Maggie shook her head. 'You tell your friend she can come to us if she likes, Rachel…'

'Not until after the wedding,' Rachel said decisively. 'We all want to be with you the night before your wedding and help you get ready that morning, Beth. Minnie will stay where she is for the moment and then I'll talk to her and see how she is getting on.'

* * *

Before she left for Paris, Sally insisted that Maggie could use the bed in their room she shared with Beth; Rachel could then offer the spare bed in her room to Minnie if she wished. Rachel spoke to Minnie of Sally's generous offer when she visited that evening, but she declined.

'It is so kind of you and your friends, Rachel,' Minnie said, a tear trickling down her cheek. 'I do not feel it would be suitable for the moment. When my sister is buried and your friend, Miss Ross, is married... perhaps then...' She faltered, unable to go on. 'I am coming to terms with my loss. I know life will never be the same, but as yet I am not sure what I want to do...' Minnie sighed. 'There was a time when I might have married...' She shook her head. 'It was all so long ago and I couldn't leave my sister...'

Rachel was surprised, for Minnie's words seemed to hint that she'd once had a chance of a different life but had turned it down for her sister's sake. It had always seemed to Rachel that Mildred was the stronger of the sisters, but now she wasn't as sure. 'As I said before, if there is anything I can do...'

'Oh Rachel, dearest, just having you here has helped me so much...' Minnie smiled. 'I still remember that lovely restaurant you took us to on my birthday last year. It was such a pleasant evening and I thought...' She shook her head. 'I wished we might go out more often, but Mildred was always so anxious about saving money. She feared old age, you see. I suppose the time will come when I can no longer sew, if I live that long. Mildred feared it and now she's gone...'

'I didn't realise...'

'Father never allowed us to have a life while he lived, but he had lost most of his money, as I believe we told you once before. I might have married after Papa passed away, but Mildred needed me and I couldn't desert my sister. Her plain sewing was good and she cut out all the patterns, but she said it was my embroidery that sold our work. She knew she would never marry and she feared that she would end in the workhouse or starve to death...'

'Oh, poor Mildred,' Rachel said and a cold shiver went through her. How many spinster women did die lonely deaths, often due to the cold and lack of decent food? Without a husband or children, there was no one to care for them and the only place they could find shelter was the workhouse. 'She must have felt so insecure.'

'Yes, she did,' Minnie said and smiled sadly. 'Together we could manage, you see – but apart she might have gone under, so I had no choice...'

'Did you wish to marry?' Rachel asked.

'Yes, very much. I loved Jonathan dearly and I think he loved me. He didn't marry for a year after I told him it was over, but then he went away and I heard he'd married a young pretty girl...'

'That must have been hurtful?'

'Oh no, I was glad he'd found happiness. I did not wish him to live alone for my sake, because I loved him. I hated hurting him and was pleased he had someone to care for him.'

How little we knew of other people's lives, Rachel thought. She'd known that the sisters lived in genteel poverty, but she'd never guessed what Minnie had given up for her sister's sake.

'Well, if you would like to share my room at the flat you will be welcome,' she said. 'Now, is there anything I can do?'

'Most of it is arranged,' Minnie told her. 'Mrs Malone says I can bring a few people back here for tea after the funeral and I've paid for flowers in the church – but I wasn't sure how to put a notice of Mildred's death in the paper. Could you do that for me, Rachel?

The coroner says it was her heart and has released her for burial – so the funeral is next Friday at three in the afternoon...'

'Yes, I will do that with pleasure and I shall be with you on Friday,' Rachel agreed. It was little enough and she wanted to do more, but now that Minnie had recovered from the shock she seemed to be coping well.

As she told Beth later at the flat, 'I thought she would be too upset to cope, but she is much stronger than I knew. I have offered her the chance to come here, but she will wait until after the funeral to decide and perhaps that is best. We all want to enjoy the preparations for your wedding...'

Beth smiled and they talked about the flowers, which Jack had arranged, and the cars to take them to church. It was to be a white wedding and he wanted everything to be perfect, even though after their honeymoon in Devon they would be living with his father.

'I really don't mind,' Beth told Rachel as they drank coffee and looked at some presents that had arrived for her that day. 'Tim isn't living at home now, so it is just Fred and us and he would never dream of interfering. It is almost as good as having our own home...'

'I'm sure Jack will arrange it as soon as he can,' Rachel said. 'Lots of young married couple start off living with their families.'

'Yes, I know, it isn't what Jack wanted – but the right place hasn't turned up. It makes more sense this way because we can save more and take our time finding what we want...'

'What is it exactly that you need?'

'Jack wants a pub or a small hotel that he can either buy with a loan from the bank or rent,' she said. 'He has a decent deposit saved and he spoke to the bank he uses. They told him he could get a loan of up to two hundred pounds...'

'That is an awful lot of money, Beth,' Rachel frowned. 'I do not think I should wish to have a debt that size hanging over my head...'

'No, and for that reason, Jack would like to lease the property rather than buy it, but the only property he has seen to let was too run-down. It was a repairing lease and that meant he would be responsible for putting it right, but it still wouldn't belong to him.'

'Not a good idea,' Rachel said. 'Has he seen a property he would like to purchase?'

Beth looked thoughtful. 'There was one, but he needed another fifteen hundred pounds and that was just too much. Even with his savings, he couldn't manage that...'

'Yes, I see...' Rachel nodded her sympathy. It was difficult for young people to get started in life and only the lucky few would ever own property. Even Rachel's husband had rented their house and he'd had a good job while he was well, their substantial savings seeing them through his long illness but leaving her with little on his death. 'It is a wonderful dream and perhaps it will come true one day...'

'We have to keep saving and keep looking,' Beth said. 'Jack thought if he took this job it would give him some experience in running a small hotel and he will be here in London all the time – not that he will have much to spare, because he has to work long hours. However, he feels the work he does now will stand him in good stead for the future.'

'Yes, I imagine he will have to work long hours as a manager,' Rachel said. 'I know when I managed a small business, I worked after time night after night. I didn't mind, but my boss wasn't very appreciative. As soon as he was well, he wanted me gone...'

'And that's when you came to Harper's...' Beth smiled at her. 'I think it was a good thing he was such an ingrate, Rachel. You're much better off at Harper's...'

'Yes... though I've been thinking of something Minnie said about her sister's fear,' Rachel explained. 'For women who live alone, there is very little to look forward to but a lonely old age and poverty...'

Beth shivered. 'Please, don't say things like that, Rachel. I don't believe it in your case. You will always have friends to share a home with – or, if you wish, a husband...'

'I'm not sure I would wish to marry again.'

'Just because William Bailey let you down, you shouldn't let it put you off marriage,' Beth said. 'He spoke out of turn, but do you think he really meant to hurt you, Rachel?'

'No, perhaps not,' she agreed thoughtfully. 'He did try to apologise, but I wouldn't let him.'

'There you are then,' Beth smiled at her. 'I'm sure you will find someone to love if you want...'

Rachel nodded. As yet she didn't know what she wanted, but Miss Hart's sudden illness and Minnie's revelations about her sister's fear had certainly made her think about the future. A life spent living entirely alone would certainly not suit Rachel. At the moment she had good friends, but Beth would be married soon after Sally returned. Rachel was fairly certain that both Maggie and Sally would follow Beth in marrying one day and then what would Rachel do? Would she have to find lodgings again or take other women in to share the flat?

Oh, why did men have to be so careless of other people's feelings? She was annoyed with herself for being so hurt by William Bailey's betrayal of her trust. It was foolish to let it upset her and she made up her mind that if he tried to apologise again, she would be friendlier.

24

They were driven on to the Southampton docks by the car Ben Harper had hired and men in uniform appeared as soon as the driver began to unload the cases and bags. All Sally had to do was look about her at the hustle and bustle. The Cunard liner SS Imperator was a hive of activity, though another large steamship was berthed a short distance away and seemed deserted, except for a sailor lazily swabbing the deck. Sally found it very noisy, with all the chattering, laughing and cries to 'look out', as cars arrived and left. Piles of luggage were everywhere, men and women in smart clothes milling around, calling for a steward in shrill voices, and a throng of people saying goodbye to friends and relatives made it a fight to get to the gangway, but Ben Harper seemed to cleave his path through with ease. Sally made hurried steps to keep up with his long stride, glad she hadn't worn one of her hobble skirts.

He turned to look at her as they walked up the incline to the ship's deck. 'All right?' he asked and she nodded, a mixture of excitement and nerves making her unable to answer.

The deck was crowded, especially at the rails as most of the passengers seemed intent on standing there and waving to the throng on the docks. The stewards in white coats had disappeared below somewhere, taking their bags with them, and Sally hesitated, unsure of what to do next. It was her first time on board a steamship and she was feeling a little bewildered by it all.

'Shall we inspect our cabins and then come back on deck?' Ben suggested and Sally smiled, agreeing. She followed him and realised that he knew exactly where he was going. He hadn't needed to follow their baggage. When he stopped outside a door, he looked back and smiled at her. 'We've got adjoining cabins. I thought it would be better because I'll be on hand if you need anything as this is your first time on board ship.'

Sally drew a shaky breath. Was that the reason he'd booked adjoining cabins or was there another? 'It is a little overwhelming,' she answered. 'I would never have found my way here alone.' Looking around her, she saw there were portholes and realised that he'd secured some of the best accommodation for them.

'You will soon get used to it – not that we'll have long on board, just this night and a few hours in the morning before we disembark, so don't unpack more than you need, Sally. You will only have to squeeze it all in again when we disembark. I don't know why, but I can never get things to go back as they were...'

Sally laughed.

The stewards had deposited their bags at the end of the beds, which looked comfortable and a decent size. She'd thought they might be narrow or small, but they weren't at all, and perhaps that accounted for the huge size of the ship. It was like a floating hotel with servants' quarters and kitchens as well as all the guestrooms.

In the privacy of her cabin, Sally touched her face with a faint blush of powder to stop the shine. She was glowing – a polite word for sweating – and felt a little too warm. Removing her gloves and hat, she fluffed up her hair and was applying a smear of lip colour when Ben Harper knocked at her door.

'Would you like to go up on deck again?' he asked. 'We'll be casting off in a few minutes. Most people like to see the shore recede...'

Sally picked up her straw hat but left her gloves and long frock coat on the bed. Everyone was packed close to the rails and it was impossible to get near them, but since she had no one to wave to, Sally was happy to stand on a raised dais and look towards the docks. People were throwing streamers and a band was playing and she thought it was like a carnival.

'We're only going across the Channel...' she observed.

'Yes, but for some of the passengers, it is the start of a longer voyage. Many of them will be sailing round the Mediterranean, calling in at Italy and Spain and various ports. It's just that we're getting off at the first port in France...'

Sally nodded. The excitement was catching and she laughed up at him as he took her elbow. 'Yes, I can see what all the fuss is about – is it like that every time you return to America?'

'More so,' Ben Harper said. 'I understand the Titanic's send-off was twice as lavish as this...'

'Yes, and that was terrible,' Sally was thoughtful. If Jenni hadn't stayed behind to help her learn the ropes as the new buyer for Harper's, she might have been on that fated ship. In her last letter, she'd talked of the General and his little boy and of what she was doing at the store in New York. Like Jenni, her letters were colourful and full of life, while her telegrams were brief and succinct.

'Shall we go and find a space to sit and enjoy a cool drink?' Ben asked and Sally agreed.

'Where are we staying when we arrive in Paris?'

'Oh, I've arranged that with a friend...' he said. 'Madame Clairmont runs a small pension – or hotel. It is a friendly, comfortable place, unlike some of the big hotels, and I've stayed with her before.

I think you will enjoy it, Sally. It is just outside Paris but not far from the workshops I want to visit...'

Sally felt slightly disappointed. She would have liked to be in the bustling heart of the city, because she wanted to see everything.

'Don't worry; I'll take you on the river in one of those funny little boats that go up and down the Seine. I think it is the best way to see the sights of Paris, unless you just wander the streets and get lost – it is very easy to do that in Paris...'

Sally nodded and smiled. She'd purchased a guidebook and had a list of things she wanted to see, like Notre Dame and the Eiffel Tower, but she thought it would be lovely to wander the streets and little back alleys to explore, just as she had in London when she'd first left the orphanage.

'Perhaps I could do that one day,' she said and gave him a teasing look. 'I think I should rather enjoy getting lost on a warm afternoon because eventually everyone finds their way back to the river and then it's easy... at least it is in London. I see no reason for Paris to be any different.'

'Are you afraid of anything, Sally?' Ben looked at her oddly.

Sally glanced away as she replied. 'Lots of things, but I try not to be...'

They found a table in a shaded spot on deck and a steward appeared as if by magic and asked what they wanted. Cool drinks in long glasses with ice and fruit and a little fan on a stick appeared. Sally sipped and smiled as she appreciated the blend of fruit juice and wine.

'This is lovely. I think I'm being spoiled.'

'I would like to spoil you if you would let me...'

'This whole trip is a treat,' Sally replied. 'I know it is work – but it is very pleasant work.'

'I think you've earned it,' Ben said and his smile caressed her. 'I haven't thanked you enough for holding the fort when I was in the States...'

'It wasn't just me,' Sally said and her cheeks were warm. 'Everyone worked hard, from the trainees right through to the manager.'

'Yes, but you held it together. Stockbridge told me that some of the stock Jenni bought just wasn't right. You bought in new stock and slightly reduced the old stuff in price and then it balanced up and suddenly all the departments were busy.'

'If I hadn't reduced some of the goods, I would have had more for the sale in January – that was our only dip in sales and it ought to have been a boost for us...'

'That wasn't a mistake, it was just a learning process,' Ben said. 'I'm hoping to make a big thing of Christmas this year, Sally. I'd like to have a Christmas grotto with Father Christmas so that children can visit him – and if we can get it, a reindeer and sled piled with gifts.'

'We had some lovely displays last year,' Sally said, 'but nothing like you're planning, Ben...' She stretched her shoulders, lifting her face to the sun, which sparkled on the sea and dazzled the eyes. His name had slipped out naturally, but it seemed right here. 'It's absurd talking about Christmas in summer, isn't it?'

'Necessary in the retail business,' Ben said. 'The shops in Paris will be filled with summer clothes and probably bargain prices, but we'll be looking at winter styles and perhaps even ideas for next spring...'

'Yes, I know...' Sally laughed up at him. 'I've already ordered winter coats and suits, but I still have space for a few special items – though next spring could be when the French stock would really come into its own...'

They talked some more about the business and then Sally said

she would like to get changed into a fresh dress for tea and Ben
went for a walk about the deck.

Sally returned to her cabin and took off her dress, which felt
creased and soiled after being worn all day. She found a pretty voile
dress that would take her through tea and into the evening, because
Ben said they wouldn't dress for dinner as they would not be seated
in the main dining room.

'We'll be disembarking tomorrow, so I thought just a light meal
in the informal dining room...?'

Sally agreed. She had brought an ankle length black velvet skirt
and two silk evening tops with her, but she only possessed one
special dress and she didn't want to unpack that on board ship.

Tea was lavish – sandwiches, cakes, tiny trifles and fruit tarts
with cream, so many little bits and pieces to choose from that Sally
thought if she tried everything that caught her eye she wouldn't
want dinner.

Ben ate two tiny salmon sandwiches and a slice of rich fruit
cake. Sally had chicken sandwiches and a strawberry tart piped
with cream. Afterwards, they walked about the deck for two hours
and then went below to look in the shops that were still open to the
passengers. Sally saw some jewellery she thought she recognised
from one of her wholesalers, but the price was horrendous. Either
the shopkeepers were being overcharged or the passengers were.

'It's hardly surprising we sell so much jewellery at Harper's –
just look at the price of that Scottish brooch. I mean, it's silver and
the stone is a pretty green – but it is too pricey.'

'Supposing you were a businessman returning home and you
hadn't had time to buy presents for your aunts or your mother,' Ben
said. 'What's an extra pound or two to purchase something as
stylish as that set of brooch, pendant and earrings?'

'Much more sensible to find time to shop at Harper's,' Sally said.
'They could buy something nicer for less...'

'That is why we're busy, because you have a good head for business...' Ben's gaze was warm. 'I feared the place might collapse when I was away so long, but I just couldn't get back...'

'Did you have so much to settle?' Sally looked at him curiously. 'I had begun to think you were not coming back at all...'

'It was always my intention to return, Sally – surely you knew that?' Now there was a chiding note in his voice.

'How should I have known? You did not write – and you seemed angry when you left and when you returned. I thought you might decide to sell Harper's.'

'At one time I thought I might have to – but then things changed and suddenly it all went my way; there are reasons why I don't feel like celebrating, although I am delighted with business...'

Something in his tone told her he wasn't ready to explain yet and so she did not push him.

'As long as you're satisfied with the business...'

'Everything is as I would wish it to be...' Ben murmured and she felt the warmth in his voice as a caress.

'I'm pleased for you,' Sally said and turned to look at some of the exotic skin bags on display in another booth. She thought the prices exorbitant, but even as she watched, a lady in a sleek black evening dress and a white fur cloak purchased a bag in pale grey snakeskin.

'It wasn't just for my sake that I stayed on in the States,' Ben said from just behind her. 'Yes, there were meetings that I had to attend, but there was another reason, a personal reason...'

'You don't have to tell me,' she said hastily.

'Don't I, Sally Ross?' Ben asked. 'Are you telling me that you have someone in your life and so whatever I say doesn't concern you?'

'No, I don't!' Sally said quickly and then blushed. 'I mean – it is up to you whether you want to tell me something private...'

'Sally, I do want you to understand...'

Whatever Ben was about to say was interrupted by a bell and the shopping booths starting to close their doors.

'It's dinner time, I think,' Sally said nervously, suddenly afraid of what he might say. 'I didn't expect to be hungry after that delicious tea, but I am – it must be the sea air, don't you think?'

'Yes, it makes me ravenous,' Ben said. 'We'll talk later, Sally – we have all week. I'm sure we can find time to talk about important things at some point...'

'Important things?' Sally swallowed hard as she looked into his eyes and saw the warmth there. He did care for her! She couldn't be wrong this time. Her instincts had told her right from the start that there was something between them, but always he'd drawn back. 'Yes, I think we should, Ben.'

'Quite soon.'

'After dinner,' Sally suggested and he smiled.

'Yes, after dinner. We'll take a walk round the deck – unless you want to see the show?'

'No, I'd prefer the walk,' she said, and her heart raced. 'Besides, I think we need to talk properly – don't you?'

* * *

Dinner was a delight. Sally wondered how the ship's cooks managed to produce such a variety and cook it so well on board a ship. She'd never visited a galley kitchen but didn't imagine it could be huge – not as big as some of the hotels in London, but the seafood starters, soup, steak and coffee mousse afterwards were delicious so they ate them all. Even the little almond finger presented with the coffee was crisp and tasty and she thought she'd hardly ever tasted better.

Afterwards, they went for a walk round the deck, listening to the sound of the waves breaking over the bows and looking into the dark sky, lit only by a few stars. From somewhere between decks, there was the sound of romantic music as a tenor sang of unrequited love.

'It feels lonely out here on the sea,' Sally whispered. 'Don't you think it must have felt terrifying for those men who first found their way across the ocean?'

'I think seamen are rather tough characters and able to live within themselves,' Ben said. 'They must spend hours with little to do, especially when it was all sailing ships. At least now it has cut down the journey by weeks. To cross to America was a feat of endurance for those early settlers.'

'Yes, it must have been...'

Sally could feel the tension in him as they approached the stern and stood against the high railings, looking at their creamy wake in the starlight.

'What did you want to tell me, Ben?' she asked and it was suddenly so natural to say his name. 'I know something is on your mind...'

'There's no easy way to say it,' he replied and she felt his unease. Something made her look up and she saw the play of emotions, sadness and grief and regret. 'When I was nineteen I ran away to get married with a young girl I hardly knew. Maribel was lovely, a year younger, headstrong and foolish, and just back from school. I wasn't much better. Her father worked in the wood yard mine owned – it was just one of our holdings and her family was nothing, which meant that our families would never agree to a match between us. We were in love, so we went anyway and we married in a little chapel in a town so small it was hardly a blip on the map – and at first we were happy...'

Sally drew her breath sharply as the pain struck. He was

married… but then she saw his face and knew instinctively that the story didn't end there.

Ben's hands were on the railings. He was gripping so hard that his knuckles had turned white. She waited silently for him to go on, sensing that it was difficult.

'Maribel was a wilful girl. I wasn't the only man who'd wanted her, but she decided she wanted me. We returned to our homes to find the doors locked against us. My father disinherited me. Not that it mattered. I didn't know it then, but his empire was failing. He was drinking too much and without me at home it got worse. He changed his will again in my favour when he knew he was dying, but there wasn't much left of his fortune. If my uncle hadn't given me a job, I would have had nothing…'

Sally waited, motionless, tingling. She knew he hadn't reached the important part of his story yet and she sensed that he needed to tell it.

'We started to quarrel within days of the wedding. Maribel didn't like living in the wooden shack, which was all I could afford then. It was no better than her father's and it made her angry. She threw up all the men at me that she might have married, men who owned small businesses. She'd chosen me because my father was rich, and she'd thought he would come round once we were wed, but he died owning very little but his personal trinkets.' Ben drew a deep breath and Sally sensed that it was painful for him to continue.

'It was raining the day it happened,' Ben went on at last and his voice sounded forced. 'We quarrelled, as we did most days. I took her into town. She wanted a new dress for the summer picnic. I gave her ten dollars – it was all I had and it wasn't enough for the dress she coveted. I was tired of arguing and annoyed that I couldn't give her everything she wanted and I snapped at her, told her she would have to make do…' He took a deep breath. 'She got out of the

truck and ran across the road. It was raining and he didn't see her...
her own father was driving like a madman and he struck her. She
went flying through the air, landed on her head...'

'Oh no, that's terrible...' Sally took a choking breath as the
tragedy of it hit her.

'If she'd died, I think it would have been easier on us all,' Ben
said and each word was forced out in a flat tone that hid the ragged
grief. 'She lived for years in a kind of coma, sometimes waking but
often dazed, just lying in bed staring at nothing. I don't think she
knew any of us, though sometimes when she saw me her eyes
would glaze over and she would start to scream. Somehow, she
blamed me for how she was, paralysed and...' He shook his head,
unable to finish. 'She must have gradually remembered a part of
what had happened to her, though the doctors denied it – but I
knew she blamed me.'

'That wasn't fair...'

Ben hadn't heard her, or if he had, he didn't answer, continuing
in the same flat voice: 'Her father drank himself to death. He
couldn't bear what he'd done and I swore at him, called him a fool
and accused him of knocking her down on purpose. Of course, I
knew he hadn't, but I had to accuse someone. He blamed himself
and his way out was to drink. It killed him slowly but still she didn't
die, lingering on, her pitiful state an accusation to us all.'

'That must have been so hard...' Sally felt the knife twist in her
heart as she understood how his wife's pain had hung over him like
a black cloud.

'It was hard to find the money to pay for her care. I didn't tell
anyone I was paying for her to be in an expensive nursing home.
Jenni didn't even know she was paralysed, because I never told my
family about the accident, only that she was delicate and didn't
want to see people. Jenni was away at school and then she went to
work for my uncle in New York. Uncle Gerry gave me a job when I

swallowed my pride and asked, and I managed to keep my wife in the best place available. Eventually, my father came to me and offered what he could afford, but I was too proud to take it. When he died, what little he had was left to me and I bought a few shares in my uncle's business. Then my uncle decided to give me the management of the London store and you know the rest.'

'Oh, Ben,' Sally breathed. 'I'm so sorry...'

'Maribel took a turn for the worse last year. I returned home and went to see her in the nursing home. She seemed to know me then and she wept pitifully. Jenni visited her once just before she died. She'd never been until then, didn't know what Maribel was like. She'd never known the whole story until I told her recently...' Ben shook his head as if to clear it of painful memories.

Sally didn't know how to answer him. Suddenly, the things that had hurt her became clear. She understood why he could not offer her marriage.

'Maribel died a few weeks ago,' Ben said. 'I spent time with her until the end, Sally. I still felt guilt that a beautiful girl had become the pale wretch lying in that bed, because it was our quarrel that put her there. She'd hated me for a long time, but at the end she clung to my hands and cried. I think she remembered somehow, though the doctors said her mind had gone...'

'Doctors are not always right,' Sally said. 'I'm sorry for all the pain – hers and yours. It was a terrible thing to happen...'

'Yes, awful,' Ben acknowledged. 'For a long time we hoped she might recover... she seemed better sometimes, but it never progressed to a recovery.'

'So she is at peace now,' Sally said and the thought came unbidden to her mind. If his wife was dead, he was free to love again and to marry if he chose.

'I believe so. She was smiling in her coffin.' Ben turned to her and his face was twisted with grief and regret. 'She looked so beautiful and I knew it was how she should always have looked – and I still torture myself over what happened.'

'You didn't knock her down.'

'No, but I was angry and that made her reckless. She ran across the road in temper and...' He shuddered. 'I've relived that moment so often, wishing I could make it not happen.'

'Everyone thinks that when accidents happen,' Sally said and moved towards him. 'It truly wasn't your fault, Ben. Maribel was old enough to know she was behaving foolishly. She should have known that you would have given her all you could...'

'So you don't think I'm a heartless monster?' He smiled oddly. 'Her mother called me that once because she'd heard I was sleeping with a woman. I let her call me names and left her to weep by her daughter's bedside. The next day she came to me and begged me not to stop paying Maribel's fees. Her husband had told her that if I didn't pay, her daughter would be in her charge because he couldn't pay for her care.'

'You did what you could...' Sally said. She slipped her arms about his waist, wanting to take the look of despair from his eyes, no thought of her own feelings in the action. 'Don't you think you should forgive yourself, Ben?' she asked sympathetically.

'Yes, and I have – at least most of the time. I couldn't change what happened and I did what I could...' He looked down at her and then bent his head. Sally lifted hers for his kiss. 'I love you... but I think you know. I wanted to tell you about Maribel long ago but couldn't...'

'I love you,' Sally said softly. 'I didn't know you before, but I do now and I love you even more...'

'What about Mr O'Sullivan?'

Sally smiled up at him. 'Mick is just that,' she said. 'He has been a good friend to me and I like him – but liking isn't loving, is it?'

'No, it isn't,' he agreed. 'So – what are we going to do, Sally Ross?'

'What do you want to do?' she asked and pressed herself closer to his body, inhaling the scent of him. 'I think we should go back to your cabin...'

'Oh, Sally...' Ben murmured and held her closer. 'I was going to ask you to marry me when I got back, but then I saw your friend kiss you and you ran through the rain to your door. I was torn between anger and fear and that made me draw back. I would rather you were happy with him than dead...'

Strangely, Sally understood what he meant. Seeing her run across the road in that downpour had taken him back to Maribel's accident and that had made him fear for her. He'd been angry the next day when they met, because he'd thought she cared about Mick.

'I love you,' she whispered. 'Come back to the cabin and we can talk more...'

* * *

Sally nestled up to Ben's warm body, feeling the strength of him and sighed with contentment. She knew that this was where she was meant to be and even if he had not promised her marriage, she would have been happy. It was the first time that Sally had lain with a man, though she knew there had been others for Ben, but only one who had meant anything. Maribel's shadow was still there somewhere in the background, but for the moment she had been banished and Sally knew she was loved as he kissed her throat and stroked her naked back with his hand.

'I love you so much, Sally,' he murmured. 'I want us to be married soon...' Sally murmured her acceptance as she arched for his kiss and held him tight. 'I have a ring for you, my darling – I've had it for a while...'

'Oh, Ben...' Sally's eyes were moist with tears. 'I can't believe I'm so lucky.'

'I want you for my wife so much, so very much,' he murmured huskily.

'And I long to be yours,' she whispered, as he drew her into his arms again. 'I can't announce our engagement before Beth's wedding,' Sally said. 'I want her to have her moment of glory and to be there for her – and then we'll tell everyone we're engaged. Do you want to wait for Christmas or marry sooner?'

'I'd like to do it properly this time, which means Jenni needs to be told and to come over for the wedding,' he said and smiled as she looked up at him. 'So perhaps a Christmas wedding, even though I would rather it was tomorrow. If I pleased only myself, I would marry you in Paris...'

'We'll wait for a while,' Sally said. 'Rachel will need time to find someone to share the rent with her. Beth is leaving and if I do too... she won't manage it alone...'

'We can promote her to floor walker,' Ben said. 'Mrs Craven has been recommended to me by Mr Stockbridge to take Miss Hart's place, so I think that would help with the finance side – but I agree that we need time to do things properly. You should visit my apartment and see if it suits you. Perhaps we should find somewhere else? I can arrange a bridging loan...'

'A move would be expensive and you put everything into the store,' Sally reminded him. 'There will be time later to think of a house with a garden...'

'My apartment has a small garden,' Ben said. 'Adequate for a while I think...'

'Yes, I'm sure of it,' Sally said, and snuggled up to him again, bringing a little moan from him and his kiss on her lips once more.

She wound her arms about him, giving herself to him without reserve. Loving Ben was as natural as breathing and she felt a thrill of desire as she felt the lean hardness of his thigh against hers. He knew exactly how to make her body sing with pleasure and she was eager for him to bring her to that blissful state once more.

* * *

They explored Paris together, walking the ancient streets and little alleys, taking trips down the Seine in the small boats that were for hire. Artists were seated by the bank, drawing views of the city in the hope that tourists would buy from them, but Ben asked one to draw Sally and declared himself delighted with the result.

'We'll have your portrait painted one day,' he promised, 'but this is very like you, my darling. He has captured your smile and the look of mischief in your eyes...'

Sally felt happier than she could ever recall.

They spent some hours in the various workrooms and showrooms, watching models displaying the current collection for winter and autumn 1913, and sometimes being given a sneak preview of the spring collection for 1914. Sally ordered some suits and a few evening gowns from the winter collection but asked if some samples of the spring collection could be sent to her as soon as they were ready. Drinking coffee in a little café, they talked endlessly about their plans for the future, for the store and themselves.

'I want to work for a while,' Sally told him. 'Don't ask me to be a housewife yet, Ben.'

'I wouldn't dream of it,' he smiled at her. 'Do you know how lovely you look sitting there in the sun – the sun suits you, Sally. I think we shall come to France every year for a holiday. You blossom in the warmth and Paris suits you, too.'

He was right. Sally drank in the beauty of the ancient buildings, revelling in the atmosphere of the old quarter and enjoying the beautiful churches as much as the cafés where music was played at night.

A greetings telegram was sent to Jenni, telling her of their marriage and asking her to visit for the wedding at Christmas. Ben's sister was important to them both and they wanted to give her plenty of time to make her arrangements. Ben also telegraphed his aunt and cousin, inviting them, though he told Sally that he did not think either would come.

'My aunt hates travelling – and my cousin doesn't much like me...' Ben said. 'So I shan't expect them – though Uncle Gerald's wife may send a gift...'

Ben had given her a beautiful diamond ring the first evening they were in Paris and formally asked her to marry him. Sally had accepted, and was wearing it on her left hand.

'I shan't tell anyone when we get back, not immediately,' she reminded him, 'but even when I take it off, I'll still be wearing it in my mind and heart.'

Ben nodded. He never argued during those sunlit days. He was a different man, always smiling, happy and eager to show her everything. Sally could have asked for the moon and he would have tried to get it for her, but all she wanted was to be with him and to make love every night.

'I shall miss this when we get home,' she told him on the eve of their departure. 'I'm tempted not to wait to arrange the wedding and yet I want to...'

'We shall wait,' he told her and kissed her lips. 'You taste of champagne...' He ran his tongue over his mouth. 'Hmm, lovely.'

Sally laughed and leaned towards him, kissing him again. 'Let's go for a last walk in the moonlight,' she said, 'and then we'll go to bed...'

25

Mildred's funeral was the day prior to Beth's wedding. It felt strange to stand in the church and listen to the burial service, watching Minnie struggle against her tears and then go home to the celebrations for Beth. However, Rachel managed to put her sorrow for Minnie to one side and join in the fun and laughter on the eve of Beth's wedding. They had bought her several small gifts. Sally had managed to get them wholesale prices on a silver coffee pot and a china tea service. Because it had cost just over half what they would need to pay in store, they'd been able to give Beth a really good present and she was overcome.

Because Beth had shown her the silver tea service her aunt had sent her, she'd managed to match it with the coffee pot and Beth had been delighted as she saw them all together on the silver tray that went with Aunt Helen's tea set.

'I shall keep this for best and give it pride of place on my sideboard,' she told them and then laughed. 'When I have one...'

'You can use the china one for every day,' Sally agreed.

'I never expected all these gifts,' Beth had said, smiling and hugging them as she opened the parcels tied up with ribbons. 'Thank you all so much...'

As a 'thank you' gift, Jack had bought all three bridesmaids a pearl necklace, which he'd purchased in New York; they were cultured pearls and large and creamy with silver clasps. All of them tried them on with their dresses and declared they were thrilled.

He'd taken Beth over to his father's house with boxes of her stuff two evenings before the wedding, but apart from that she hadn't seen much of him because he'd been busy with his new job.

'I'm sorry, love,' he'd told her. 'But once we're married we shall have all the time in the world...'

Jack had bought pearls for Beth too, but hers was a double strand and had a gold clasp. The necklace fitted into the square décolletage of her gown very well and when she was dressed she looked beautiful. After an evening of laughter and talk, they all went to bed and finally even Beth fell asleep.

* * *

The next morning was bright and fine, the sun shining soon after breakfast. Sally went into Harper's for an hour, just to make sure everything was in place and their replacements knew what they were doing, but the others had a leisurely breakfast with Beth. Sally came home with a wistful look on her face and a dreamy expression in her eyes. She brought back a large box from Harper's and inside was a dinner service to match the tea service; it was a gift from Ben Harper.

'I suppose you told him what to buy,' Beth said after she'd peeped inside the box at the generous gift.

'He asked and I told him, but it was his idea to buy you a present.' Sally's smile was secretive and Rachel wondered what was behind that look, but Beth hardly noticed in all the excitement.

Several of the staff had clubbed together and bought Beth some table linen, but the dinner service was something she certainly hadn't expected. Rachel was surprised that Ben Harper would give such an expensive gift to a junior minor member of staff, but he must surely have done so at Sally's urging.

Sally hadn't said much about her Paris trip to any of them. When Rachel asked her if she'd had a nice time, she was non-committal and simply said she'd enjoyed seeing the clothes being made. Rachel had thought she might open up a bit more as the evening wore on, but she hadn't so she didn't press her.

On the day of the wedding, Rachel, Sally and Maggie followed Beth down the aisle, and Rachel took her bouquet when she knelt for the blessing. She thought Beth looked very happy when she and her husband came from the vestry after signing the register. Rachel stood with the other bridesmaids and well-wishers outside to throw confetti over the bride. Sally had some rose petals and dried lavender, which smelled nice.

'Beth looks radiant, doesn't she?' Sally whispered as the bride lifted her face for her new husband's kiss and then they came down the aisle to the sound of church bells ringing and triumphant music from the organ. The happy couple clearly had eyes only for each other.

Outside the church, one of Fred's neighbours stood with a little girl and she came forward to offer Beth a horseshoe tied up with blue ribbons for luck. Beth was given several little trinkets from friends of Fred's family and the reception was for thirty people, almost all of whom were Jack's friends. On Beth's side, there were only her three friends from Harper's and Fred, who had given her away, standing in for the father she had lost many years before. Aunt Helen was nowhere to be seen and hadn't attended the service.

'Where has her aunt got to?' Rachel whispered to Sally, who shrugged. 'She said she was looking forward to the wedding...'

'I bet her husband has something to do with it,' Maggie whispered. 'I saw Beth looking round – and I reckon it's mean, upsetting her on her wedding day.'

'Perhaps her aunt couldn't get here,' Sally frowned. 'She isn't on the telephone or I'd ring...'

'I'll tell Beth that one of us will go round later and see if she's all right,' Rachel said.

Beth was standing with her husband, welcoming her guests to the reception. When Rachel kissed her, she looked anxious and said, 'Have you seen my aunt?'

'She isn't here, Beth – but you mustn't worry. Sally and I will go round this evening and see if she is all right...'

'Thank you.' Beth frowned, still clearly anxious. 'She must be ill – or he has shut her up in her room again...'

'Surely he wouldn't – not on your wedding day, Beth?'

'I'm not sure anything would stop him,' Beth said. 'I wish she'd never married him...'

'Well, don't let it spoil your wedding day, love...' Sally advised with a smile.

'No, I won't,' Beth replied, but her smile didn't reach her eyes. Sally cursed Beth's aunt for not making the effort to get there, but Rachel was sure it wasn't her fault.

Apart from the absence of Aunt Helen, the wedding went off well, the sun shining the whole time and everyone looking smart and happy. Beth told Rachel she'd caught a glimpse of Sally's friend, Mick, at the back of the church, though he didn't come to the reception. He'd only met Beth once, but she told Sally and Rachel at the reception later that he'd sent her a set of pearl handled fruit knives as a gift.

'I would never have expected a gift from your friend,' Beth remarked. 'I didn't even invite him to the wedding...'

'Mick obviously liked you,' Sally said and shrugged. 'He's a good friend and I need to see him soon and explain...'

Beth questioned with a look, but Sally shook her head and whispered that she would tell her some news when she returned from her honeymoon...

When the wedding was finally over and the bride and groom had departed in a cloud of rose petals, Rachel and Sally decided to go together to find out where Aunt Helen had got to but when they reached the house where Beth's aunt lived, the windows were closed and the curtains drawn.

'What's going on here?' Sally asked Rachel. 'Something is wrong – I'll go and ask next door...'

'You're right,' Rachel said. 'Let's ask next door...'

She marched round to the back of the neighbour's house and after a while a woman came to the door. She shook her head when Rachel asked if she knew where Aunt Helen or her husband had got to.

'I haven't seen him for more than a week,' the woman said. 'Come to think of it, it might be two weeks – she was here the day before yesterday. I thought she was going to her niece's wedding today...'

'She didn't arrive,' Sally said and took a notebook from her bag, scribbling her address. 'If she turns up, can you let me know please?'

'Yes, all right,' the woman said. 'I'll send you a letter...'

'Thank you...' Sally gave her two shillings for the trouble and left.

Rachel had walked round to the back of the house, but she saw no sign of anyone and the back door was locked. That in itself was a pointer, because most folk left their kitchen unlocked unless they were out.

'There's no one here,' Rachel said. 'I don't know what to think...'

'Beth's aunt was here on Thursday, but the neighbour hasn't seen Gerald for a couple of weeks...'

'It's odd – but it happened once before and then Aunt Helen turned up and said everything was fine.' Rachel wrinkled her brow. 'I can't believe she let Beth down like that...'

'Maggie told me she was a bit odd sometimes,' Sally said. 'There's no more we can do for her at the moment, Rachel. I'll come over again tomorrow evening and see if she's around then...'

Rachel looked back at the house again. For a moment she thought she saw the curtain twitch and then told herself it was her imagination. Why would Beth's aunt hide up in her bedroom? Yet why hadn't she attended the wedding? She made the bridesmaids' dresses and given Beth a nice gift – surely she would have wanted to be at the church if she could?

Rachel could only feel for Beth, because it must have cast a shadow over her wedding, even if she tried not to let it upset her.

* * *

'I shouldn't let it upset you,' Jack said as they sat on the train that evening.

Beth had told him she was worried about Aunt Helen, but when she suggested they go round to investigate, he was reluctant.

'There's little you can do, Beth – besides, didn't your friend say she would go round?'

'Rachel and Sally were going to see if she was all right,' Beth agreed. She knew if they'd missed the train they wouldn't have been able to get to the hotel that evening and Jack had gone to a lot of trouble and expense to make things right for their honeymoon. They were breaking their journey to stay one night at a hotel just outside Oxford and would continue in the morning to their holiday destination. Jack had planned it all as a surprise and Beth was determined not to let her aunt ruin it for them both. 'I think she must be unwell,' Beth said. 'But you're right; I can't do anything, Jack. I begged her to leave him...'

Jack nodded, a grim line to his mouth. 'Your aunt is a proud and stubborn woman, Beth. We tried to help her, but she wouldn't let us – I'm just sorry she upset you today.'

'No, she hasn't.' Beth moved closer, looking up into his face. She smiled at him and took his hand, holding it to her cheek. 'I love you, Jack, and I want to be here with you. I know that if there is anything to be done, Rachel and Sally will do it...' She shook her head. 'She won't let me help her anyway...'

Jack put his arm about her, drawing her in close. He looked into her eyes. 'Try to forget Aunt Helen and her husband and let's enjoy ourselves for a few days. Once we're back I'll be working hard and we shan't have much time for having fun...'

'I know...' Beth lifted her face for his kiss. 'I am happy, Jack. Honestly, I'm really looking forward to our week at the sea...'

He smiled and kissed her softly but with an underlying passion. 'I've been looking forward to this ever since we met,' he said and she understood that he wanted the physical love that they had denied themselves. Beth had preferred to wait for marriage and Jack hadn't wanted anything to spoil their wedding and so they'd waited, but she knew he was eager for their wedding night. She sighed and leaned into him, letting the feeling of love wash over her. Beth felt she knew Jack so well that passion and loving held no fears for her – and so it proved.

They arrived in the hotel just outside Oxford late at night and went straight to their room, having ordered a light meal in the dining car on their train. The room Jack had booked for their first night was very special, even though they would only spend a few hours there as they had to catch a train early in the morning. It had been prepared for a bride and groom, with flowers, sparkling wine, chocolates and sheets that smelled of rose petals. Yet it was Jack's tender loving that Beth would always remember. She'd gone to him without fear and even when it hurt her a little, she'd still trusted him and felt pleasure in his relief. Jack had made love to her twice during the night and again in the morning before they rose and went down to breakfast. Beth didn't feel the shuddering delight that he so clearly gained from their loving, but she was happy. It was nice being in bed together, cuddling and kissing and talking of the future, and she was content, glad that she was married and looking forward to the rest of their lives.

They continued their journey after breakfast at the hotel, had lunch in the dining car and arrived at their final destination in Torquay just in time for tea at three thirty. The hotel was small but comfortable and set at the top of a steep hill, which gave them wonderful views out over the sea. They changed after tea and walked down to the beach, wandering at the edge of the sea for a while in the sunshine. Jack talked of his plans to have a hotel near the sea one day and Beth nodded, letting him talk, just enjoying the sunshine and the feel of the sand between her toes.

'You are happy, Beth?' he asked and she nodded, smiling up at him.

'Yes, of course I am – why do you ask?'

'I just wondered. I thought...' He shook his head. 'It doesn't matter...'

Beth laughed, broke from him and ran further up the beach. Jack came pounding after her, caught her, swept her off her feet and swung her round, kissing her passionately on the mouth as he set her down.

Beth clung to him and smiled up at him. 'I do love you, Jack,' she said and saw the fire in his eyes.

Later, after they'd washed and changed for the evening, they went to a show at a theatre in the town and had a pot of tea in their room when they got back. That night, Jack made love to Beth again, slowly, taking his time to bring her to a trembling awareness, and for the first time she felt more than just a warm comfort at being in his arms. She moaned softly and he held her closer.

'You do like making love?' he asked in her ear and she pressed herself against him for answer.

'Yes, of course I do,' she whispered and kissed the side of his face. 'I love you...'

Yet she didn't feel the overwhelming joy in their loving that he did. Beth sensed that he was a little disappointed in her responses to his lovemaking, but she didn't know how to respond or what he needed from her. She was happy, but she knew that something was lacking when they made love, but she didn't know what it was or what she ought to do to make it right.

* * *

Jack made love to her every night for the first five nights and then on the sixth he just yawned, said he was tired and went to sleep. Beth lay awake for a while, wondering what she'd done to upset him.

The next day was their last before they had to go back to London and they spent the morning shopping, buying small gifts to take home, and the afternoon lazing on the beach. It was a small private cove they'd found and very few people ever used it. That afternoon no one else was about and after they'd been into the water to cool themselves, Jack dried her back. He kissed her all the way down her spine and Beth shivered, giving a little moan of pleasure. She arched back against him and then turned into his arms, pressing herself into his body. He looked down at her and then laughed.

'You really want me this time,' he said and drew her closer, a look of delight in his eyes. 'So now I know what turns you on, Beth...'

Beth laughed up at him and then they were lying on their towels and Jack was making love to her, but this time she went to him eagerly and suddenly it was good. Her body moved beneath his and shivered with pleasure as she gave herself up to his loving.

Afterwards, when she'd cried out and shed a few tears, Jack lay stroking her cheek. 'I thought you didn't really want me...' he whispered. 'You seemed so remote when I touched you...'

'It's just... I didn't know how...' Beth whispered back and kissed him. 'You make me happy, Jack...'

'Yes, I know,' he said and looked happy and confident. 'Let's get dressed and have tea – and then we'll go dancing again...'

They'd been dancing twice at the ballroom that week. Neither of them were good dancers, but the music was nice; they could hold each other and get through the slower dances and it was a nice way of spending the evenings. Beth knew that once they were home there would be little time for such things and she was pleased that she'd given Jack the response he wanted on the beach, even though she had let him think she felt more than she really did... but now she knew how to please him.

It had been a wonderful honeymoon, but she couldn't help wondering about her aunt now and then...

* * *

Beth went to see her friends at the flat the evening after they returned to London. Jack was going to be late back and she'd told him where she was going. She took the sweets she'd brought home and found them all sitting on the sofa drinking cocoa.

'Did you have a wonderful time?' Sally asked. 'You've got a nice colour, Beth – it was lovely weather all week...'

'Yes, it was and we went on the beach most days,' Beth said. 'I had the best time... but did you discover why Aunt Helen didn't come to the wedding?'

'Oh Beth, I'm so sorry,' Sally said. 'It's bad news, love.'

'I'm so very sorry, Beth. We didn't phone the hotel as we didn't want to spoil things for you – but Helen is in the hospital,' Rachel said, looking upset. 'They say she must have fallen down the stairs and she lay there for a couple of days. When Sally couldn't find her again the night after your wedding, she fetched a police constable and he broke in. He discovered her lying at the foot of the stairs unconscious. She is very ill and hasn't recovered her senses yet and the doctors aren't sure she ever will...'

'Oh no!' Beth went cold all over. 'Poor Aunt Helen – to lie there all alone and not be able to get help...' She felt faint suddenly and sat down.

'I'm so sorry,' Rachel said again. 'Can we get you a drink, love? I know it is a terrible shock for you...'

'But how...?' Beth whispered. 'What happened...' she was shivering and felt a little sick. Poor Aunt Helen lying there while she was enjoying her honeymoon! She felt guilty, even though she knew that was silly.

Sally took up the story, her expression grim. 'Your uncle returned home the next day. Helen's neighbour let me know he was back and Rachel and I went to see him. He said he was worried about his wife and looked nervous... but I think he knew she was lying there at the bottom of the stairs... I think he pushed her down...' Sally said baldly.

'Sally, you mustn't say such things,' Rachel scolded and shook her head at her. 'We have no proof that he was there when it happened. He says he was travelling for his business and—'

'He was lying,' Sally said. 'You saw the bedroom curtain twitch on the night of Sally's wedding. Someone was there – either he'd got Aunt Helen shut up there or she was already lying at the foot of the stairs. He must have left her there to die...'

'Yes, I did think it twitched, but I thought perhaps Beth's aunt didn't want to answer the door to us, so we just went away...' Rachel looked apologetic. 'Now I feel terrible and wish we'd fetched the police then, but we couldn't have known.' She hesitated then, 'We didn't know whether to tell you before you came home or not...'

'I wouldn't let Rachel ring the hotel,' Sally said. 'Besides, we couldn't know what had happened and even when I approached the police, they told me I was probably making a mistake, but I just had a feeling. I told the constable that if he wouldn't break in I would and so he did. He was very good once he found her, summoning the doctor and getting her to hospital. She was being looked after and there was nothing you could do...' Sally looked uncomfortable. 'I'm sorry if I was wrong but I didn't want to ruin your honeymoon...'

'If you'd rung I'd have wanted to come home,' Beth said. 'That would have ruined Jack's plans, so it's best you didn't...' She sighed. 'I've still got tomorrow off and I'll visit her in hospital.' Tears sprang to her eyes, but she wiped them away. 'I think you may well be right, Sally, but we can't prove he pushed her down the stairs. She would never provide evidence against him.'

'Some men don't realise their own strength,' Rachel suggested. 'It might have been an accident...'

'I doubt it. He was angry because he felt she cheated him,' Beth said, her throat tight with emotion. 'He thought she had money, but she didn't – nowhere near as much as he expected. My grandfather owned a big ironmongery store once, but he lost most of his money before he died by investing in worthless shares. Aunt Helen inherited more than my mother, because she nursed grandfather, but she earned her living – and the house was never hers. Gerald thought she had a small fortune in the bank, but it was just a couple of hundred pounds...'

'Poor Aunt Helen.' Sally scowled. 'He should be strung up!'

'I think he mistreated her, I know he hit her,' Beth replied thoughtfully. 'But when anyone else was around, he was all kindness and caring – and I'll bet he has people who will say he couldn't have been there...'

Rachel nodded. 'You'll do no good by making false accusations. If, God forbid, your aunt dies, there is sure to be an inquest. We can only hope they indicate that there is reason for suspicion – but even then it would be difficult to pin the blame on Gerald...'

'I shan't try unless she wakes up and tells us what he did,' Beth said. 'What good will it do if she dies? I suppose he might go to prison for a while, but that won't make her well. I wish she'd never met him...'

26

Sally looked at her ring in its box before she went to bed that evening. It was so beautiful and she longed to show it off. She'd planned to tell her friends when Beth got back from her honeymoon, but the news about Helen had made her hold back. Sally couldn't show them the magnificent ring Ben had given her when Beth was so distressed and so she must wait for a better time.

Ben wanted her to wear her ring and she did when they were together, but the few times they were able to be together as they wanted were nowhere near enough. Ben had cabled his sister a second time, to tell her that he was getting married a week before Christmas. As yet Jenni hadn't replied but she would certainly come for the wedding, however busy she was, which meant they had to make the arrangements soon. If they wanted to book a good venue, they needed to do it now or everything would be gone – and that meant Sally would have to tell her friends shortly.

She sighed as she got into bed, tucking her ring back into her handbag. She knew that Ben felt frustrated that they could not be together at night. In Paris they'd had their own rooms side by side but had slept together every night. She missed him now when he wasn't there and knew he felt the same.

'I want you in my bed all the time,' he told her passionately. 'Can't you move in now?'

'You know I can't,' Sally had said. 'I wish I could – but it would be awful to just walk out on Rachel and Maggie now...'

'I thought you said Rachel wants to bring a friend of hers to the flat?'

'She did mention it, but she isn't sure if Minnie wants to come. She's proving stronger than Rachel thought and may choose to stay where she is...'

'Well, once I offer Mrs Craven the new job she'll be able to afford the rent anyway...'

Sally had nodded. She knew what Ben said was true, but it was only impatience talking. He wanted Sally with him, but she knew she had to give Rachel time to sort things out. After all, it was Sally who had suggested they move into the flat. If Beth had still been there, it wouldn't have been so bad, but she was married and living in her husband's home.

* * *

Sally went into work as usual the next morning. She was busy at her desk when the door opened and someone entered. Looking up, she was a little surprised to see Mr Marco, because she hadn't arranged a meeting and he didn't often come without an appointment, but looking at his face she could see that something was wrong.

'What is it?' she asked and stood up, moving towards him instinctively. His face was working with emotion and she knew he was fighting his tears. 'Something terrible has happened – please tell me...' She took his arm, guiding him towards her chair and urging him to sit.

'It's Julien,' he said in a choked voice. A sob broke from him and he sat down heavily in the chair. 'Mon Dieu! May He forgive me for I can never forgive myself...'

'What happened?' Sally asked, feeling chilled.

'His father found out about us... that we were lovers...' Mr Marco said, tears running down his cheeks. 'I went to his home at the weekend to see him before he left on his trip and... we couldn't help ourselves. We were in the summerhouse embracing when his father walked in and saw us.'

'That was unfortunate,' Sally said, 'but perhaps in time he will understand...'

'No – it is too late,' Mr Marco said and he gave a deep sob. 'Julien couldn't bear his father knowing. He told me to leave and I understand there was a terrible row and then...' His grief was choking him now. 'Julien returned to the summerhouse where we'd met during the night and hung himself...'

'No! That's too awful,' Sally gasped and her heart went out to him. 'Just because he loved a man... it isn't right he should be made to feel ashamed or evil...'

Mr Marco looked at her, his eyes filled with the horror. 'I am sorry to load this on you, Sally Ross – but I knew you would understand. So few accept us...'

'I know and it isn't fair,' Sally replied. 'Love comes where it will and it was wrong of Julien's father to despise him...'

'He is devastated, so I've been told – but I've been warned not to attend the funeral. They don't want me near and they're hushing it up...'

No wonder Mr Marco was in such distress. 'You should wait until they've all gone and then lay your own tribute after the funeral,' she said, looking him over in concern. 'Are you all right to be at work? Wouldn't you rather go home until you're calmer?'

'I couldn't bear being on my own,' he said. 'I'll be all right once I start work – it's all I have now.'

Sally nodded. She understood perfectly what it was like to be so lonely that you had to work to forget. 'If there is anything I can do...'

'No one can,' he said and took out a white handkerchief to wipe his face. 'But you have helped, thank you. I shall go now and somehow forget...'

Sally felt her eyes moisten as he left. The laws that made the love of two men unacceptable were wrong, because in Mr Marco and Julien's case their love for each other was true and it was a tragedy that bias and prejudice had caused the death of a young man just because his love was considered unnatural.

Just then the door opened and Ben entered. He took one look at her face and came round the desk to embrace her. 'What is it, my darling?'

'Mr Marco had some bad news...' She hesitated, not knowing how much to say.

'Marco is my friend,' Ben said. 'I know his secrets – what has happened?'

Sally explained as briefly as she could and he frowned.

'Thank you for telling me. I'll go after him, do what I can.'

Sally dabbed her eyes. She was glad Mr Marco had a friend in Ben. At least he need not be completely alone.

27

Jack had stared at her in horror when Beth told him about her aunt's accident. They were in their room preparing for bed, Beth in her petticoat and Jack with his shirt off, his braces hanging over his hips.

'I feel we should have done something the day we were last there...' he'd said looking at her apologetically, but Beth had shaken her head.

'How could I have prevented what happened? I begged her to leave him – what more could I do?' she'd asked, her eyes wet with tears. 'I feel so sorry for her, Jack. She lived alone all those years and kept a roof over her head – and mine for a while – and then he came along and made her think he really cared...'

'He deserves a good thrashing – and if the worst happens and your aunt dies, he should hang...' He'd looked grim. 'He'll get away with it! He's sly and clever and he'll lie his way out of it.'

'Not if I can help it!' Beth had retorted.

'We don't have proof he did this...' Jack had said and then, seeing the look in Beth's eyes, 'I'm sure he did, but we just can't prove he pushed her.'

'Even if she fell, it was because of him. He made her miserable and ill and I think he pushed her...'

Jack had nodded angrily 'It won't be easy to prove his guilt, Beth. I'll bet he has an alibi all set up to make the police believe he was miles away.'

'Yes, I know...' She'd sighed. 'I just hope Aunt Helen recovers so that I can talk to her, make her see sense. She should leave him and start up her own business again.'

'We'll help her,' Jack had promised and put his arm about her. 'Try not to worry, love. We'll do all we can to protect her in future...'

'If she has a future...' Beth had said because she had a cold feeling at the nape of her neck. She wasn't sure Aunt Helen would recover...

* * *

Beth knew why she'd felt that sudden chill as soon as she told the young nurse at the hospital who she was and why she was there.

'Oh, Mrs Burrows, I'm so sorry – your aunt passed away this morning, about five, I'm told. I wasn't on duty, but Sheila – the night nurse – told me she was very peaceful.'

Closing her eyes for a moment, Beth asked, 'Did she say anything at all before she died?'

'No, I think she never recovered her senses,' the nurse said. 'Would you like to see Sister Norris?'

'I should like to see my aunt to say goodbye, please.' The tears were close but she fought them back.

'Yes, I'm sure Sister will arrange that,' the nurse replied, looking sad. 'Please wait in this room, Mrs Burrows, and I'll tell Sister you're here.'

Sister Norris was a thin, efficient looking nurse who told Beth that Aunt Helen had irrevocably damaged herself during the fall.

'She struck the side of her head hard on something and her spine was broken; I think death was quite possibly the kindest thing. She might have been paralysed or even impaired in her mind... so perhaps this is best, Mrs Burrows.'

Beth didn't reply. 'May I see her please?'

'She isn't here,' Sister Norris frowned. 'Her husband was very efficient and her body was almost immediately taken to a private funeral parlour – I'm afraid I wasn't told the name or address. You will have to contact her husband.'

'I see...' Beth was barely able to control her anger, but Sister Norris was not to blame and so she inclined her head, thanked her, and left.

Beth caught a bus to her uncle's house and banged loudly on the front door. Gerald answered, looking sheepish and slightly furtive as he saw her.

'Where is she?' Beth demanded. 'I want to see her...'

'The name of the funeral parlour is Winter Brothers,' he said. 'It is in Howard Street. The funeral is next week. I am having her cremated...'

'I don't think Aunt Helen would have liked that...' Beth objected, but he merely stared at her coldly.

'I will let you know the details if you wish to attend – and it will be in *The Times*. If you will excuse me, I have things to do.' The door was closed firmly in Beth's face.

She felt her temper rise and was tempted to throw a brick through his parlour window but knew that it would give him reason to ignore her or even send for the police and say she was making a nuisance of herself.

Pushing the letter box open, Beth shouted into it, 'You think yourself clever, Gerald Greene, but I know what you did. It may take me a while, but I'll make you pay, you murdering brute...'

A man had stopped in the street and was staring at her. Beth threw him a defiant glare, lifted her head and marched off. Her moment of defiance had done no good at all, but she felt better for having told Gerald what she thought of him.

Beth took a bus home. The house was empty, because both Jack and Fred were at work. She put the kettle on and then burst into noisy tears. It wasn't fair. Why should that brute get away with Aunt Helen's murder? Because there was no doubt in her mind that it was his fault she was dead. She wished she dare go round there and do something to hurt him, but knew she must let the law deal with him despite a burning desire to make him pay. He would pay somehow, she just didn't quite know how to make sure of it yet.

* * *

Fred and Jack both did their best to comfort her when they got home that evening. She'd cooked a tasty casserole for their supper and she managed to eat some of hers, though it tasted like ashes in her mouth.

'The worst thing is that Gerald is so arrogant,' she said. 'He is so sure that he has got away with murder...'

'If he has...' Fred's was the voice of caution.

'I know it inside,' Beth told him. 'She was frightened of him, Fred. No woman should have to be frightened of their husband, should they?'

'No, Beth, they shouldn't,' Fred agreed. 'If either of my boys hit a woman, I'd disown them. It is the worst sin, in my opinion – and I despise your uncle for it, but it still doesn't prove he's a murderer.'

'I know...' Beth smiled oddly. 'It's just the way he looked at me when he opened the door this morning. He's never been friendly, but he just couldn't wait to slam the door on me...'

'Do you want me to go round there and thrash the truth out of him, Beth?' Jack offered.

'No, Jack, I don't,' she cried, alarmed. 'That's the very last thing I want – you would be locked up and you'd lose your job. He mustn't be allowed to touch our lives any more.'

'He already has – because he has upset you.'

'I shall be all right soon,' Beth said touching his hand gratefully. 'I'm just angry and sad. When the funeral is over, I'll never have to see him again and I'll forget...'

'I think it will rankle and you won't rest,' Jack said. 'We could employ a private detective, Beth. Get someone to find out where he was when your aunt had her so-called accident. He might be able to settle things one way or the other...'

'Could we do that?' Beth looked at him in surprise. 'Would it not be very expensive?'

'Yes, it would cost money, but I'd rather spend a few pounds and know you were happy...'

'Thank you, Jack. I'd just like to be sure. I know it is a waste of your savings but...'

'I told you, I want you to be able to rest and feel your aunt has been avenged, because otherwise you'll never be happy...'

'I know someone...' Fred said, surprising them both. 'He's my age, but he was in the police force until he retired. I heard he did a bit of private sleuthing – mostly for divorce cases, rather sordid, Harold felt, but something to keep his mind busy. He wouldn't over-charge you...'

'If you give me his address, I'll go round,' Jack said, but Fred shook his head.

'I'll speak to Harold myself. We were at school together – and he owes me. Let me do it for you. I'd be glad to help.'

'Oh, Fred, thank you,' Beth said and smiled gratefully. 'I just don't want Gerald to get off scot free... it isn't fair.'

'I'll have a word with Harold tomorrow night,' Fred promised. 'Now, you just stop worrying and drink your tea.'

28

Back at work the next day, Beth told Rachel what they'd planned and she approved.

'I know how you feel, Beth. He should be punished if he killed your aunt and if your private detective can help prove his guilt it will help set your mind at rest.'

'I know it won't bring her back,' Beth admitted. 'Nothing can change that she was unhappy for the last months of her life, but I feel better knowing we're doing something.'

'Poor Aunt Helen,' Maggie said when she learned that Beth's aunt had died in hospital. 'I'm so sorry, Beth – she was lovely to me. It's really sad...'

'Yes...' Beth swallowed hard. 'But I'm angry, Maggie. If that rotten devil killed her, I want him to pay.'

'Yes, so do I,' Maggie said fiercely, which made Beth smile and eased her tension a little.

Being busy behind her counter all that morning helped Beth come to terms with her grief. She enjoyed serving the customers, keeping her stocklist up to date and setting out her displays.

It wasn't until they left work that evening that she thought to ask Maggie how they'd got on with the replacement assistant while she was away. They were standing on the pavement, waiting for the road to clear. It was busy, the motor buses queuing up to take passengers on board at a stop nearby when a young woman dashed across the road, narrowly escaping being mown down by one of the vehicles.

'Janice was fine,' Maggie said in answer to her question. 'I like Janice, but she isn't you, Beth. I do prefer Marion, but she has been off sick three times since she started working here...'

'Yes, I wondered where Marion was,' Beth said. Because she'd started not long before Beth's wedding, she hadn't really got to know her yet. 'How long has she been off?'

'Three days while you were away – and again this morning. I think Rachel is going to talk to Mr Stockbridge about her. I mean, we do need a junior sometimes, but she isn't much use if she is off sick half the time...'

Maggie was exaggerating, but still it was happening too often and Rachel would have to bring it to the attention of the manager if it continued.

Beth's bus came to a halt at the stop and she got on, nodding to Maggie, who was walking down the street. She glanced at the evening paper she'd purchased earlier, noticing that the headlines were about the deaths caused on London Streets by Motor Buses. Beth thought it was hardly a surprise that street deaths from motor buses had risen fivefold since 1907 when she saw the way some pedestrians simply dashed across the road.

Fred was late back for supper that evening. Beth had made something simple and she offered to cook Welsh rabbit for him when he finally arrived, but he shook his head.

'I had a pie at the pub with Harold,' he said. 'He was pleased I'd gone to see him. His wife died six months ago and he's feeling it a bit – told me to tell you he'll be pleased to help and he's looking forward to lunch on Sunday. Do you think we could have roast beef, Beth? I know old Harold is very partial to roast beef...'

'Of course we can,' she said. It was a favourite with the whole family. 'Have we got any fresh horseradish in the garden to make our own sauce?'

'Yes, I noticed it was coming on well the other day,' Fred said. His vegetable plot normally kept them going with fresh food of various kinds. Tomatoes and salads, peas, runner beans and strawberries through the summer, and cabbage, carrots, sprouts, potatoes and parsnips in winter. He also had an asparagus bed in spring and some mint and horseradish plants, which were really tasty when they were ready to be picked.

Beth had settled into her new life easily. The house was easy enough to keep tidy and Fred did as much as he could for her, bringing in coal, coke for the range and chopping wood. Jack often washed dishes or took scraps out to the chickens in the coop at the far end of the small garden. They had a cock bird and five hens. The hens laid a few eggs most days and were kept for that purpose, though sometimes they let them sit on eggs and reared a few chicks. The pullets were killed and cooked when the right age and it made Fred almost self-sufficient in the kitchen, though he ate a more varied diet now that Jack and Beth lived with him.

Most evenings, Fred was content with something on toast and if Jack worked late, Beth had the same. One evening a week, they had a proper meal and she cooked on Sunday, when Jack would be at home for most of the day. His assistant was supposed to take care of things on a Sunday, but that first Sunday back at work Jack went in for an hour in the morning just to make sure that everything ran smoothly.

'You don't mind?' he asked Beth and kissed her before he left. 'I know it is officially my day off...'

'Go and do what you have to, but remember we're having a big lunch and your father's friend is coming...'

Jack promised not to be late and Beth got on with the lunch. Fred's kitchen was big and comfortable, with armchairs close to the range and an old settee against one wall. The large table was scrubbed pine and the chairs were all what was loosely called country style, wooden slatted backs and seats worn smooth with use and covered with bright cushions that Beth had brought with her when she moved in.

Fred fetched a root of horseradish from the garden and scraped it, then shredded it and mixed it with vinegar and cream. Beth tasted a little on her finger and it was hot and delicious, just the way she liked it. She had runner beans from the garden, some baby carrots Fred had pulled while they were still young and tender, and some good-sized potatoes, which she put into roast.

The meat cooked slowly in the range while she whisked the batter for Yorkshire pudding, cut the beans and scraped carrots, and the smell was delicious. For afters, Beth had made a treacle sponge pudding and it simmered fragrantly on the range as she assembled the trappings of a delicious roast dinner.

Harold Brooks, Fred's friend and former Scotland Yard detective, arrived five minutes early and Fred opened a large bottle of stout. After the introductions were made, Fred took Harold off round the garden, glasses in hand, and when they got back, Beth had the table set, the meat resting, waiting to be carved and the vegetables in dishes. She glanced anxiously at the clock, but Jack arrived just fifteen minutes late. He murmured an apology, kissed her on the cheek and shook hands with Harold.

When everyone was seated with a plate of perfectly roasted beef, Yorkshire pudding and vegetables, the conversation began. Beth found it easy to talk to the private detective because it was an informal occasion and everyone was enjoying the food.

'From what you tell me, your uncle shows all the characteristics of a bully,' Harold said after swallowing a piece of beef. 'Delicious meat, Mrs Burrows, done just how I like it – and I agree that Mr Greene might easily have killed his wife, but whether it was planned or an accident I couldn't say at this point. In my experience, it takes a cold intelligence to plan a murder perfectly. Bullies can kill and frequently do so, but normally in a temper or by using more force than they intended.'

'I think he is cold and clever enough to have planned her death...' Beth said, cutting a piece of pudding soaked in gravy. 'He looked as if he would like to murder me when I went there...'

'I would advise you to keep well clear of him. Watch him at the funeral by all means – but don't go to the house.'

'I never want to see him again,' Beth said. 'My supervisor has agreed that I can have time off to go to my aunt's funeral next week, but I shall stay away from him...'

'Yes, that would be wise,' Harold nodded. 'I'll get on to the case immediately. I have a couple of divorce cases at the moment, but they are straightforward. This sounds worth my time and will keep me interested for a while...' He smiled at them. 'The problem is, you see, we need a motive. Your aunt didn't have much money so that probably isn't enough – unless your uncle had another target lined up...'

Beth stared at him. 'I don't understand... target...?'

'If he chose your aunt for the fortune he thought she had, he was probably looking for someone else he could either marry or swindle out of some money. Some men specialise in looking for older ladies, women who have been left a fortune and are lonely...'

'Yes, Aunt Helen would have seemed to fit those criteria,' Beth agreed. 'She received most of what her father left in his will, but it wasn't as much as Gerald expected...'

'He is a very unpleasant man,' Jack said. 'I didn't like him at all, Inspector.'

'Please call me Harold; I'm no longer in the force,' Harold said and smiled. 'Your aunt's husband does sound a very unsavoury character and I shall be very interested to observe him. I shall attend the funeral, Mrs Burrows, but please don't speak to me or show that you know me. We'll save that little mystery for Mr Greene to discover.'

'I'm sure she would still be alive if she'd never met him...' Beth said and there was a sob in her voice. 'He controlled her, though she didn't realise it until it was too late...'

'Yes, I imagine so,' Harold agreed. 'I can't promise you'll I'll get conclusive proof of his guilt, but I'll find the truth, if that's enough for you.'

'Yes, thank you,' Beth said and looked round at the empty plates. 'If everyone has finished, I'll serve the treacle pudding next.'

* * *

Beth felt much better after her talk to Harold Brooks. He had obviously served many years in the police force and knew what he was talking about, and more than that, he seemed to understand the criminal mind. He'd told Beth later as she washed the dishes in the scullery that criminals nearly always made a mistake.

'There will be something somewhere,' he'd said. 'It might be that we get him for something unconnected with your aunt's death – but it would prove his guilt by association and see him punished. Leave it with me, Mrs Burrows, but if anything comes up that you think I need to know, please be in touch...'

'Yes, of course,' Beth had promised.

She didn't think anything would happen that she could report but kept an open mind as she waited for the funeral. She'd asked if she could have the time off, but because she'd had a lot of time off recently, she'd worked through her normal half day to make up for it.

'I hope you will not make a habit of taking time off now you're married, Mrs Burrows. I do hesitate about employing young married women, because they have babies at most inconvenient times,' Mr Stockbridge had said a little severely.

Beth had assured him she wasn't thinking of starting a family just yet. However, she noted that asking for extra time off would be frowned on.

The morning of Aunt Helen's funeral was chilly. It was only the end of August, but the lovely warmth of the summer was suddenly gone and there was an autumnal feeling in the air. Beth wore a dark grey coat and a black hat with a veil. She felt very subdued, because only Fred had been able to get time off to be with her. Jack had apologised but was just too busy, Sally had appointments she couldn't break and Rachel was needed in the department. Maggie had asked for time off but been refused because she was told one missing assistant at a time was sufficient and she must work.

Beth stood with Fred in the chill of the church and shivered. Gerald was in the pew in front of her and had two male friends with him. They all wore dark pinstriped suits and looked grave, their voices deep as they sang the austere hymns that Gerald had chosen.

He never looked at Beth once during the service or afterwards when she followed the small procession out to the graveside.

Beth was aware of Harold watching the proceedings gravely; he had a young woman with him but did not attempt to speak to her, though after the service she saw Gerald approach him. Harold told him something that seemed to satisfy Gerald and he went off in a large black car without glancing at her, accompanied by his friends.

He had not asked her to a reception and she doubted there was one. So she and Fred went for a cup of coffee and a bun before returning to work at Harper's.

'I agree with you, Beth,' Fred said over their lunch. 'Not a pleasant man – and I would say capable of anything, but don't break your heart over it, love.'

'No...' Beth shook her head. 'I'm not going to cry any more, Fred. It doesn't do any good. I can't bring her back, but I hate that man...'

'Well, we'd best get back. I've got work to do and so have you, Beth.'

They caught a motor bus back to Oxford Street and went into Harper's, Fred heading for his basement domain and Beth to her department. Marion had been holding the fort on the scarves while Maggie worked on hats, but Maggie gave up her place when Beth entered.

'How was it?' she asked sympathetically.

'I'm just glad it is over...' Beth said and Maggie nodded her understanding.

'I've sold two red hats and a black one this morning,' she told Beth, as if she understood that Beth would prefer to think about work. 'The black one had a lot of veiling and the red ones were trimmed, one with roses and the other a feather.

Beth nodded. She could see that Maggie had replaced the hats on the stand with a mauve cloche and a pale blue felt trilby with a floppy brim; the trilby was very mannish but had a large cream bow on the side to soften it. Only a few younger women felt comfortable with a hat like that and Beth would move it as soon as possible for something prettier. Sally had tried it for their stock, because she liked to give the customers a big variety, but Beth didn't like that kind of design, preferring the softer, more feminine styles.

Almost as soon as Beth had her coat off, she was serving customers, and continued to do so all afternoon. She sold six hats, most of them the new autumn stock that Sally had bought in recently, and to her surprise the trilby was sold to a young lady who was wearing the colours of the Women's Movement in a brooch on her suit lapel. Her jacket had a rather mannish cut to it and her hair was cut short in the nape of her neck.

'I think I've seen you at our meetings,' she said when Beth handed her the stylish box. 'We're going to make Mr Asquith pay for his treatment of Sylvia Pankhurst. You watch the newspapers and see...'

Beth nodded and smiled but made no comment. The suffragettes had been busy all month disrupting meetings and bombing ministers' country homes. However, Rachel had impressed on her that she wasn't to express an opinion while at work, even if invited to by a customer.

'Well, good luck,' she said when the young woman took her leave and saw her smile.

After that, the stream of customers slowed to a trickle and then it was time for them to close the department. Beth draped her hats with silk squares to keep them free from dust and checked her stock book before she went to get her coat.

'You were busy this afternoon,' Rachel said. 'It was a good thing that you were here, Beth. Maggie sold several pairs of gloves and I was also busy. Marion was helpful, but she doesn't know enough to manage for long on her own yet.'

'At least she came in...'

'Yes, I impressed on her that she needed to and warned her I would have to go to Mr Stockbridge if she continued to be off sick. She blushed and apologised.' Rachel frowned. 'I doubt she was ill any of the days she didn't come in, Beth. She's hiding something, but she wouldn't tell me...'

'Would you like me to speak to her – ask her what's wrong?'

'Maggie is nearer her age and they get on well. I'll ask her to speak to the girl and see if she will tell her what is wrong. Tomorrow, I'll send them on their lunch break together.' Rachel looked at her. 'I imagine you're glad this morning is over?'

'The funeral – yes I am...' Beth sighed. 'It still seems wrong that Aunt Helen has gone. She was never ill in the past. My mother was the invalid, but my aunt was strong and stubborn. I still think...' She shook her head. 'I'm going to put it behind me, Rachel. I have a husband and a home to run and I owe them my full attention.'

'Good...' Rachel smiled at her. 'William came into the department this morning. He bought some gloves and a scarf from Marion – he says he has something important to tell me and asked if I would meet him for lunch this weekend...'

'What did you say?'

'I decided I would...' Rachel hesitated, then, 'Did Sally tell you that Miss Hart is not returning to the store?'

'I haven't seen her today...' Beth was shocked. 'Is Miss Hart too unwell?'

'The doctors say she may never recover the full use of her arm and she will be lucky to walk. It seems she has a cousin, who is a widow, and she has offered to take her in when she leaves hospital, but...' Rachel shook her head. 'She will have to give up her own home and I know she was proud of it. She told me it was small but just as she liked things...'

'Yes, it is sad if she has to give up all she has worked for...' Beth was silent for a moment, then, 'It means they will need someone to take her place here...'

'Yes, that is what Sally said when I saw her earlier. They want to replace her with someone who already works here and recruit new staff to junior positions. Apparently, Mr Harper thinks it is better to move staff up so everyone knows they can improve their standing in the firm...'

'You could do her job,' Beth said and saw Rachel's slight nod. 'Is that what you'd like?'

'It's more money,' Rachel said. 'I'm not sure whether to apply or not – but it would be a step up...'

'We should need a new head of department...' Beth was thoughtful. 'It would have been Sally if she was still on the counters...'

'Yes, perhaps – but you could run the department, Beth. I'm sure you're capable of more than you do already. If I did apply and if I got the job, I would recommend you to take my place...'

'Rachel! I haven't had anywhere near as much experience as you or Sally.'

'I've trained you well. We could have another trainee, although Marion isn't ready to move up yet.'

'Janice did well when she was here.' Beth thought about her suggestion. 'Do you think you will apply?'

'I wanted to talk to you – and also to Sally,' Rachel said. 'She was feeling upset because Miss Hart had resigned and I don't want her to think I'm taking advantage...'

'No one could think that,' Beth assured her. 'I think you'd be just right and I hope you get the position.' She smiled as Maggie came up to them.

'I wanted to say how sorry I am, Beth, Maggie told her. 'I couldn't be at the funeral but I hope you know how I felt?'

'Of course I do,' Beth said. 'Aunt Helen was fond of you and I was sorry you couldn't get the time off...' she linked her arm with Maggie. 'Shall we have a cup of coffee together now?'

* * *

Beth's mood lifted in the days following the funeral. She began to feel easier in her mind and to think of her future and Jack's instead of dwelling on her aunt's sad fate. Jack loved his job and was doing very well, though his hours were longer than either of them liked, but, as he said, it was a small price to pay for their future prosperity and once they got their own hotel they would live on the premises.

'We'll see each other more often then and you can choose your own job, Beth – something that fits in with having a family...'

Beth had nodded and smiled. His arm was about her and he was nuzzling her neck, which gave her a lovely warm feeling inside. Jack was a passionate husband and liked to make love often and she was used to it now and found it easier to respond and to make the sounds of appreciation, which he seemed to expect. She suspected that she was not the first woman he'd made love to and that pricked a little, but she'd decided, sensibly, that as long as she was the last it didn't matter. Jack had been a sailor and they were noted for having a lady friend in every port which in her husband's case she thought probably wasn't true – but she was certain he had experienced physical love before their marriage. However, because she was happy, Beth didn't ask about the past.

It was a week after Aunt Helen's funeral, as she left work, standing for a few minutes on the pavement to bid her friends goodnight, that Beth felt a sudden push in the back and went sprawling into the road. Fortunately, the motor van coming towards her was slowing down and it managed to screech to a halt seconds before it would have hit her.

'Beth! Are you all right?'

Both Rachel and Maggie plunged into the road after her and one of the male staff stood in front of an oncoming bus and held his arms out on either side, bravely stopping the traffic until Beth was safely back on the pavement.

'What happened?' Sally asked, coming towards them. 'Are you hurt, Beth?'

'She tripped and fell into the road,' Maggie said.

Beth was shaking, but at that she lifted her head and looked at her friends. 'No, I didn't trip,' she said. 'I was pushed...'

'Oh no!' Maggie cried. 'Did someone knock into you?'

'I think it was deliberate,' Beth replied. 'I felt a hard push in the back and I just went flying...'

The van driver had got out and come to investigate. 'Yer give me a right shock, lass,' he said. 'I saw you go flying after that rogue barged into yer...'

'You saw it?' Sally asked and he nodded.

'It was what made me brake hard. If I hadn't seen it happen, I might not have stopped in time...'

'Good,' Sally said and took out her notebook. 'We may need you to give evidence – will you?'

'Yeah, why not?' he said and gave her his name and address. 'I don't hold with buggers like that...'

Sally thanked him, and after asking again if Beth was all right, he went back to his van and drove off. A small crowd had gathered out of curiosity, but they dispersed as the three friends guided Beth back into the store and sat her down. Her silk stockings were torn and there was a small cut on her shin, which had bled, but other-wise it was just shock that was making her tremble.

Fred came to them and asked what had happened. He swore softly when they told him and looked angry.

'I'm going to get some brandy from the office...' Sally said, but Beth stopped her, holding her arm.

'No, I'm all right now. Thank you all for helping me, but I'm fine...'

'We'll go home in a taxi,' Fred said and smiled at her. 'You others can get off home. Beth will sit here quietly while I lock up and I'll have a taxi out to take us home.'

Sally insisted on telephoning for a cab and then she, Rachel and Maggie left. Fred went off to lock the main doors of the store and then they exited by the staff entrance. Once they were in the taxicab, Fred looked at her anxiously.

'It wasn't an accident, was it, Beth?'

She shook her head. 'No, I think I was meant to be hurt, Fred. It was only luck that the van driver was so alert. I could easily have been killed. He has given Sally his details, because he saw it all.'

'We should tell the police...'

'What can we tell them except that someone pushed me? And it could've been an accident... except that I don't think it was.'

'Nor do I, love,' Fred said and pressed her hand. 'You know what I think – that uncle of yours doesn't like being investigated. He's found out we've set someone on him...'

Beth took a deep breath. 'Yes, perhaps.' She looked at him, feeling a little frightened. 'What does he have to hide, Fred? What does he think we shall discover?'

'Let's hope Harold can find out,' Fred said grimly. 'Once I've got you safe home, I'll be popping round there to tell him about this development – because if someone tried to kill you, they may try to dispose of him too...'

Beth nodded, feeling slightly sick. It had seemed a good idea to hire a private investigator, but this made her wonder just what they had stirred up.

29

'I'm sure it was either her uncle who pushed her or someone he hired to do his dirty work,' Sally told Ben when they were together later that evening. He looked at her in silence for a moment and she could tell he didn't want to believe her.

'It sounds a bit dramatic, Sally. Do you really think he would kill just because she set a private detective on him?'

'He clearly has something to hide,' Sally said. 'I felt really angry. How could he do such a thing?'

'Well, if he deliberately pushed his wife down the stairs, he'd hardly hesitate to shove his wife's niece in front of a van – and yet he must have a stronger motive surely. Even if he was angry or a bit scared of what her private detective might find, there must be a reason he needs her dead. He could just clear off. The police might never find him, especially if he went abroad.' Even with the telegraph and the help of newspapers, it was easy enough for criminals to disappear if they left the country.

'Money,' Sally said. 'I'll bet it has something to do with money...'

'Yes, perhaps – but I thought the aunt hadn't got very much?'

'Beth says not, but perhaps there was something she didn't know about...'

'Possibly...' Ben frowned, looking at her intently. 'So you didn't tell them about us then? You were going to let them know we're engaged.'

'I couldn't,' Sally said. 'Beth was too upset – but I shall tell them tomorrow.' She smiled at him. 'I'll invite them to dinner one evening – and we'll take them out somewhere nice, but I'll tell them at work tomorrow.'

'Good...' Ben said and reached for her, kissing her sweetly on the mouth. He smelled of a fresh light soap mixed with his own musk and it set her senses tingling. 'Are you hungry? I have some steak in the refrigerator and we can make a meal ourselves or go out...' Although the refrigerator was quite new for home use and a luxury, Ben had been accustomed to an ice house at home and had bought the largest one he could find.

'Let's cook something here,' Sally said and put her arms around him. 'Have you heard back from Jenni yet?'

'No. I expected she would cable me straight back,' Ben said. 'It's not like her to leave something like this – but she may have been away. I'm sure she would have replied if she'd got my telegram...'

'Yes, it isn't like Jenni,' Sally agreed, feeling slightly worried. She would hate it if Jenni was upset by their wedding plans. Ben's sister had always been her friend and it made her slightly uneasy that she hadn't replied.

'You prepare the salad and I'll grill the steak,' Ben said and poured some wine into two glasses. 'We've got some fresh bread.'

Just as Sally finished slicing the large ripe tomatoes on a plate, the front doorbell rang. Ben was busy with the steaks, which had begun to smell delicious, so Sally went to open it and discovered who was there. For a moment she stared in disbelief and then smiled. 'Jenni! We didn't know you were coming...'

Jenni stepped forward and threw her arms around Sally. 'I came as soon as I could get a berth,' she said, her eyes glowing with pleasure and a hint of amusement.

'That's lovely,' Sally said. She laughed, because it was just like Jenni to do something mad and wonderful. 'We were wondering why you hadn't cabled...'

'It's a long story,' Jenni said as she stepped inside and Sally helped her off with her smart coat. 'I've got something to tell you – and I didn't want to put it in a cable...' Her eyes lit with laughter. 'You're not the only ones getting married...'

'Jenni – has he asked you?' Sally said, because she'd known how Jenni felt about her General when she last visited.

'Yes, and he wants an early wedding, which means I shan't be able to come at Christmas, and I wanted to ask if you wouldn't mind getting married sooner so I can be here...'

'Jenni! My God! What's wrong?' Ben said, staring at her in shock. He hadn't heard what she said in the hall but swept across the kitchen to embrace her. 'We were wondering why you hadn't replied.'

'I was lucky enough to get a decent cabin in a Cunard liner, so I thought I would come and surprise you.' She wrinkled her nose. 'That smells good – do you have enough for me?'

'Of course – those steaks are huge,' Sally said. 'We'll share one – but come and sit down and tell me about you and your General. Did you really just say you were getting married at Christmas?'

'About time too,' Ben grinned at her. 'I wondered when he would get around to it.'

'Yes...' Jenni laughed with delight. 'Henry proposed the week before last and I said yes – but the only time he has free is Christmas. He's such a busy man, Sally. If we don't do it, then we'll be waiting for ages...'

'That's great, Jenni,' Ben said and hugged her. 'I like Henry – always have...'

'He's always been the only one for me,' Jenni replied, her cheeks pink.

'So you want us to get married sooner?' Sally looked at Ben and found she was laughing. Jenni's excitement was infectious. 'I suppose we could bring it forward...'

'The sooner the better, as far as I'm concerned,' Ben said. He lifted his brows, his eyes questioning. 'I know you want a church wedding, but do you think you could buy a dress rather than have it made?'

'We'll go to one of the best designers in London, perhaps Hartnell...' Jenni said. 'They're sure to have something that will fit, Sally, and your bridesmaids can wear something off the peg...'

Sally hesitated, because she'd wanted to enjoy the weeks before her wedding, making the arrangements and inviting her friends, but she knew it could be done sooner and she couldn't disappoint Jenni.

'All right,' she said. 'When do you have to be back?'

'I'm here for five weeks,' Jenni said. 'I thought I could hold the fort while you take a holiday – it's only fair if you're bringing your wedding forward for my sake.'

'Yes, of course we will,' Sally said and hugged her. 'I'm glad you'll be here for our wedding...'

'Thank you. I wouldn't miss it for the world,' Jenni said. 'Ours will just be a small private ceremony with a few close friends. We'll have a few days away, but Henry is always busy and I never thought he would ask me...'

'Why has he asked, Jenni?' Ben enquired. 'Is it because he loves you – or because his son needs a mother?'

For a moment Sally thought Jenni wouldn't answer, but then she painted on a bright smile. 'I expect it is a bit of both,' she admitted, 'but he is the only man I've ever loved and I would have him whatever his reasons...'

Ben looked at her long and hard and then nodded. 'I suppose – if you're happy,' he said and then gave her another bear hug. 'I'd like to be there for you, love, but Christmas will be busy in the store and I'd hate to miss it. I did that last year and it caused problems.' He looked directly at Sally and smiled. 'We'd planned to have a weekend off and then take a longer holiday in the New Year...'

'Come over and stay with us when you can,' Jenni invited with a smile.

Ben brought the food to the table. He'd cooked huge T-bone steaks and there was more than enough meat in one for the two ladies, though Ben made short work of his. Sally and Jenni enjoyed the salad with the dressing and did the washing up between them.

'You two will have to get busy arranging that wedding,' he said. 'It means you can't wait any longer to tell your friends, Sally...'

'I'll definitely tell them tomorrow,' she agreed and accepted the glass of champagne Ben had poured while they were disposing of the dirty dishes.

'A toast to all of us,' Ben said. 'May the gods smile on our weddings and give us long and happy lives...'

The three of them touched glasses, laughing excitedly because it wasn't often that two weddings happened in the same family so unexpectedly.

'I know I'm lucky to be marrying Sally, but I hope your General knows how fortunate he is to get you, Jenni Harper.'

* * *

'I'm sorry I didn't tell you before,' Sally said when she gathered her friends together the next morning. 'We were going to arrange the wedding for just before Christmas, but now it will be in September...'

'Gosh, that is quick,' Maggie said and then blushed. 'I mean – will you be able to arrange it all in that time?'

'Ben is seeing to the church and the hotel this morning,' Sally said. 'Jenni and I are going to see some dresses this afternoon – and I wondered if we could use the bridesmaid's dresses Helen made for Rachel and Maggie. Beth would have to be maid of honour and wear something different...' Sally saw the way Beth's smile dimmed. 'I didn't mean to upset you, Beth. I thought it might be a tribute to Helen, to remember her happy times...'

'I'm not upset,' Beth said staunchly. 'I'm very pleased for you, Sally, and I think it is a good idea to reuse the dresses. I could wear something similar.' She smiled. 'When did he ask you?'

'In Paris,' Sally said. 'He already had the ring, but we would have waited until Christmas for the wedding if Jenni hadn't come over and asked us to bring it forward.'

'It's very exciting,' Rachel said. 'Two weddings – and after the tragedy of past times that is something special. Jenni must have been through quite an ordeal after her friend died on the Titanic.'

'Yes, she did,' Sally agreed. 'It's why I couldn't refuse her. We're going to shop for her dress as well as mine so that we can share some of the fun, but I know it seems quick and I haven't forgotten that Beth has had troubles enough...'

'You mustn't worry about that,' Beth said and went to hug her. 'Aunt Helen's death is something I shan't forget for a long time. I'm convinced that Gerald murdered her and until he has been punished...' She shook her head. 'That's my problem and doesn't matter for the moment. I'm very pleased for you, Sally, and for Jenni of course. I don't know her as well as you do, but she is always pleasant when she visits the department so I wish her well.'

After that, they all talked about Sally's dress, what they would choose for the wedding, and her beautiful diamond ring, which she was wearing for the first time at work.

'That is so gorgeous,' Beth said. 'I think you deserve it and I shall look forward to being a matron of honour. Will Jenni be a bridesmaid too?'

'Yes, I think so,' Sally said and her excitement bubbled over. 'We're going to a designer for the dresses, but they will be from the collection – there isn't time to have everything specially made. If we use your bridesmaids' dresses it makes things easier...'

'Yes, of course,' Rachel nodded her agreement. 'Your happiness is what counts. I think it is a like a fairy tale, Sally. I had no idea – you've kept it all quite secret.'

'For a long time I didn't think it would happen,' Sally said and smiled. 'There was always something between us, but I didn't believe Ben Harper would ask a girl like me to marry him.'

'Why not?' Rachel said. 'You're lovely, Sally, honest, hard-working – the ideal wife for a man like that.'

Sally shook her head. 'Ben was married years ago,' she said sadly. 'He wasn't free to marry again – but his wife died in a nursing home a few months ago. She had been an invalid for many years and it was a happy release for her.'

'And everyone who loved her, I imagine,' Rachel said and a shadow crossed her face. 'My husband was ill for a long time. It hurt to see him in pain and in the end I could only be thankful for an end to his suffering.'

'How awful for you,' Beth said, looking at her with sympathy. 'I knew you'd lost your husband, of course, but I hadn't realised how bad it was...'

'It isn't something you talk about,' Rachel said. 'Ben Harper wouldn't have wanted to speak about his experiences either.'

'It was hard for him,' Sally acknowledged, 'but he told me – even Jenni didn't know the truth until recently.'

Rachel nodded. 'Those involved tend to keep it inside,' she said, 'but it will be better now it's no longer hanging over him like a shadow of doom.'

'Oh, don't!' Maggie said and shivered. 'Don't spoil Sally's news by sad things. We've all had our share of those...'

'Yes,' Rachel said and put an arm about her waist, because Maggie had seen too much sorrow for a young woman. The deaths of her parents and then her break-up with Ralf had changed her, taking the look of youthful wonder from her lovely eyes. 'We've all had our own troubles to bear, but sharing them has made it easier – we're all Harper's girls and we help each other.'

'We'll go out to dinner soon,' Sally said. 'Just us four and Jenni. Ben said it would be best that way, but he is going to treat us to a special meal – would Jack be too busy to come?'

'Yes, he wouldn't be able to come out to dinner,' she agreed. 'He only gets Sunday off and he's late home every night...'

There was a faint note of regret in her voice and Rachel took her hand and squeezed it. 'He's working hard to make a better future for you both.'

'Yes, I know – but it was more fun when we could get out more often.'

'Jenni's husband-to-be has hardly any time to be at home with her and his son. That's why we had to rearrange the wedding,' Sally said. 'I like my work too and I've no intention of giving up just because I'm married.'

'What if you have children?' Beth asked.

'I'll find a way,' Sally replied. 'I want a family, but I don't see why I should give up my career at Harper's...'

'Good for you,' Beth said and shook her head because the idea was very modern and radical. Most women were expected to stay at home once the children came. 'Let's think about Sally's news and celebrate it.'

30

Maggie sold several pairs of gloves and three expensive silk scarves all to one gentleman. She was excited afterwards when Beth told her she'd heard she was the leading sales girl for the week, seeming pleased that she would be the one earning the bonus.

'I'm saving for a new coat,' she told Beth. 'I've seen one in Harper's dress department and now I can put a deposit on it. Mrs James says I can pay for it every week until I've paid it off and she'll keep it by for me.'

'That's good of her,' Beth said. It wasn't Harper's policy to keep goods to one side so the supervisor of the dress department must like Maggie a lot to do it for her. Beth tried not to ask favours but Maggie was popular throughout the store and Mrs James had probably volunteered.

'How are things with you?' she asked Maggie. 'Is Tim all right?'

Maggie nodded, her smile a little regretful. 'I don't see him as much as I'd like but when I do we get on well.'

Customers entered the department and they returned to their positions. Beth was busy at her counter and sold six hats that afternoon, but Sally's assertion that she didn't intend to give up her job when she had children kept running through her head. Jack had made it clear that Beth would be expected to stay at home and look after the children once they arrived. He spoke vaguely of her working with him in their hotel once he managed to get his own premises, but she believed he was thinking that the children would be toddlers by then or even older. If they were at school most of the day it would give Beth time to work in reception or the kitchen, wherever she chose.

However, to conceive now would mean she would be at home in Fred's little cottage all day on her own, coping with a baby as best she could. There would be no friends to share her worries or her triumphs with – or only very occasionally, when the child was asleep and she could leave it with Fred for a while. Jack would be at work most of the time and she would be alone.

Beth wanted children one day, but she wasn't ready yet. She'd been married just a short time and she enjoyed working with her friends – also, her concern about her aunt's death would play on her mind if she was on her own too much. It was something she was able to forget at work but often in her mind at other times.

It had frightened her when she was pushed into the road, deliberately she was sure, but she hadn't let it make her afraid to come to work. Fred had spoken to his friend, alerting him to the possible danger, and he'd seemed to think that whoever had taken the chance to shove Beth into the road had done it on the spur of the moment.

'Tell her not to worry too much,' Harold had said. 'I'll get a couple of men I know on the job and we'll see if we can't bring this rogue to book...'

So Beth's fear had receded. She was actually more worried that she might be pregnant already. If she was, it must have happened on her honeymoon, but surely it didn't happen like that? Rachel had been married for ten years and never carried a child full term and many women had to wait years: women who longed desperately for a baby and had almost given up all hope. Surely Beth, who wasn't ready for motherhood yet, had not conceived so swiftly? It just couldn't be possible, could it?

* * *

Fred insisted that Beth wait for him each evening after the incident outside Harper's and he made certain he had hold of her arm, escorting her to their bus and making sure she was safely seated on board. That evening, he was a few minutes longer closing up and apologised to Beth for keeping her waiting, but she shook her head.

'I would rather wait for you, I feel safer,' she said, smiling at him as he came out, accompanied by the young lad who helped him in the stores. 'Thank you for looking after me, Fred. I hope you don't find it a burden?'

'Goodnight, lad,' Fred said to Willie. 'Don't be late in the morning...'

'Night, Fred,' Willie said with a cheeky grin. 'Night, Mrs Burrows...'

Fred turned to look at her as his assistant went off whistling. 'You could never be a burden to any of us – Jack, Tim or me. We all care about you, Beth,' he said stoutly. 'You're my daughter now, and I would do anything to keep you safe from that scheming devil. I shall be glad when he is safely under lock and key.'

'If we can ever prove he was responsible for my aunt's death...'

'Goodnight, Fred, goodnight, Mrs Burrows.' They both turned as they heard Mr Marco's voice. 'I'm waiting for a taxi – on my way to meet some theatrical friends this evening.'

'How lovely,' Beth called as his cab drew up. 'Have a nice time, Mr Marco.'

'I like that young man, always polite and cheerful,' Fred

remarked, smiling as Mr Marco waved before getting into his taxi. His frown returned almost immediately, though, as he went back to their earlier conversation. 'Harold says it may be difficult to prove your uncle's guilt, because as far as we know there were no witnesses, but he won't get off scot free, Beth. Harold thinks he is closing in on him in other ways and that's why he attacked you, hoping to scare us off.'

'Did he tell you what he meant by other ways?' Beth asked, a little trickle of ice sliding down the back of her neck.

'I think Gerald may not be as good at covering his tracks as he thinks he is,' Fred said and smiled mysteriously. 'Harold told me that he'd tracked someone down who knew our Mr Greene in the past and he was going to speak to them this week – if he gets the answers he thinks he might, he will take the evidence to the police.'

'So he's done bad things in the past?' Beth enquired and Fred nodded.

'Yes, I reckon your aunt wasn't the first unsuspecting lady to fall for his silver tongue. Once Harold has finished exposing him, he will be safely locked away for a long time.'

Beth was thoughtful as they journeyed home. As she'd feared, it was unlikely they would ever prove that Gerald had murdered Aunt Helen, but if it could be proved that he'd done similar things in the past, perhaps that would be enough. Nothing would bring Aunt Helen back or take away the unhappiness that man had caused her, but maybe he could be stopped before he harmed another unsuspecting woman.

At home, Beth got on with cooking and cleaning as usual and she had just finished washing the dishes when Jack walked in. He apologised for missing supper but explained there had been a small crisis at work.

'I had to stay to sort it out myself,' he said. 'One of our visitors had lost something – a valuable gold bracelet. We searched the hotel and were just about to ring the police when it turned out that her husband had taken it to the jeweller to have the clasp repaired without telling her.'

'Oh, Jack,' Beth said and kissed him. 'How upsetting for you! You must have been worried that someone had taken it...'

'She practically accused the maid and the girl was hysterical. I could hardly walk out of a situation like that and leave them to sort it out, could I?'

'No, of course you couldn't,' Beth sympathised. 'You look tired – can I get you something to eat? I can fry some bacon and egg or make something on toast?'

'I had some sandwiches an hour ago,' he said. 'I'm not hungry, Beth. I just feel annoyed that I missed being with you this evening.' He frowned. 'I'm wondering if we should move into a room at the hotel. I'd hoped there might be a small flat we could have, but there's only a large double with its own bathroom.'

'I don't think I should like that...' Beth said and Jack nodded.

'It isn't satisfactory,' he agreed. 'I really need to live on the premises, Beth, but I can't ask you to live in a room with no facilities. I shall have to see if I can find some way of making us independent accommodation within the premises.' He nodded, more to himself than her. 'I'll speak to my boss about it.'

Beth smiled but made no comment. She didn't mind living here with Fred; she just wanted to see her husband more often.

Later, when they went up to bed, Jack seemed to be in a serious mood and sat on the bed, watching her undress. She took the pins from her thick fair hair, letting it cascade about her shoulders in a shining mass.

'I love your hair,' Jack told her. 'It is so beautiful, Beth – and you're gorgeous like that.' She stood in her silk petticoat, no corset or restricting skirts to hide her curvaceous body. 'You have wonderful breasts.'

'Jack!' Beth blushed furiously, because even after four weeks of marriage she hadn't got used to intimate remarks like that one. His gaze narrowed as he saw her confusion.

'You don't regret what we did, Beth?'

She looked at him in surprise and saw that he was anxious. 'No, of course I don't. I wish we had more time together – but I understand that sometimes you have to work late.'

'I'm taking you out somewhere nice this Sunday,' Jack told her and smiled. 'I do love you, Beth, and I want things to be perfect for us...'

She went to kiss him and he pulled her down to him so that she fell to the bed; he began to kiss and touch her passionately, turning her beneath him in the bed. 'I love you, Jack. Please, don't ever doubt that... whatever happens.'

Beth wondered if she should tell him that she thought she might be pregnant, but it was too soon to be certain. She would book an appointment with the doctor soon and if she was with child, she would tell him then.

She looked up into his face and invited his kisses, inhaling his scent and slipping her arms about him, her hands moving over his back beneath his shirt.

'You know I adore you?'

Beth laughed softly as she pressed herself against him, her lips kissing his throat, knowing that he was aroused and wanting her, wanting him too. In that moment she was happy and she knew Jack was the man she wanted and really nothing else mattered.

31

'I'm so glad I came over,' Jenni said as she tried on the wedding gown they'd chosen together. It was a froth of organza and silky lace and looked wonderful on her, its waist high and the hem just swishing above her ankles. 'I might have found a lovely dress back home, but I've had fun shopping for it with you, Sally.'

'Yes...' Sally smiled at her warmly. She'd chosen a slender sheath of ivory satin with long sleeves and a deep V-neck at the back with a diamanté strap holding it together; the kind of dress she could wear to go dancing if she chose. It was simple but stylish and made her look elegant, almost regal, and she'd known it was the right one the moment she saw it. 'I'm glad you came over too, Jenni. I wish we could be at your wedding – but perhaps we'll get to visit soon.'

'I'd love to spend more time with you and Ben.'

'You have a store to run,' Sally said and Jenni nodded.

'I've been training a junior back home and she will gradually take over the buying, though I'll go in for consultations and keep an eye on things until she's confident and then I'll leave it to her. I'm hoping to have a big family and I don't want work to get in the way...'

'You won't remain as the buyer for Harper's in New York?'

'No, why should I?' Jenni said and smiled softly, her happiness showing through. 'I was pushed into it by my uncle and I had no choice, but now I do. I'm part owner of Ben's store and I know he'll make a success of it – and I shall be the wife of a rich man, Sally. Henry wouldn't want me to work and I'll be busy entertaining his friends, looking after his children and being his wife. I don't need the responsibility of the store.'

'I love Ben, but I don't want to give up my job as buyer,' Sally said as the salesgirl unbuttoned the back of Jenni's dress and took it away to pack it for her. 'He understands and he wants me to keep working. Of course, I'll need time off when we have children, but I'm lucky, I can choose my own hours and Ben says we'll have a nurse for when I need to work.'

'I could have a nanny,' Jenni said, 'I may do because I don't want to be in the nursery all the time – but I don't need to work. I suppose we're just different that way.'

'Yes, I suppose so,' Sally agreed. 'Where are you going on your honeymoon – or hasn't the General told you?'

'He says it will be somewhere skiing,' Jenni said. 'We all like that – it's fun and we'll be taking little Tom with us.'

'On your honeymoon?'

'Yes, I'd like him to come. It still isn't long since he lost his mother, Sally. I don't want him worried that we won't come back. He'll have his own room and we'll have fun together on the slopes – perhaps in Vermont, although it's better there earlier in the year.' Jenni smiled at Sally as they went through to the reception area to pay for their gowns. 'Has Ben said where you two are going?'

'I think just a weekend in the country. We haven't long been back from Paris. We might go somewhere after Christmas, when we're not so busy.'

'Christmas is usually our busiest period at home,' Jenni told her. 'But I've booked my time out and they will just have to manage.'

Jenni smiled as she paid the girl for her dress and they left the store together, having arranged for their purchases to be sent to Jenni's hotel. 'I need some shoes, but I don't have to buy them here – what about you, Sally?'

'I shall buy some satin shoes,' Sally said. 'I saw some pretty ones in Harrods the other week. I like to visit all the stores in London – that way I know what my opposition is selling, though, of course, we've never done much in the way of shoes. I have no idea why...'

'Harper's of Oxford Street isn't big enough to sell everything,' Jenni said. 'We have a bigger linens department, shoes, furniture and drapes in New York – but we're about twice the size of Ben's store. That's why it was such hard work to fill it. My uncle was there to advise me at the start, of course, but we soon needed a full-time assistant buyer – and I'll keep an eye on the stock for a while for my aunt's sake.'

'So you won't give up completely...' Sally laughed and linked arms with her. 'I'm glad. Harper's wouldn't be the same without you...'

'Oh, they'll manage,' Jenni said. 'We're all replaceable, Sally. My uncle told me that at the start. He said that he would give me a chance to shine, but if I let him down he would give my job to someone else.'

'He sounds a bit of a tartar?'

'Yes, he was in a way, but he made me keen to work and it helped me. I learned fast because I knew that being his niece was no guarantee of keeping my job. It was the same for Ben. My uncle left him some shares but not enough to take complete control – he was meant to earn that and none of us were certain that Ben would do it. He never told anyone where his money went. No one at the store knew that Maribel was being cared for night and day...'

'It must have been expensive...'

'A small fortune,' Jenni said. 'My uncle thought he spent his money on gambling or women or something. I suppose I thought the same until Ben told me that Maribel was dying...'

'Poor woman,' Sally said. 'I feel dreadful sometimes, Jenni. I'm so happy and I couldn't have been while she lived.'

'You must never feel that way,' Jenni said. 'It's the same for me – Henry would never have noticed me while my friend lived. He was in love with Marie and I was just her friend. I couldn't help the way I felt about him, though I never let either of them guess while she was alive. I sometimes wonder if she did sense something, but I was careful not to show my feelings.'

Sally's arm hugged her. 'We share that – being second wives. Do you think the first wives watch us and feel jealous or upset?'

'Perhaps...' Jenni shrugged. 'They've gone, Sally. You make Ben very happy.'

'He makes me happy too,' Sally said. 'I never thought it would happen.'

They smiled at each other. 'Let's go back to the hotel and have coffee and cake,' Jenni said. 'You don't have any appointments today, do you?'

'No, I kept it free especially.'

'Good.' Jenni hugged her arm. 'I'm glad we're to be sisters, Sally. It means we shall always be friends, whatever happens.'

32

Maggie was serving a customer with white cotton gloves and a pale pink silk scarf when she noticed the young girl watching her. After her customer had paid and gone, the girl approached her hesitantly.

'Are you Miss Margaret Gibbs?' she asked shyly.

'Yes, I am.' Maggie looked at her curiously. 'May I help you?'

'It depends if you want to,' the girl replied. 'I'm not quite seventeen and I know you're eighteen and I'm not sure you would be interested...' She took a deep breath, then, 'I'm Becky Stockbridge. My father said you were kind to him when I had that operation...'

'Becky Stockbridge!' Maggie smiled in delight. 'I'm so glad to meet you. Are you better now?'

'Yes, much better, thank you,' the girl assured her. 'It took me a while to recover, because I was ill for weeks after I left hospital – and that's why I'm no longer at school. My father said he would let me have lessons at home, but it does mean that I don't have any friends and... I was wondering if you would come to tea on Sunday...' She finished in a rush, her breath coming fast as if she were nervous of asking.

'I should love to have tea with you.' Maggie smiled. 'Is it your birthday?'

'No, but it's a celebration of my feeling well again,' Becky said. 'My father told me to ask you if I wanted, but I thought you might find it a bore.'

'Not at all,' Maggie assured her. 'I've asked Mr Stockbridge how you were and he said you were getting better, but I'm so pleased to see you looking so well, Miss Stockbridge.'

'Oh, no, you must call me Becky,' the girl smiled. 'I hope I can call you Margaret?'

'I'm Maggie to my friends – and I think we shall be friends, Becky.'

'Yes, please,' the younger girl said. 'I want to be a secretary, Maggie. That is why I'm having lessons at home, because I need to pass exams before I can apply to train – and I have to be eighteen too, so that is just over another year. My birthday is in October.' She gabbled on excitedly, clearly pleased to be talking to a girl of a similar age.

'Mine is August,' Maggie told her. 'We're not really that much apart, Becky.' She saw a customer approach. 'I ought to get on now – but leave me your address and I'll come on Sunday.'

Becky smiled, passed her a small envelope and left just as the customer came up and asked for a blue silk scarf. Busy for the rest of the morning, Maggie didn't have much time to think before her lunch break, when she opened the little card with the invitation to tea and Becky's address. It made her smile because she had another new friend and it was good, because Beth was married and Sally was getting married, which meant she wouldn't see either of them as much as she had and with Tim often busy with the Royal Flying Corps at the weekends it sometimes left her with not much to do.

* * *

Beth leaned over the toilet and vomited into it, her stomach heaving. It was the third morning in a row that she'd been sick and she knew she'd put on a little weight, even though she only noticed it because her best hobble skirt felt too tight about the waist. It had always been a snug fit and now it wasn't truly comfortable. She felt a sinking sensation inside: her suspicions had proved true and it looked as though she was pregnant.

It was Sally's wedding the following week. Beth hoped she would be able to squeeze into the beautiful pale blue dress Sally had purchased for her. Jenni Harper had a similar dress to Beth's, because she'd liked the flounce at the hem and so they would be two and two because Rachel and Beth were wearing the dresses Aunt Helen had made for them for her wedding.

Wiping the vomit from her lips and rinsing her mouth with cold water, Beth patted her face and looked in the mirror. Was her condition showing? No, she looked fine; it was just her queasy stomach that she feared might not let her eat her breakfast again.

She went downstairs to the kitchen. Fred had toasted some bread and buttered it and was crunching a slice spread with honey. He turned and looked at her, his eyes thoughtful as they scanned her face.

'Not feeling too good this morning?' he asked.

'Just a little tummy upset,' Beth said. 'I don't know if something we ate yesterday wasn't quite right.'

In saying that, she was maligning the wonderful dinner Sally had bought them, which had been at Mathieu's, an expensive French restaurant where they'd had prawns in a fancy basket made of lettuce with pink sauce and white asparagus. Followed by sole in white wine with sauté potatoes and green peas and surpassed by brandy snaps, black cherries, cream and a touch of liqueur and ending with coffee and petit fours, Beth had never tasted anything quite like it.

'Perhaps,' Fred agreed good naturedly, but Beth saw a knowing look in his eyes and knew that she couldn't put off telling Jack any longer. It wasn't fair if his father had guessed the truth before Jack had any inkling of her condition.

Beth managed a piece of toast with a scraping of honey but forwent the butter, which she just couldn't face. Even the smell of melted butter made her want to bring it all up again. It was odd, but it was the smell rather than the taste of things that made her feel queasy.

Why did she have to fall for a baby so quickly? Beth was annoyed as she caught the bus for work. As yet, it only affected her first thing in the morning.

By the time she arrived at work, she was feeling fine, but that wasn't likely to be the case for the whole of her pregnancy, and, if she was unwell, she might not be able to work as long as she'd hoped. If she got too big, it would be awkward and might embarrass the customers, because many ladies liked to keep such things private. She was sure that Mr Stockbridge would not have agreed that she should be the new supervisor if he'd guessed that Beth was pregnant.

Rachel had been offered the job as floor walker. She hadn't even applied. Mr Stockbridge had summoned her to his office one evening after work and told her that they wanted her to take over Miss Hart's job.

'We're very sorry that Miss Hart cannot return to us,' he'd said, 'but her illness has left her in difficult circumstances and she felt it would be better to take the pension from her annuity now rather than try to hang on.'

Miss Hart had apparently paid into a scheme for a private annuity that had been arranged for her by her late father's lawyer, and which she would receive on top of the small pension Harper's had promised to pay her.

'It was lucky for her that she took out the private annuity,' Sally had told Rachel after she accepted the job. 'She can pay for her board at her cousin's and won't feel that she is beholden to her, as she might have had she been hard up...'

'I didn't even know it was possible,' Rachel had replied and looked interested. 'That is something I may look into myself...'

'I think everyone should if they can,' Sally said. 'No one knows when something bad will happen. I am sure Miss Hart expected to work for several years to come.'

'Yes, I expect so,' Sally replied.

'You're married now so it isn't so important for you,' Rachel told Beth when they discussed it. 'But I shall certainly invest in something of the sort – after all, a little extra money when you retire is a good thing.'

'Yes, of course.' Beth agreed with her, though her own thoughts were far from annuities and retiring.

She'd hoped to work a bit longer, to save for the future and have a little money of her own put by, but that was no longer an option. Any money Beth had managed to save would get eaten up in buying things for her baby. Once she gave up work, she would be reliant on whatever Jack gave her. He was generous and the housekeeping was always more than she needed, but her own money had been so useful and it made her feel independent, something Beth knew was important to her. She loved her husband, wanted to be his wife and have his children, but there was a part of her that needed more, far more, and she couldn't explain it. If she tried, it would sound as if she were complaining, dissatisfied with all she had, and that wasn't true. She didn't understand this part of her that could never just accept and stand still, nor where it had come from, but she knew it had grown slowly somewhere at the back of her mind.

There was no use in regretting what could not be changed. Beth loved her husband and Jack was a passionate lover. She knew that he would not wish to use restraint in their loving in order to minimise the likelihood of her becoming pregnant. In reality she could expect to give birth often in the next few years, unless she sought some kind of contraception herself. It was a subject Beth knew nothing about, considered taboo by many women, and she did not think her husband would approve of her using it even if she consulted an understanding doctor.

She was a little anxious, because in truth she hadn't had time to get used to being a wife and now she would be a mother too and she found the idea a little frightening. Her future was all wrapped up and set, whether she liked it or not, and she couldn't help feeling a faint resentment. Why couldn't she have been one of those women who took a while to conceive? Had she been married for a year or two, she would have been delighted to be told she was pregnant; it was just too soon.

'You look a little pale,' Maggie said to her when she came to tell her she could take the first break that morning. 'I'm all right, Mrs Burrows – if you need a little rest yourself...'

'I'm fine,' Beth assured her and she was. The sickness never lingered on into the morning and she knew she was lucky, because some women had it far worse than she had so far. 'You go first and then Janice and Marion can go together.'

Maggie smiled and went off, returning a minute before her time. Beth sent the other two girls to their break together and she was about to take her own break after their return when Sally sent a message down that she would like to see Beth in her office.

Beth took the lift up to the top floor, wondering why she'd been summoned. Surely she hadn't done anything wrong? She'd been surprised but pleased when she was moved up to be supervisor of the department, though she knew now it wouldn't be long before she was handing over to someone else.

Sally had a tray of coffee and some biscuits waiting in her office.

She smiled as Beth entered and indicated that she should sit down. 'I wanted to show you the hats I've bought for the wedding,' she said and pointed to a pile of smart boxes. 'I think these will go with your dresses well – and I know they will suit you, Beth.'

The boxes revealed four identical hats made out of straw, silk flowers and veiling in a combination of pale blue, navy and white. Beth took one out and tried in on in front of the wall mirror.

'Oh, that's lovely,' she said and turned to smile at Sally. 'I'll bet you're looking forward to next week.'

'Yes, I am,' Sally agreed. 'I've bought my dress and shoes and a suit for going away in – but I still have plenty of new clothes from my trip to Paris. Some of the designers gave me bits and pieces from their collections and so I haven't bought much.'

'Has Jenni bought her wedding dress too?'

'Yes, she was delighted with it,' Sally said. 'How are you getting on in the department? I know Janice is an experienced salesgirl and Maggie is gaining in confidence all the time – but Marion is just a trainee.'

'She doesn't learn as fast as Maggie did,' Beth said, 'but she is a pleasant, friendly girl and I've heard no complaints – have you?' Sally shook her head. 'I miss seeing Rachel all the time, but I'm glad she is the floor supervisor now. She deserves it.'

'Everyone likes Rachel, of course. I have to admit that all the girls seem happier now she is the floor walker. Miss Hart was never a favourite with them, though the male staff didn't mind her.'

'Poor Miss Hart,' Beth said, nodding her agreement. 'She wasn't very popular, I'm afraid – and she was awful to you. Not many women would have visited her in hospital and tried to help her if she'd spoken to them the way she did you.'

'I felt it could have happened to me if I hadn't met Ben,' Sally said. 'I might have ended up like her, alone and frightened.'

'Was she frightened?'

'Yes, of course,' Sally said. 'It was her fear of loneliness that made her jealous of us, Beth. She told me she envied our comradeship and the way we all got on.'

'I suppose we were lucky,' Beth admitted. 'It was meant to be that we all turned up for a job at the same time and became friends.'

'Yes. I think we always shall be.'

Beth nodded and then a sobbing sigh escaped her. 'Will you visit me when I'm stuck at home with a baby?'

Sally looked at her hard and then arched her eyebrows. 'You're not – are you? It's so quick, Beth...'

'I know.' Beth made a face at her. 'I love Jack, but I'd hoped for a bit longer at work before this happened... I haven't told him yet, but I shall this evening. His father has guessed, so I have to tell him now.'

Sally came towards her and Beth stood. They embraced and Sally laughed. 'Don't look so gloomy, love. You don't have to give up too soon – and I'll be sure to pop over every week and you must come here to visit when you have time. You won't lose us just because you have a baby.'

'Won't I?' Beth stared at her, hope dawning. 'I just felt it was the end of my life here...'

'You'll always be one of us, an original Harper's girl,' Sally said. 'Yes, you're married and you'll have babies, well, so shall I – God willing – but I intend to keep up with my friends. You and Rachel and Maggie are my best friends. I love Jenni as my sister but no one can replace you and the others. I shall cling to you down the years, so don't think I'm going to wave goodbye and watch you disappear for good.'

'Thank you.' Beth felt much better. She glanced at the clock. 'Gracious, I'd better go! I'm going to be late back for the first time ever and I am supposed to set a good example to the others.'

'Blame me,' Sally said and smiled. 'Go on, you daft thing, and be happy. You have so much to be thankful for – a husband who adores you, a father-in-law who thinks you're the best thing that ever happened to his family and now you're having a baby. I think that is just about perfect.'

Beth laughed on her way to the door. 'Yes, well, put like that, I suppose I am lucky. You always did know how to cheer me up, Sally.'

* * *

Jack was over the moon when Beth told him that evening. He grinned from ear to ear, hugged her, kissed her and swung her up in his arms, his delight brimming over.

'How do you know?' he asked. 'Have you been to the doctor – what does he say? When will it be born?'

'Oh, Jack,' Beth laughed, happy in that moment because he was so delighted. 'Let me answer one question at a time. I've been sick every morning for the past three days and I'm three weeks late with my period. The doctor said he would do a test, but he hasn't confirmed it yet – but I know. I've put on a little weight already.'

'Let's hope you can fit into the dress Sally bought for her wedding,' Jack said, still grinning like a Cheshire cat. 'I'm so happy, Beth. I knew we'd have kids one day – but this is so quick.'

'It probably happened on our honeymoon,' Beth said and giggled, caught up in his enthusiasm. 'We shouldn't be surprised after the way we've been carrying on.'

'I'm a lucky man,' Jack said and hugged her, but gently, so as not to harm her. 'You'll have to do less, Beth, take care of yourself and the baby.'

'I'm well, Jack. I don't need to stop work until the last two or three months. It will be better for me to work than sit at home twiddling my fingers. Besides, I'm in charge of the department now and there's no way I'm going to overtire myself.'

'Just make sure you're all right,' he said and looked serious.

'Fred looks after me,' Beth told him seriously. She understood his concern, which was very real for both her and the baby, because with Gerald Greene lingering in the shadows, anything could happen.

33

Even though September could sometimes be less than perfect, for Sally's wedding the sun shone both sides of the hedges, making it a perfect day for all the finery. Sally was beautiful in her simple cream silk gown with lace insets, which made her look beautiful and serene as she walked ahead of her four attendants carrying a bunch of flowers.

Sunshine filtered through the ancient stained glass of the old church, warming its cold stone floors and throwing a myriad of colours over everything it touched. The thick pillars of white turned grey by the ages sparkled with light and the flowers in tall vases were a scented background to the quiet vows taken by bride and groom. The old oak benches were packed with smartly dressed guests and the aroma of lilies and roses mingled with the scents of the old church. Jewels flashed in the light of the candles and discreet overhead lighting, because some of the guests were rich friends of the Harpers'.

Sally smiled all the way through the ceremony, her heart swelling with love as she looked at Ben and saw the warmth in his eyes when they were pronounced man and wife and, afterwards, the signing in the vestry. Outside in the sunshine, she saw all her friends, as well as many people she hardly knew, friends of Jenni and Ben. Maggie had been told she could bring a friend and she'd chosen to bring Mr Stockbridge's daughter, Becky, with whom she'd formed a friendship recently. The girl stood with others from Harper's and threw rose petals over her, the scent of heavy perfumes from women in expensive dresses and wonderful hats wafting on the breeze.

Sally turned to her new husband, feeling pride as she saw how handsome and confident he looked in the sunshine. How had this happened to her – a girl from an orphanage who had never known the love of a family? Suddenly, she had a husband, sister-in-law and friends all here smiling at her and her heart overflowed with happiness.

And then the cars came to take them all to the reception in the hotel Ben had booked. Standing in the large room, which was dominated by three long tables dressed with the magnificent buffet, the centre one bearing a beautiful three tier wedding cake immaculately iced and decorated with tiny figures of a bride and groom, Sally smiled until her cheeks ached. More confetti had been thrown and it littered the polished wood floor. Bowls of white roses were set at intervals all around the room and their perfume billowed towards her every time the door opened to admit another waitress with more food.

Ben had spent lavishly on the reception and every little morsel was delicious and delicate, whetting the appetite for the next: prawns in a pink sauce and crispy pastry, scallops on a bed of green asparagus puree and lobster in a creamy sauce that vanished on the tongue. There were salads of every description, rice, and luscious fruit piled high, ham with ripe red tomatoes, crusty bread, cold chicken, tiny green peas and crispy potatoes.

Then there were all the sweet things: meringues and cream and strawberries and black cherries in kirsch and pineapple slices in sweet liquor, brandy snaps and cakes so light they melted in the mouth. This entire feast was accompanied by champagne or a cool fruit punch for those who did not care for alcohol.

'What a lovely wedding,' a woman wearing heavy perfume wafted up to Sally and kissed her cheek towards the end of the reception, when the speeches had ended. 'How lucky you are to have caught Ben in your net, Sally, and how do you expect us to buy you a gift, Ben darling, when you own a department store?'

'Half a store, Lady Bridges,' Ben said with a twinkle in his eyes. 'Jenni owns the other half – Have you seen her yet? I'm sure she'd love to have a word...'

Sally didn't even remember the woman's name, though she recalled Jenni murmuring it in her ear when the woman had first entered on the arm of a rather short man with thinning hair. Now she was staring at Ben and looking slightly annoyed before her husband led her away.

Sally found Jenni at her shoulder again almost instantly. 'Take no notice of her, love,' she said. 'Margery never stood a chance even if she hadn't been married to poor Rodney. I'll bet she puts him through hell.'

'Is she American?' Sally asked, because she'd thought she caught a faint accent.

'Yes. She used to work for my uncle in his office – until she met Sir Rodney Bridges. He's rich and she couldn't wait to get her claws into him, poor man, but she always had an eye for Ben. She would happily sleep with him if he was interested, which he never has been.'

Sally was conscious of Lady Bridges' green eyes watching her as she moved between her guests, kissing cheeks and thanking them for gifts and for making her wedding perfect.

Rachel, Maggie and Beth had put together and bought Sally a

tiny gold locket on a chain. They knew Ben had most things the couple needed in his apartment and wanted to give Sally a keepsake of the day. She'd cried and kissed them when they'd given her the small box, declaring that she would always treasure their gift and she was wearing it now. Ben had given her a diamond and platinum cocktail watch as his wedding present and Sally was wearing that on her wrist.

'Shall we go now?' Ben asked, slipping an arm about her waist. 'We could stay forever and they'd keep us talking – but we should be on our way.'

Sally looked up at him and smiled. 'I've just said goodbye to the girls,' she told him. 'The others don't matter – most of them I don't really know.'

'Nor do I,' Ben said, his eyes laughing. 'Jenni said to invite everyone we knew in London to make it special, so I did – but we know who matters.'

Sally met his eyes and inclined her head, a little smile on her lips. She took his hand and they left the reception to the sounds of some cheers from a few male friends he'd invited. Ben lifted his hand in acknowledgement but didn't pause. They left the huge room that had looked so immaculate and was now strewn with confetti, waste food and abandoned dishes, going quickly to the lift and up to the room Ben had reserved for them to change their clothes.

Sally's suit, hat, shoes, gloves and bag were on the bed waiting. Ben slipped out of his tailored suit into slacks and a casual jacket while she removed her wedding gown and pulled on the smart suit.

'You looked so gorgeous in that dress,' Ben said and kissed her on the lips. 'You will wear it again just for me one day?'

'Yes, if you wish,' Sally said and laughed as she saw the heat in his eyes. She knew what that meant, but if they gave way to the urge to make love they would be here all night. 'We should go...'

'Yes, we should...' His eyes were hot on her and she shivered as he ran his finger down her cheek and her throat, making her sway towards him, ready to abandon all their plans for the touch of his lips on her flesh.

'Ben...' she breathed.

'We're going, Sally.' Ben grinned at her. 'I want to be on our way before six or we'll never get there.'

He'd arranged a short break for them down at the Sussex coast, near to the town of Hastings-on-Sea, and Sally knew everything would be perfect, just as it had been today for their wedding. She picked up her bag, gloves and her hat. Their suitcases were already in the car that would be waiting for them downstairs. Ben hadn't wanted to drive himself, so he'd arranged for a hired car to take them and it was a long black vehicle with a high roof that smelled of leather.

Some of their friends had been on the watch for them and rose petals were showered over them as they got into the car and settled on the comfortable padded cushions. Sally turned to wave to the friends who had thrust a lucky horseshoe into her hand at the last minute and then smiled at Ben.

'We're married,' she said and laughed for sheer joy. 'It took me a while to believe it could really happen, but it has.'

'Yes, lucky me,' he said and leaned forwards to kiss her. 'I love you, Sally Harper, and I feel so blessed to be with you. For a long time I thought my life was over...'

'No,' she whispered and her fingers strayed up the back of his neck into his thick hair. 'For us this is just the beginning, Ben. We're going to make Harper's a big success, have lots of children and live happily ever after.'

Ben grinned and pulled her to him. 'When you say it, Sally, I believe it.'

'Forget the past and the pain,' she whispered. 'From now on, it's us all the way and it will be good.' The confidence brimmed out of her and no one could have doubted her belief and sincerity.

* * *

'Didn't she look lovely?' Maggie said as she, Beth and Rachel collected their things and left the reception. Mr Stockbridge had arrived in time for the reception; having closed the store early on Ben Harper's instructions so that his staff could attend the reception if they wanted or simply have a few hours off. He'd taken Becky home with him, even though she would rather have stayed with Maggie.

'Beautiful,' Rachel agreed. 'Happy, too – that is the main thing. I'm so glad Sally has what she wants at last. I think she'd had a lonely life at the orphanage and when she left... until we got together.'

'Harper's girls, that's what she calls us,' Maggie said and looked at Beth as the cab set off through the busy streets. 'Did we tell you that Minnie is going to move in with us?'

'I knew Rachel asked her if she wanted to,' Beth said. 'I didn't know she'd agreed.'

'Yes, she's decided to share Rachel's room and I'm to have yours and Sally's old room, Beth. We might ask someone else to share in the future, because it makes the rent cheaper, but not just yet. It would have to be the right person.'

'Minnie has been taken on at Harper's in the alterations department,' Rachel said. 'It is a steady wage for her and she can still do embroidery for her old customers if she wants. I've advised her to keep in touch with them for the time being.'

'So she will be a Harper's girl, too,' Beth said. 'How do you feel about it, Maggie?'

'Oh, I like her,' Maggie replied and smiled. 'Rachel asked me if I was sure I didn't mind before she offered the share to Minnie. She's rather sweet really, and determined to do well at her new job.'

'It will be a whole new life for her.' Rachel looked at Beth as the cab drew up outside their apartment. 'Do you want to come in, Beth, or take the cab on?'

'I think I'll come in for a while,' Beth said. 'Fred would have gone home by now, I'll take a bus back later.'

The three of them went up to the flat after paying the driver. Beth sensed the changes immediately. Sally's things had gone and it seemed a bit empty without her and that wasn't just because of the furniture she'd taken. The others would notice the difference when she wasn't there – but it might help having Minnie, though she wasn't Sally Ross.

Rachel made coffee and they talked about the wedding. Beth stayed until she knew the shops would be closing and then left her friends, walking swiftly through streets that still thronged with people. She called in to the grocer's and bought a bag of sugar, which she'd suddenly remembered they were short of when at the flat. Once or twice she felt she was being followed and glanced uneasily over her shoulder but couldn't see anything to alarm her. Just as she approached her usual bus stop, she saw one draw away and mumbled a curse beneath her breath.

It was too far to walk home and the heat of the day had gone, leaving a thin wisp of mist in the air that felt as if it might turn to rain. She would either have to wait for the next bus or take a taxi and, as she looked about her, there was no sign of a cab. A shiver went down her spine as once again she felt as if she were being watched and for the first time was nervous. The nearest phone box was halfway down the street and she wasn't sure she knew the name of the taxi firm. As she stood hesitating, feeling the first drops of rain on her cheek, a small car drew up at the roadside and a man looked at her from the open window.

'Beth – would you like a lift?'

She looked and saw Mark smiling at her. He'd been angry the last time they'd met, when she was on holiday with Sally, and she hesitated, but the alternative was to wait in the rain for a bus. Her eyes caught a glimpse of a man in the shadows and she was certain he was staring at her. She walked towards the car and Mark got out and opened the door for her.

'Get in and I'll drive you home,' he said. 'It will save you getting a soaking – and that dress wasn't meant for standing in a bus queue.'

'No, I've been to a wedding,' Beth admitted. 'I stopped to have coffee with friends and I missed my bus. I don't fancy waiting half an hour for the next.'

'No need. I've got a good idea of where you live – it's across the river, isn't it?'

'Yes. We're lucky, because we back on to the river with the garden. Fred's cottage is at the end of a small terrace – St James' Terrace and we're number five...' Having a garden big enough to grow a few vegetables was a luxury in London and it was another reason Beth wasn't keen to move into a room at Jack's present hotel, which did not have a garden for the guests.

'I really just want to say goodbye, because I'm leaving London,' Mark said, surprising her.

'Will you go abroad again?' she asked.

'Yes, I think I might,' he replied. 'I've been offered a place at a German hospital. They want me for a three year residency because I have some experience with psychological problems.'

'Well, good luck, wherever you go.'

'Thank you, Beth. That means something, coming from you.'

They drove in silence for a while. Mark had crossed the bridge and now turned into a maze of streets, finally pulling to a halt in the little cul-de-sac of terraced houses. The smell of the river was pungent after the heat of the day and the cloud ridden sky seemed to trap it so that it seemed worse than usual.

'Thank you – I'm grateful,' Beth said. 'Take care and have a good life.'

'You too – I'm glad you're happy with your husband, Beth. He's a decent bloke.'

'Yes, he is, thank you.'

Beth got out, clutching her things, and ran across the road, letting herself into Fred's kitchen. Her father-in-law was making a pot of tea. He smiled at her and was about to speak when the hall door opened and Jack entered.

'Where the hell have you been?' he demanded furiously. 'We've been worried to death...'

'No, surely not,' Beth said, taken back by the anger in his voice. 'After Sally left on her honeymoon, I went back to Rachel's apartment and then stopped to buy sugar but missed my bus...'

'So who brought you home?' Jack asked and she knew he'd seen her get out of Mark's car.

'Calm down, Jack,' his father said. 'Beth isn't on trial here.'

'I want to know who she was with...' Jack said furiously.

'That was Mark,' she said. 'He pulled up near the bus stop and asked if I wanted a lift. It had just started to rain so I said yes...'

'You should have come straight here in a cab after the wedding.' Jack glared at her. 'Anything might have happened to you and the baby.'

'I'm sorry. It got late suddenly,' she offered, knowing it was a lame excuse. 'Besides, I didn't expect you to be home yet...'

'I took time off because I thought we might go somewhere nice – but it's too late now,' Jack growled.

'Why is it too late?' she asked. 'It's not quite seven.'

'Because I say so,' Jack muttered. 'I may as well go back to work.'

'Don't be daft, lad...' Fred said, but Jack threw him a murderous glance, went out and slammed the door after him.

'Jack...' Beth started towards the door, but Fred touched her arm.

'Let him go, lass. He was in a bad mood when I got home. He won't listen to reason until he's worked it out of him.'

'He's angry because Mark gave me a lift, but I was safe with him,' Beth said. 'It wasn't nice standing there on my own as the light faded because of the storm clouds and I saw someone watching me. I thought it wouldn't matter if Mark gave me a lift – he knows it is over between us. I chose Jack...'

'Of course you did, but something is gnawing at him,' Fred said. 'I think it must be work, but he wouldn't tell me.'

'Yes, perhaps.' Beth sighed. 'It was such a lovely wedding. I wish he'd been there.'

'He should've been,' Fred agreed with her. 'No job is worth denying yourselves the pleasures of life. I know he wants it to be a success, but he could have had the day off if he'd insisted.'

Beth nodded, but she knew Jack worried about his job. There was a lot of responsibility and the owners expected the hotel to make a substantial profit. If things were not going as they ought, Jack would feel responsible.

* * *

Beth was asleep when she heard the noise downstairs. The back of her neck prickled and she reached for Jack, but he wasn't there. She got out of bed, pulled on her thick robe, slipped her feet into her shoes and then went quietly down the stairs. The noises were louder now. It sounded like someone was banging into things.

When she entered the kitchen, Beth saw Jack was lurching about, obviously drunk and unable to walk straight. He knocked into a chair and swore and then slumped down on the old daybed, his eyes closing.

'Jack...' Beth touched his shoulder, but he'd fallen into a deep slumber. She loosened his shoes and eased them off and then covered him with his overcoat that she took from a hook on the back door. There was no possibility of getting him upstairs, so he would just have to sleep it off in the kitchen.

Fred entered as she was about to leave. He frowned as he looked at his son. 'It's years since Jack got drunk,' he said. 'He's a fool, Beth. I hope he wasn't abusive?'

'No, he just lurched about and then collapsed on the daybed. Do you think he will be all right like that?'

'Yes, let him sleep it off. He will be sorry in the morning.'

'I imagine he will have a terrible headache.' Beth smiled at her father-in-law. 'I was going back to bed, but I could make a cup of tea if you fancy one?'

'No, we'll leave him to sleep,' Fred said. 'In the morning he'll apologise, Beth. This isn't like Jack – and I don't think it was all down to you being late back either.'

Beth nodded and went back to her room. It was a while before she settled down, but eventually she slept and was woken in the morning by the curtains being drawn and when she opened her eyes she saw Jack with a tray of tea for her.

He looked awful and any irritation she might have felt over his behaviour vanished. 'I'm sorry, Beth,' Jack said. 'It was stupid of me to be angry last night and getting drunk was a mistake.'

'Have you taken anything to help?'

'Dad made me a raw egg in milk with a swig of whisky – it made me sick but I do feel a bit better.'

'I think it is supposed to line your stomach,' Beth said. 'Poor you.'

'Are you very fed up with me?' He gave her an apologetic smile.

She smiled and patted the bed. He sat and she poured tea for herself and him. 'I'm not fed up with you, Jack. I'm sorry if you were worried – and if you thought there was something going on with Mark.'

'I didn't and I know you wouldn't – but I *was* worried, because of that devil who tried to hurt you before.'

'One of the reasons I let Mark bring me home was because I thought I might have been watched,' she admitted. 'I ought to have come straight home after the wedding, but I should be free to walk where I like.'

'Yes, you should. Perhaps we should have gone to the police when it happened, Beth.'

'Would they have believed us?'

'Probably not.' He sighed, hesitated, and then shrugged in resignation, 'It's no good – I have to tell you. There's a good chance that I'm going to lose my job...'

'Why?' Beth stared at him in dismay. 'You've worked all hours to make that job a success – why would they sack you?'

'It's not my fault. The hotel is failing, Beth. It was long before I took the job. Don told me he hoped a new manager would fix it, but the bank has told him he has to repay some of the loan and I don't think he can.'

'Oh, Jack, all your hopes will be gone if they close. You'll have to start looking for jobs again.'

'There were other jobs I could have taken, but Don offered me a better wage and the freedom to do things as I pleased. I thought I could pick trade up, Beth, and I have – but there is so much wrong with the place. If I had my way I'd install new bathrooms and basins in all the bedrooms and improve the dining area and the reception. I've got rid of some of the staff who were dragging their feet, and we were almost full this past week. I believed it was going well – and then yesterday I got a formal letter from Don to say that unless I could double the profits in the next three months the hotel would close.' He shook his head. 'It's impossible, Beth.'

'I'm sorry.' She leaned forward to kiss him. 'What will you do if it folds, have you thought yet?'

'I'll find work, even if I have to go back to the ships – but I was learning such a lot and I thought it might be a good idea to invest in the hotel. I might have offered to inject some cash, but the debt to the bank is far beyond my savings.'

'Oh, goodness,' Beth said. 'I know you're disappointed, Jack, but it isn't the end of the world. You'll find a job. You could never just give up. Keep looking for a place for us – it might turn out to be a blessing in disguise.'

'Beth, my darling,' Jack said. 'What did I do to deserve you? I was worried about letting you down – and our child. I promised you a home of your own and all I gave you was a bed in my father's home.'

'I'm happy enough,' Beth replied. 'Your father is one of the kindest men I know and he makes me welcome. Don't despair, Jack. It will come right for us.'

'Bless you, my love,' he said and kissed her, or would have done had Beth not had to scramble out of bed and rush to the toilet, where she was violently sick.

She returned to the bedroom feeling a bit dizzy and looked at him apologetically. 'Sorry, Jack. It's the morning sickness. It will go in an hour or so, but I smelled Fred's breakfast and that made me vomit.'

'Poor you,' he said sympathetically. 'Why don't you stay in bed longer this morning? You look as if you could do with a rest.'

'I'll be all right when that smell has gone,' she said ruefully. 'I love fried bacon but not at the moment. A piece of toast and honey is all I can manage in the morning.'

'Shall I make you some?'

'When I come down,' Beth replied. 'Don't you have to go in and check things are all right this morning?' He normally went for an hour or so even though it was his day off, but he shook his head.

'If they can't manage without me for a day they ought,' he said. 'I've given all the staff training and they don't need me all the time. I just wanted to make the place a success.' He smiled at her. 'You should come for tea one day, Beth. I'd like you to see it – because I know with a bit of money invested it could be so much better.'

'Yes, I'm sure,' she said. 'I'm sorry that your dream has gone wrong, Jack.'

'I'll just have to start looking again...'

After Jack had gone, Beth thought for a while, but there was nothing she could do to help Jack get his own place and it would be disappointing for them both if he had to return to the ships.

She sighed as she got up and went downstairs. If they'd found their own hotel and bought it, she would have been settled in modern surroundings and none of these inconveniences would have affected her. Of course, many women lived in homes like Fred's, some much worse than his, which was dry and warm and didn't have bugs crawling out of the walls every time you touched them. Other women brought up their children in slums and would gladly change places with Beth. They worked in factories and the laundry for less than she'd been paid when she started at Harper's and often got knocked around by their husbands. Beth knew she was lucky to have both Jack and Fred. It was just that she'd known better and had hoped her own home would be more like Aunt Helen's house had been.

Jack was tidying the kitchen when she got downstairs. He made her some toast and a fresh pot of tea and told her how much he loved her. Beth smiled. She was lucky to have such a loving family to take care of her and she would just have to make the best of things as they were.

34

Sally stretched and sighed with contentment, watching Ben as he stood in front of the bedroom window doing some stretching exercises. She'd known him long enough to be aware that he did the exercises each morning to keep himself fit. He was a strong, attractive man and her eyes moved over him lovingly and with a feeling of surging happiness. She'd never known she could be as happy as she was now.

Ben turned, saw her watching him, smiled and came towards her, bending to kiss her sweetly on the mouth.

'Sleepyhead,' he chided but with laughter in his eyes. 'I've been up half an hour. I was just thinking of taking a run on the beach.'

Their hotel was not one of the big ones that Hastings-on-Sea boasted but a smaller, country home with comfortable rooms, deep seats on a cosy veranda that overlooked the coast and wonderful soft beds that hugged you in comfort. In pale colours of faded pinks, greens, blues, and a splash of bright orange, the rooms welcomed visitors as much as the charming hosts. Mr and Mrs Stevens ran what they termed a family hotel and half their staff had been with them for years, the others were sons and daughters. The food was prepared by Mrs Stevens with help from her eldest daughter and was always delicious, though simple, local fare with fish included on the menu every day.

Sally and Ben walked each day on the high cliffs overlooking the resort. Many of the beaches consisted of large pebbles and there were long breakers that went out into the sea and caused it to spend itself in white foam that rose high in the air. It was a restless sea and the winds that often swept the coast sometimes made it treacherous so that reckless swimmers could find themselves in trouble at high tide on a windy day.

However, the hotel had a path that led down to a small sheltered and sandy cove where the swimming was safer and there was a patch of golden sand; it was there that Ben had been patiently teaching Sally to swim her first few strokes. She wasn't very good yet but had no fear of the water with him there to hold her and he was confident she would be able to swim in the warmth of the Mediterranean Sea by the time they were able to take holidays abroad.

'If you wait, I'll come with you,' Sally said and jumped out of bed, not caring that she was naked. Any shyness she'd had concerning her body had long gone and she walked about their room without clothes, knowing that he watched and enjoyed what he saw. They were lovers in the true sense of the word, their bodies fitted together as if it had always been meant to be and Sally had discovered pleasure beyond any dreams she'd ever had. Ben was considerate, strong and passionate and she adored him. She knew that no other man could ever have made her feel quite this way and wondered why she was so lucky.

Dressing quickly, Sally took Ben's hand and they went downstairs, sneaking out the back way so as not to be seen by their kind hosts. A swift run would make them both hungry for the massive breakfast they knew would be served in about an hour. Time enough to run on the sandy beach, return to the hotel, have a wash in the warm bathroom, and change into fresh clothes, before going down to the dining room. They'd had breakfast in bed two mornings running, but this time they would be eating downstairs for a change.

Sally felt the cool breeze in the air as they left the cosy warmth of the hotel. It had been warm when they first arrived, but it was nearly the end of September now and you could feel the change, as if autumn was preparing you for the cold of winter with a little taste of what Mother Nature could do.

They ran swiftly down to the beach, laughing like children as Sally tried to keep up with Ben's long legs and failed. She knew he would always beat her and he reached the sea before her, standing to look out at the horizon and breathe in the bracing air. It was more sheltered here in the cove than on the main beaches, but it felt too cold for swimming that day, though Ben had kicked off his sandals and was paddling at the edge, his trousers getting soaked in the process. He beckoned to her to join him, but she shook her head and just watched. He was braver than she was because she knew the water would be very cold today.

'Coward,' he challenged her, but she just laughed and he ran to join her, sweeping her up in his arms and carrying her into the foaming grey water, swinging her back and forth and threatening to drop her. Sally screamed and hung on to him, and then laughed as he took her back to the beach. 'Time for breakfast,' he said and they linked hands and walked back. 'It's wonderful to be alive,' Ben said and his eyes dwelled on her, because she was what made it wonderful and he was telling her so with every breath he took. 'I hope Jenni is as happy when she marries her General...'

'Do you think she will be?' Sally asked and looked at him thoughtfully. 'I know she loves him and she wants to be his wife and little Tom's mother – but is she doing it just because his wife went down with the Titanic?'

'She loves Henry,' Ben said. 'I'm sure she thinks it is what she wants – but I'm not sure she will be happy. He is a man dedicated to his job and he travels all the time. Sometimes, she will be able to go with him, but at others she will have to stay at home. I'm not sure it will be enough for her. She has worked since she was sixteen. I think she may miss the cut and thrust of business.'

'Yes, I wondered about that,' Sally said. 'Do you think he loves her – or does he just want a mother for his son?'

'It's my main fear,' Ben admitted. 'I would hate for her to be unhappy, Sally. She was always loving towards me – the one member of my family I felt was truly on my side.'

'And yet you didn't tell her about Maribel being in the hospital.'

'She would have wanted to help me pay the expenses,' he said. 'I couldn't ask her, Sally – and I didn't want her to worry.'

'Yes, I understand,' Sally replied. She squeezed his hand. 'We can't tell Jenni what to do with her life, Ben, but we can be there for her when she needs us.'

'Yes, just as she would be for us,' Ben said. 'I do worry for her a little, though I know she would tell me not to – but Jenni is strong. She will survive whatever happens.'

Sally felt a chill go over her at that moment and shivered. She looked up at the sky. It had clouded over and the clouds were gathering. There was a sudden change in the weather and she thought there was bound to be rain before long and perhaps a storm. Even as she thought it, thunder rolled and a streak of lightning forked across the sky and over the sea.

'No wonder the surf was rough,' Ben said. 'It looks as if our lovely weather has gone, Sally. We'd better run for it before we get soaked.'

35

Harold called at Fred's cottage that Sunday afternoon.

'Sorry to pop in unannounced,' he said, though he accepted an invitation to stay to tea. 'I had a bit of news for you and so I thought I'd come right over and tell you.'

'Have you discovered Gerald was here in London the day Aunt Helen died?' Beth asked, but he shook his head.

'No, he will have covered his tracks there,' he said. 'Sorry to disappoint you, Beth, but I don't think we'll get him for your aunt's murder – but we might get him for another woman's unlawful death...'

'Good work, Harold,' Fred congratulated him.

'How did you manage that?' Jack asked, looking surprised.

Beth stared at Harold. She wanted Gerald punished for making her aunt unhappy in the last weeks of her life, but she didn't much mind how. 'What do you mean?'

'He has been married three times,' Harold said and looked pleased with himself as she stared in astonishment. 'And his name hasn't always been Greene. He was born Gerald Makepeace and he married a woman called Elizabeth Jenkins ten years ago in Margate. She owned a small bed and breakfast and had a few hundred pounds in the bank that her first husband had left her. She died of what the doctors thought was a heart attack eighteen months after she was married and six months later her husband sold the property and left town.' He paused, looking at them expectantly. 'If she died of a heart attack, how could Gerald be blamed?' Beth asked.

'He couldn't, of course,' Harold said. 'However, her brother returned from a trip to South Africa a few weeks after Gerald had scarpered and smelled a rat. He persuaded the police to dig his sister's body up and, though they couldn't prove poisoning, the examining doctor thought it unlikely she'd died of natural causes. He said her heart was perfect and the inquest returned a verdict of unnatural death...'

'That didn't prove murder,' Fred said, seeing the doubt in Beth's eyes.

'No, but Gerald's second wife died after a mysterious illness only twenty-three months ago,' Harold said, 'and I managed to convince her eldest son that her death may not have been natural. He was suspicious and didn't like the way Gerald sold the house immediately and then left the area. He demanded the police dig up her body – and this time arsenic was found, enough to point to murder. So Gerald Makepeace is now wanted for murder by the police in Bournemouth.'

'But how do you know about those other crimes?' Beth asked.

'I used my police contacts and traced women of about your aunt's age who had recently died, and discovered at least two that were thought unnatural, and there may be others we yet know nothing of.'

Beth took a gasping breath and felt the blood drain from her face. 'Are you sure that he is the same man?' she asked, her pulses racing wildly. She felt a little sick and short of breath. 'Can we prove it?'

'That is the thing,' Harold said. 'I was fairly certain that the two men were the same, but I couldn't prove it – even though I knew it in my guts, but now I can...'

'How?'

'When your aunt married Gerald Greene, a photograph was taken,' Harold said. 'He'd told your aunt he didn't want a photographer and he took a lot of pictures of her and their guests himself with a small box camera – but I found a picture of them both taken by a local paper. You arranged for the wedding to be reported and the enterprising young reporter took a picture of the happy couple. Your uncle obviously didn't see it in the paper.'

'But I did,' Beth said. 'It wasn't very clear of him, because he turned his face away.'

'But the newspaper had two others at their office,' Harold said and now he was triumphant. 'Both caught him full face and they let me have copies – and the son of his second wife, Anne Morton, knew him at once. He took the evidence to his local police and they are liaising with the police here in London to find him. Gerald Makepeace will have a lot of explaining to do when they catch up with him.'

'Oh, that's wonderful!' Beth looked at him in awe. 'So he will be arrested for one murder, even though he has probably killed three women.'

'They are the ones we know about,' Harold said grimly. 'I always found when I was in the force that these men killed again and again; it's as if they think they're invincible. Once they get away with it, they do it over and over, only this time he made a mistake. He married a woman who had a suspicious niece and so he won't get away with it.'

'Thanks to you,' Beth said and smiled at him. 'I'm so grateful. I can't believe you've done all this. I wasn't even sure my suspicions were right.'

'I only did it because you asked,' Harold told her with a smile. 'I've spoken to some colleagues of mine and they will be looking out for him here in London.'

'I think he is still here, I'm almost sure he followed me the other evening when I walked from my friends' apartment, but why? Surely, he would've been better just going away and changing his identity once more.'

'I wondered too, but Mrs Morton's son said he insured her life for five thousand pounds...'

'Aunt Helen said something about an insurance policy once,' Beth gasped and Fred glowered. 'She told me she had made sure he wouldn't get anything more from her – or something to that effect. I didn't take much notice. I was more worried about her than insurance money.'

Fred spluttered with anger, 'That's what the bugger is after, the insurance money. He has to stay around to get his hands on that...'

'But that doesn't explain why someone tried to push Beth in front of traffic,' Jack said, frowning. 'He must have known there was a chance his past would catch up with him.'

'As it happens, I know the answer to that one too,' Harold said. 'Because Mrs Morton's son was suspicious and asked questions after her death, Gerald got clever this time. He got your aunt to take out her own insurance policy on both of them. She insured him for five thousand pounds and herself for the same amount, even though he'd told her he had his own policy.'

'So he thought that would deflect suspicion,' Beth said and frowned.

'Yes, but he was too clever,' Harold said. 'Your aunt made a will and in that will she left the insurance money to you and also any money she had of her own.'

Beth looked at him in disbelief. 'Surely, if my aunt left money to me I would have heard from her solicitor?'

'Yes – and the solicitor says that he wrote to you immediately before your wedding – but, either it got lost in the post, or, somehow Gerald must have intercepted it...'

'It could have been taken from the post at the apartment,' Beth nodded. 'The letters are put in racks downstairs. One of us takes them up at night when we get home – but if someone got into the reception area, they could have taken it, I suppose.'

'It may simply have gone astray,' Harold said. 'It comes down to the same in the end – if you were dead, Gerald would get everything, unless you married, which you did, of course. That is, if he gets away with her murder. If there is no proof that it was anything but an accident, the insurance will pay out and the will says it comes to you – but by law it would probably revert to him if you'd died.'

'Surely not?' Fred frowned. 'If Beth lived long enough to inherit the money, it would surely come to her husband by law.'

'Yes, true enough,' Harold agreed. 'That was the bit that puzzled me. Maybe it was just spite then or anger because he felt you'd cheated him of what should have been his.'

'He did that himself by being too clever,' Jack said. 'Anyway, it hardly matters because we know Helen's death was suspicious and the insurance would surely have refused to pay out.'

'Yes, but perhaps there is something else your aunt had that she hid from her husband.' Harold shrugged. 'I'm not sure why he decided to attack you, Beth – but it was his undoing. It was that act that brought you to me and I have a good record of unravelling these sorts of puzzles.'

Beth nodded and looked sad. 'So my aunt was right – he did marry her for money. When he discovered she didn't own her house and had only a few hundred in the bank, he decided to insure her, but she suspected and arranged for me to be the beneficiary. I suppose that made him angry enough to try and harm me even if he couldn't get that money, and if I hadn't married he might have got it anyway, because he would still have been my closest relative.'

'Who knows what goes on in the mind of a man like that?' Fred muttered.

'I believe the mind of a criminal is centred on himself and nothing else,' Harold said. 'In my years as a police officer, I found that murderers were nearly all cold, calculating and supremely arrogant.'

'Thank you for telling us,' Beth said. 'I understand now and I pray he hangs for his crimes – but I just wish Aunt Helen had never met him. She thought him so kind and generous at the start...'

'He knows how to charm women,' Harold said. 'However, he made a mistake with you, Beth. He should have tried to be your friend rather than setting you against him.'

'I never liked him from the start. He must have felt that even though I tried not to let anyone see it.'

'Well, several police forces are looking for him now and the photographs I have of him will be circulated. Wherever he goes, someone will recognise him – unless he changes his appearance, though he hasn't in the past, just his name.'

'I noticed someone wearing a cap pulled low over his eyes the other night, but I don't know if it was him,' Beth said and shivered at the memory. 'He is still out there watching and waiting for the chance to get me alone.'

'You make sure to wait for Dad when you leave work at night.' Jack scowled. 'I'll be glad when they have the murdering devil under lock and key.'

'We'll all be glad of that,' Harold said. He finished the slice of cake he'd been eating and stood up. 'I'd best get back. I've got someone coming to see me this evening – your case has given me a taste for more of the same and one of my colleagues from the station wants me to help them sort out another mystery.'

Beth went to the door with him herself. He offered his hand, but she kissed his cheek impulsively. 'Thank you for everything you've done for me,' she said. 'I'm so glad we asked for your help.'

'It was an interesting case and I enjoyed pitting my wits against Mr Makepeace. I don't think you need worry too much, Beth. My friends at the Yard will soon have this rogue in their cells.'

'Good.' She smiled and watched him walk away before returning to the warmth of the kitchen, where her husband and father-in-law were talking earnestly. They looked at her as she entered the room.

'Sit by the fire, love,' Jack invited. 'Dad and I were wondering whether you should stay home for a while – just until they've got that devil...'

'No, I won't let him win,' Beth said and lifted her head. 'I shall write to the solicitor. Harold left us the address on the table.' She scooped it up and read: 'Messrs Pickford and sons, lawyers of London. Yes, I'll tell them that we suspect my aunt was unlawfully killed and the insurance money should not be claimed. I do not want blood money.'

'No, certainly not,' Fred agreed. 'That is the right thing to do, Beth. It is a lot of money, but you would feel wrong if you took it.'

'I couldn't.' She shuddered at the very thought. 'That despicable man – when I think how he took three women's lives for money and still hadn't enough...'

'It makes you feel sick,' Jack said. 'I wish she hadn't left it to you. It must be the reason why Gerald attacked you and yet he must have known it would never come to him.'

'Revenge or anger.' Fred shook his head. 'It is a mystery though – because he couldn't have hoped to get it once you were married.'

'There must be something more,' Jack said. 'Surely, a cold-blooded killer like Harold said he was wouldn't let anger cloud his judgement...'

'Please, don't let's talk about him any more,' Beth said. 'When I think of what he's done I want to scratch his eyes out – but I know he is going to hang and that is all that really matters.'

The subject was changed and Beth started to clear the tea things into the scullery. Jack came to help her with the washing-up. She looked at him uncertainly as he took a china plate and started to dry it.

'I'm sorry about the money, Jack. I know it would have meant the world to us, bought you all you need for your own business and set us up for life...'

'You were right when you called it blood money.' He smiled at her. 'I wouldn't expect you to accept it even if they pay out.' He leaned in and kissed her. 'I'm proud of you, my love.'

Beth nodded and sighed. 'It's a pity she did it, she must have known in her heart why he'd asked her to take out the insurances.'

'Perhaps she wasn't thinking straight – just wanted to punish him...' Jack suggested.

Beth made an effort to change the subject. 'So what will you do about your job?' she asked. 'Given that the doctor confirmed I'm pregnant I shan't be able to work for more than a few months longer.'

'I'll hang on and make them fire me,' he said, setting his mouth stubbornly. 'Why should I make it easy for them? I'll take my wages and in the meantime look for something else.'

Beth wiped her hands. 'I think I'll have an early night...'

'I'll come with you,' he said and put his arm about her. 'Don't worry, Beth, we'll manage.'

36

Rachel pulled her scarf a little tighter around her throat. The wind was chilly and she shivered, thinking she would be glad to be home. She'd been to the little corner shop near their apartment, filling her basket to the brim, and it was heavy on her arm. Shifting it from one arm to the next, she sighed, feeling a little down. Her job was enjoyable and she liked living with Maggie and Minnie, though she missed Sally and Beth in the evenings. Maggie went out quite often, with Tim Burrows or to Becky Stockbridge's house, and her first-aid classes, which she'd begun soon after her mother's tragic death, and Minnie often sat at her needlework for hours.

'That looks heavy – may I carry it for you?' Rachel turned her head and saw William Bailey looking at her. 'You've done a lot of shopping...'

'Yes, I have. We were getting low on butter, tea and other essentials. Beth and Sally used to shop regularly. Now it is mostly down to me.'

William reached out and took the basket from her. 'I was hoping I might see you earlier, but you must have left Harper's before I got there. I was visiting in the area and I knew you lived here somewhere...' He offered a hesitant smile. 'Do you think you might like to have lunch with me on Sunday? I am visiting an elderly aunt in Hampstead and I thought she would like to meet you – she so wants me to meet a nice lady and settle down...' Now there was laughter in his eyes. 'Could you possibly bear it? I would call for you at half-past ten...'

Rachel hesitated and then relaxed. Unless she allowed herself to make friends, she could spend the rest of her life regretting it. 'Very well, William,' she said. 'I do hope you won't let me down regarding the Movement again.'

'I promise you I am converted,' he said. 'I've decided to take up another cause – one that I believe you will approve of. I want better working conditions for the miners of Britain.'

'Now that is a cause I heartily agree with,' Rachel said. 'I believe the conditions they are forced to endure are terrible... Perhaps you would like to share supper with Minnie and I this evening? We are having soup and sandwiches, plain food, I fear – but I promise you it will be good.'

'I would enjoy anything in your company,' he promised and smiled. 'Thank you – I shall be happy to help prepare it if I am able.'

'Oh no, I don't think we'll make you work for your supper,' Rachel said, 'but you can tell us more about this project of yours over supper if you wish.'

Rachel smiled. Having another friend would help to ease the emptiness left by Sally and Beth. She knew they were both happy and wished them well, but she did miss them.

* * *

Beth received a letter two days after she'd sent hers to the solicitor. They thanked her for her honesty and said they would refer the matter to the insurance company. However, her aunt had also left her another small bequest.

Your aunt's late father – your grandfather – invested in a goldmine in South Africa some twenty or thirty years ago. However, his shares were deemed worthless when the mine was thought to have run out. When your aunt inherited them, she was advised they were worth nothing, but quite recently another valuable mineral, palladium, was discovered in the mine. It is not sure how extensive the seam is, but we have been made an offer for your grandfather's shares. That offer is for the sum of two thousand pounds. We are taking advice on this and at the moment we would advise you to wait. It is possible that we might raise at least twice that sum at a later date. Perhaps you would like to come in and discuss the possibility of a sale in the future.

Beth had opened the letter while sitting on the bus to work. Fred was beside her and she clutched his arm, handing it to him. He read it and then stared at her in surprise and dawning pleasure.

'That's a wonderful surprise for you, Beth – your grandfather's shares are worth a lot of money.'

'I can't believe it,' Beth shook her head. 'I'm sure my mother had some of the shares, I have them with her personal things, because her belongings came to me. She said her father divided them between his daughters and told them to keep them safe because the mine might open again one day.'

'If they are the same shares you might get twice as much...' Fred stared at her. 'You'll be rich, Beth.'

'It will be for us.' She smiled at him. 'Jack will invest whatever we get and it means he can buy his own place.'

'I'm so happy for you,' Fred told her. 'Be sure what you want before you tell him he can have it, Beth. You might want to save some for yourself and the baby.'

'A few pounds perhaps,' she agreed. 'I'll miss my wages when I leave work – but most will go into Jack's business.' The smile left her eyes. 'I wonder if Aunt Helen knew they were worth money. Mum thought they were worthless – just another one of Grandfather's reckless schemes. He had a good business, was a rich man – until he lost it all...'

'They say a fool and his money is soon parted,' Fred said, nodding sadly. 'That's another reason you should keep a bit of the money back, Beth. Look after this windfall, it won't come again.'

'It's such a lot of money – even the two thousand...' Beth frowned. 'I wonder if Gerald knew about the shares. He would think they should belong by right to him, no wonder he is angry. He lost the insurance money and now the shares.'

'We must hope the law deals with him appropriately,' Fred said. 'Don't let your aunt's misfortune spoil your pleasure, Beth. These shares belonged to your grandfather and in the circumstances he would want you to have them.'

'Oh, I shan't refuse them,' Beth said and smiled. 'I couldn't take the insurance money knowing Aunt Helen had been murdered – but the shares are different. It will make so much difference to our lives.'

Fred looked at her thoughtfully. 'Will you still work until the baby is almost due? I know it was in your mind – but now there's no need...'

'I love my job now I've been promoted,' Beth said and sighed, because she knew he was right, but she wanted to stay at Harper's. 'Let's wait and see what happens. Until we actually get the money, I shan't be sure.'

'Your lawyers know what they're doing,' Fred said and tapped her arm. 'Time to get off now, Beth. In all the excitement we nearly missed our stop. You'll have to talk to Jack this evening – hear what he has to say about it.'

'Yes.' Beth frowned. 'It's my half day today, Fred, I think I'll take a cab home when I leave work. I might try ringing Jack from the telephone box at the end of the road. He will be so excited.' She smiled at him in sudden excitement. 'He was upset over his job – but now it doesn't matter.'

'No, it doesn't.' Fred took her arm and steered her safely into the store. 'I'll see you this evening, love.'

Beth nodded as they parted, he departing to the basement where he was in charge of the stores and she to the first floor. Her news was burning inside her, but she had made up her mind that she would not tell any of her friends until Jack had been told.

It was difficult to calm herself down and see to the customers. Beth's mind kept wandering and she had to pull herself up sharply, because she needed her wits about her when dealing with the expensive bags and silver jewellery. She sold just one leather bag and two bracelets that morning and when the time came for her to leave, she handed over to Rachel, who would stand in and keep an eye on the department for the afternoon.

Outside, Beth was fortunate enough to see an empty cab and hailed it immediately. She'd always felt in the past that it was an extravagance because it cost twice as much as her bus fare, but today she relaxed. Fred couldn't take her home and she was safer with the cabbie, who chatted to her in a friendly way, commenting first on the Zeppelin L2 exploding with the loss of the twenty-eight passengers on board, and then on the way the authorities had tried to deport Emmeline Pankhurst from America.

'I reckon it was despicable the way they treated the lady,' he said. 'She's only standing up for her rights – that's what my missus says.'

'Your wife is right,' Beth replied.

She gave him a threepenny-bit tip when he dropped her by the telephone kiosk at the end of the lane. The box had only been put there a few months earlier and Beth was a bit nervous when she entered it and followed the instructions to press the button and insert her money when the pips went.

'This is the Hotel Maddison reception...' a girl's voice answered.

'May I speak to Jack Burrows please?'

'Mr Burrows is engaged at the moment, madam, may I take a message?'

'Please tell him that his wife rang with important news – if he could possibly get away early tonight I should be grateful...'

'Very well, madam.' The phone went dead with such alacrity that Beth stared at it in surprise. How very odd! The girl had been barely polite. If that was the way she normally spoke to clients then she was no asset to the hotel.

Beth walked the few yards to her home and let herself into the kitchen. She hung her coat up and put her bag on the kitchen table. First of all, she made up the fire and put the kettle on to boil. Then she went into the scullery and took the sheets she'd changed that morning, transferring them from the sink where they'd been soaking to the washtub. There was warm water in the copper and she poured that on top of the sheets in the tin bath, adding soap flakes and giving it a stir with the poss stick. The wooden stick was the best way of moving washing in hot water and she gave the tub a thorough stirring and then left the sheets to soak again. By the time she returned to the main kitchen, the kettle had boiled and Beth made a pot of tea.

As she drank, Beth read the letter through again, still too shocked by its contents to truly take in the difference it would make to their lives. She had never expected to have so much money, though she knew her grandfather had once been wealthy. He'd left a little money in trust for his daughters, a few pieces of his late wife's jewellery and the shares, which none of them had thought worth a penny. Of course, they hadn't been until recently, but if her solicitor was correct they were worth a great deal now.

Her drink finished, Beth ran upstairs and got out her mother's writing slope. She'd put it under the bed for safety's sake because it contained personal papers, a few pieces of jewellery that she didn't choose to wear and those shares. Studying them, Beth still wasn't sure whether or not they were the same – but it didn't matter, the solicitors would find out for her. She ought to write and let them know she would come to see them next week on her half day.

Penning her letter, Beth signed it, wrote on the envelope and placed the relevant postage stamp on it. She decided she would take it down to the box before she finished her washing. Slipping on her jacket, she ran down to the post box in the lane and back home, waving to her next-door neighbour, who called a cheery greeting as he got on with weeding his garden.

Beth went back inside and rinsed and mangled her washing until the water ran clear and then put the sheets into a basket made of rushes to carry it into the back garden. She hung the sheets on the line, looking anxiously up at the sky. It was overcast but the wind was blowing, so it was better than having to dry them inside. As she went into the kitchen again, she stretched to ease her aching back. All that mangling was hard work, but as she tried to straighten up, an arm went around her throat and she gave a stran-gled cry as a voice hissed at her ear.

'Bitch.' Gerald's voice sounded low and harsh as it rasped. 'You thought you could get away with spoiling my plans, but no one gets the better of me.'

Beth kicked back violently, catching him on the shins. He gave a cry of pain and swore, grabbing at her again. Beth ducked out of his way and tried to reach the door, but he was there before her, blocking her way with his arm. He leered at her, eyes filled with a wild triumph as she saw her doom in his face.

'You won't get the money if you kill me,' she said desperately. 'I've made my will and everything will go to Jack.'

'I don't care about the money,' Gerald sneered. 'I'll make some other woman pay for what you've stolen for me – but you'll pay for setting the law on me before I've finished with you.' He lunged at her again, grabbing her by the waist and wrestling her, trying to bring her down.

Beth guessed what he meant to do and screamed for all she was worth. He pushed her back and she felt the warmth of the range, uncomfortable at her back. She reached behind herself and grabbed the kettle she'd used earlier to make tea, bringing her arm back swiftly and hitting him in the face. He staggered back, swearing loudly because the remains of the boiling water went into his eyes, and made an angry lunge at her. Beth screamed again in terror, managed to avoid him and yanked open the back door, shouting out for help at the top of her voice. If her neighbour was still in his garden perhaps he would hear...

Gerald swore and moved towards her purposefully. His face looked red and sore where the water had struck him, but he'd recovered enough to grab her from behind before she could escape and his arm was around her throat again, cutting off her cries for help. The last scream died in her throat as he flung her down on the floor and then stood over her, leering at her as he fumbled with his trouser buttons.

'No!' Beth screamed again and again, scrabbling to get up and bucking in an effort to throw him off, but he was on her, his weight pinning her to the ground, and his intent was plain, to humiliate her and rape her, inflicting as much pain as possible.

Beth bit his hand, wriggled and kicked as she tried to throw him off but his hands were clawing at her skirts and her strength was almost spent. She knew he would have his way, for there was nothing she could do to stop him, but then she heard voices, figures barged through the back door and she was vaguely aware that someone pulled the heavy weight off her. She heard shouts and yells and a groan of pain just before she passed out.

When she opened her eyes a short time later, Jack was bending over her anxiously and her neighbour was standing there, pitchfork in hand, glaring down at her attacker. Gerald was on his knees, head bowed and another man was behind him, clicking on what looked like handcuffs. He glanced at her, nodded and went off to report to the police, leaving Fred's neighbour, Bob, on guard with his fork.

'Jack...' Beth tried to rise but felt dizzy and fell back against the cushions of the old daybed. Someone must have lifted her on to it after she fainted. 'How— when did you get here?'

'I came as soon as Phyllis at the hotel gave me the message,' Jack said. 'Bob heard you scream and was on his way to see what was wrong when I arrived. We dealt with the bugger, and Harold's man, who had been patrolling the street, was here seconds after. Gerald had got past him somehow, probably across the gardens from the river, and he's gone to summon the police now.'

Beth felt sick but struggled to hold it in. She managed to push herself up against the cushions so that she was sitting and looked at him. 'I'm so glad you came,' she whispered. Her throat was sore where Gerald had pressed his arm against it. 'When I rang earlier, I had some good news – but then he sneaked up behind me. He must have got into the house when I went to hang out the washing.' Beth took a shaky breath, her limbs quivering. She'd sensed someone watching her earlier when she went to the post box at the end of the lane, but Gerald must have crossed the neighbouring gardens to avoid him. She threw a look of shuddering disgust at her aunt's widower.

At that moment, the man who had left earlier entered the kitchen with a sturdy young police officer following in his wake.

'Now then, what's all this,' the constable said and looked from Gerald on his knees, still breathless and subdued, to Beth. 'Are you all right, ma'am?'

'My wife was set on by this man,' Jack said furiously. 'He is a murderer, officer, and your people are looking for him...'

'Perhaps you would tell me what happened, ma'am?'

Beth nodded, taking a deep breath as she controlled the trembling. 'This man attacked me from behind and I believe he intended to rape me. I tried to fight him off, but then my husband came.' She took a shaky breath. 'He calls himself Gerald Greene, but it is not his name. We have proof that he has killed at least once and perhaps three times or more. He was going to punish me for setting the law on him...' Beth was shaking, trembling all over despite her attempts to stop. 'If Jack and Bob hadn't come when they did...'

'Well, we did and now he's the one that will pay,' Jack said, looking grim as the police constable read Gerald his rights and took a firm hold of his arm. The officer turned to Jack with a grin.

'My old boss, Chief Superintendent Brooks, will be pleased with me – and so will my current boss. I reckon I'll get a commendation for this.'

'Thank you,' Beth said. 'Thank you all for helping me...'

The officer pushed Gerald in front of him, brandishing his truncheon. 'Just try to get away from me, laddo. Just you try...' He looked as if he relished the idea of hitting him hard.

Gerald had a bruise on his face, several cuts to his mouth and cheek and his hand was bleeding. Someone had tied a handkerchief round it. He also limped and winced as he walked. He didn't look capable of making a break for it, but Bob told the police officer that he would go with him to the station and Harold's man went too, to give his account of events.

Bob brandished the pitchfork at Gerald and grinned, pleased with himself. 'I sharpened it this morning,' he said. 'Care to test it?'

Gerald looked at them sullenly but didn't answer. Then, at the door, he turned his head and spat in Beth's direction. 'Witch,' he muttered. 'I shan't forget...'

'You can think about it while you wait for the hangman,' Jack said and shut the door behind them. He looked at Beth. 'I'm so sorry, love. I didn't get your message for half an hour...'

'You came sooner than I expected. I asked you to come home early, not right away – and I didn't expect Gerald to be watching me here. I had some good news I wanted to share, Jack... but I'm so glad you were here...' She gave a strangled cry and the tears slipped down her cheeks now they were alone. 'I never even thought of locking the kitchen door while I hung the washing out...'

'You shouldn't have to,' Jack said bitterly. 'You should be safe in your own home. Sit down and I'll get you a drop of brandy for the shock.'

'I'd rather have a cup of cocoa,' Beth said and he nodded.

'Whatever you want, love.' He looked pale and angry. 'When I think of what that bastard might have done to you...'

'He didn't,' Beth said, 'because you came and so did Bob and Harold's man – I didn't know he had someone patrolling outside...'

'Harold told me he would just for a few days until they caught Gerald – but his man didn't help much.'

'How did Gerald know to come here?' Beth shook her head.

'He probably followed you home at some time.' Jack poured milk and water into a little saucepan and set it on the range. He fetched two mugs and spooned cocoa powder into them and then took the warmed milk and made their drinks. 'You are all right – he didn't hurt you?'

'A bit,' she admitted. 'I'll have bruises, but never mind that, let me tell you my good news, Jack.' Beth fought down her shudders determinedly. She wasn't going to let Gerald get to her. Making an effort, she got up and went to the table, taking the letter from the solicitor and placing it on the table. 'Read that – and I have some shares in Mum's box that may be the same...'

Jack read the letter and stared at her in stunned silence. 'Two thousand is a huge sum, Beth – and they may be worth more.'

'Perhaps twice as much if my shares are the same...'

'What will you do with it?' he asked, still seeming stunned by the news.

'What we dreamed of,' she said. 'With your savings, we can get the property you've always wanted, Jack. Our own hotel...'

'It's your money – are you certain it's what you want? Hotels are not always easy, Beth. We'll make money, but you might make more by reinvesting into more shares.'

'That's how my grandfather lost the fortune he inherited,' Beth said. 'No, we'll put it into a business we know will bring in a living. I don't want riches. I want security and a life we can share.'

Jack looked at her a few moments longer and then he smiled. 'We'll invest the money well, Beth. As you said, we want a good living – a good way to live. A family hotel, and I'll make it work, I promise you.'

'I know you will,' she said and smiled at him. 'It's what you deserve, Jack – it's what we both deserve.'

'It's a reward for your honesty,' he said and laughed. 'Well, I never – I can hardly believe it. I could never have bought something as good as we'll get now. I'll come with you when you visit your lawyer, Beth, and we'll get him to act for us – squeeze as much as he can from whoever wants the shares and then we'll know what to do next.'

'Yes, that's what I thought,' Beth said and he put his arms about her. 'It's wonderful, Jack. I feel so lucky.'

'Not half as much as I do,' Jack told her. 'Drink that cocoa up,

Beth. I'm not going to leave you today. You've had a nasty shock and I intend to stay with you until you feel better.'

* * *

Beth allowed Jack to look after her, making her sit still and tending the fire so she was warm and comfortable. He even went to bring in the sheets from the garden and when Fred got home, Jack went off to fetch their supper from the pie shop. Neither of them would allow her to do a thing. Beth tried to persuade them she was all right to carry on as usual, but neither would listen and later that night when the cramping pain woke her she knew they had been right. Beth clawed out of bed, clutching at her middle and bending double as the dragging pain grabbed at her insides. She felt the wetness on her thighs and looked down, seeing the blood on her nightgown just as Jack woke and saw her in agony. He was out of bed in an instant. Beth looked at him with tears in her eyes.

'You'd best get the doctor,' she whispered. 'I think I'm losing our baby...'

'The bastard...' Jack muttered and for a moment his eyes were wild. Had Gerald been there that moment she knew Jack would have killed the man who had attacked her.

Jack went from the room as Beth whimpered in pain. She heard him wake his father and a short argument. Jack came back to their bedroom.

'Dad went for the doctor. He told me to stay with you. Can you lie down, love?'

Beth shook her head. She felt the pain was enough to tear her apart. 'Go down and put the kettle on,' she begged him, wanting now to be alone.

Because there was no upstairs toilet, they had a commode in an alcove off their room and Beth went and sat on it. She felt the urge to push and it was like trying to pass waste elements when constipated and then, suddenly she felt something come away from her and she knew it was Jack's child and her heart broke. He would never forgive her for losing their baby...

Looking down at the mangled mess of blood and flesh, which would have been a baby in another seven months, Beth staggered back to the bed and collapsed onto it, closing her eyes. She was crying now, tears trickling down her cheeks. When Jack returned with tea, she couldn't look at him or speak, the tears telling their own story. She felt ashamed and miserable. It was her fault. She hadn't wanted to be pregnant yet and now she wasn't – what should have been their baby was just a mess of blood in a chamber pot.

'What's wrong, Beth?' Jack asked, desperate to help. She managed to point towards the commode and heard his gasp as he found the evidence of her guilt. 'Oh, Beth love, I'm so sorry – that wicked devil is to blame for this.'

'I lost our baby...' she managed to get the words out. 'My fault...'

'Never,' Jack said loyally. 'It was him – what he did to you. The doctor is coming, Beth, he will tell you the same. It wasn't anything you did.'

They could all say the same thing, but Beth knew. She hadn't wanted a baby yet. She'd felt it too soon, preferring to have more life with her husband before she was tied to the home with children. It was her fault it had died and she would never forgive herself.

37

Sally took the telephone call in her office. She'd only just got in and Jack's news shocked her, making her feel both angry and upset.

'Give Beth my love and tell her she must stay at home until she's feeling better,' she said. 'I'm so sorry, Jack. Is there anything I can do – or Ben? I know he would want to help if he could...'

'No, the police have Gerald under lock and key and they won't let him out of their sight. The evidence is piling up against him and it looks as if he might have duped several women out of their savings, some of whom are still alive to give evidence. His photograph has been circulated to other forces and he's been recognised as an offender.'

'If only he'd been caught sooner...' Sally said and Jack made a guttural sound in his throat. 'I'll come and see Beth in a couple of days, when she feels a little better.'

'Thank you. I'm sure she would like that,' Jack replied. 'I've taken a couple of days off, though Beth says she's all right...'

'She isn't though,' Sally said. 'How could she be?'

Jack muttered something and rang off.

Sally sat staring at the wall for a few moments and then opened the silver compact Ben had given her as a wedding gift, peering at her reflection to tidy her hair, which she'd grown a little longer because her husband loved her hair. Satisfied that no tears streaked her face, she went downstairs to the hat department. Sally needed to tell Beth's friends what had happened. Rachel and Maggie would want to know that she was all right – although she wasn't all right. How could she be when she'd just been savagely attacked and suffered a miscarriage? Jack hadn't said much about that, but in Sally's mind that was the most painful bit of it. Beth had been saved from the worst of her uncle's attempt to harm her, but in losing the baby she had suffered far more. It must have upset her terribly.

Sally decided to visit the florist in her lunch break and send her friend some flowers. She was busy most of that day, but would make time to see Beth the following morning, because she knew Beth would be holding the hurt inside her, letting it fester.

Rachel and Maggie were both upset and asked Sally to accept a contribution to the purchase of flowers for Beth. They both spoke of visiting her later in the week. Sally spent a few minutes talking to them and then set out for her appointment in Hatton Garden. The jewellery department at Harper's was doing very well and she wondered if they ought to expand it. Janice Browning had been brought up to stand in for Beth and she wasn't truly up to handling both the bags and the jewellery in Sally's opinion. Jenni had never expected the silver bangles and pendants she'd purchased to sell as well as they had and it might be time to reorganise the hat department. It would be difficult if Beth was away for some time. Either they needed another counter or the bags should go down to the ground floor and be displayed with the suitcases and other leather goods. She would have to ask Mr Stockbridge what he thought and speak to Ben, because it was a big decision.

It had been Ben's idea to offer Rachel the position of floor walker when Miss Hart was forced to retire because of ill health, but it had left the department vulnerable. Maggie did well on her counter but wasn't ready to take charge, nor was Janice, in Sally's opinion, which left them in some difficulty. Perhaps they should look for an older woman again, someone who wouldn't leave to have a family.

Not for the first time, Sally regretted Miss Hart's departure. The floor walker hadn't always got on with other members of staff but she'd been an excellent employee and Ben's business needed good people. Perhaps Sally should just take Beth's place for a few days if necessary...

She was on the path outside the store hailing a taxi when a car drew up beside her and she turned her head to see Mick grinning at her. 'Can I give you a lift anywhere, Sally?' he asked.

'That's kind of you,' she said and smiled. 'But I've hailed a cab – he's coming over now. Thank you for offering, though.'

She moved towards the cab and opened the door, giving the address in Hatton Garden that she wanted. Sally had seen the disappointment in Mick's eyes, but she didn't look back. Ben would be annoyed if she accepted a lift with the Irishman. Her husband was still jealous, even though he knew he need not be. Ben had asked Sally if she wanted to invite Mick to their wedding and she'd sent him an invitation; he'd been at the church but not the reception.

Sally hadn't expected him to attend and she didn't want to travel some distance with Mick in his car, perhaps because she felt a little guilty. Mick had been good to her when she'd been feeling lonely and let down, and she'd allowed him to take her out a few times. He might feel he had the right to be aggrieved because she'd married Ben and she didn't want to risk an argument so had avoided him, though she felt a bit of a coward for it. Mick was a friend but he'd wanted to be more and Sally should have made sure he knew it wasn't going to happen. Perhaps she hadn't been fair to him.

* * *

'That's rotten luck for them both,' Ben said that evening after they'd settled down in their apartment with a glass of wine and she told him about Beth's loss. 'I'm really sorry for your friend, Sally, and if you want to take on a replacement, to give her time to get over her loss, I think that's the best thing in the circumstances.'

'I'm sure she will want to return to work,' Sally said. 'We promoted Rachel and that has left my old department a little bit short of experienced staff. Janice Browning is fine as a salesgirl, but I don't think she is ready to run the department. The jewellery is expensive and needs to be properly overlooked and a strict check kept on the stock or it could easily get misplaced.'

'Speak to Stockbridge,' Ben said and smiled at her. 'I think you could run this place without me...'

She looked at him oddly. 'You don't really believe that, Ben? I wouldn't want you to think I was trying to take over...'

Ben burst into laughter. 'Don't look like that, my love. I always knew you were capable and I'm proud of what you've done at Harper's.'

Sally hugged him, feeling ridiculously like weeping. Perhaps it was Beth losing her baby, but Ben's words had made her feel emotional.

'Shall we go out this evening?' he asked. 'Or shall we cook something together?'

'Let's cook,' Sally said and jumped up, pulling him to his feet. 'We have some nice chops and they won't take long – and I'll do some creamed potatoes and beans to go with them.'

'I'll make us a nice salad for starters,' he promised and followed her into the kitchen, putting his arms about her waist to nuzzle her neck as she started to prepare the vegetables.

Sally turned and kissed him. 'I love you so much,' she said. 'I'm the luckiest girl in the world. I'll find someone to stand in for Beth for a few days, because I don't want to make things worse by putting someone in over her head – but I shall ask Mr Stockbridge to look out for another senior assistant.'

'Whatever suits you,' Ben said and smiled as he started to prepare a fresh salad. 'But your friend may not wish to return.'

* * *

Beth told Jack he should return to work the following day. 'I'll be all right now,' she said, though her heart was aching. 'You need to keep things right, because it will be a while before we can get our own place, Jack. Even if the lawyer manages to sell all the shares, it will take time to find what you want.'

'Yes, I know...' Jack looked at her intently. 'Are you sure you're all right, Beth, love?'

Beth took a deep breath and then forced a smile. 'Yes, I'm fine,' she lied. 'Truly, Jack, I'm not frightened to be here – besides, I think I shall go back to work tomorrow...'

'The doctor said you should rest for at least a week,' he reminded her. 'What happened – it must have pulled you down at the very least. You should take a few days to rest and get your strength back.'

'I'll give it one more day,' Beth said, 'but I'm needed in the department – and I would rather be there than here.'

Jack looked at her again and then sighed. 'If it's what you really want, love, I shan't stop you – you know that...'

'Yes, I know,' Beth said and smiled at him. This time the smile was genuine and he kissed her. 'I love you, Jack, but I need to be alone for a while – and then I'll go back to work. If you fuss over me I'll just keep thinking about it...' She shook her head because the tears sprang to her eyes.

'I've told you, Beth. Losing the baby wasn't your fault. I should have had the doctor to you immediately.'

'He said it wouldn't have helped.'

'He told me it might have happened even if Gerald hadn't attacked you, sometimes the child doesn't form quite as it should...' Jack's eyes darkened. 'It may have been for the best, Beth... and we'll have others one day.'

'Yes, perhaps,' Beth agreed and then, as she saw his expression, 'it's just too soon to think about it yet.'

'I was just trying to cheer you up, love.'

'I know...' She sighed. 'I'll be all right – I'm just so sorry...'

Jack nodded and ran his fingers through his hair. She knew he wasn't sure what to say and it was his uncertainty that made her feel she would rather be alone for a while.

'You go on,' she urged. 'I promise I'll be fine. I've got some ironing to do and then I'll sit down and rest, I promise.'

'All right,' Jack agreed and kissed her cheek. 'I'll go for a couple of hours but I'll be back early.'

After Jack had gone, Beth kept busy doing little jobs that were not strenuous. She'd been told to rest, but resting only made her dwell on her loss and her guilt. Jack was being so good to her, trying to make her feel better, but she knew he was upset. He'd been so proud to think he would be a father and now... Beth swallowed a sob. The doctor had told her that after what had happened it might be some time before she became pregnant again, and, remembering that she had been an only child, Beth wondered if she'd lost her only chance to be a mother.

She had just sat down with some sewing when someone knocked at the front door. She went to answer it, taking a deep breath to steady herself. No one was going to hurt her now that Gerald was in a police cell. When she saw Sally standing there with a huge bunch of roses and carnations, she gave a cry of pleasure and hugged her, almost crushing the delicate blooms between them.

'Come in,' she said and there were tears on her cheeks. 'I couldn't think who was at the front door, everyone uses the kitchen entrance.'

'It's the first time I've been here,' Sally said. 'I'll remember next time.'

Beth smiled and shook her head as she led the way into the comfortable kitchen, which smelled of clean washing and baking. 'It doesn't matter which door you use, Sally. It's just so good to see you.'

Sally smiled at her. 'Rachel and Maggie send their love. Maggie wants to come and see you but wasn't sure if you were ready for visitors. You've had a nasty shock.'

'Yes,' Beth admitted. 'Jack and his father are being kind and fussing and somehow that makes it worse. I'll be glad to get back to work. I think I shall come in tomorrow.'

'Are you sure you're up to it, love? We'll be glad to have you back. Janice isn't quite ready to head the department and Maggie isn't either. Both do well at selling, but as you know, being supervisor takes more.'

'I was enjoying it,' Beth told her, 'but you may need to look for someone to take over, Sally. I've had some good news as well as bad.' She outlined her good fortune regarding the shares. 'So Grandfather's investment is coming into its own at last, which means Jack will be able to start his own business sooner rather than later. He was worried he might lose his job, but now he will take what time is left to him to look round for something that suits us both. I'll probably work in reception and hope to oversee things – though I might do a bit of cooking, but that depends whether we find a brilliant chef.'

'So we shall lose you at Harper's in a few months?' Sally frowned.

'It won't be before Christmas,' Beth said, knowing that the countdown to what was normally the busiest period of the year had started. 'I'll be there to look after things into the spring. Jack has a contract to fulfil and unless he's sacked he can't just walk out – so we think it will be next August before we can open our own hotel.'

Sally nodded and thanked her for making it clear. 'Now that you've told me we can plan for the future, Beth. Do you think you could train Maggie to take over from you?'

Beth considered for a moment. 'I don't see why not – but if you don't mind my saying, an older woman might be better in the senior job. We all looked up to Rachel and an older woman is less likely to become pregnant or leave to get married.'

'Yes, that is true,' Sally agreed. 'Well, I have about ten months or so to solve the problem. I like to promote other women, but it isn't always easy. We haven't had any changes of senior staff elsewhere and that's because men are in charge of all the other departments, other than the fashions, and Mrs Chambers is a widow who will be there until she's forced to stop.' She laughed. 'Yes, you've convinced me, Beth. I wasn't sure what to do – and I didn't want to upset you.'

'I wouldn't mind if you found someone to take over,' Beth assured her. 'I know you have to think of Harper's and... I may have another child...' She drew a ragged breath, making Sally look at her sharply.

'Did the doctor say you might not?'

'He said that it might be a while before I became pregnant again...'

'That isn't the same as saying you won't,' Sally's eyes were on her face. 'Is that why you're blaming yourself – because you think you might not have another chance?'

Beth nodded, her face working with suppressed emotion. 'My

mother only had one child and my father was an only child… I feel it was my fault, Sally – because I wasn't ready to have a baby. I didn't want to give up my job so soon and stay here alone looking after the house and a child…'

Sally looked thoughtful. 'Yes, I can see why you might feel that way, love, but it isn't why you had a miscarriage. The baby might not have been just as it ought – and being attacked so brutally was the cause of it happening.' She reached forward and took both of Beth's hands. 'You're not to blame, Beth, and you will have another child. I promise it will happen.'

Beth gave a shaky laugh. 'You always make me feel better. I believe you, Sally, even though I know you are just saying it to make me feel better.'

'No, I'm not,' Sally said. 'I've never said this to you or anyone before, Beth – but there are times when I feel things will happen and they do. It's a bit worrying sometimes, especially if it is a bad feeling…' She gave a little shiver and then shook her head. 'I know you will have a child to love, perhaps more than one and so shall I, and we'll always be best friends. Even if you leave Harper's, you will always be one of the first Harper's girls. That makes you special to me.'

'Oh, Sally…' Beth was suddenly crying, but the tears were a release of the grief she'd stored inside her, not just for her lost baby, but her aunt's murder and, even before that, the unhappiness of her mother's long illness and the heartache that had brought. It was as if a dam had burst and suddenly her feelings were no longer numbed. 'I do love you, Sally. You're special too – the sister I never had.' She smiled. 'I feel so much better now – and yes, we'll always be friends and keep in touch, even when Jack finds his hotel and I leave Harper's.'

'Good,' Sally said, 'and now, do you think we could have a cup of tea and a slice of that delicious cake I can see under that glass dome?'

'Yes, you can have as many slices as you like,' Beth said and got up to slide the kettle on to the range. 'Now, please, tell me about all the plans you've made for Christmas at Harper's this year.'

38

'More than four hundred men were trapped underground by an explosion,' Rachel told Beth as they talked over a cup of tea in their lunch break some days later. 'I think I told you that William had taken up the miners' cause, didn't I?'

'I saw the headlines this morning as I travelled in on the bus,' Beth said. 'It said the pit was on fire, but I haven't had time to buy a paper. We've been busy all morning.'

'The pit is in the Aber Valley in Wales and they could hear the explosion in Cardiff, eleven miles away. The shaft entrance was shattered and the works were mangled. It must have been terrifying for those underground and their families...'

'Yes, terrible,' Beth agreed and shuddered. 'Those miners have a hard life.'

'Yes, they do. I understand that many miners have been lifted to safety, but those still trapped – well, there isn't much hope, if any.'

The two friends looked at each other in shared sorrow. 'It makes you realise how lucky we are,' Beth said and held her hand.

Rachel sighed. 'William came to tell me, he has decided to go down there and do what he can for the families. There's nothing he can do for those poor trapped men – but he can start a fund for the widows and children, and he will lobby the government to do something. He's been selected for a seat and at the next election he will be standing for Parliament, but his cause will be the plight of the miners – and it is something I can share with him, Beth.' Her grip tightened on Beth's hand. 'You've had your own tragedy. I haven't spoken of it, because I know how it feels to lose a child that way.'

'Oh, Rachel, yes, I believe you told me. I'm so sorry.'

'I don't often mention it – it was a long time ago.'

'Yes.' Beth smiled and touched her hand. 'I'm glad you've made friends with William, Rachel. It is always good to have friends...'

'Oh yes,' Rachel agreed and smiled. 'William is a friend. We may become more in time, his aunt wants him to marry me – she is an absolute dear and invited me to lunch with her on my own. She told me she longs for William to marry again and it seems she approves of me.'

'Shall you marry again?'

'Perhaps; I thought once I would not – but now...' Rachel nodded. 'Yes, perhaps I might.'

Beth glanced at the wall clock. 'I must get back to the department.'

'And I to my rounds.' Rachel nodded as they both stood. 'We have to set an example to the younger staff, Beth – and especially as Harper's grows. I'm wondering how long it will be before Mr Harper starts looking round for bigger premises...'

* * *

The weeks since Beth's miscarriage had gone quickly and it was almost Christmas. At Harper's, Christmas was something special, Beth observed as she let her eyes travel round the ground floor. Mr

Marco's incredible windows with their pantomime themes were pulling in the crowds, who stood staring at his magical scenes for ages despite the cold. As well as a Christmas tree and various lanterns, sparkling decorations and baubles, a part of the ground floor had been converted into Santa's grotto for the children. Ben Harper had purchased toys, sweets, puzzles, picture books and games and he and Sally had sat for hours wrapping them in paper and tying them with ribbons. Father Christmas was sitting on his sledge with a large sack by his side and a life size model of a reindeer was standing by the sleigh. A small queue of children had been brought in by their mothers and nannies to see him and looked excited, their faces scrubbed and shining clean.

Beth liked the poster on the wall, telling the tale of Saint Nicholas who had visited the poor in the snow, taking a sledge filled with firewood and food for the families he chose to bestow his gifts on. It was the origin of the myth of Santa Claus and had begun many centuries ago. Sally had commissioned it and a talented young artist on the staff of Harper's had illustrated it beautifully. It was something different and had caused many people to read it and exclaim that they had never known where the legend originated. The children didn't much care. All that mattered was that for one shilling they could talk to Santa, the bolder ones sitting on his knee and whispering what they wanted for Christmas. Ben, who was beneath the padding, red suit and white beard, had told Sally that most boys wanted a set of lead soldiers or a train set and that the girls wanted dolls, a doll's pram or a pretty dress.

'At least the mothers get good value for their shilling here,' Ben had said to Sally as they wrapped their parcels, for each contained not only sweets, a picture book or a quality jigsaw puzzle and either a tin whistle or a bead necklace but also a silver sixpence.

Beth knew what was in them, because Sally had told her. She

made time most days to visit Beth or sent someone down to ask her up for coffee in her office.

'I told him he would never make a profit this way.' Sally had confided that she'd scolded her husband when he'd shown her what he intended to give the children in their parcels.

'Of course you did,' Beth had said and laughed at her, because Sally was joking. 'What did Ben say?'

'He just grinned at me – and then what do you think he said?'

Beth had shaken her head.

'Just what I expected, "I didn't intend to," he'd said, laughing all over his face – and then he told me the clever bit, "I'm hoping the mothers will come back to buy Christmas presents and clothes for themselves. What I'm doing is investing in loyalty, Sally. I want to make Harper's the store that gives value and cares for its customers..." so what could I say to that?'

'Kiss him might be the best...' Beth had suggested and laughed as she saw the truth in Sally's face and knew that was just what she'd done.

'I told him we already did that – but I love it that he's done this for the children. It is something no one else is doing – not like this anyway – and it gets even better on the afternoon of Christmas Eve. We're having a party. We'll close the departments upstairs early and everyone can come down to the ground floor. Ben has invited an orphanage to bring its children here and he plans to give them gifts for free – and free drinks. Sausage rolls and some sort of iced and decorated sponge, to be offered to the children and all the staff. Orange squash for the kids, of course, but sherry for the rest of us.'

Beth had smiled and nodded. There was no doubting Sally's happiness for it shone out of her. Beth's own life was easier now and she was happier too, more content than she had ever been. She'd enjoyed buying surprise gifts for Jack, Fred and Tim, and her friends at Harper's, and putting up decorations at home, something she'd missed in the years of her mother's illness.

Now, it was the day before Christmas Eve and the shoppers were queuing early in the morning. Beth's department was decked with tasteful decorations that she and her staff had made at home and brought in. They had a Christmas tree made out of coloured paper and silver ribbons and several tiny glass balls, also a large figure of Father Christmas made out of papier-mâché, which Beth and Fred had spent ages making in the evenings when Jack was still working at the hotel. Standing near the large figure was a sack, really a box covered in red paper, and inside it were scarves, gloves and a handbag, suggesting that they made lovely gifts.

'How are you doing on hats, Janice?' Beth asked when they had a brief pause mid-morning.

'I've sold some of those velvet berets and three felts,' Janice told her. 'It's not the best time for hats, Mrs Burrows, we'll get that in the spring and summer.'

'Yes, I agree with you,' Beth said. 'You can have a turn on the bags and jewellery while I go to lunch. Marion and I have been rushed off our feet all morning.'

'Yes, I noticed,' Janice replied, a touch of envy in her voice. Her hair was a reddish brown and inclined to curl about her face, though she brushed it back and pinned it tight each morning. However, by midday it was already escaping its bonds and suited her very well, for she had a pixyish look about her face.

'Thank you, Mrs Burrows. I do love handling the jewellery. It is such lovely quality. I'd never seen silver pieces like this until I came here.'

'Well, I am going to leave you in charge for a while and Marion will help you. Do not forget the golden rule – only two pieces of jewellery on the counter at a time and do not leave it unattended...'

'I shan't forget,' Janice said and smiled. 'Thank you so much for giving me the chance.'

Beth had left her and come downstairs to look at how the rest of the store was faring. Every counter was busy and the cash machines were whirring as they flew back and forth to the office. It was a safe way of handling large sums of money, because none was ever kept on the floor, but it did take time and Beth wondered if it was the most efficient way of doing things. She thought that she might speak to Sally after Christmas and hear what she thought. Sally had already brought in many changes and she would bring in more as time went on.

Returning to her department after having a quick cup of tea with Fred in the basement, Beth discovered that there was a queue at the jewellery counter. She went to help out, because there were more customers than staff and the two younger girls were having difficulty coping. The rush continued until about four thirty in the afternoon and then began to tail off. During that time not one hat had been looked at or tried on, though Maggie had done a brisk trade on the scarves and gloves, which also made acceptable gifts. Janice had looked so bored standing there that Beth had sent Marion to take over, telling her she could assist Maggie if she had no customers, and she and Janice served the jewellery customers non-stop. In the end, Beth had called Marion back to help and left the hat counter unattended, because no one was interested.

'Well, that was exhausting,' Maggie said when the floor began to empty and then, almost magically, everyone had gone. 'I do not know how you coped on your counters, Mrs Burrows.'

'No, it wasn't easy,' Beth said. She smiled at Marion and Janice. 'Thank you both for coming to the rescue. I couldn't have coped alone.'

'It was exciting,' Janice said, her face alight. 'Everyone was happy and wished us a Happy Christmas, and it made it feel like fun rather than work.'

'It was a bit hectic,' Marion acknowledged. 'I wondered if we would run out of those silver bangles – but I didn't know you had more locked in the office, Mrs Burrows.'

'We kept some back especially for Christmas,' Beth told her. 'Mrs Harper stocked more than usual last month and we decided to keep some in reserve. Otherwise, the display cabinets would have looked empty by now.'

'Isn't it strange how most customers wanted similar items,' Janice said. 'I know there were several styles in the bangles, but I sold at least ten and I think you sold as many again or more.'

'I sold fifteen and Marion sold two and three brooches,' Beth said. She was still meticulous about using the girls' surnames when anyone else was on the floor, but when they'd finished work she relaxed the rule because she felt it made the girls more at ease. Had it not been a rule at Harper's, she would have used first names all the time.

'I sold a gold bracelet, too,' Marion said. 'I ticked it off in the book, Mrs Burrows – and a ruby and pearl dress ring.'

'Goodness me – were they all to that gentleman who spent a long time choosing gifts?'

'Yes.' Marion beamed at her. 'He asked me what I liked in the rings and I showed him and he chose that ring and the bracelet and two silver brooches, for his aunt, he said.' Her cheeks tinged with pink. 'He thanked me, told me I was a nice helpful girl and he would come back when it was his niece's birthday.'

'That was nice,' Beth said and Marion's blush deepened. She didn't often speak up, usually just doing as she was told once she was on the department. For the past few days she'd managed to arrive on time for work and Beth hadn't had to warn her a second time that persistent lateness might lead to dismissal.

'Well, we'd best get off and all of you get an early night,' Beth said. 'We shall only work until two o'clock in the afternoon tomorrow. After that, this department and the others above ground floor will close and we shall all go down for the party and the visit of the children from the orphanage. Mrs Harper wants us to have a good time, enjoy the food and drink, but we may also give a hand with looking out for the children – making sure that all the little ones get their presents and their share of food.'

'I'm looking forward to it,' Marion said shyly. 'My little sister wanted to visit Santa, but Ma couldn't afford a shilling, even though I told her it was good value...' She stopped and blushed again.

Beth looked at her in silence for a moment. 'Tell your mother to bring your little sister tomorrow afternoon and she can visit Santa for free.'

'Could I really?' Marion looked at her, clearly uncomfortable. 'Ma won't come – but my middle sister will bring her. Kathy is twelve and she looks after Milly when she isn't looking after Ma.' She took a deep breath. 'My mother isn't well, Mrs Burrows. Some days she doesn't get up at all – Kathy and me look after Milly and the two lads, they're eleven and thirteen, and the eldest works down the wood yard.'

It was the longest speech she'd ever made and Beth looked at her in surprise, understanding now why she was so often late for work. 'You've never mentioned looking after your brothers and sisters before, Marion?'

'No, Mrs Burrows. Ma is proud – she doesn't like me to talk about the family, but Milly does so want to see Santa.'

'Tell Kathy to bring your sister and your brothers, Marion,' she said. 'I shall treat them all to a visit to Father Christmas and they can have some of the food too. It is an extra little bonus for you for working so hard.'

Marion stared at her uncertainly and then her face lit up. 'Thank you so much, Mrs Burrows. I promise I won't be late again.'

'Don't promise what you may not be able to keep,' Beth said, smiling. 'If your mother is ill and things go wrong, I'll understand – but tell me, don't try to keep it all inside.'

Marion's eyes filled with tears but she didn't let them fall. Beth saw Maggie go to her and the two talked for a while. Maggie had shown Beth some parcels she'd prepared for Marion's family.

'It's just little things from the market mostly and a little silver dressing table mirror that was my mother's for Marion,' Maggie told Beth. 'I have several things of my mother's and I know Marion has it hard at home so I thought I would just make Christmas a little more special for them...'

'You're a lovely girl,' Beth told her and smiled. 'Happy Christmas, Maggie – and I hope you'll spend some if it with us. Tim is coming home for a couple of days so be sure to visit then...'

'Yes, I shall,' Maggie said. 'You and Sally and Rachel are my family now – and I'd love to come over when Tim is home...'

'We'd better get on then,' Beth said, as a few last shoppers entered the department.

They had two gentlemen rush into the department just as Beth was about to tell them to close up for the night. She and Janice served them as they both wanted jewellery. Beth sold a large silver locket on a chain and a gold-link bracelet and Janice sold two silver bangles. They were the last ones with stones set into the metal and there were no more in the office safe.

After the last two customers left, the department was tidied. Beth looked at her silver cabinet. She would have to change the display the next morning before the customers came because it looked a bit thin, and the bangles were nearly finished.

Everyone got their coats and bags and left. Beth went downstairs and met Fred. She had fallen into the habit of waiting for him to close up and so they travelled home together, either on the bus or in a cab if it was cold and wet. It was cold that evening but dry and they were both wrapped up.

'We've been rushed off our feet,' Beth told him as they sat together on the bus. 'What about you?'

'I've been taking stuff up to the fashion department and the men's – they had a rush on the shirts and woollens, so Mr Stockbridge told me, and of course socks always sell at Christmas.'

Beth smiled at him. Fred was like her father in many ways – kind, thoughtful and considerate. He'd never mentioned her miscarriage, though she knew it had upset him, but he was too kind to say anything that might distress her.

They talked comfortably all the way home, looking at each other in surprise as they saw the lights on in Fred's cottage. Both were wondering what was wrong, for it was unlike Jack to be home early.

When they entered the kitchen, it smelled of fish and chips, which were warming on plates in the range, and the kettle was boiling. Jack grinned at them.

'Not bad timing. I thought I wouldn't be far out.'

'What is wrong?' Beth asked. 'Have they closed the hotel or something?'

Jack shook his head. 'Just the opposite, Beth. Don – my boss – told me that we've turned the corner and he made me a proposition – he's offering me a fifty-fifty partnership for two thousand pounds...'

'Jack!' Beth stared at him in surprise, not sure what to think. 'Is that what you'd like? You've always said you wanted your own business...'

'In time it will be,' Jack said. 'Don is sixty. He reckons to retire in another three to five years – if we build the business up, I can buy him out when the time comes.'

'But...' She looked at him, bewildered. 'I thought this was just to gain you experience. Will you like being a partner, Jack? Doesn't it mean you have to agree on things? Only a few months back you were cursing him for being a fool...'

'Don isn't a fit man, Beth. He had let things slide, but I've got the hotel back in profit – only just, but it's there. I think I can expand and improve it – and then it will be what I want. This way I don't take much from your money – at least, not until we buy him out.'

'It's up to you, Jack,' Beth said. 'Make sure the contract is water-tight, love. My lawyers will look at it for you if you like. I wouldn't trust him too much – you'll build the business up and then he'll want twice as much for his share...'

Jack grinned at her. 'I'm getting it cheap,' he said. 'By the way, there's a letter from your lawyer on the table.'

Beth picked it up and read the contents with a little frown. 'We've been offered six thousand pounds for all the shares; my lawyer got them up a thousand on Aunt Helen's and apparently mine were worth as much as hers; it is far more money than I've ever thought of having. We could buy our own property now if you wanted...'

Jack nodded, looking pleased. 'I'm glad for you, Beth, and if we need some of your money we'll use it. I've got five hundred saved and I can borrow some from the bank. Your lawyer can help you invest the rest safely – not in shares, though. We'll think about this over Christmas and decide in the New Year – it's what I told Don we would do.'

'All right.' Beth caught a whiff of their supper as the plates were brought out. 'I'm starving. We've been so busy and I only snatched a sandwich with Dad...' Beth saw him smile as she used the term, because it had taken her a while to do it but now she really thought of him as a father and he was very dear to her.

'Are there any of those pickled onions you made, Beth?' her

father-in-law asked. 'They're the best I've ever tasted and I can polish off this lot with a few of them.'

Beth laughed and went to fetch the jar from the larder. Jack had sprung his idea on her and she wasn't sure why she felt it was risky, but something was telling her he ought not to trust the man who had promised him a good job and then almost folded the business after a couple of months. He was the kind of man who would benefit from Jack's hard work and then cheat him if he could – or that was Beth's gut feeling.

'Shall you come to our staff party tomorrow, Dad?' she asked. 'I think it is going to be lovely.'

'Wouldn't miss it,' Fred said. 'Mrs Harper came down and asked me herself. Lovely smile that lass has got.'

* * *

'This was so kind of Mr Harper,' Beth said to Sally the next day as they watched the orphanage children line up to receive their gifts from Santa.

'You've done your bit for Marion's family,' Sally said and nodded towards the little group who clutched their parcels and now were eating iced sponge cake and sipping orange squash. 'You needn't have paid – Ben would have been happy to let them come for free.'

'Marion wouldn't have brought them then,' Beth said. 'I told her it was a Christmas bonus for working so hard yesterday and she accepted that, so all's well.'

'Yes, you had quite a rush on yesterday,' Sally agreed. 'The department has been almost empty this morning, I think?'

'Yes, they all came yesterday to make sure they got what they wanted. We've sold a few bits and pieces today, mainly scarves, bags and gloves. One customer was disappointed that he couldn't get a silver bangle with stones set round it, so he bought an expensive leather bag.' Beth looked thoughtful. 'He ordered a heavy silver bangle set with sapphires or aquamarines for next month. It is his daughter's birthday and he wants it for her. I said we would be having new stock after Christmas and he should come and view the fresh bangles.'

'Yes, I'll be restocking then.' Sally smiled at her. 'You and your girls have done really well, Beth. Thank you – and Happy Christmas to you and Jack. I hope you will like the gifts we bought. Ben chose Jack's himself.'

'We'll open them tomorrow,' Beth said. 'We hope you like what we bought you, Sally.'

Beth had bought Sally and Ben a beautiful crystal glass vase from Harrods and she'd sent them some flowers from an exclusive florist, which should arrive when they got home from work. She'd sent a card from her and Jack and she'd also given Sally a pretty red scarf that she'd bought in a shop in Bond Street. Beth had also bought gifts for Rachel and her staff, several of them from her own department, using her staff discount wherever possible. Jack had given her five pounds to do her shopping for Christmas and she had some she'd saved besides. Beth's money from her aunt would – all but a few pounds – be put aside until such time as they needed it. As far as Beth was concerned, she would continue to live on Jack's wages and her own, just as they had since their marriage.

'I'm sure we shall,' Sally told her and squeezed her hand. 'I have to talk to everyone, Beth. Enjoy your holiday – you and Fred can leave whenever you're ready.'

'We'll stay for a while, until the children go,' Beth said and moved off to speak to some of the others. It was such a lovely Christmassy atmosphere and one of the few times that the staff of Harper's got to mix. Everyone was laughing and chattering and Beth enjoyed having a word with the girls from the fashion department. She spoke to Mr Stockbridge and his daughter, Becky, briefly and then talked to Rachel for a few minutes. The next moment, Mr Marco swooped up with a sprig of mistletoe and kissed her on the cheek.

'Happy Christmas, Mrs Burrows,' he said. 'Have a lovely time...' She laughed as he passed on and caught Rachel with his mistletoe.

'How are things with you?' she asked. 'Is Minnie settling in well at the flat? I know she likes her job because I saw her in the fashion department discussing a gown alteration with a client; she was busy but she looked happy.'

'Yes, I think she is happy,' Rachel said. 'How are you, Beth – feeling better now?'

'Yes, thank you.' Beth didn't want to speak of the miscarriage more than she needed, even to friends like Rachel. Sally was the only one she'd really opened her heart to and she tended to dismiss any mention of the miscarriage, even though deep inside it still hurt. 'I've been busy, Rachel. I don't have time to dwell on it.'

'Good. I always think it's best to keep busy. Work is the best medicine,' Rachel agreed. 'I found it so after my husband died.'

Beth nodded and looked at her. 'What about you – have you been out with your gentleman friend again? He came to the department yesterday and bought a couple of things.'

'He took me to lunch and he showed me the speech he intended to give in the House if he's elected in the next by-election, Beth. It seems that he is now a convert to our cause as well as that of the miners.' Rachel smiled, a faint colour in her cheeks. 'I think perhaps I may have had a hand in that – and I am glad of it. We need men to stand up for us and make the world see that we should be treated as equals. Women are as strong as men in many ways, but different. Just because we have our vulnerable sides, it doesn't mean we are weaker or less deserving. Also, not all of us agree with the militancy in the Women's Movement.'

'And does your friend understand that now?'

Rachel laughed softly. 'Oh, yes, he does – and his sweet aunt is completely on my side.'

'Well, that sounds good.' Beth smiled at her. 'Happy Christmas, Rachel. I hope you have a wonderful time.'

'I am sure we shall. I'm taking Minnie and Maggie out to lunch at a friend's restaurant for Christmas and on Boxing Day we shall all be with William for the day. He invited us all, though Maggie is going to tea with Becky Stockbridge, and I know it will be perfect.'

'Jack has arranged for us to have Christmas lunch at the hotel,' Beth said. 'He said it was to give us a rest – but I shall cook a large joint of beef at home on Boxing Day.'

She parted from Rachel and then spotted a small child crying and went to discover what the problem was; a quick visit to the toilets made the tears disappear and by then the children were departing with their tummies filled with Christmas treats and their gifts clutched in sticky hands.

As the ground floor finally emptied, Fred and Ben Harper made a tour of the store together to make certain no child had got lost or trapped. Ben had taken off his costume, which he said had been very hot by the end of the party. Beth took the opportunity to wish the staff 'Happy Christmas' as they left in ones and twos, sometimes with friends from other floors. Almost everyone had gone when Ben and Fred returned, only Rachel and Maggie were lingering to say goodbye to Sally.

'Well, that went off well,' Ben Harper said and sighed when they took their leave. 'I'll lock up tonight, Fred. Happy Christmas to you – and you, Beth. And thank you for all your hard work. We've had a wonderful Christmas at Harper's and you've all played your part.' He smiled at her and Sally who were embracing. 'I had a cable from Jenni, she says her wedding was wonderful and she will be sending pictures.'

'I would love to see them,' Beth said. 'Sally told me it was going to be a real Christmas wedding.'

'Yes, it is a pity we missed it,' Ben said, looking regretful, 'but we'll visit in the New Year.'

'Goodnight, Mr Harper.'

Fred held the door for Beth and they went out, carrying various parcels and bags with them. Fred saw a taxicab pulled up on the opposite side of the road and hailed it.

'We'll treat ourselves tonight, love,' he said. 'Mr Harper gave me a five pound bonus this evening – and he told me I'll be getting a raise in the New Year. He says the store wouldn't run half as well without me.'

Fred was looking like a cat that got the cream and Beth smiled happily. It was things like that that made her proud to work for Harper's. She loved being a Harper's girl and hoped her life wouldn't change too quickly. Jack had made up his mind he wanted to buy into the hotel but there was no room for them to have their own suite. He'd told her he would look out for something close by, hinting that he had something in mind, and asked if she would be disappointed if they continued to live with his father for the time being.

'I'm fine at the moment,' Beth had said and meant it. Since Tim no longer lived at home, it would leave Fred on his own if they moved out and she felt that would be a little unfair. In time they would work something out, but for the moment she was happy to continue living in Fred's house.

Tim was coming home on leave on Boxing Day and Beth would talk to him then. She knew he still took Maggie out sometimes but didn't know if they were courting. Perhaps Tim would have something to tell them, but Beth would let him confide in her if he was ready.

Sighing, she realised she felt a little tired now that the excitement was all over. She was glad they were going to Jack's hotel for dinner the next day so that she could have a rest.

Sally was excited about cooking her first Christmas dinner in her own home. She'd bought all sorts of stuff to decorate their apartment and treats to please the guests she'd invited for drinks and lunch on Boxing Day. Beth smiled as she thought of all the secrets shared. She hoped that Sally would be telling her husband the most important one of all that night.

* * *

'Well, how did our first Christmas together at Harper's go?' Ben asked as he stretched out in the hired car taking them home. 'Did your friends enjoy it – did you?'

'It was wonderful, Ben,' Sally said and reached for his hand in the dim interior of the car. 'I loved every minute and so did those children – I gave Marion's siblings a few things to take home. Extra food that I told them would only be wasted.'

'Of course you did,' he said and leaned forward to kiss her. 'Spending all my profits again, Mrs Harper?'

'You can talk – do you think I didn't notice you slipping shiny silver shillings into the kids' hands?'

'Guilty as charged,' Ben grinned. 'Can't help it – I love kids...'

'That's good,' Sally said and snuggled up to him. 'Because you're going to have one of your own quite soon... well, about seven to eight months or so from now...' She giggled as he shot forward in his seat and looked at her. 'So shocked, Mr Harper? It happens, you know. Especially if...'

Whatever Sally was about to say next was muffled as she was enveloped in a bear hug, but it caused Mr Ben Harper to give a shout of joy and the taxi driver to glance in his driving mirror and grin at what was going on in the back seat of his car.

MORE FROM ROSIE CLARKE

We hope you enjoyed reading *Love and Marriage at Harpers*. If you did, please leave a review.

If you'd like to gift a copy, this book is also available as an ebook, digital audio download and audiobook CD.

Sign up to Rosie Clarke's mailing list for news, competitions and updates on future books.

http://bit.ly/RosieClarkeNewsletter

The next book in this series, *Rainy Days for the Harpers Girls,* is available to order now!

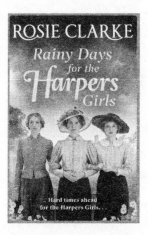

ABOUT THE AUTHOR

Rosie Clarke is a #1 bestselling saga writer whose most recent books include *The Mulberry Lane* series. She has written over 100 novels under different pseudonyms and is a RNA Award winner. She lives in Cambridgeshire.

Visit Rosie Clarke's website: http://www.rosieclarke.co.uk

Follow Rosie on social media:

 twitter.com/AnneHerries

 bookbub.com/authors/rosie-clarke

ABOUT BOLDWOOD BOOKS

Boldwood Books is a fiction publishing company seeking out the best stories from around the world.

Find out more at www.boldwoodbooks.com

Sign up to the Book and Tonic newsletter for news, offers and competitions from Boldwood Books!

http://www.bit.ly/bookandtonic

We'd love to hear from you, follow us on social media:

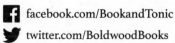 facebook.com/BookandTonic
twitter.com/BoldwoodBooks
 instagram.com/BookandTonic